ticity and heart, this trilogy will touch your life and spark many conversations.'

Isabelle Felix, author of *Deafinitely*

'In *The Beautiful Ones*, O.M. Faure offers us a chilling glance into a world not so very far from our own, and paints a compelling picture of a dystopian future that may be closer than we think.'

Clare Kane, author of *Dragons in Shallow Waters*.

ALSO BY O. M. FAURE

THE CASSANDRA PROGRAMME SERIES:

The Disappearance (prequel)

THE BEAUTIFUL ONES (TRILOGY):

Book 1: *Chosen*

Book 2: *Torn*

Book 3: *United*

UNITED

BOOK 3 OF THE BEAUTIFUL ONES TRILOGY

O.M. FAURE

FORWARD MOTION PUBLISHING, LTD.

ISBN: 978-1-9164370-3-6

Published by Forward Motion Publishing, Ltd.

Cover design by Stuart Bache of Books Covered | Cover images ©
Shutterstock

The events in this book are an extrapolation of what the future could be, based on real scientific data, UN forecasts and current studies.

However, this is a work of fiction. Names, characters, places and incidents are either the product of the author's imagination or are used fictitiously, and any resemblance to actual persons, living or dead, or to actual events or locales is entirely coincidental.

If you would like to know more about the sources and data, please consult the bibliography at the end of this book. A list of book club topics will also be provided to readers who subscribe to the newsletter.

Visit www.omfaure.com to join the conversation today.

For Nicole, my closest friend,
my inspiration, my anchor.

'It's going to destroy it all. Democracy cannot survive overpopulation. Human dignity cannot survive it. Convenience and decency cannot survive it. As you put more and more people onto the world, the value of life not only declines, but it disappears. It doesn't matter if someone dies.'

— Isaac Asimov
(1920–1992)

UNITED

1

OLIVIA

M*arch 2082*

BURKE IS on top of me, his weight like a slab of marble, suffocating me. I wriggle and fight him with everything I've got but he's too strong. My nose is clogged with dried-up blood and snot and my mouth can't remember how to breathe anymore. His hands are digging into my throat, squeezing my scream into silence, crushing my windpipe. I struggle with everything I have. I can't breathe. I can't breathe. I CAN'T BREATHE.

Gasping for air, I inhale in long gulps and touch my throat gingerly. The cell is dark and the walls are too close. I try to focus on my lungs expanding and contracting but they're having none of it. Panic grips me as I struggle to loosen my collar.

The singsong voice in my head moans, *Murderer, you're a murderer. Murderer, murderer.* The merry-go-round starts again in my mind. I let it run its course, knowing that I can't stop it: *I should have talked to DeAnn sooner. I should have learned to drive better. I should have run away from the village as soon as I saw the dead bodies. I should have let Anthony kill me. I should... I should... I should...* I think I left something behind in Africa. A piece of me is missing. But I can't remember what it is exactly.

The inky darkness is pressing against my chest like a vice, as I peer anxiously through the bars, trying to guess who will come to process me. I need to get out of here. It's too dark. Too small. I get up and grope around in the dark. Fighting with the door handle. Out, I need to get out. Gasping.

A movement on the other side of the bars. I freeze.

I can't see my interrogator. I don't want to say too much. I can't betray... I mustn't reveal the Programme's secrets. But I need to say something to be released.

The man is silent, the weight of his presence and his expectation pressing down on me.

'God, please help me,' I whisper, as the little barred window slides open, letting in a latticed sliver of light.

The shadow bends his head. I suppose he can't see me either.

'Forgive me, Father, for I have sinned. It's been six months since my last confession. I accuse myself of the following sins...'

'My child, there is no need to use the old formulas. There is no accusation. Just a place to unburden yourself. I am listening.'

'I... I killed a man, Father.'

The priest stays silent.

'He was going to kill me. I had to.'

He listens to all of it quietly. Relief and guilt wash over

me, alternating like waves as the story spills out of me, soaked with tears.

'... and I stabbed him until his hands let go of my throat. Until it didn't hurt anymore.'

The priest stays silent for a long while.

Then his warm voice pulls me out of my nightmare. 'All life is precious, my child. But what's done is done. This man now rests in the hands of God. He will receive his judgement. You, on the other hand, are still alive and can still be redeemed. And the first step is to forgive yourself.'

'But how can I? I've killed a man. I've broken the most important of God's commandments. I can't forgive myself.'

I shake my head and sob into a ball of soggy tissues.

'My child, I will let you in on a little secret. God does not really need you to confess. God is all-seeing, all-knowing and he has already forgiven you.'

His voice is like a buoy thrown to me as I drown.

'How? How could he forgive me? I'm a murderer.'

'Because God loves all of you. Your light *and* your darkness. He loves you just as you are, because he made you so. There is nothing you've said today that could make God love you less. You are accepted and forgiven.'

I just sit there and sob, stunned.

'Dedicate three novenas to Mary. Ask her for solace and healing. I absolve you of all sin. Go in peace.'

'Thank you, Father.'

Bowled over by this man's kindness, I stumble out into the light of the church, blinking. The sound of small children singing and laughing greets me, like a salve on my soul. I miss my choir kids so much. I used to go to Mass every Sunday in London and I miss the lovely, chaotic ensemble of kindness, giggles and song.

'Do we want any fishes in the choir?' I used to ask the

kids, as I opened and closed my mouth with a smack, mimicking children who pretended to sing yet remained silent.

'Nooooo,' they all replied, smiling.

'How do we sing?'

'Loud!'

'I'm sorry? I can't hear you.' Every week, I would cup a hand around my ear and they loved the ritual. 'How do we sing?'

'LOUD!' the children replied, laughing.

'Anna, who do you sing for?' I asked the little girl who wore frilly pink dresses every Sunday.

'I sing for the last person in the church, the one on the last bench, Miss Olivia.'

'That's great, Anna.' This was a trick I'd taught them to project their voices. If they sang for the person who was farthest away from them, then everyone sitting in between would hear them too.

I turned to Anna's twin brother. 'And who do you sing for, Raymond?' He wore tiny suits and ties, and was the choir's most diligent child, singing already at the Royal Albert Hall. I'd given advice to his mother on how to get him a music scholarship, and hoped he would continue on this path; he was a wonderful child.

'I sing for the lion, Miss Olivia,' the little boy answered.

I crinkled my eyes and smiled at him proudly. Raymond didn't sing for the people on the last bench, he sung even further; for the lion who drank from the river on the stained glass window. I'd pointed out the scene to him once and told him I sang for the lion and now he did as well.

I mussed up his hair. 'Well done, Raymond.'

≈

LIKE A DREAM, the edges of those sunny days blur, as I walk towards the sound of children's voices raised in song. Who knows where my choir kids are now? That time of my life is gone forever, slipped through my fingers like water. I wonder sometimes if I didn't imagine it all. The happiness I felt, the ease of life back then.

We're so far away from everything in 2082. In the middle of nowhere, just the two of us lost in this horrible future, and so helpless. How will we ever get home?

The memory of my last day with Mum in our cottage twists in my gut and a sob clogs up my throat. I didn't know that I would never see her or my choir kids again. If only I'd known.

I get a bit closer and listen to the small choir's rehearsal. They're singing '*Shine, Jesus, Shine*', my favourite hymn, so I sit quietly on a pew, drying my tears.

'And who are you singing for?' says the young woman who's directing the choir.

The kids laugh and shout, as one, 'For the lion!'

What? I turn around and look at the stained glass window. There's no lion there. They keep singing, all of them are adorable, some serious, some mischievous, all of them earnest.

I stay back as the rehearsal ends. The choir director shakes the hands of all the parents. Ruffles the kids' hair and starts to put away the hymn books.

'Excuse me, miss?'

She looks up and smiles.

'Sorry, I just wanted to ask you, why do you teach the children to sing for the lion?'

She laughs, 'Oh, it's just something Father Raymond says his choir leader taught him when he was a child. The children love it.' She smiles and leaves.

Father Raymond? I turn around and see an old Asian man exiting the confessional and shaking hands with a parishioner who just confessed.

It's Raymond.

The little twin boy who sang in my choir sixty-five years ago.

Heart beating, I hide behind a pillar and, making sure he hasn't seen me, I hurry out of the church and emerge into the bustling Manhattan street and the din of morning rush hour traffic.

2

DEANN

S t. Louis, Missouri, USA, March 2082

'I'M SO SORRY, HON,' the fat white woman smiles, 'the room's just been rented out.'

'Are you sure? It was still available when I called to arrange a viewing, half an hour ago.'

'Was it? No, my assistant must have made a mistake.' She tries to push the door closed but I wedge my foot in.

'Listen, I'll pay double, OK? I won't be any trouble. I'm a single woman, no dependents, no pets, I've got a good job. I just need a place to rent.'

'You go away now, you hear?' Her face dissolves into fear. 'Remove your foot now, or I'll call building security.'

'But I'm... why the hell would you do that?'

She starts to shriek, 'Help! Help!' and rummages behind her with one hand as she strains to close the door with the other.

No sense in getting myself arrested or worse. I pull out my foot and the door slams in my face.

Repressing a groan, I leave the pristine residential building and emerge into the sunshine outside, taking in the flowery bushes lining the front yard and the American flag flapping above me, cheerfully oblivious. A group of kids stare at me slack jawed, their games and happy cries silenced as I pass by, tapping on my iMode.

I'm deep in white suburbia, a few miles from the St. Louis city center, and I might as well be on the set of a fifties movie where everyone looks like fucking Doris Day and James Stewart.

Olivia and I have split up to cover more ground; she's in New York, infiltrating the law firm that facilitated the medical tests and I'm going undercover at GeneX, the research facility that supplied the drugs. None of that is getting us any closer to home, but A. pledged to search for a way back to 2017 if we do this. Olivia and I both wanted to get to the bottom of the medical experiments anyway. I still haven't met the mystery woman, but I hope we're right to put our hopes in her. She doesn't strike me as overly concerned with our safety. This could be a huge mistake. And it could be our last.

Huge mansions are planted in the middle of perfectly green manicured lawns. Everyone looks blond, rosy cheeked and fat. Front porch swings sway gently in the warm breeze and brand new cars shine in driveways. An ice cream truck's melody drifts gently toward me and the air smells of mowed grass and chlorine. I ignore it all and focus on my search.

The hotel has given me notice. They're threatening to report me for vagrancy if I don't find more permanent housing tonight. Anyway, my budget would run out fast if I kept living there and I can't stand the glares the staff give me anymore. It's Sunday and I need to find a room to rent before I start my job tomorrow morning.

After Africa, this feels obscene. So hollow. So vapid. Stepford wives with perfect bottle-blonde hair give fake smiles to their neighbors as they pick up newspapers on the front lawn. Toned joggers wearing pastel colors chat together as they make their morning tours to survey their domain. A few stop to stare and then tap their iMode collars, no doubt reporting my presence to the police.

I'm an anomaly here. An unwelcomed guest. I'm the wrench in the works. I'm the reminder that their perfect existence is fake. I'm a visual cue that says: your world is built on the blood of my people, you look clean but your hands are stained, your food is tainted, your water is stolen. They know it and hate me accordingly.

I hate them too, yet I'm trying to live among them, as I used to. I don't know where else I could go.

Well, that's not true. I throw a look at the next address on the listing and sigh. After a dozen rejections of the type I just went through, my spirit's deflated. I can't take on the whole damn system today. I order myself a cab.

At least driverless vehicles don't care about the color of my skin; well, no actually, they do. They care about my skewed social rating, my undesirable destination, my dwindling bank account. So I wait for a good fifteen minutes before a car appears, getting more and more worked up. Finally, a banged-up car of doubtful cleanliness shows up and I climb in, sensing eyes on me. Swallowing the defeat and shame, I ignore them and focus on my objective. Apartment today, job tomorrow.

Gradually, detached mansions of absurd proportions, swimming pools and lawn sprinklers give way to more modest terrace houses, with pick-up trucks and geranium planters on sooty window sills.

Then the view outside the cab's cracked window worsens. Now, all around me, the inner city is displayed in all its apocalyptic glory.

Dilapidated family houses, their windows boarded up, their walls tagged, crumble where they stand, in the general indifference. Soon even these give way to squat project buildings riddled with bullet holes. Burnt car husks sit like animal carcasses on garbage-strewn streets as music blares from a boom box and young men watch me go past.

The cab lazily rides through it all, respecting every speed limit, every stop and crossing. At a red light, we come to a halt and I glance at a group of young children, none older than ten or so, who are playing in the dirt of a vacant lot and who now start running toward my car. Most are black, wearing ripped up t-shirts, their faces consumed by curiosity and something else. Something familiar. But it can't be. Not here. The group of kids flock around the car and bang on my window.

'You have arrived at your destination.'

'Uh, no, I haven't,' I say, checking the iMode for the apartment listing. I'm a half a mile away from my destination, but no matter how much I tap on the pinned location on the map, the car refuses to drive on.

The cab's metallic voice intones: 'This vehicle cannot take you any further. Should you wish to exit here, Alles declines all responsibility. Under no circumstances shall Alles, or its affiliates, partners, suppliers or licensors be liable for any indirect, incidental...'

'Oh, fuck off!' I slam the door shut and kick the tire for good measure, as it drives away. A ping on my iMode informs me that my rating has gone down by two points and that my fare has been increased by twenty dollars.

Furious, I unglue my eyes from the driverless cab as it glides sedately away and focus instead on the children gathered around me, begging for food. So it was hunger that I saw in their eyes, after all.

Feeling a crack fissure my heart, I put on a happy face and say, 'Who wants to earn a few bucks today?'

'Me, me, me!' They smile and touch my clothes, my arms.

'OK, kiddos, you can all have a little something if you help me find this address.' I show them my iMode bracelet.

A little girl with Bantu knots slides her hand in mine and pulls me forward, checking over her shoulder from time to time to make sure I'm still there, her features split by a huge grin. I close my eyes for a second and, as always, behind my eyelids, Kitsa falls like a puppet whose strings were cut, slowly, her knees buckling for the hundredth time as her head hits the white cream carpet with a muted thud and I stare into her empty eyes.

This time, instead of clamping my hand on my mouth, I burst into the room and grab her little body and hold her close to my chest, screaming. Yesterday, I burst into the room, grabbed a letter opener and stabbed Omony before he could kill her.

But none of this happened. I just left her there. My little, fierce, beautiful Kitsa. I allowed her to be killed and then I left her there and I ran. Like a coward. I never used to second-guess myself. I usually just did whatever had to be done and never looked back. But nobody really mattered much to me before, so I don't know what to do about all these... these *feelings*. If only they could go away. If only I could flip a switch and turn this pain off, I would, in a heartbeat.

Instead I mourn.

The kids make an unholy racket, laughing, asking me questions, showing me the neighborhood, and I give in to the pull of the little girl's hand in mine, letting her tug me once again into the flow of life.

3

OLIVIA

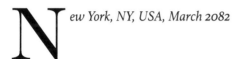

N *ew York, NY, USA, March 2082*

THE SKYLINE of New York City stretches outside my window, like a steel giant awakening from slumber as flurries of snow swirl against the dark grey sky.

The city looks strange. New skyscrapers have changed its familiar silhouette; huge buildings rise miles above the ground, twisting, shining and reaching for the clouds like greedy fingers.

My iMode pings. I read it and bite my lip.

'Identities ready for first day. Good luck.'

I fiddle with the brand new bracelet in the lift and my fake identity appears on the screen: Olivia Sinclair.

As I emerge into the weak morning sunlight, Manhattan greets me in all its drab grandeur and surreal modernity. The snowstorm is in full swing by now and the temperature is polar. I zip up my coat all the way to my nose and trudge forwards, boots sinking in the knee-deep snow.

Buffeted by the wind, I dive into the subway station where the crowd engulfs me. Moist, thawing bodies press against mine, their squishiness and proximity uncomfortably intimate. Fending for my place in the tunnel's flow, I'm shuffling forward when someone jabs me in the ribs with their elbow. I glare at the man who did it but he doesn't apologise or even acknowledge that I exist; he just continues jostling his way through the crowd and staring at nothing, as if I weren't here.

As I'm swept into a maze of corridors, claustrophobia grips hold of me. The crowd is so dense that I thought there was a technical fault on the line. But this is just the normal morning rush hour nowadays. I'm carried by the throng, barely needing to hold straight, propped up as I am by the moving mass of bodies. The platform is so full that there is hardly enough space to breathe and we all stand there, the bravest ones oscillating on the platform edge.

A high-pitched whine intensifies as the stale air whooshes in anticipation, and a mouse, sooty and fat, darts along the electric tracks, running away from the approaching train. The doors screech open and people surge forwards, dragging me in their irrepressible wake. The crowd squeezes through the narrow door and expands again inside the already crowded carriage.

Wrapped inside their smoke-screened iBubbles, commuters sway as the train brakes and accelerates. I'm drowning in people. The smell of sweat and stale air mixes with the accumulated grime of centuries wafting from the tunnels every time the doors open.

I'm suffocating. An amorphous dread rises, as I shove through the crowd with my shoulders and elbows, the faceless bubble-headed bodies like reeds, parting and swaying but rooted to the spot. I gasp and shove and swim against the current. The shrill warning spurs me on and I burst onto the platform just as the doors close. Panting, I cling to the closest wall, slumping against the interactive map, as I gulp down big breaths of humid air and at length, I muster enough courage to get back to the surface.

The crowd on the street is just as dense, but at least here, if I crane my neck back and look straight up, the snow-laden sky is visible between the skyscrapers. My breathing returns to normal as I clutch the subway's banister and get my bearings.

I'm nearly there and also nearly late but I don't care, I'll go the rest of the way on foot. There's no way on earth I'm diving down into those rat tunnels again.

Walking is nearly as bad as taking the subway, the pavement is so crowded. Snowflakes swirl around the crowds as warmly clad New Yorkers shove their way through the throngs, completely ignoring me. I'm bloody transparent. Mounted on self-propelling devices, platforms and hovering shoes, passers-by bump into me and don't apologise. They look through me, above me, around me, their faces blank, self-absorbed. Frowning, encased in their notional bubble, New Yorkers wish themselves alone in the middle of a crowd and I'm in their way, walking too slowly, taking too much space, impeding the flow.

The streets are lined with homeless people, sitting on cardboard mats, looking emaciated and hirsute, huddled against the arctic cold while they try to avoid being trampled. I never liked New York much, but it's sad to see the grand old lady fallen on hard times, overrun, decrepit and poor.

I thought the future would look more... I don't know...

futuristic. I expected more flying cars, outlandish technology, *Star Trek* teleportation and *Back-to-the-Future* food. But in reality the future is disappointing. It's so mundane, dirty and ordinary. Here, people dress in the same close-fitting weird suits as they do in London, but they're definitely much taller than me here and verging on the morbidly obese. The streets are filthy, there are potholes everywhere and rubbish bins are overflowing with disposable cups and food remains staining the already grey piles of slush and sooty snow. It's depressingly more of the same, just worse.

In some ways, it's subtly different, though. I forget for a minute that I'm in 2082 and then something small reminds me: people seem to wear much tighter, more revealing clothes, but their postures have slumped; and everybody seems more willing to do private stuff in public. The language has slipped as well, and it sounds to me like they're all teenagers, their vocabulary limited, their grammar appalling. This future is hardly the stuff dreams are made of.

A large, scuffed and dented robot bumps into my hip when I get too close to the kerb. Jerking me out of my sombre thoughts, I move out of its way and it continues to sweep the streets, its aggravating beep the only sound in the eerily silent, milling crowd.

Finally, I arrive at my destination; a vertiginously high building, made of glittering steel and glass. Wiping a hand on my skirt, I push the revolving door and approach the throbbing red line on the floor. Oh God. The scan.

Hundreds of employees walk across it, holding mugs, chatting to colleagues, folding coats on their arms. Their bracelets flash red when they cross over the line and they don't even blink. But I'm frozen.

I don't think it will work. Our previous iModes' ear buds

took our blood samples and there were several scans of us taken in London. A., my Cassandra Resistance handler, says she's hacked the records and swapped our identities so that our DNA, fingerprints and scans are now linked to these new identities and wiped clean from the Programme's database.

But as I walk into the official-looking building, I realise I'm going to be scanned from head to toe – and they'll know who I am. I'll be arrested, tackled to the ground and sent back to London to be executed by the Programme. I'm effectively giving myself up. Knees shaking, I approach the red line across the floor and pretend to rummage in my bag. A security officer frowns and starts to walk over as I remove my snow covered coat and fold it over my arm to buy some time.

I don't think I can do this. I don't want to die. Why can't we just hide for eight months and work on a way to travel back to 2017? Stopping the Ugandan medical experiments isn't really in our job spec, is it? We're not even agents. I was supposed to be a back-office member of staff, safe and sound behind a desk. I shouldn't even be here.

The security guard is approaching now, pushing on his ear bud with three fingers, his lips moving. He's staring right at me.

Bugger, bugger, bugger.

Holding my breath, I step across the Rubicon, wincing.

And nothing happens.

The security guard stops, hesitates and doubles back to his post. I release my breath and will my knees to stop shaking.

It worked. Of course it did, I admonish myself. The Programme would have found us already through our iModes if the identity switch hadn't succeeded. Groebler probably thinks we died in the Kampala riots. I stop by the lifts, resting a hand against the black glass wall to steady myself, and deploy my iBubble, pretending to make a phone call, to buy a few extra minutes.

Something starts moving on the wall next to me; startled, I step back and see a group of senior golf players looking up at me. I seem to have interrupted their putt. It looks like their image is projected on the wall but it's in 3D and if I weren't in the middle of Manhattan, I would be convinced I was on a golf course in Scotland. I'm mumbling an apology and stumbling back when one of the golfers strides over and steps out of the screen.

He's an absurdly handsome sixty-year-old man, with a Mayfair vibe, perfectly coiffed grey hair and a suntanned complexion. A peach jumper is wrapped around his neck and his too-perfect white smile is positively beaming.

'Hi there.'

I look behind me but the man really seems to be talking to me. Did I trigger a videoconference?

'Erm... hello?'

'I see you're joining our law firm today as a paralegal. Welcome to the team, Olivia,' he says, holding out his hand. 'What can I do for you?'

I reach out and grab a handful of air. Of course, he's not really there; I'm such a dolt. The hologram laughs – a rich, warm sound.

'What the hell am I doing here?' I mutter, glancing over my shoulder at the exit. The AI takes it literally though.

'You're here to support Carapadre and Dergrin's client, GeneX. Ah.' He pauses. 'Very interesting project they've got you working on.'

'Is it? Oh, I mean... yes it is. Could you give me a run-through?'

'I'm afraid not, your clearance is still being finalised.'

'Can you brief me more generally, then?'

'With pleasure,' he beams. 'GeneX are the American leaders in the field of genetic research.' The handsome man's face disappears and, in its place, a video is projected against the inside of my iBubble.

I see thousands of people gathered outside a gleaming white building bearing the silver GeneX logo. Speakers on stage make happy noises and stare at an enormous digital display screen. It looks like New Year's Eve in Times Square, but it isn't. The huge crowd is counting up, not down. 'Nine hundred and ninety-five! Ninety-six! Ninety-seven! Ninety-eight! Ninety-nine! Six hundred million! The crowd erupts with joy as fireworks and the American national anthem starts to play.

The crowd scene is replaced by snippets of video, photos and newspaper clippings. A Supreme Court judge declares Roe vs. Wade overturned. A smiling journalist against a red, white and blue background explains that contraception is now illegal with a big grin on her perfect face. Newspapers announce a recession and a fertility incentive programme. An article requests that the population make every effort to replace the dying Millennial generation in order to boost the economy and save the pensions system.

Historic footage from 2032 shows a pasty man standing at a podium, who lowers his hand after swearing on a Bible in front of a crowd on the front steps of the Capitol building. He proclaims, 'I am a Christian, a family man and a Republican. In that order.' The crowd cheers and the man continues, 'Thanks to the immense inroads we have made during my predecessor's four mandates, we will restore America to an age of purity' – his voice gathers momentum – 'to a time when values meant something,' the crescendo builds up,

'when family, work and nationalism were not swear words!'
He opens his arms and people clap, waving flags.

A naked woman with words scribbled on her chest in
marker pen launches herself at the podium, interrupting
the speech, but she's dragged away by security. The pallid
man chuckles but his oddly emotionless face doesn't move.
He shouts, chopping his hands down, 'The moral decay and
turpitude of the Liberal age is over!' The crowd goes wild. 'I
will restore America's greatness and usher in a Golden Age
of prosperity and growth for the worthy, for the faithful, for
the chosen. The American people deserve an Empire—'

The video clip stops and the golfer reappears. 'Thanks to
GeneX's medical advances, we can live to our full potential
of one hundred and twenty years, we can delay ageing and
we have cured all communicable diseases. Ever-increasing
growth is now not only possible, but a reality. We are the
fourth most populated country in the world thanks to
GeneX's tireless efforts. The future is bright – and the future
is now! So you see, Olivia, how lucky you are to be helping
the law firm's largest client to bring—'

'You can't be serious. What about overpopulation, for
God's sake?'

I feel something brushing against my arm and jump,
startled. A man is standing right in front of me, blending
eerily with the Mayfair AI's silhouette. As their two faces
blur and vacillate, he raises his hand and I flinch.

'There is strength in growth, Olivia, and capitalism
needs never ending—'

The iBubble retracts and the Mayfair man dissolves in a
shower of blue sparks.

My heart beating slightly faster, I focus on the real
person standing in front of me. A very tall man in his thirties is squinting at me through horn-rimmed glasses.

'There you are. You're the new paralegal, right?'

I nod, holding out my hand to shake his. 'Yes, Olivia S...
Sinclair,' I say.

He smiles, amused and instead of taking my hand, he
scans my iMode, confirming my identity.

Oh bugger, I forgot that shaking hands is no longer
accepted practice. People do a weird half-hearted wave or
avoid greeting each other altogether.

Raking his fingers through his brown curly hair, he says,
'My name is Michael Quisling. We're going to be working
together. Come on.'

I hurry after him, as he heads towards the lifts.

'Arguing with the AI and late on your first day.' He
shakes his head. 'Off to a great start, aren't you?'

4

DEANN

S t. Louis, Missouri, USA, March 2082

I GET out of the cab, adjust my work outfit and close the door distractedly, as I look up the name of my new manager and the department I should ask for at reception.

'Get in! Quickly! The storm is coming!' A young black woman is gesturing urgently from the R&D building's entrance. What is she talking about? The weather's hot and it's dry as bone, not stormy. No clouds.

Puzzled, I look up from my iMode and see people running past, panicked as they point at something behind me. A rumbling roar grows in intensity, mixing with crackles of thunder and people's screams. With a sinking feeling in my stomach, I turn around. A huge cloud bank of red dust at least three hundred feet high, stretching for miles on the left and right, is careering toward me, devouring buildings, cars and people, like a tsunami.

'Come on, run!'

I sprint as fast as I can, tripping over my own feet, but the rolling wall of dust is already upon me and in the blink of an eye, I'm swallowed up. The wind slaps my hair against my face and fine dust swirls, getting into my eyes, my ears, my nose. I can't hear anything aside from the wind. It howls and pushes, wrestling me in its violent embrace. Every exposed part of my skin stings and burns. I scream and dirt gets into my mouth. I'm drowning in red sand.

All is dark, so dark that, as I run, I try to hold out my hands in front of me, but I can't see them. I keep walking anyway – I saw the door just a few seconds ago, but now I have no idea where the building is anymore. Struggling to open my eyes, I take a few more steps and stumble on something hard, at knee height. Hands outstretched, I fall forward, flailing. My leggings rip and my kneecaps get scorched against the asphalt.

Choking, I'm about to curl into a ball when the door opens again and light shines out like a beacon, cutting through the dark. I get back up and start running, holding my shirt in front of my nose. Sand in my eyes, tears streaming down my face, I lunge forward and collapse inside, as the young woman fights with the wind and finally manages to slams the entrance shut. The storm shakes and rattles the door, as it clamors to be let in, whistling under the threshold and wailing with frustration.

'You nearly bought the farm there,' the young woman pants, sliding to her knees. 'What the hell were you thinking? Out so close to an alert with no shelter lined up?'

She pushes my hair away from my face as I lie on the floor gasping and spitting. Something that looks like blood comes out. Maybe it's red dirt. Coughing, throat burning, I try to catch my breath.

'Thank you—'

'Never mind. Come on, I'll feel better once we get away from the door. I'm Jada, by the way.'

She's a light brown color and her long cornrow braids sway against her waist, beads clinking as she walks away, not waiting for me to introduce myself. She's wearing a monochrome power suit with a statement necklace, but the effect is ruined by the red sand covering her from head to toe. Dusting myself off and wiping my mouth on the back of my hand, I follow her, limping from my fall.

We round a corner and find ourselves in a huge reception area, surrounded by glass walls. The dust storm hasn't reached here yet. It's still light and the sky is deep blue but a handful of people are running across the parking lot, yelling and pointing, as trees shake violently. Jada and I edge closer to the glass wall and watch, mesmerized, while the red cloud crests above the left side of the building and engulfs everything and everyone in its path.

The rust-colored flood spills and crashes against the glass, and I stand there, stunned, as darkness falls on the large atrium and the world disappears under a blanket of swirling sand.

I'm staring at the electrical charges that zigzag across the roiling cloud when a face appears through the murk, a few inches away from mine, smashing against the windowpane. I jump back, yelping, as the old white man screams for me to let him in, our eyes locked.

I run to the glass doors and try to open them but they're sealed. The man is at least eighty and as he pounds his fists on the glass, his cane bangs again and again, its frantic beat the only sound in the vast, dark reception area.

'We have to let him in through the door, at the back.'

'It's too late,' she says, shaking her head.

The old man can't hear us, but his expression is a mask of despair and terror. He knows. A gust of wind smears the old man's face against the glass. He yells but the sound is washed away by the storm's roar.

Something bumps against the glass a few yards to the right. Then another dull thud makes us jump. And another.

We stumble backwards and backpedal across the marble floor toward the steel reception desk. In the eerie red gloom, the old man's cane on the glass rhythmically marks the seconds, but it's getting slower and slower.

There's a loud metallic clang against the glass, followed by a cracking sound.

'Shit,' Jada says grimly.

She drags me behind the reception desk and pulls me down as we both stare at the crack snaking its way along the glass wall. My heart is in my throat, as the glass fissure grows, little white cracks branching out against the swirling red wave. Still crouching, the young woman is rummaging in the drawers.

'What are we waiting for? Come on, we need to get out of here!' I yell, over the pulsing thumps of the old man's fist and the dust storm's howls.

'Wait, we'll never make it without these.'

When she turns, there are two gas masks in her hands; she throws me one. The whole building is shaking. I fumble with the mask and figure out how to put it on just as the sound of breaking glass rings out and dust and shards explode inward. The old man is projected against the marble wall above us. I rush to help him and am leaning over his prone body when I hear her scream 'Come on! What the fuck are you doing?'

I can barely make out Jada as she runs toward the elevator bank. Before she disappears, I slide my hands under the old man's armpits and drag him in the general direction where I last saw the young woman. I can barely see anything, the mask's visor is obscured by dust particles and the wind's howls drown out everything but the sound of my own breathing, ominous and labored, in the claustrophobic mask. Walking backward, pulling the old man, I struggle to drag his inert weight as I search for the young woman and find only dust. I'm starting to flag when a light pierces through the gloom. Panting, I manage to pull him into the elevator cab just as the doors close.

Before I have time to do anything, she yanks the mask off my face.

'What the hell? Risking our lives to drag a corpse. Are you out of your fucking mind?'

Ignoring her, I start to give the old man CPR, but his mouth is coated with dust. I open his jaw and plunge my fingers in, trying to dislodge the red slime but it's formed a paste that's plugging his throat. Not enough air gets through.

With growing desperation, I administer mouth to mouth, wincing as my lips touch the red slobber.

Come on. Come on.

I could have been him. I could have suffocated out there. I could have been thrown against the wall like a dislocated puppet.

Come on. Breathe, damn it. Breathe.

Notes of bland elevator music trickle through my concentration, absurdly trivial as my intertwined fingers pump down on his ribcage.

'It's over, stop,' Jada whispers.

I can't stop the compressions. There's still hope.

Still kneeling next to the poor man, I try to push air into his lungs as the elevator stabilizes on level forty-one.

Jada shakes her head, swearing under her breath.

'We've got to get you out of here before someone realizes I let you in. I could lose my jo—'

The doors open and a high-pitched screech makes us both flinch.

'Oh, for God's sake,' Jada mutters as she steps out of the elevator cab.

A receptionist, sporting very curly blonde hair, too-long bright red nails and pastel-colored spandex shorts with a matching twin set is screaming as she stares at us, her face the picture of terror. She waddles around the reception desk, cellulitis bulging above her knees, the folds of skin under her arms quivering with every movement as she shrieks, 'Get away from him!'

'I'm a doctor, I'm trying to help,' I tell the woman between breaths.

'Don't touch him.' She pushes me roughly away and I fall backward, shocked.

Gawkers have started to gather around us by now and the elevator is blaring an alarm, as the receptionist has pressed the stop button.

'Call security!' someone shouts.

I try to get back to the man's side but the woman is yelling for me to get back, rubbing the old man's mouth with disinfecting wipes. People are getting agitated and a few young men interpose themselves, pushing Jada and me back with small, aggressive shoves.

A hysterical woman shouts, 'Oh my God, is that blood on her mouth?'

'What did you do to him, you fucking coons?' a balding man splutters in my face, his spittle flying.

'Nothing, just mouth to mouth...' I'm trying to get back to my patient, but there are too many of them now.

'You killed him.'

We're backing carefully out of the growing circle of onlookers when a couple of rent-a-cops jog along to the corridor toward us, keys jingling, guns drawn.

Jada lifts her hands up, saying to me over her shoulder, 'Come on, what are you waiting for? You'll get shot.'

'Over here, officers! Two intruders killed a man,' the white receptionist yells, as tears make her voice wobble.

'Hands up!' the larger guard barks at me, holding his gun with both hands, eyebrows furrowed in concentration.

Fear descends on me and I slow down. No sudden movements. No angry retort. Just do what the security guard says.

I lift my hands up slowly, but he grabs my wrist and twisting it behind my back, brings my hand up and squashes my face against wall, pressing his palm on my cheek so hard it forces my lips open. I stay very still.

The other guard is checking the elevator, using his iMode screen as a sort of scanner.

I feel cold handcuffs loop around my wrists. Then, the guard splits my legs open with a few insistent taps against the back of my knees.

'Name, ID,' he barks.

'DeAnn, C... Campbell.'

He scans my iMode bracelet. 'What are you doing here? You know what the penalty is for niggers breaking and entering in this part of town?'

'Probably looking to score some high-tech drugs,' a woman sneers.

The guard's hands are inching up my thighs, as he interrogates me. No sudden movements. Don't say anything. Stay calm.

'There's been a mistake,' I say, trying to stay calm.

'Shut up.' His search is rough, his pats more like bruising

hits; I flinch and force myself to breathe as he moves up to my waist.

'I was doing CPR to save the man's life.'

'I said shut the fuck up.'

EMTs arrive and start to busy themselves around the old man. The receptionist is squeaking by the elevator door, crying into a tissue and gathering support. She seems genuinely frightened and a couple of people are consoling her.

'I'm a geneticist, I'm starting work here today.'

The first policeman snorts, 'Yeah, right and I'm the King of England.'

'I work here too,' Jada chimes in. 'Look, I have a badge.' She makes no move to touch it, her hands remain raised as she stays very still.

One of the paramedics walks out, snapping rubber gloves off his hands. 'Who tried to save this guy's life?'

The guard who holds me hesitates and then walks over to the elevator cab. The two guards and EMTs exchange a few terse words.

'OK, show's over people. Get back to your day.'

'What? But, what about the intruders?'

'It's fine, we're taking care of it. Move along now, folks.'

People disperse, mumbling and chatting among themselves. It takes a few minutes and when everyone's gone, the guard unclasps my handcuffs, a bitter slant to his lips.

'Looks like your story checks out. You're free to go, for now. You're goddamn lucky there was CCTV footage.'

Rubbing my wrists, I open my mouth to berate him but Jada catches my gaze and shakes her head. I'm here undercover and my first day is already a catastrophe. I try to smile.

'No harm done, officer. You're just doing your job, I understand.'

'Watch yourselves now, you hear. That's strike one.'

I nod and bite the inside of my cheek.

'Now get your asses back to the lobby, so we can process you. You have no business being on the executive floor.'

The ride back down is tense and silent. When Jada reaches her floor, she steps over the old man's body and exits the cramped elevator. I feel a twinge seeing the back of her but nothing else happens; they let her go and when we reach the ground floor, the guards escort me to the desk and start making my badge.

'That one was from Oklahoma, I reckon. You can tell by the color. The ones from Kansas are black,' one of the EMTs says, leaning against the desk, vaping something that smells like skunk.

'How long till waste disposal gets here?' his colleague asks.

'I don't know. They gave me a ten-minute ETA. But you know how it is.' He shrugs.

I stand very still, a fake smile still on my face, throwing the occasional backward glances at the devastation. The reception area's glass window is shattered, shards hang from the steel frame and small sparkling fragments are strewn across the entire lobby. Outside, the red sand has formed dunes against every lamppost, every wall, every car.

People are emerging, blinking into the sunlight, their faces smeared with the fine particles. Some are already shoveling the dirt away. The mounds of sand reach waist high and the whole parking lot where I was standing, not half an hour ago, has become a desert. A proper dune-and-camel desert.

'Ah, here they are.' The EMT puts his vape away and gestures to his colleague as a convoy of trucks and street cleaners appears in the parking lot and men in hi-vis fluorescent overalls start busying themselves with the cleanup.

One of the garbage collectors tugs a human arm out of a dune. He doesn't even bother to look for a pulse. He just pulls the arm and the limp body of a woman follows. Her face is covered in red dust and her mouth hangs open. She looks like she's screaming but it's only sand pouring out of her mouth. Her empty eyes, coated with a fine layer of carmine powder, stare at me, as her body is thrown on a pile of cadavers. One of the men blows a bubblegum as he removes her jewelry and pockets it while the others continue clearing out the sand with leaf blowers strapped to their backs, creating red clouds as they walk across the parking lot.

The paramedics carry the old man's corpse outside and dump it on the pile.

'Look here,' the guard says, as the camera scans my face and irises. 'And put your fingers here... and here.'

As the screen logs my fingerprints, a beeping sound makes me glance behind me again, despite myself. The garbage collectors are swinging the old man's body and, on cue, they let him go and he flies into the waste compactor mechanism. I hear crunching sounds and feel bile coming up.

'All done,' the security guard says, reluctantly handing me my iMode where a new badge is revolving against the lit screen. 'Wait here. I've called your manager. He's coming to pick you up.'

5

OLIVIA

*N*ew York, NY, USA, April 2082

I'VE BEEN WORKING my arse off for over a month. Staying until midnight, going the extra mile, shouldering other colleagues' workloads.

And nothing.

I'm still no closer to finding out anything about the medical experiments than on my first day.

I've scoured the archives from top to bottom, searching for likely keywords, poring over records until my eyes burn; I've tried talking discreetly to colleagues without giving the game away; I've applied for extra clearance, ingratiated myself with the PAs with sandwich runs and compliments. All to no avail.

I pull out the High Commission memo from my purse. The paper is soft by now and the creases have nearly torn the sheets in pieces. Smoothing it down, I re-read it for the hundredth time.

FROM: Mr. John Bartlett
  Partner
  Carapadre & Dergrin
  New York, NY, USA

TO: Mr. Hugh Mees-Brogg
  Head of Trade and Investment Department
  KEW High Commission
  Kampala, Uganda

DEAR SIR,

With reference to the discussion we had with you on June 3rd, 2079, we write on behalf of our client, GeneX, Ltd (ID number: 03256HLC67850081), to follow up on relevant issues pertaining to the business venture previously registered.

Carapadre & Dergrin are acting with Power of Attorney on behalf of our client and hereby lodge a formal request for the KEW High Commission's assistance in obtaining the necessary authorizations and permits to allow our client, GeneX to conduct their medical tests in the district of Kisenyi.

Accordingly, we submit for your approval the following provisions governing our client's engagement in Uganda and the necessary forms, filled out as per your instructions. If you are in agreement, please sign the enclosed copy of this letter in the space provided below. If you have any questions about these provisions or the form attached, or if you would like to discuss possible modifications, do not hesitate to contact us.

. . .

I FLIP the page and read through the second request, for similar tests in Bwaise, two years later.

'Sinclair?'

It's right there, in black and white. I'm in the right place. So why can't I find out anything?

The voice insists. 'Olivia Sinclair?'

I don't react immediately.

Bloody hell. That's my fake name.

Flinching, I turn in my chair and look up. The senior barrister who showed me around on my first day is leaning over my cubicle separator, staring at the piece of paper I'm reading. He works directly for John Bartlett.

Sucking my breath in, I plant my elbow on the memo and lift a hand to my hair, leaning over the desk in a weak pretence of nonchalance.

'Yes?'

'Is that paper?' He squints through his horn-rimmed glasses, trying to get a better look. 'Where on earth did you find that? I didn't even know you could procure any in the office anymore.'

'Oh, it's nothing,' I say, folding the paper and cramming it in my handbag. 'What can I do for you?'

'Have we—' He frowns. 'Ah yes, I remember you now. You're the odd duck from a few weeks back. You were having a philosophical conversation with the orientation holo, weren't you?'

I blush. 'Erm...'

'Well, congrats. You're moving on to the big leagues. Get all your stuff and follow me.'

I gather all my possessions, grab my coat and thirty seconds later, I'm trotting behind him, as I try to keep up with his long strides down the busy hallway. En route, he explains, 'We've been waiting for a long time to find a paralegal with the kind of work ethics, erm... profile... and security clearance that you have. We sorely needed an extra pair of hands but we had to be sure about your credentials. You seem to have made an excellent impression downstairs and we need your kind of talent and ... pedigree.'

I nod, wondering exactly what vetting they might have done, and getting retrospective chills about what might have happened if they had seen through my new identity. And what the hell does he mean, pedigree? Did they do a bloody DNA test?

We take a lift to the highest level and he continues, eyeing the floor numbers as they scroll away and we climb to dizzying heights, 'Our firm is part of the magic circle, as you know. We specialise in political law. We help politicians and very large corporations to navigate the murky waters of lobbying, regulation, bribery, compliance, that sort of thing.'

I resist the urge to tell him that I have been working in law for the last fifteen years. I'm supposed to be a lowly admin, I'd better keep my mouth shut so I just nod.

'My team works on the firm's biggest account, GeneX. We're the highest revenue generator for Carapadre and Dergrin for the seventh year running.' He pauses, no doubt expecting obsequiousness, so I oblige.

'Thank you so much for your trust, Mr Quisling, I really appre—'

He interrupts me with a small wave of his hand. 'This morning, we're getting a visit from our client, who has just invented a new... "technology", and needs to know how likely it is that they'll get sued for making it... "available" to the wider public.' He looks at me and probably sees that I am not completely *au fait* with what he's talking about. 'You're English, right?'

'Yes, sorry, I would really appreciate it if you could bring me up to speed on the context.'

He frowns. 'Well, the technology our client has invented is still illegal here. The government may pass a law to make it permissible soon. But it will take a few more months to make it legal and that's assuming the law makes it through all the hoops. Our client needs to know how to navigate that period while at the same time starting to ... "market" and use that new technology. Does that make sense?'

'Yes, perfect sense. Thank you,' I say, wondering what the heck this is all about. Through the thick forest of euphemisms, could he be talking about the drug they were testing in Uganda?

'Whatever you hear during your assignment in my team, it's obviously highly confidential and you can't repeat it to anyone aside from me. Do you understand? Not even other colleagues within the firm.'

'Yes, of course. Client confidentiality is paramount, I understand.'

'I've already forwarded you an NDA, make sure you sign it asap. Then I need you to help take notes this morning. Just find a chair at the back of the room and record the verbatim of the meeting, alright? We'll sift through it later.'

'Yes, Mr Quisling, will do.'

'Sinclair, was it? You really are an odd duck, aren't you?' He laughs. 'Don't get me wrong, as a fellow vinter, I enjoy the retro touch, as you can see.' He gestures to his nicely cut suit. Come to think of it, that's probably a twentieth-century cut. 'Just maybe tone it down up here. Don't shake hands or curtsy or whatever.' He chortles and rubs his bearded chin, looking at my lips.

As we enter the vast conference room, Michael leaves me and goes to talk with an older man, adopting the body language and deferential tones of someone interacting with his manager. That must be John Bartlett, then.

The view is stunning from up here. High-rises, busy streets and traffic unfold as far as the eye can see.

My mood considerably lifted, I choose a chair in a corner, as far away as possible from everyone, sign the non disclosure agreement and then absorb myself in finding out how to record the minutes on the work computer that's perched on my knees. It's paper thin, hard and translucent. By the time I'm done smearing fingerprints all over the screen, the room has gone silent and everyone is sitting around the large conference-room table.

Michael's manager gets up. 'Mr Viles, thank you for joining us this morning.'

All eyes are on a small, grey-looking man, with too much makeup on. A simpering smile stretches his collagen-enhanced lips. He has the taut, leonine look that comes with too many nips and tucks.

I nearly jump out of my skin when Michael's deep voice says, 'He's the CEO of GeneX', inside my head.

Michael's sitting five metres away, at the conference table. His lips move again but no sound comes out.

'Ready?' he rumbles in the curve of my ear.

His iMode collar must be recording the movements of his throat and translating them as a voice in my ear bud.

Bugger, how do I respond? I try to hold my finger to my collar and silently mouth the words, 'Yes, I'm ready.'

'You can start recording the meeting's audio now and take notes as well, so we can write proper minutes later on.'

'Yes, Mr Quisling.'

He smiles and covers his mouth with his hand. 'Call me Michael, odd duck.'

The CEO of GeneX starts with an intro and my ears

prick up when I hear '... and very successful tests in Africa. We are now confident that we'll be able to start selling the technology to our Coalition allies within a few months. However, we need to be certain that the US government will protect us from any repercussions associated with the use of this new technology. As you can imagine, this will be controversial and there is likely to be considerable backlash from public opinion.'

I scan the room for any reactions. No one looks outraged. No one looks surprised. These people have essentially no qualms about helping GeneX conduct medical experiments in Africa. Or helping the company deploy an illegal technology ahead of a hypothetical change in the law.

After weeks of hard work, it looks like I'm finally in the right place to find out what happened in Uganda.

I've made it into the inner sanctum.

6

DEANN

*S*t. Louis, Missouri, USA, April 2082

I'M SITTING down in my cubicle, blocking out the sounds of white-bred people chatting to each other about the difficulties of finding dependable maids, their upcoming weekends of barbecues, inflatable kiddie pools and the latest AI self-improvement app or whatever, when my boss comes by my desk, sweaty and gross. He peers at me above his glasses and seems mildly shocked all over again to realize I'm black.

'Staying late again, Diane?'

I glance up at the fat mountain of him; he's got a triple chin and looks about eight-months pregnant. Probably expecting twins: heart attack and diabetes. He pushes back his glasses with a pudgy hand sporting too-long nails.

'You know me. I'm all about the work, Dick.'

That's really his name. Why anyone would purposefully

choose to be called that is beyond me. Turns out, it suits him perfectly.

'We just got a great big data dump from one of our testing facilities, they had to close and we've been tasked with analyzing all the information. We need someone who won't be too... judgmental about the work.'

'No problem at all. I know that everything GeneX is doing is for the greater good.'

All this simpering makes me sick to my stomach. But I'm learning so much here that I can't afford to jeopardize it. I smile and grit my teeth. My cheek muscles are sore from all that fake smiling and it hurts in more ways than one. My face remembers doing it for years.

I hadn't realized how good it felt to be authentic in Uganda. I was more truly myself there than I'd ever dared to be before. But now that I'm back home, all the old masks are snapping back in place, locking in. I need to pretend in order to be accepted here. My soul flails against the restraints and I quiet it down.

He lingers for a while longer, pressuring me about the deadline. Nothing's worse than a petty man with a small amount of power. He tries his best to undermine me but he can probably sense that it's in vain. He leaves with a thoughtful look on his face, his comb-over floating as his massive body wobbles away.

At first I was amazed by the amount of information I was given access to. But then, I started to realize that to them this is just a drop in an ocean of ethically questionable experiments. Jada, a few floors down, is an analyst working on genetically modified crops and she tells me her friends are researching vaccines, cloning, organ farming, longevity experiments... The building is over forty stories high, there's no way of knowing what else might be in play here.

Most of their medical research and testing are conducted in underdeveloped countries. There is no appetite for testing in developed countries. These days, when even one test subject dies, they consider the entire test as failed and the drug gets canned.

This is why GeneX test their drugs in Africa, away from prying eyes, on unsuspecting subjects. It's the only way to get anything approved for the American market.

Meanwhile, rich patients in the USA and Europe don't really care about how new drugs are tested, as long as a brave new world of ever-lasting life, endless youth and imperviousness to disease is ushered in. So the system perpetuates itself without much scrutiny from anyone at all. There's nothing I can do about it. So I set my qualms aside, sift through the data and learn as much as I can.

A LONG WHILE LATER, looking up from my screen to rub my eyes, I'm startled to find the lab plunged in darkness. I didn't notice the time pass. I'm so close. I need to understand what this drug does. I'm not entirely sure why it should matter to me more than the other innumerable experiments that GeneX is conducting. Maybe because Kitsa died for this one. Maybe because Omony tried to kill me for it.

My iMode pings and Olivia's face appears on screen. She looks distraught as she waits for me to pick up. I toy with the idea of rejecting the call but my eyes snag on the angry pink scar that now slashes through her upper lip and I decide to take it. We promised to work together and communicate. I can't shut her out. Not anymore.

'Hey, Snow White, how's the Big Apple?'

'Ha ha. Very funny.'

She tells me about her promotion and what she found out today then asks me, 'Any progress on your side?'

'It looks like GeneX has reverse engineered a chemical compound from a substance found in a patient zero.'

'You know, I've been wondering about something Anth... something I heard.' She bites her lip. 'Do you think the chemical could be from the future? Maybe a returning agent was patient zero. Wouldn't that explain why they don't have free access to the formula and have to reverse engineer it?

I mull it over. 'Yeah, I think you might be on to something. Given the current medical progress, this is way too advanced for 2082. It only takes one exposure to the compound to trigger an irreversible genetic modification. It's quite clean and efficient actually. I really admire the science behind it.'

'Until we figure out what it actually does,' she says, frowning, 'I'll reserve my judgment.'

'Mmh. Well, whatever it does and however they got it, it looks like the Programme tried to replicate the chemical with the help of GeneX and came up with formulas that were close but not perfect.'

'That would explain why the Programme conducted field tests on the variants for years. They weren't getting the correct composition,' Olivia says.

'Yeah, looks like it. Reading all the autopsy results chronologically, I think at first the drug must have been too potent and it caused immediate death. Subsequent formulas caused cancers. That seems to tally with what Rosebell and I observed in Kampala. A rash of cancers in the populations exposed to the molecule.'

'That's huge, DeAnn. Is that what Itungo had? A cancer caused by the wrong dosage?'

I keep forgetting that she met Itungo and her husband,

that she went to Bwaise regularly and for the umpteenth time, I feel a twinge of regret about what we could have accomplished if only we'd spoken earlier. Kitsa's face flickers and fades.

'Yes, that sounds about right.' I say.

'Itungo must have been an early experiment subject, when they were testing in Kisenyi in 2079.'

'I remember Itungo told me that she'd moved from Kisenyi to Bwaise. It all fits. By 2081, they probably started getting the dosage right and the last phase of the field test in Bwaise must have yielded the results they were looking for.'

'I heard Colonel Groebler and... I overheard a conversation saying the substance worked and that's why the Programme wrapped up the tests.'

'And I saw them gathering the barrels of the formula that worked for repatriation. Presumably they sent the successful batch back here, in St Louis for analysis. So I think they succeeded... I wish I knew what they succeeded in creating though.'

'Whatever it was,' Olivia says pensively, 'they needed to check that the results remained permanent. So they probably followed a few dozen test subjects and collected these poor people a few months or a few years later. Murdered them and cut them open.'

She shivers. She told me what she saw in Camp Askaris. 'Do you think you can find out the objective of the chemical? What they were looking for in those autopsies?'

I shift in my seat and look behind me. Nobody can hear me inside my iBubble. But still, the darkness and the deserted offices are making me nervous.

'I'm sifting through the data methodically and chronologically. It's very slow going because they've chosen each person in this lab to have a very limited set of skills and assigned them a small piece of the puzzle, so no one can actually figure out what they're working on. I only have access to my case load – and I'm only an analyst.'

She smiles encouragingly and I brace myself, ready for her to say something chirpy and encouraging. She doesn't disappoint.

'Except, you're not just an analyst, are you? You're much more senior and skilled than anyone there. You'll figure it out. You're brilliant. Look how much progress you've made in only a few weeks.'

I smile, oddly not annoyed and even a little pleased.

'You should talk to your colleagues, make friends with them so you can access their jigsaw pieces.'

'Huh. That's a good idea.'

'Try not to sound so surprised.' She grins.

We chat a little more after that and then hang up. I check the time again. Probably way too late to text, let alone call. But I try anyway and Jada picks up, looking grumpy, her hair in an turquoise wrap.

'Hey, Jada.'

'Have you seen the time?'

'Do you know someone who could get me access to the lab? I need to figure out a few things about my project but I don't have access. I've only got clearance for the analysis and reporting section. I really need this data for a project that—'

'Yeah, yeah, yeah. Save your sob story for someone who cares.' She thinks for a minute. 'Sure. I know someone who could grant you access. But on one condition.'

'If you're going to put conditions, I don't know if—'

'I'm hanging up now. Good luck with your project.'

'OK, fine, fine. Don't be like that, for God's sake. What's the condition?'

'I saw you perform CPR on that old guy the day I saved your life. You're a doctor, right?'

Oh, here we go. 'Yes, so what?'

'There's a clinic not far from where we live. If you want my help getting access to the lab, it'll cost you five evenings of volunteering a week at the clinic for a minimum of a year.'

'Out of the question, I have a full-time job. Come on, Jada.'

'You don't give a shit about anyone but yourself, do you? Money, comfort, career – that's all that matters to you, isn't it?'

For someone who's known me for half a minute, she's annoyingly good at pricking my pride.

'One evening a week for one month is all I can do,' I counter.

'Three,' she says, crossing her arms, 'for nine months.'

'Two evenings a week for six months. Deal?'

'OK, deal. Can I get back to sleep now?'

'You drive a hard bargain.' I smile. 'Hey, Jada?'

She pauses, her finger on her collar, grumpy as ever. 'What?'

'Why do you care so much?'

'Why don't you?' She hangs up.

7

OLIVIA

N*ew York, NY, USA, May 2082*

I TRY hard to integrate in my new team but I don't like any of my colleagues and none of them seems to like me much either. Except maybe Michael. We're pulling an all-nighter at the office again tonight so I've tagged along to a midnight run for dinner. As soon as we arrived at the upscale grocery store, everyone scattered and now I'm a bit lost in the endless aisles of the enormous supermarket.

The lurid neon lighting illuminates every corner of the store, where row upon row of food is displayed in garish colours. Unfamiliar music blares and strange-looking people loiter along the endless aisles. I can't help but stare at a man with thick bifocals and a long ponytail that reaches down to his bum. He's fixes the strap of his horse-hoof shoe, neighing and shaking his head as I go by.

I spot three of my colleagues, Cressida, Imogen and

Blythe, who are gossiping while they wait for their sand-wiches. They're all wearing skin-tight pantsuits, their hair is perfect and they're beautiful in an intimidating sort of way. Sighing, I edge closer to the group of immaculate lawyers and try to blend in.

'... so I told Travis: I know we already have four children, that's not the point. You make me another or I leave you,' Imogen says, with a toss of her blonde hair. She's pregnant to her eyeballs and clearly the queen bee of this hive.

'So what did Travis say?' Cressida asks with rapt attention.

'Well, he said...' Imogen draws it out and then squeals with delight: 'Yes! He said we'd make another baby as soon as he had his promotion and his raise... and here we are, expecting twins.' A smug pout on her face, she gestures at her distended belly, encased in hot pink spandex.

'Twins!' the sycophants gush.

But on their faces I see only envy and disgust. I'm guessing they've both heard this story a thousand times before, and now their veneer of enthusiasm is wearing thin.

I can't say I blame them. As always, when I see a preg-nant woman, I feel a wave of dislike and jealousy rises up. They're forever waddling along, rosy cheeked, talking about cervical mucus with abandon, endlessly stroking their bumps and getting all the attention. I'm such a failure. Why does she get to live the life I want? What does she have that I don't? Too many good answers occur to me as I detail her perfect complexion, shiny hair and elegant, manicured hands.

Suppressing my feeling of inadequacy, I try to join her little posse. 'Sorry, do you know the shop well? I'm looking for—'

'Oh. You're the new girl, the *paralegal*,' the dominant

blonde says, looking at me as if I were the help. Which I guess I am. There was only this small role available on the project I needed to join, and DeAnn and A. felt that I would be better able to go under the radar in a low-level job.

The other two look at each other with a smirk.

'Yes, hello there, I'm Olivia.' I pretend to be oblivious to their snubs even though I can't help but blush and hate my cheeks for it. 'Thank you for inviting me along tonight, that's very kind of—'

'Oh your accent. You're English, how soop.' Imogen puts on a mask of civility. 'I hear you're forty-one and child *free*.' She smiles. 'You're the smartest one of us all, aren't you? Can you remember all the free time, girls?'

'Not to mention the disposable income. You must do so much shopping,' adds the younger one, Blythe, but she looks me up and down and suppresses a smile as she says it.

Cressida, the brunette, turns to the other two. 'It's so expensive to raise a family these days, don't you think? Makes you wonder whether they do it on purpose, to discourage people from having too many kids?'

'Well, it would discourage only a certain type of people,' Blythe chimes in, her eyes sliding over my mediocre outfit and frizzy hair.

'I don't think it's a question of money. Otherwise, Lord knows inner cities would be empty. I think some people are just selfish,' Imogen says with practised outrage. 'They'd rather prioritise their work over starting a family. Personally, I think it's so self-centred it's shameful. Can you imagine dedicating your entire life to your own whims, never caring for anyone but yourself? What about our duty to the country and to God?' She gracefully takes the sandwich that the attendant is passing over the counter.

The familiar sting rears its ugly head. Cold. Selfish. Self-centred. If only they knew how hard I tried. How it crushed me to fail.

'We don't mean you, of course, Livy.' The pregnant blonde's laughter sounds as artificial as a sitcom's. 'You're a foreigner, it's different.'

'Ah. Sinclair, there you are.' Michael barges in, unaware that he's interrupting a hazing session. He seems like such a nice guy and he's been taking an interest in me – or maybe he hasn't. It's hard to tell. He's close and also distant. Sometimes like today, he seems to genuinely like me. Other times he's absorbed in his work and I think I've imagined his interest. I don't know how to deal with this. Life. Normal life again. How do I reconcile all these petty concerns with my nightmares?

'Did you find what you need yet? We should get back to the office.' Michael smiles down at me. He's very tall and slightly chubby, with smiley puffy eyes.

'Not yet. Can you help me find the salad bar?'

He laughs, a big heartfelt chortle, head thrown back. I like the sound of his laughter. It sounds clean and warm. His deep baritone voice lends it depth.

'Yes, coming right up, milady. Will you have some caviar with that?' He looks at me fondly.

'No fruit either, then, I'm guessing?' I smile, trying to pass my mistake as a joke. 'What is this dump you've taken me to, anyway?'

'Well, I don't know what kind of lifestyle you've been accustomed to before coming here, but this isn't a gourmet shop for millionaires, you know.'

He offers me his arm and we go in search of my dinner. I don't turn back to check on the group of vipers.

'Why so gloomy, Sinclair? You OK?'

'Oh, it's nothing. Everything just seems a bit... alien I suppose.'

'You don't like my city?' he says in his charming New York accent.

With surprise, I realise I actually miss Uganda. 'I'm afraid not, sorry. It feels like someone dimmed the lights here, the sky is always grey. The air is foul. People feel too washed out, too polluted... I don't know.' I shrug.

'Jeez Louise, don't sugar-coat it for me,' he laughs.

'There's also a ruthlessness, an absence of compassion here that I find disturbing.'

'Well, that's just not gonna work.'

'I'm so sorry, I didn't mean to—'

'Mission accepted, Sinclair. I'm going to make you love my city.'

I smile and we shake on it.

The shop he's taken us to is obviously upmarket and the food is showcased with care. We're in quite a good neighbourhood from what I can tell, so this must be what yuppies have access to here. Row upon row of corn derivatives. Corn flakes, corn flour, corn syrup, in a myriad of chemically flavoured incarnations. It all looks colourful and tasty. But it doesn't really feel like food.

'Um, I guess bread and something to put in it, then.'

'We're going to make a sandwich from scratch? Very old school – I like it, Sinclair.'

We go in search of bread. It's a struggle to find a loaf that's actually made of wheat and has no sugar, no flavours, no additives, preservatives or added colours. Just plain old bread. Michael gamely reads all the labels to help me.

Remembering the Ugandan stores' empty shelves is making this innocuous shopping trip seem completely surreal. In Kampala, I used to find empty, dusty shelves in the small corner stores where I traded spices for a few tin cans. I feel sick to my stomach thinking of how desperately we tried to gather food for our church drives.

Here it seems that there is everything one might want and more and while food is not healthy or nutritious, there's still just about enough to feed the rich. People don't starve, but they're malnourished, eating processed food that contains no vitamins, no fibres. Their lives are not in immediate danger yet, but all the preservatives and colorants hide the basic truth that their food is empty of nutrients. It seems that the same is true of their culture. The more garish and strident it gets, the less truth it contains. It's all so sugary sweet and absurd.

'All that food,' I sigh, feeling overwhelmed by the quantity and choice. 'Do you know, Michael, how the French cook frogs?'

'I've never eaten a frog, have you? I hear it was a delicacy.'

'Not my point at all,' I chuckle. 'If you put a frog in a pot of cold water and only gradually increase the temperature, the frog won't try to escape. It won't actually realise that the rising temperature is killing it until the water's boiling.'

'I'm not following, Sinclair.'

'You do know that the world is overpopulated, right? You're nearly at boiling point and you don't even know it. Overpopulation has been slowly increasing over generations. So by the time it's your turn to have children, you all think that this is... normal because no one alive can remember what it was like before there were billions too many of us.'

No one except me, I think sadly. I know what it was like when the water was cold. The year I was born, there were only four billion people in the world. And the oceans were teeming with life, the air was pure and food tasted like food.

He pops a pretzel in his mouth, takes a moment to chew it and says: 'We don't have an overpopulation issue.'

'What?'

He looks around and gestures at me to keep it down. 'We have a water shortage issue. A street violence issue. An infrastructure decay issue—'

'But all these things are related to overpopulation: water and food shortages are happening because there isn't enough food in the world to feed everyone anymore. There aren't enough jobs for all of them, so: mass unemployment. Then the street violence is a result of the employment crisis because people are too poor to buy food, so they resort to violence to fend off starvation.'

We finally find a loaf of bread and he takes me towards another aisle. 'And the infrastructure decay?'

'Well, obviously the more of us there are, the harder it is to keep everything functioning. For example, your country's population has doubled in fifty years. It would have been impossible for you to also double the infrastructure – the schools, the roads, the number of nurses, teachers, postmen. No wonder things are getting worse; you can't keep up with your population growth.'

'You can't mention this topic. It's in poor taste.'

'I beg your pardon?'

He's frowning. 'Overpopulation is mostly down to the poor and immigrant populations being too fertile. So you can't say anything about it. It's racist.'

'No, no you misunderstand me. I'm saying that all of humanity is exceeding Earth's carrying capacity. It's not about skin colour, it's about our species in general.'

'Still. It's taboo. I'm a Democrat. We just don't talk

about that sort of thing. The topic is too sensitive and it's practically impossible to rally activists behind it. Any politician who tries to bring it up is pretty much sure he or she'll never be re-elected again. It's much easier to rally people behind the slogan "save the children",' he air quotes, 'than behind "stop making so many goddamn children".'

We pass by a morbidly obese white woman who is only wearing a hot-pink thong, a very transparent nightie and feathery pink slippers. Her cart is full of diet products.

'So everyone ignores the problem, then?' I feel so dejected.

'It's not so bad. Look around, we have enough.' He shrugs.

'People are starving throughout the world in order to get these shelves fully stocked. There just isn't enough for everyone anymore.'

'I disagree. Hunger is always manufactured for political reasons; there is no penury at a global level, just glitches in distribution and market dynamics that occur in certain countries. There's enough to feed America, we'll just have to pay more, that's all. Maybe fight other countries for resources as well.'

We're at the till now and there's no sign of our colleagues. They must have gone back to the office already. I have a loaf of bread, some sort of sandwich spread, a bag of crisps and a bottle of water. The bill is close to $150. He carries my plastic bags and we walk back to the subway. Seeing the dozens of homeless people between us and the subway entrance, I falter and ask him to show me how to give them money, since there is no cash anymore.

'You just program it. You can choose a particular home-less guy and give only to his iMode by swiping yours against his. Then from that point on, every time you cross paths, the transfer of money will take place.'

He gently takes my wrist and the contact of his fingers against my skin startles me.

'Here, I'll help you set it up.'

'What about the ones who don't have an iMode?' I ask while he programs the device.

Just as he opens his mouth to answer me, we hear screaming tyres and a car rams into a homeless man kneeling on a square of cardboard a hundred yards away from us.

I stand there, frozen with horror, but Michael's already moving. He pulls me into a narrow alleyway, holding his finger in front of his lips.

'You fucking SCUM!'

I poke my head carefully around the wall. A young woman is yelling as the homeless group scatters, scrambling to get away from her. A nice-looking car is crashed against the wall, blood splattered on the bonnet and the wall behind it. The homeless man's body is lying beneath the car, beheaded.

Two young men and another girl are getting out of the car, wielding baseball bats. They look so young and preppy that my mind is refusing to accept what I see. They're white, they look wealthy; blonde-pony-tails-and-pastel-jumper-draped-around-the-shoulders kind of wealthy. What in the name of God is happening here? Pale faced, Michael pulls me back further and we crouch behind a rubbish container as the smell of rot and urine invades my nostrils, acrid and pungent.

The group goes on a rampage. We hear them laugh and egg each other on drunkenly. The shrieks are heart wrench-ing. One of the homeless men sprints past our alleyway, just a few feet away. He stumbles and falls flat on his face. I try to get up to go help him but Michael pulls me back down with a sharp tug, wrapping his arm around my waist and holding me against his chest, as we shrink into the dark shadows.

Just then, one of the girls enters our range of vision, holding a bloodied baseball bat and wearing a demented grin. She pummels the homeless man to death in front of us with shrieks of rage. Spattering the man's brains on her pristine white shirt and her peach sweater. Bile rises in the back of my throat as the bat thumps against the soft moistness of the man's body.

A rat scurries across my foot and I recoil involuntarily, making the grocery bag rustle. The girl looks up abruptly, glaring in our direction. Her face is so round, rosy and soft. She starts to walk down the alley towards us, the expression on her pretty face cruel and focused. A hunter.

Michael shrinks in the shadows, crushing me against him, a hand on my mouth. My palms start to tingle with sweat as I remember Burke holding me captive, his hands on my throat. My lungs stop working. Gasping for air, I start to squirm as terror rises like electricity along my nerves.

The girl with the sweet, full face approaches, the sound of her footsteps heading towards the spot where we're hiding, as she scans the pitch-black alley. The night is still concealing us but she'll see us any moment now. Panicking, I start to fight Michael's embrace and my movements dislodge the rat. It runs past us and out towards the main street.

The girl stops. With a snort, she has a last look at the rubbish container and then leaves. As soon as she's out of sight, I yank Michael's hand off my face and take long, silent gulps of air. We stay like this for a long time. His arms around my waist, crouching in the filthy alley. Immobile.

Listening in the dark, as the screams die down and the street falls silent.

At length, when the stillness has returned and my heart rate has calmed down, I twist out of Michael's embrace and, treading cautiously to the mouth of the alley, I peek around the corner. They're gone.

Michael dusts down his suit and runs his hands through his curly brown hair, as he walks over to me. 'That was freaking close. You OK?'

I nod, swallowing with difficulty as I discover the massacre beyond.

'Come, we need to go.' He tries to drag me away but I stop to take a homeless man's pulse. Nothing. It looks like he was slashed open, the lacerations deliberate. Like... torture.

There are six dead in the street. One of the homeless was a teenage girl. Her face is half gone, the missing part splattered all over the pavement. I bump into her naked foot and when it twitches, the entire contents of my stomach come rushing up. The brick wall rough against my palms, I throw up, eyes closed.

When I open my eyes again, wiping away a tear, the night is pulsing with red and blue lights and Michael's face is contracting with tension as he hesitates between waiting for me and running.

'Quickly, Olivia. We don't want to be here when the police arrive.'

I let him pull me away and we sprint to the subway, grocery bags knocking wildly against our shins.

In the carriage's stark lighting, the few people around us all look defeated and old. Some seem drunk. None look preppy. Sagging with relief, I sit on the plastic moulded chairs as the train rattles away. Michael doesn't seem particularly shocked or surprised. Just grim. He sits next to me, pulling his leather satchel onto his lap. His kind, plump face twisted with something that looks like fear and shame.

'I can't believe we witnessed the Rage, and lived to talk about it,' he whispers.

'Where were the authorities? How could this happen in the middle of the street?'

'Ssh. Keep it down.' He looks around, but the people who surround us don't seem to register anything. 'The police let it happen. These kids are usually really wealthy. They're Alphas, the sons and daughters of Senators, CEOs; no policeman on minimum wage wants to antagonise their parents. The ones who try are fired. Or worse.'

'But why do the kids do it? If they're rich and powerful, they must have enough to eat, enough of everything?'

'They don't need any of that. No one really knows why but they're violent. Angry. They take it out on the weak.'

'I don't understand.' I shake my head.

'No one understands it. It's only the teenagers, the youngest generation who do it. Some psychologists think that it's behavioural sinks.'

'What's that?'

'Violence, aggressiveness, frenetic behaviours triggered by overcrowding.' He shrugs. 'Who knows? Main thing is we survived. We were really lucky.'

8

DEANN

S *t. Louis, Missouri, USA, May 2082*

A DISHEVELED HOMELESS man holds a sign by the side of the road, looking straight at me as the driverless car rides placidly past him.

'The LORD will turn the RAIN of your country into DUST and POWDER,' he bellows. 'It will come down from the SKIES until you are DESTROYED! Repent sinners! This is the WRATH OF GOD!'

As his silhouette fades in the rearview mirror, I glance at Jada and Lashelle. They haven't asked why I really need access to the lab. They're just helping out in good faith. We're on our way to meet someone who has the right privileges and has agreed to help me out.

Jada's VRing her children and Lashelle's working during the trip, her long brown fingers flying across the transparent iMode screen.

'How much longer?' I ask her.

The woman lifts up her delicate face. 'About an hour.'

She's wearing a plunging décolleté made of some silky material over the usual leggings, and manages to look feminine and blasé, despite the danger of our collaboration.

This could get them both fired. I hope they won't live to regret it. Biting the inside of my cheek, I ask, 'Are you really sure you—'

'Jada vouched for you,' a wicked smile stretches on her lips, 'and none of the pasty boys in IT have any clue. Don't worry. They won't be able to trace it back to any of us. I'm very good at what I do.'

Suburbia recedes behind us and soon we're out in the countryside. Or what should be the countryside, but it's devastated.

The driverless car struggles on the road, as it's completely covered in the red sand, which swirls in our wake. Outside, through the dust, I can make out the outlines of cornfields, the plants long dead.

The car swerves around a set of bones and tanks violently to the right. My head bangs against the window and we go off road as the car tilts dangerously above the ditch, and withered corn stalks lash at the windscreen like hands begging us to stop. I rub my temple and look out as the car rights itself and we continue on our way.

Lashelle and Jada chat about inconsequential things, shoes, food, celebrities. I tune them out while we pass through farmland submerged under orange sand. Carcasses of cars, the paint sandblasted off them, gleam in the sun, looking oddly like the half-submerged steel skeletons of strange desert beasts. Farmhouses with collapsed roofs and caved-in doors litter the landscape, their walls licked by amber dunes, as they drown, flooded in a sea of sand.

Finally, the car slows down and Jada turns to me.

'Ready to see the future?' she smiles.

Absorbed in the landscape, I jerk awake and stop myself from making a quip. *I've seen quite enough of the future, actually.*

They walk ahead and I follow, my heels finding little purchase as my shoes fill with hot grains of sand. Then, over the crest of a dune, I see them. Strange-looking plastic domes protruding from the ground like gigantic fly eyes. For a moment I think I've landed on Mars, as I take in the hexagonal panels fitted together to form futuristic hothouses embedded in the red sand.

A slight buzzing emanates from one of the round domes; I place my hand on the frame and jerk back when a swarm of small dark shapes skitters toward my palm on the other side of the plastic.

'What is this place?' I ask.

'Experimental biofarm,' an older woman says, ambling toward us in knee-high rubber boots and a farmer's overalls. She hugs Jada in a warm embrace.

'Hey, Shanice,' Jada says, emerging from the hug with a smile, 'this is DeAnn and you know Lashelle, right?'

'Welcome, welcome,' Shanice says, smiling as she tightens the scarf holding her dreadlocks in a lose bun.

'How did the last batch do?' Jada asks.

The old woman's smile falters, she shakes her head.

'Shit,' Jada says. 'Show me.'

The older woman places her hand on a fingerprint panel and the doors open with a hiss of cool air. Glancing at the GeneX logo stenciled above the door, I start to follow them in but have to stop on the threshold, startled; we're in an oasis.

The dome's round ceiling rises up to at least thirty-five

feet height and through the blurry patchwork of windows, red sand is visible as it laps against the outside of the circular structure, reaching high above our heads. A cool mist kisses my face and the sound of running water tinkles somewhere nearby.

Jada and Lashelle are already off, asking technical questions about the project, as Shanice leads them to a small patch of corn. I stand still for a moment, taking in the wonder of this poignantly green Eden in the middle of the blighted desolation outside. Plants grow in neat little fields, delineated by pathways, and scientists in white lab coats take measurements and tend to the experiments. Nobody spares me a glance as I catch up to my small group.

'Well, that doesn't look so bad,' Jada starts. 'Do you think it will finally work?'

Shanice tugs on a corn stalk and the roots lift clean out of the orange soil, offering no resistance. Sand rains down and the white roots appear, barely one inch long.

'God damn it!' Jada kicks a bucket, swearing as she walks away from us, to check other stalks.

'Aren't these hybrids supposed to hold the soil together?' Lashelle asks, peering at the plant as she holds the tablet against her chest.

Shanice nods, peeling away the yellow wrap of fibers to uncover a withered cob. 'Native prairie grasses might have held back the sand. But we've killed those. We don't even have the heirloom seeds for anything that used to grow here. It's all gone.'

'What's wrong with these plants?' I ask, glancing at the one in her hand.

'Nothing, as far as we can see. But they just die,' Shanice says. 'From the start, the genetically engineered plants required more fertilizers, more synthetic pesticides, more irrigation than traditional plants to produce their high yields. This deteriorated the soil and caused a massive ecosystem disruption.'

'So the plants we invented caused the situation we're in?' I ask.

'In part, yes. It's a mix of factors. Climate change, drought, soil erosion, gullying...' Shanice clamps her jaws together, staring at the giant honeycomb pattern all around us, lost in her thoughts.

We walk toward Jada, who's kneeling near a small field of wheat at the back of the lab.

'How many years have we been working on this together?' Jada asks the old woman, her face grim. 'How can we still not have found a way? We've got the best scientific tools at our fingertips; we should have a solution by now. What are we doing wrong?'

'It's not your fault, Jada. I just don't think it's possible for anything engineered by us to reverse the Dust Bowl.'

'Why not?' I ask.

Shanice shrugs. 'We probably lost something along the way. For decades, we just kept tweaking the plants in labs, creating clones of clones, copies of copies, and the seed stock kept weakening. We lost touch with nature. We only care about profit and yield these days.'

'Well, we have to, don't we? To feed everyone,' Jada says, frustrated and angry.

Shanice frowns. 'You know how I feel about this. The only solution now is to hold back and let nature recover. More of the same won't produce a different result, Jada.'

'So what? We just throw up our arms and give up? You can't think like that. We'll create a plant that can put an end to the storms. We will. We have to. If we fail, millions will starve,' Jada says. Then she turns and stomps back toward the entrance, looking dispirited.

'Let her go. It's not you,' Lashelle says, putting a hand on Shanice's arm as she watches Jada's back pensively. 'It's just harder for her. She worries about her kids' future.' She sighs.

We follow Jada out of the dome and into the barren dunes outside. The wind rises and a mournful howl whistles through the metal doors as we walk toward the exit.

'Surely technology can fix this?' I ask, puzzled, as I gesture toward the desert around us.

'No one can "fix it", girl,' Shanice says. 'For centuries, they've planted thousands of acres of the same heavily engineered crops over and over. The soil is depleted. They didn't let the land rest, none of it was ever left fallow. And all along, they were plowing just a couple of inches of top soil that were barely holding together a desert.'

'Like what? The Sahara? Under the Midwest's topsoil?' I chuckle.

'Where else did you think the sand came from?' she asks me.

Looking around me at the endless dunes, I believe her. After a moment of silence, I ask, 'But the region will recover, like it did after the Dust Bowl of the 1930s, won't it?'

'This isn't recoverable. This isn't temporary. The sand dunes under our feet are miles deep and the desert has taken hold. It grows every day. It's over.'

I'm at a loss for words.

'Well, it is what it is,' Lashelle sighs.

'No, it isn't.' Shanice says. 'This isn't fate. We did it to ourselves. We could have avoided all of it. Raping the earth for profit, global warming, intensive mono-crop farming, weak genetically modified plants that couldn't hold the earth together. It was all avoidable.'

Lashelle sighs and pats the old woman on the shoulder. I feel suddenly the loss of Rosebell and Kitsa more acutely than ever since leaving Uganda.

These women all seem so close. The bonds of their friendship make me feel like I'm on the outside looking in. I wish... there's no point in finishing that thought, is there? Rosebell and Kitsa are gone and it seems like no one will ever fill me up again. It feels like I've forgotten how to laugh and how to love. I wonder if I'll ever care about anyone again.

Lashelle says to the old woman, 'I know, I know. Well, there's nothing we can do about it now, is there? We just have to get on with it.' She holds the door for me as we exit the biofarm. 'Which reminds me – we should take care of DeAnn's little problem, shouldn't we?'

We file into a surprisingly quaint farm, the mosquito-net door biting at our heels as we pile inside to shelter from the sun.

'Make yourselves at home,' Shanice says, as she removes her boots on a bench at the entrance. 'You're staying for lunch, right?'

Jada thanks her and accepts on our behalf, while I walk over to the sink and swill some water around my cheeks, then spit out the sand in my mouth.

'Hey, don't drink the water.' Shanice closes the tap. 'You want to die or what? Jesus.'

She opens the fridge and offers us bottles of soda. I take a coke and drink it, relishing the cold fizzing liquid as it washes down the last of the dust in my throat.

'None for me, thanks,' Jada says. 'I don't drink sodas.' She chooses a bottle of water instead.

'OK, down to business then,' Lashelle says, as she sets up her electronic equipment on the kitchen table.

We all exchange a look.

'Are you sure you want to help me with this? It could be dangerous—'

'You're not pulling out of our deal, are you?' Jada glares at me, frowning. 'After we arranged to come all the way over here.'

'No, no. I'll help out at the clinic like I promised, regardless, but your jobs could be at risk and—'

Shanice holds up a hand. 'Jada said you're doing this to help our brothers and sisters, is that right?'

I nod.

'OK, then in that case, let's get this done,' Shanice says, firmly.

Lashelle pulls a chair and holds out her hands. 'iModes.'

A solemn mood descends on the kitchen as we unclasp the devices from our wrists and entrust the slender woman with them.

'So this is how it will work. It's a bit of code I've come up with that could land me in jail, so I'll be grateful if you're fucking careful with it.'

I bite the inside of my cheek and glance at Shanice.

Lashelle continues, 'Basically, every time you tap here, DeAnn, your iMode will switch and think you're Shanice. This should give you access to any laboratory and all the test results and biological material you might need. Meanwhile, your access profile for the Analysis and Reporting section of the St. Louis building will go dormant and, with it, all your privileges, so make sure you switch back before you enter your office or you'll trigger every fucking alarm in the joint, as Shanice doesn't have the right to be there.'

I nod, feeling a tremor of anticipation at the perspective of finally getting my hands on the samples.

'OK, so let's go over this one more time...' the IT specialist says, looking at Shanice and me.

I can't see any other way to discover what my team is working on. The case load I've been given is an endless procession of data, names, DNA profiles. Rows upon rows of numbers and statistics that I will never be able to break down into meaningful clusters. I need to understand the bigger picture. With my current profile, I can't check any of the samples, blood draws, biopsies; I can't have access to the autopsy results; I can't use any of the lab equipment and robots.

I need access to the labs or I'll never figure out what the Ugandan medical experiments were about.

But this could get me caught.

This could get all of us killed.

9

OLIVIA

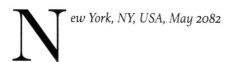

New York, NY, USA, May 2082

'DAYDREAMING?' a deep, warm voice says in my ear.

Michael is at the conference table, apparently listening to the meeting, but he's hiding his mouth behind his hand. I check that the hard plastic collar is pressing against my trachea and mouth the words without making a sound.

'None of your business.'

His hand can't hide the grin. 'Alright, alright. Don't bite my head off. But let's pay attention to this next bit, OK? We'll need it for the minutes.'

'Sure, sorry.'

'I think you mean: sorry, sir.'

'Idiot.'

'You coming to the team lunch, right?'

'Maybe. I might have something else to do.'

'Like?'

'Reorganising the stationery cabinet, sorting through the archives – I don't know, more important stuff.'

'Wow, way to display team spirit, Sinclair. You're going to be a shoo-in for the next promotion, obviously.'

'Yes, because that's clearly the important thing in the world right now: winning the rat race.'

'I don't care at all if you come or not, anyway,' he says.

I smile and look down at my tablet.

When the meeting ends, we all go out to lunch, forming awkward clusters as we walk down the crowded Manhattan pavement. Imogen and co. radiate the usual mix of toxic barbs and vacuous nonsense, so I do my best to ignore them and focus on Michael, who's looking for all the world like a *Casablanca* character in his silly hat and flappy suit. He's been talking about the restaurant we're heading to for a solid week.

As soon as everyone's slid into the moleskin booth, Michael starts to tinker with a small, grease-stained jukebox on the side of the table.

'Any preferences?'

'Sorry?'

His cheek is practically lying on the table, his nose close to the dial. His hair is thick and brown and my hand wants to run through his curls. I don't let it.

'Nineteen-thirties jazz, sixties rock, eighties pop, nineties rap?' He looks up, squinting at us through his horn-rimmed glasses.

Blythe groans. 'Don't they have normal 2080s music?'

'Just go with it, will you?' he says.

She rolls her eyes. 'Vinters. Why can't you guys just be normal?' She glances pointedly at my skirt with a raised eyebrow. She's young and at the cutting edge of fashion.

All our colleagues are wearing leggings and rubbery

jackets, but I find the leggings so unflattering that I wear skirts or normal trousers and compromise by adding one of the neoprene jackets on top. They obviously all think it's weird. Except Michael; he likes it, I think.

'Thirties jazz, please.' I breathe in the artic AC and look back at Michael fondly.

'Ah. A woman after my own heart.' He extracts coins from his jacket pocket, glances at the two quarters and puts them in.

'I didn't realise that cash still existed over here.'

'It doesn't. You buy those at the entrance. It's just to make the experience more real. So what do you think?'

He's organised this team event and I can see why now; everybody else in the diner is dressed normally. Well, they look normal to me, so they must be eccentrics who like turn of the millennium memorabilia. Everywhere around us are jeans and shirts, fit and flare dresses, normal hair. It all feels so reassuring.

'I love it, Michael.'

He beams.

An old-fashioned TV hanging above the bar is showing *Happy Days* on low volume. The Fonz is preening and strutting around the all-white cast, as if doing a song and dance in exchange for pre-recorded artificial laughter.

The image on the screen shifts and an announcer blares: 'Are you tired of the food shortages? Do you wish you could have your very own place and a job for life? Have you always wanted to go on an adventure? Then we want you.'

A red barren landscape appears on the screen. 'Mars, the new land of the free and home of the brave,' says the deep bass voice, as if advertising an upcoming film.

'Who would be stupid enough to go?' Imogen snorts, rubbing her enormous belly.

'How can you say that?' Aubyn, a young lawyer, chimes in, overkeen and pimply. 'They're pioneers, heroes. I hope I'll go some day.'

Blythe made sure to sidle up next to the young man as soon as we arrived. 'Wow, that's so brave,' she smiles prettily at him, 'but don't you want to wait until the terraforming's done? It's still too dangerous.' Her thigh is glued against his. He doesn't seem to mind.

'I don't care. It's the only place left where we can strive and grow again, a new frontier.'

I whisper a question to Michael: 'Did it at least act as a sort of exhaust valve, to relieve overpopulation?'

He leans in. 'Stop saying that word. Politically incorrect, remember?'

'What word?' Imogen says.

Ignoring Michael's elbow in my ribs, I answer 'Overpopulation, you know... the root cause of the mess we're in.'

'Overpopulation is just fear-mongering. Everybody knows it's a myth,' Imogen says, frowning. 'It's a well-known fact that fertility is declining all over the developed world and GeneX is making great strides in helping every family know the blessing of children.'

'Um. Sorry but if fertility is declining, how come the world's population doubled over the last sixty five years?'

The blonde looks disappointed and despite myself I lower my chin and feel like I've just said something silly.

'Overpopulation is a non-issue, it's all a hoax. The entire population of the world could fit in Texas and the planet can accommodate all of us comfortably. Foreign countries are conspiring to make our great country weaker by asking the US to curb our population growth. Meanwhile, they continue to grow their own numbers in order to gain power over us.'

'How could being fewer make you weak? I don't get it.'

She smiles condescendingly. 'There's always been strength in numbers. The power of a religion is largely determined by how many people follow it. The clout of a country depends on how many citizens it can send to war. The rise of China was in large part due to the sheer size of its consumer market. No government and no religion would ever willingly make their population smaller. That would reduce their weight on the international scene.'

Her point made, Imogen loses interest in the conversation as it's not about her and turns her attention back to Cressida, Aubyn and Blythe.

Michael whispers 'I told you not to bring it up,' then grinning, he adds 'anyway, Mars isn't the solution. We've only sent about one hundred thousand of us up there; it's not about to solve the overcrowding down here. You could say it's even worsened the situation by creating the artificial perception of additional space for growth. Did you know that in the years following the first Mars landing, we registered a definite baby boom on Earth?'

I shake my head, incredulous.

Blythe's been trying to convince her crush to stay on this planet. When I pick up the conversation, she's saying, 'It would have worked if Everett hadn't died. Since then it's been a freaking mess, with the Indians, American and Chinese throwing each other out of airlocks to grab resources every time an Earth shipment lands.'

'Earth isn't perfect but better the devil you know... that's all I'm saying,' Cressida adds.

Imogen laughs. 'Well, at least it makes for soop entertainment. Have you guys seen the latest trailer?' She silently mouths something and as her collar picks up the request, the programme on the TV screen changes to a sleek last-week-on-the-show recap.

A woman is sprinting through a metal corridor, wearing a flight suit. She stares behind her, stumbling and panicking, as she runs. She reaches a locked door and starts to bang on it, the sound of her laboured breathing emphasised ominously. Seconds start to tick, increasing the sense of suspense until, finally, the door slides open and she lunges inside. The next shot is from her point of view, as she lies panting on the stainless steel floor. Three crewmembers are standing around her as she screams, 'Lock the door! Lock the door!' and the camera pans out to show that behind their turned backs, a man is sprinting towards them, blood on his face and an axe swinging from his hand. The woman on the floor screams and the screen blacks out. Then the announcer's voice rumbles seductively: 'Mars, the last frontier. Tune in tonight.'

'This isn't a horror movie? It's real?' I ask, aghast.

'Oh, yes,' Imogen says distractedly, as she looks at the menu, 'it's really good rTV. Have you placed your bet yet? I'm rooting for Nadia. I think she'll make it.'

'I don't bet. It's rigged.' Cressida twists her earrings and I notice that her sleeve is fraying and one of her nails is chipped. 'All of it has already happened two years ago, we just don't know the outcome yet because of the distance. I'm sure some people must know in advance and cheat on the odds.'

Michael asks what we'd like to eat and without thinking, I order a cheeseburger with chips and a chocolate milkshake.

'Nice. Guys, by the way, don't worry, right? The firm's paying for this. It's going right on the client's account. We might as well enjoy ourselves.'

'Why would anyone want to go to Mars after what you've just shown me?'

'The Tinmen have taken all the unskilled jobs,' Cressida says, motioning to the kitchen. Through the glass panel, the cooking robot has started preparing our burgers. The interactive menu-table must have triggered the robot's eight steel arms. Knives twirl around its faceless head and I can't help but stare at the fascinating yet disturbing choreography for a while, losing track of what they're saying.

'...and as we don't have unemployment cover, health cover or any other kind of support system for the poor here—'

Imogen sniggers. 'Here we go – Michael's about to rant about welfare. Give it a rest, for God's sake. You Democrats are all the same.'

'How about you guys get off my case and focus on Sinclair for a change? The Brits are practically commies. The food rationing alone—'

Aubyn leans over Blythe and says, dripping with earnestness, 'We believe in free enterprise and resilience over here. Every man for himself, you guys should try it, it's called capitalism—'

'Yes, quite,' I reply. 'Because it's working so well for your poor, your wretched, your huddled masses...'

'Hey, less sarcasm, OK, red menace?' Michael smiles, glancing at my hair.

'Everyone should find a way to succeed and if they can't, then we don't owe them anything and they're just a drag on society,' Imogen says.

'Don't look at us like that, Olivia. It's who we are.' Aubyn shrugs. 'That's what's made America great; survival of the fittest and all that. It's in our cultural DNA.'

A loud ping makes us look towards the kitchen. Our

burgers have been pushed through a small automatic glass door and are sitting on the faux fifties diner counter.

We get our plates and tuck in. It tastes nearly the same. Not quite. I can't put my finger on what it is. Vat-grown beef, probably.

'Thank you, Michael, this is delicious.'

'Well, it better be, it'll come to $700 each.'

He's obviously relishing this food, savouring every bite with shiny eyes and full cheeks.

'With prices like that, no wonder your people are starving.'

Aubyn shrugs. 'You really gotta hold on to your job, you know.'

'What if you're made redundant?' I ask.

Cressida looks away as she pats her lips with a paper napkin, lost in her thoughts.

Imogen shrugs, oblivious to her friend's unease, 'The market is wise in a way – the Invisible Hand culls the population so that the demand for food decreases and it triggers a lowering of the prices. The problem solves itself naturally and it all balances out. You see?'

'Yes, I see,' I say sadly.

I glance around the diner at the plastic decorations, the neon displays and the garish costumes. Fake meat, fake place, fake people. They all seem so hollow and sad. Can't they see that Earth is dying? Why are they spending their time on useless pursuits instead of changing the world for the better? They're like hamsters on a wheel, pedalling faster and faster and wondering why they're going nowhere.

10

DEANN

S *t. Louis, Missouri, USA, May 2082*

RUBBING the back of my neck, I look up from my work and realize that everyone else has gone home. I'm going cross-eyed, looking at all these figures and the rows upon rows of numbers, names, locations. It's hard to make sense of any of it, especially since I'm only allowed to analyze a fragment of the data set.

I get up and glance over my cubicle wall. The lights are off and the office is plunged in darkness. There isn't a sound except for the quiet whirring of the air conditioning. As I stand there, in my small island of light, the whirring shudders to a halt and silence descends. Even the air has stopped. It must be eight o'clock.

I press my finger to the iMode collar and as soon as the call connects, whisper: 'Jada, get your ass down here, we're on.'

Trying to remain as natural as possible, I grab my purse and walk around every single row of the office, glancing at the empty cubicles, and when I'm sure that I'm alone, I stride to the lab. Just as I get there, Jada arrives, out of breath.

'Nobody saw you?' I ask.

'No, no, I made sure.' She looks excited.

'Jada, you're sure you want to come along? It could be dangerous, I don't want to—'

'Yes, yes, I'm sure, do it already.'

An exhilarating current of fear quivers through me as I tap on my iMode and just when I reach the glass door, Shanice's wrinkled face starts revolving on the bracelet's screen.

'Damn, it's working,' Jada says, sounding surprised as she glances at my wrist. 'The iMode thinks you're Shanice.'

'Yeah, but the question is, will it fool the building's security system?'

Holding my breath, spine tingling, I swipe the iMode and wait. The seconds slip away and nothing happens. I'm starting to back off, heart pounding, when the pad flashes blue and the door opens with a whoosh of released air that mirrors my own.

We stand very still at the entrance of the changing room, poised and alert, listening to the lab beyond. No sound.

'There's no going back once we step in there,' I say, giving her one last chance to ramp off.

'Are we going to stand here all night or are we going to do this?'

I snort and step over the threshold, holding my breath, but nothing happens. She squeezes in as well and the door closes behind us.

'OK, what next?' she says. I think I detect a hint of fear in her voice but I don't mention it. She insisted on helping me and gratitude and guilt are warring inside me. I shouldn't involve her but I'm also glad she's here.

Palms sweating, I rummage through the lockers and locate white coveralls and shoe covers for the both of us. I quickly step into mine, then make sure the nitrile gloves are encasing her sleeves, leaving no part of her skin exposed. She checks me as well, then I carefully remove a small plastic pouch from my purse and, making sure it isn't punctured or damaged, I slide it carefully into my coverall's pocket and leave the purse on the steel bench.

We slip our hair into the caps and approach the next obstacle; mouth dry, I swipe my iMode and the lab door slides open, so I step over the steel threshold of the lab, followed closely by my friend.

No one's there. I rush over to the closest lab bench, suppressing a small leap of joy in my chest. This is where I belong. Every surface is covered with pipettes, Eppendorf tubes, centrifuges, molecular biology kits. Finally.

'DeAnn?'

'Oh yes, sorry.'

I log on at the nearest computer pad, biting the inside of my cheek as I wait for Shanice's profile to be declined and alarms to start blaring.

We both flinch when the computer says: 'Welcome, Professor Curtis.'

Heart beating in my mouth, I press my hand against my chest and smile as Jada laughs nervously.

'We're in!'

The login screen dissolves and in its place a directory appears. I select the project code.

'Holy shit.'

'What?'

'It's all of the Uganda data, everything GeneX learned in Kampala is right here: the autopsy results, the different samples from Kisenyi and Bwaise, the cheek swabs, the tumor biopsies, the blood draws. All of it. This is incredible.'

She whistles softly and rolls a chair closer to my work-station.

Time passes as we absorb ourselves in the data. I'm starting to understand it better, now that I can see the samples. What felt like meaningless statistics next door, with row upon row of sequencing reports and perplexing numbers, is now starting to look like a complete picture shimmering like a mirage just beyond my reach.

'Hey, DeAnn, have you noticed? There's one test that keeps reoccurring.' She's pointing at a sequence of blotches aligned vertically on her screen.

'Yeah, it's a western blot, it's used to gauge protein expression.'

'Why are there hundreds of those tests on file? It makes no sense.'

I frown. 'You're right. I thought they were testing a drug against a communicable disease, maybe trying to find a cure for Zika or dengue. Why would they be separating proteins and conducting gel electrophoresis?'

I'm staring at the hazy inkblots, screwing up my face in puzzlement when a loud sound starts to blare and we both freeze, staring at my stupid iMode; it's my alarm. We need to get out of the lab. We've already been here for an hour.

Jada stands up. 'We should go.'

I glance at the lab door. Beyond it, the changing room and the offices are probably still deserted and the security guard won't patrol for another fifteen minutes or so, just enough time.

'You go. You've taken too many risks already. You have a family. I don't want you to lose your job because of me.'

Jada's eyes flicker toward the door but she lowers her shoulders and says, 'Screw it, if you're staying, then I can't leave. Tell me what you need.'

'You're awesome,' I beam.

'Yeah, grandma, thank you for the obsolete vocabulary, why don't you tell me what I can do, instead of gushing?'

'I need fifteen minutes to analyze a sample. Keep a lookout for the guard, he should start his patrol soon and we definitely don't want to be here when he comes.'

She gets up and posts herself by the glass wall, looking out of the lab and into the darkened corridor. Adrenaline gives me a surge of energy, as I sit back down on the stool and extract the small pack carefully from my pocket. Hands shaking, I've nearly opened the first plastic pouch when I suck my breath in.

Shit! Pulling back my hands, I stand up and dart to the nearby shelf to retrieve two gas masks. Feeling like an idiot, I throw one to Jada and pull the other one on, tightening the straps and then take a minute to re-check my gloves.

'Is this necessary?' she asks, her voice muffled.

'Better safe than sorry,' I shrug as the sound of my own breathing starts to hiss rhythmically in my ears and the lab becomes dimmed behind the mask's visor. Abruptly everything I'm doing tonight takes on a dangerous and ominous hue. I walk back slowly, overalls rustling against my thighs, and sit on the stool to consider the small plastic wrapped object on the lab bench.

The rubber glove that once held the shape of Kitsa's hand looks like a strange blue jellyfish that washed up on a beach. A crest of finger-shaped spikes wobbles as the round blob settles indolently on its side. The visor ripples and blurs. I curse under my breath at the plastic's poor visibility and the fogginess of the mask. Then I feel something wet on my cheek and fall silent.

The scalpel is strangely reluctant to cut open the glove's knot.

But she won't be hurt by this slash. Nothing can hurt her anymore.

Swallowing, I cut the knot and the glove's rubber skin splays open with repulsive abandon. Inside, the white powder Kitsa picked up at the Mazzi water treatment plant lies in a grainy heap.

With careful movements, I scoop a small quantity of the substance with my scalpel and transfer some to a polypropylene tube.

While the incubator shaker extracts the substance and blends it with the methanol, I glance nervously over my shoulder and Jada gives me a thumb up. Turning back, I move the tube to the centrifuge, my shaky fingers fumbling with the unfamiliar flap of the machine. This is taking too long. We can't be found here.

'What are you doing?' Jada whispers, her words muffled by her mask, as she leans over the GCMS vial.

'Analyzing a sample of the drug which I brought back from Uganda to try to figure out what kind of chemical GeneX is testing.'

'You were in Uganda?' she says, gasping.

'Mmh. Yeah.'

While the robotic arm swipes over the sample, I rush to the working station and program the gas chromatography and mass spectrometry. In the dead silence of the dark lab, the whirring, stabbing noises of the robot's syringe seems to echo too loudly.

'You never said.'

'Didn't come up,' I say, feeling a stab of guilt again. 'Any sign of the guard?'

Even through the mask, I can tell from her face that she'd like to say more. But she just turns around and resumes her watch. Minutes trudge by. How long does this thing take?

Somewhere close by a small pinging noise rings, sounding ludicrously loud.

'DeAnn, he's coming!'

The shine of the elevator cabin illuminates the darkened corridor. Jada and I crouch under the workbenches as the loud machine continues its to-and-fro above my sample.

Dread layers itself in my stomach like lead as I stare at the computer pad in my gloved hands. It took twenty minutes to do this analysis in 2016. How long would it take nowadays? Surely not much longer with this modern equipment? Sweat gathers on my palms, under the slippery gloves.

'Come on. Come on,' I mutter.

'What's taking so long? We have to go!'

'I can't stop the machine now anyway,' I hiss. And I need to know. What is this powder that cost Kitsa her life? Why would Omony kill for it?

The guard's progress lights up the automatic lights, illuminating the corridor in successive stripes, as he gets closer. He's only a few rooms away. He'll see us as soon as he gets to this section of the floor. Everything's made of glass here.

'Come on, DeAnn, just leave it. We have to go,' Jada pleads, pulling my elbow as she straightens up.

Finally something pops up on my screen. My breath of relief fogs up the mask and I have to wait a few seconds to see the results: I don't recognize this compound.

Jada's already put away the signs of our intrusion and she's approaching the door, motioning for me to follow her.

'Please, DeAnn, I can't get caught.' Something wavers in her voice.

Desperate, I click on the computer's library to look for a match. The result is instantaneous: MSA8742.

A part of me was vaguely hoping that Kitsa's sample would be chlorine. But it clearly isn't. I recognize the sequence of letters and numbers. MSA8742 is the drug name that's plastered all over the sequencing reports I've been studying for months. It's the medication that the samples in this very lab are testing. It's the drug that disrupts normal protein expression in certain subjects. So it's one and the same as the powder that Kitsa found in the blue barrels. It's the white powder that Omony dissolved in Kampala's water supply.

I scroll down and look at its components. Oh my God.

'DeAnn, *move!*'

Jada pulls me to my feet and slams the computer tablet on the workbench as she drags me to the exit.

I follow her out of the lab and into the changing area, where she wrenches off her overalls and throws them away. I yank the mask off my face and undress, trying to focus on the ramifications of what I've just discovered.

Maybe I could run a liquid chromatography, just to be sure? I glance at the lab door.

'Don't even.' Jada grabs my hand and swipes my iMode against the pad, the door opens and we step through, hurrying to my cubicle as the office lights blink to life. We can't see the guard but we can hear something metallic jangling as he approaches.

Jada says very loudly, 'So are you going to pull an all-nighter or what?'

Wincing, I search her face, as adrenaline bites and I have the irrational urge to run.

'What are you still doing here?' the guard barks, his hand hovering over his holster.

Jada taps on my wrist as she turns to him. Oh yes, of course, I need to change the ID on my bracelet.

'Hi there, Officer... Sean. That's exactly I was saying to my friend. They don't pay us enough to work this late. Am I right or am I right?' she chuckles.

The guard looks uncertainly from her face to mine and then holds out his scanner to check our wrists. I'm still fumbling with mine and I don't have time to make sure the switch has happened. I extend my wrist and hold my breath.

With a suspicious glare, the guard checks the ID on his screen, then my face.

'OK,' he says reluctantly, 'but you need to leave, now.'

'Thank you,' Jada says, sounding like she's talking to the only guy in the room who gets the joke. 'That's what I've been saying all along.'

As soon as he's kicked us out of the building, Jada stomps toward her car, all pretense of levity evaporated.

'Jada, wait.'

But she continues to walk away, as I plead with her back.

'Come on, talk to me Jada.'

'What the fuck, DeAnn, you could have gotten us arrested. Are you completely nuts?'

'I had to be sure.'

'What was so important that it was worth taking such a huge risk? Are you a corporate spy, trying to steal the formula of the cure for malaria for a competitor or something?'

'No, trust me, it's nothing like that,' I say, catching up with her.

Halfway through the deserted dark parking lot, she turns on me and hisses, 'Trust you?' You didn't even tell me you'd already infiltrated GeneX in Uganda. That seems like it might have been worth revealing, don't you think?' She shakes her head. 'Now I've gone and involved Shanice and Lashelle in this as well. Shit.'

'It's not like that.' I pad closer to her, trying to placate her.

'What is it like then, DeAnn? Tell me. Because from where I'm standing, you've manipulated me, you stole a sample from the company and I have no idea who you are anymore.'

'It's not espionage, I'm not a thief. You've got to understand.'

'Then what do you want with GeneX? What was so important that you were ready to get us both arrested tonight?' she yells.

'The drug they're testing. It's not a drug at all. It's a toxin, Jada. It's poison.'

11

OLIVIA

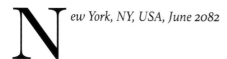

ew York, NY, USA, June 2082

I PUT the pack of vegetarian chicken nuggets back in the supermarket freezer. I wish I'd bought some two months ago. I can't afford them anymore. Walking away, I tap on my iMode bracelet and it confirms my suspicion; my bank balance is pulsing amber on the bracelet's screen. Nearly at zero.

Hiking up my shopping basket into the crook of my elbow, I take another tour of the shop. There's not nearly as much food on the shelves as when I arrived in the city. The media says it's because the drought in the Midwest is getting worse and the Dust Bowl's perimeter has grown, swallowing up the remainder of Texas, growing westward into Wyoming and climbing as far north as Montana.

No one knows what DeAnn is telling me: that it's irreversible. Nothing will grow in the breadbasket of the US for generations to come and California's run out of water decades ago. Soon, we'll be completely dependent on imports for most of the country's food supply.

I should stockpile a few tins before it gets even worse. But with what money? It takes every last dollar of my pay check to stay afloat now. The scarcity has made prices skyrocket and only the wealthiest don't feel the pinch yet. I'm on the lowest rung of the ladder at the firm so I struggle but I can't complain; I still eat three times a day. What worries me the most is what will happen when shops completely run out of stock. What will my money buy then?

My stomach growls as I pass by the semi-empty shelves and walk to the till, a tin of beans and a potato rattling at the bottom of my wire basket. That will have to do for tonight.

As usual, I start to worry about being stuck here forever when the clock strikes midnight on 31 October, the day we're supposed to return. And, as usual, I distract myself by thinking of Michael.

There's no point in denying the pleasant and painful build-up of infatuation any longer. I've become obsessed with every little word and gesture Michael throws at me. As the familiar febrile mood grips me, I spend hours mulling over the secret meaning of each one of his comments, each graze against my back, each lingering glance.

He would probably help me if he knew I was struggling. Or maybe not, I don't know anymore; we argued a few days ago.

When DeAnn told me what the trials were really about, my work at the law firm took on a sinister hue. It had been easy to forget before, surrounded by prosperity and wealth, so far removed from the charnels and autopsy tables of Uganda. I got lost in the office banter, the politics, the shiny steel-and-glass aesthetics and the glamour of New York life.

But the truth is hard to ignore now. Not only is my law firm's client testing drugs on unsuspecting patients who haven't given their consent, which would be bad enough, but GeneX is not even creating a new treatment to cure a disease and help patients. It's much worse; if DeAnn's right they've been poisoning people all along.

Just after I learned this disturbing news, I had to spend the day listening to the partners of Carapadre & Dergrin talk casually about the medical experiments and how to ensure GeneX was never prosecuted or even fined. Each boardroom joke seemed monstrous that day. Each smug burst of laughter grated on my nerves.

So when Michael mentioned in passing at the water cooler that he was going to get a raise, thanks to his work on the GeneX project, I shouldn't have snapped – but I did.

'That's great. No doubt you'll be celebrating in style tonight.'

'I thought you'd be happy for me,' he said, looking hurt. 'Are you OK? You've been moping around all day. What's wrong with you?'

'What's wrong *with me*? Are you kidding? What's wrong *with you*? All of you?'

He was obviously taken aback.

'How can you listen to the partners discuss human medical experiments and all the other horrible things they casually mention in there? You know what they're doing, don't you?'

Michael looked like I'd punched him in the face; he grabbed me by the wrist and pulled me into a conference room, closing the door behind us. 'Olivia, get your shit together. No one can hear you say this. Ever. Or they'll have your job. Or worse.'

'That's it? That's all you can say? We need to shut up

because we could get in trouble and lose our precious jobs?'
I breathed in, trying to calm down.

'Of course, I understand that it's wrong,' he whispered,
glancing around us. 'But it doesn't affect us directly. Nowadays that's all you can hope for – to survive and carve out a
good life for yourself and the ones you love.'

He tried to touch my arm but I batted his hand away.

'Why are you so angry with me? You're the racist one.
Always going on about overpopulation and how we need to
reduce our numbers. You should be happy that we're now
short a few thousand Africans.'

'You're making jokes now?' I said, incredulous as I
wondered why I was always surprised when he failed to
display the imaginary qualities I'd attributed to him? Like
common decency and empathy, for example. 'Don't you care
that your money is soaked in blood? GeneX is killing
people, experimenting on them – and you want me to
congratulate you for doing well out of the murder of
innocents?'

'Our law firm isn't technically doing anything wrong.
We're simply protecting our client and upholding the law.
It's how the system works,' he said, getting worked up.

'Yes, but the system is rotten and you're defending
people who are not working for the greater good.'

'So are you.' He said, crossing his arms.

'All it takes for evil to triumph...'

'Oh please. Give me a fucking break, Olivia.' He lost his
cool at that point. 'How naïve can you be? If we don't repre-
sent them, do you think GeneX will just stop doing what
they're doing? Of course not. Another law firm will get the
account, that's all. We all need to eat and there are worse
jobs. We could be doing worse things. We're just helping a
pharmaceutical company to make drugs and chemical

compounds which will help everyone in the long run. Neither our firm nor GeneX can be held responsible for how these are used. The tool is not evil. Only the one who wields it.'

'I still think we should do something...'

'Like what?' he snorted. 'Get real. Have you seen the supermarkets lately? How long would we last without a job, without a salary? Do your grandiose ideals feed you?' he sneered. 'What's that? Nothing? You've got no clever retort? Yeah, I didn't think so.'

I opened the door and left without a word. We haven't spoken since. It was days ago.

Maybe I was too harsh on him. He's not responsible. We're all just cogs in a machine. Aren't we?

12

DEANN

S t. Louis, Missouri, USA, June 2082

IT'S 6.35 A.M. and I'm the first one here as usual. My 5 a.m. exercise routine done, I don't see the point in twiddling my thumbs in my dingy flat, so most mornings I come and work on the project. It's become an obsession.

With the limited dataset on my screen, it's impossible to figure out what MSA8742 does. I could sneak into the lab again but it would take me weeks, months to understand the whole experiment. Sooner or later I would get caught.

What I need is a clue. Just one pointer to propel me in the right direction. I could solve the puzzle if I could just understand why they're testing for protein expression. I would even settle for a hint of how the data is coded, so I could understand why there seems to be subjects on which the toxin worked and others on which it doesn't. I stare at the columns of names, characteristics and figures but no pattern emerges.

'Here already, Campbell?'

I would normally ignore Dick but he's in unusually early today and we're completely alone in the office, so it's going to be necessary to interact. I make an effort and turn toward him, a fake smile on my lips.

'Hi, Dick. Yeah, I couldn't sleep, so I figured I might as well come in.'

'Well, don't expect extra pay or anything.'

I swallow and smile again, then bend my head down and wish I were alone to think about the toxin in peace.

But that's not going to be possible now, with Dick puttering around, watering his plant, disinfecting the work surface or whatever. I hear a grunt and wheel backward, to find him on all fours, tinkering with cables under his desk. It's impossible to concentrate with this idiotic walrus wheezing so close. Just as I'm thinking this, there's a loud ping and he immerses himself in an iBubble conversation for a few minutes, his features comically distorted by intense surprise, then greed and finally shiftiness.

When he collapses his bubble, he stays at his desk for a while, his puffy eyes squinting at something outside the window and then with a theatrical inhalation he walks over and stands behind me, shuffling.

'Diana, listen.'

I ignore him for a beat too long, which gives me a small jolt of perverse pleasure, and then turn around in my chair, features blank.

'I hope you don't still mind about what happened last week,' he chuckles.

Last week he had me work until midnight for days to make a deadline and then claimed the credit for it.

'It's all water under the bridge, right?' he falters when I don't respond.

He may be a scientific genius but clearly he's not qualified to manage anyone. If this were my real career, I would have eviscerated this guy and taken his job by now. As things stand though, I need him on side.

'Don't mention it, Dick. It was my pleasure. You know you can count on me. I'm a team player.'

'Well, I'm so glad to hear you say that. You know, you're very lucky to even have a job. Most people aren't as... open-minded as me when it comes to—'

He shuffles and looks at his flip-flops. His pruned toes are displayed for all to see, a hint of yellowing on the nails, a few hairs on the pallid phalanges.

'I know. I'm really grateful for it.' The words physically hurt on their way out of my mouth.

He peers at me over his glasses, then asks the question he's really here for. 'Say, could you do me a favor?'

Suppressing a sigh, I answer, 'Sure thing, boss. Anything I can do to help.'

'I... well... A friend just called me from a black market and said there's several pounds of real coffee to be had there if I can make it in the next hour and... well, to cut a long story short, an opportunity like that isn't going to present itself again soon or maybe ever. It's on the other side of town. But the problem is that I need to complete a report for management before ten. So I was wondering if—'

'Say no more. I'll take care of it for you.'

'Really? I mean... of course you will. You're a good girl. Thank you.'

He hurries to his cubicle and comes back with his tablet. He *tries* to give it to me inconspicuously, but I don't want any part of it. What is this, a set-up? A way to get me fired since I won't take the hint and quit on my own? Next thing I know, he'll be crying out that his tablet has been stolen.

'Don't pull out on me now, Diana. I can't miss that coffee. Do you have any idea how many people are bidding for it as we speak?' His eyes dart to the door.

'And you can't just swipe me the draft report because...?'

'If you work on it from your computer, there'll be a log and a stamp, and questions that could come back to me. Whereas if you access the sources from my tablet, you'll be able to whip up a report for me before I come back, no problem... and no traces.' He anxiously glances at the time, then back to me. 'Are you going to help or not? Because I've been very generous with you up to this point.'

I give him my most ingratiating smile. 'Yes, of course Dick, just leave it with me, I've got your back.'

'Then it's settled.' He hands me the tablet and tells me his password, the overconfident idiot.

'Oh, wait,' I say, stopping him. 'Before you come back for the meeting, make sure you change into close-toed shoes. You know, more... managerial.' I smile again.

He smirks and nods.

As soon as the door closes, I pull out my leather notebook and start jotting down notes as I scroll through Dick's tablet, looking for something, anything that will reveal what the toxin is for. Its purpose is continuing to elude me, and I need a shortcut.

I glance at the door and wonder when the first employees will start to trickle in. How will I justify having a personal paper artifact and Dick's tablet? I also need to complete the report before he comes back. Stressed, I continue clicking at random and find myself in an altogether different section. I scramble to get back to where I was, but something catches my eye. The folder simply says 'CONFIDENTIAL'.

As I open the file, the dominoes fall into place and I read on, unable to believe what I see, yet unable to stop either.

The toxin...

...it targets people based on their genetic profile.

MSA8742 binds itself irreversibly to a certain combination of markers and prevents the expression of the protein sequence.

My mind reels from the discovery; this is beyond any medical advances I've ever seen. I read through the notes and reports as fast as I can, but soon realize that I can't absorb all of it in one go, so I decide to take a huge risk. I send the whole thing from Dick's account to an outside email address that I'd created in order to receive A.'s instructions. It's completely untraceable so I should be fine, and no one will associate it with me if they find out. Then I delete the message in Dick's 'sent' folder and start working on the report he asked me to write, feeling fear pool in my stomach.

Gene targeting.

I didn't even think it was possible.

But clearly it is.

Fuck.

13

OLIVIA

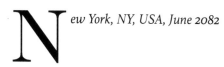 *ew York, NY, USA, June 2082*

OVER THE LAST TWO WEEKS, I've learned that you disagree with an American at your own peril. They don't seem to cope well with debate and disagreement.

I thought Michael would never talk to me again, but this morning, he plopped a paper bag and a latte on my desk, kissed the top of my head and walked away. My heart beating madly, I watched him go, as my crush returned with a vengeance. There was a doughnut in the brown bag and a note: 'Meet me at this address tonight.' Written in fountain pen. I smiled. So vintage. So Michael.

Now, I'm standing next to him as he knocks on an unmarked door in a street in the seedy end of the Bronx. A few roaming groups pass us by in the twilight. Remembering the Alphas, I shudder and step closer to him.

'Erm, Michael?'

A peep-hole rattles open and a scowling face appears behind the bars. Michael squeezes my hand.

'Password?'

'There are people in the world so hungry that God cannot appear to them except in the form of bread.'

The heavy black door swings open and we step into the gloomy corridor as a strong smell of mould, mushrooms and damp saturates my nose. A low hubbub of conversations intensifies as we climb down a metal staircase and when we arrive at the bottom, we find an arched entranceway shielded by rubbery curtains.

'What is this place?' I whisper, staying close to him. I hope it isn't some kind of sect meeting.

'You'll see.' He smiles over his shoulder and pulls me behind him, his fingers intertwined with mine. My heart beats a little faster as he pushes through the plastic folds and an enormous concealed space with vaulted brick ceilings comes into view. Hundreds of people are grouped around long trestle tables, looking, like a writhing mass of rats. Sellers tout their wares in loud insistent voices and the assembled crowd is bidding, their bodies pressed greedily, trying to push away competitors. Sensing my hesitation, Michael smiles encouragingly and guides me through the milling mass of people.

We push past a glut of women bidding on a pack of coffee and elbow our way past several dozen people haggling over a case of wine. As Michael pushes confidently through the throng, I can't help but focus on the feel of his fingers around mine as my heart pulses.

People are crowded tightly in the warm, airless cave; they push each other out of the way, jostling to be at the front, yelling as bouncers look on, arms crossed, guns prominent on their belts. I scrunch up my nose as we pass by a table displaying ripe French cheeses, their awful odour mixing with the smell of fruits past their prime, sweaty unwashed bodies and the black fungus on the walls.

'It's wonderful, isn't it?' Michael beams at me, his puffy eyes swallowed up by his dimply cheeks as he smiles. It's hard to hear him. Someone stomps on my foot.

'Right, yes, wonderful.'

'Come on, there's an auction I want to go to.' He pulls me forwards eagerly.

An overpowering, salty, rotten odour greets us as soon as we've passed the next set of rubber curtains. The crowd is denser here. We shove our way through to a bricked vault filled with people who are bidding vociferously. Flaccid, pungent carcasses are lying on ice behind steel bars and people are thrusting their hands through the bars, bidding, shouting, trying to be heard.

'Fish! I've never had any.' He grins, squeezing my hand. 'Oh my God, they have oysters!' he says, craning his neck.

Something lumpy gets stuck in my throat but I smile back. He places me near the wall, protecting me with the bulk of his solid body and starts to bid, yelling as he flaps a ticket through the bars. At last, he gets what he wants and the attendant wraps it efficiently in two plastic bags, then thrusts Michael's prize through a small window between the bars.

'Come,' he says, looking exultant, as he elbows our way to the other side of the vast underground space. There, he shows his iMode to a pair of bouncers, who admit us into a calmer area reserved for VIPs. We climb up a small flight of stairs and Michael grabs a table on a mezzanine overlooking the throngs. The clamour and chaos below recede and I breathe more easily, taking in the speakeasy vibe of the joint, the red velvet armchairs, the spirit bottles lined like condemned men awaiting their firing squad, their backs to a mirrored bar.

'Wait here, Sinclair.'

Michael strides over to the walnut counter and with a suspicious look over his shoulder, he unwraps the packages away from the prying eyes of nearby patrons and entrusts the two parcels to a slot in the glass partition. He taps on the glass keyboard and his iMode flashes blue. A few seconds later, a multi-armed robot delicately retrieves the packages and starts preparing the contents, its long arthropodic limbs gleaming in the dim vault, knives swishing, a disturbingly impassive expression on its chrome face. Relieved of his precious cargo, Michael is now visibly relaxed, happily chatting to surrounding people who stare at the robot, pointing, oohing and ahing. A few of them throw him envious looks and assess his girth and tall frame. Not worth the fight. They retreat and after a long wait, Michael swipes his iMode against the wall and walks back to the table, carefully balancing a bottle, two plastic cups and four small cardboard boxes with the care usually reserved for live bombs.

He places two boxes and one cup in front of me. A wide grin splits his face in two as I open the small white parcel and discover, arranged artfully in small colourful bundles, perfect in every way, six sushi. In the other box, one oyster is sitting prone, on a bed of ice. Michael is devouring me with his eyes, so I arrange my features to display awe and delight and push down the pity and sorrow.

Meanwhile, he's pouring us a drink and offers me a glass. I sniff the bubbly liquid and gasp.

Champagne.

Real champagne, made of grapes. It can't be.

'Michael, it's too much. I can't afford—'

'To you, Sinclair!' he interrupts me, holding his glass up. 'You make me a better man.'

Pink heat rushes to my cheeks and I bury my nose in the plastic cup, taking a tentative sip. It sparkles and dances down my throat like liquid happiness as I watch him eat his meal. He relishes every bite so I eat half of mine, then give him the rest.

'Are you sure? You don't like it?' His smile falters.

'I love it, Michael, I really do. You're a wonderful man.' Something flutters in my chest. 'You just look like you're enjoying it so much. I want you to have some of mine.'

He grins and acknowledges receipt of my precious gifts, pleasure transforming his features as the precious flavours come into contact with his tongue.

When the exquisite moment is over, we walk back downstairs and he holds my hand again, as he pulls me through the crowd, through the haggling, the fist fights and the clamour. I stop and blow half of this week's wages on half a pound of cherries, wrapped in a pack that proclaims in garish colours: 'DRONE POLLINATED. AS GOOD AS THE ORIG-INAL.' We eat them as we walk through the stalls, observing everything. Here, an elegant man in an expensive suit is buying a rack of bloody beef. There, an old woman offers a bright red apple to her granddaughter and the child's eyes go round. She's not sure how to eat it, so sniffs it and flicks its stem, puzzled. Further away, a fight breaks between two young women I saw arrive earlier. Then, they were joking and laughing, but now they're hurling vicious insults at each other over a small piece of brownie. People are pressed together like vultures over a corpse, jostling each other for strips of the carcass.

Michael navigates us through the crowd, licking the red cherry juice off his fingers while I savour the burgundy pop of sweetness in my mouth, careful to leave most for him, as he's never had cherries before. I try not to stare at his lips when he closes his eyes in inward communion.

While Michael negotiates for some spice, I nibble on a plump cherry and spit it out when I find it crawling with thin wriggly larvae. Spitting like a cat, I fumble through my bag to extract a bottle of water and rinse out my mouth, making disgusted noises. Michael comes back, a big grin on his face, carrying a minuscule pouch of spice and looks at me curiously as I spit on the floor in a corner and generally behave in an undignified manner.

'What's wrong?'

'Worms.' I wince, making for the rubbish bin with the remaining cherries.

He catches the box in the air and then makes a big show of eating them, as I laugh and shudder, pulling faces.

'Extra protein,' he grins. 'Come on, we'll miss the show.'

He takes me to a cinema room, deep in the bowels of the underground space, its arched brick ceiling encasing the red velvet seats like a cocoon.

Our two tickets bought, he pushes our way to the front, then hands me a sort of mouth guard crossed with a plane's decompression mask. I follow the tube down to the space between our seats, raising my eyebrows.

'It's a... You... Wait, I'll just show you, it'll be simpler.'

My skin tingles when his hand brushes against my neck, as he pulls my hair back over my shoulders. He unfurls the tube and places the rubber strap over my head, letting the mask hang loose around my neck.

'There you go, all set.'

God, he makes everything sound sexy. I try to figure out what makes his voice sound like... melting chocolate, and lose my train of thought when he reaches over to brush something off my cheek.

His eyes linger on my lips.

I imagine his mouth on my neck and shiver. He swallows and takes a few seconds to remember what he was doing, then pulls the mask on his own face.

'Ou bull id on lie dis,' he mumbles.

The mouth guard and mask over his nose look completely ridiculous, so I burst out laughing and his eyes crease over the breathing device. I pull on mine as well, chewing the unfamiliar rubber and probing around it with my tongue. Then I breathe in and adjust the strap. I bet I look preposterous, but hey, when in Rome.

Soon the 'film' starts; it's a collection of scenes spliced together from various 2D vintage movies and at first I can't understand why all these people would gather here to watch such a low-tech offering. The mix is nonsensical. But soon, as the mouth guard starts to tickle my taste buds and smells are pumped through the coiling transparent tube, I understand.

An elderly Asian man starts us off with the opening sequence of *Eat Drink Man Woman*, in which the actor prepares an elaborate meal from scratch, chopping chilli peppers, frying fresh fish, as the cinema audience emits a hubbub of appreciative moans. Then Bill Murray devours a breakfast with typical American gluttony in *Groundhog Day*, smearing cake icing over his face and drinking from a jug as the ghost scent of real coffee hits my nostrils. We move on to *Tampopo*, *Burnt*, *Babette's Feast*, *Paris Can Wait* and countless other movies in a swirling sickening mix. The scenes tumble across the screen, and my mouth waters against my will, my stomach grumbling like an echo of meals past.

In the darkness around me, the hundreds of spectators

in their awful masks start to remind me of medical experiments in a horror movie. Plugged in like dead foetuses, their eyes blank, they drool around their mouth guards and most of them don't even wipe themselves.

A couple of rows down, a man is masturbating, his limp white penis like a German veal sausage in his hand. Maybe he should put some mustard on that, I think, sensing a hysterical laugh bubbling to the surface, muffled by the mask.

Michael's profile is tilted towards the screen, his eyes glazed, his plump cheeks working. Is he chewing? Uneasy, I glance at the screen; we've reached the *Indiana Jones and the Temple of Doom* banquet; the guests eat eyeball soup and frozen monkey brain as the tube sends me odours of offal mixed in with Indian spices and suddenly it's all too much. The walls press down on me, the crowd becomes unbearably oppressive and the room starts to spin. I can't breathe. Anthony's hands wrap around my throat and my lungs panic. Yanking the mask off, I gulp in stale air as the disgusting mouth guard drips saliva. I wipe my chin, throw it down on my seat and stumble across Michael's feet to get out. I can't breathe. I can't breathe.

The vaults are empty now, custodians are sweeping up as a few stragglers pick through the left-over fruit rotting in abandoned boxes and crates. I rush back to the entrance and when I reach the surface, I stop outside the club to drink in big mouthfuls of evening air. I'm starting to relax when a hand loops around my waist and I yelp with fear.

'You OK?' Michael leans around me solicitously.

I inhale deeply and nod. 'You should stay, enjoy yourself. I just need some fresh air and then I'm going to go home.'

I do feel comfortable around Michael. He's soft and kind

and a bit chubby. He doesn't feel dangerous, like Anthony did. He feels reassuring.

But even if I were considering dating him, it would be idiotic. I have to go back to 2017, I can't stay here.

With an apologetic smile, I start to leave as my singsong voice intones in the back of my mind: *Well, good luck getting back to 2017. How are you supposed to pull that off exactly? And what would you go back to, anyway?*

Oh shut up, I tell my bloody singsong voice.

'Can I walk you home?' Michael asks with a side-glance.

'That would be lovely,' I say, against my better judgement. *At least he cares about you, who would give a hoot whether you live or die in 2017?* Shush. It's just a fling. Be quiet. There's no sense in getting overexcited about a crush that can't lead to anything but a dead end.

He smiles a big goofy smile and my heart leaps as he offers me his arm and we start the journey back to my place, choosing to walk in the crisp spring night.

'YOU LIVE HERE?'

His eyebrows are raised and he's looking up at the handsome building a few metres from Central Park.

'Yes, don't get too excited, though; I just rent a room at the back.'

The family is rich but they still need lodgers to make ends meet and they don't want it widely known. I struck gold when I found this sublet, it's a discreet arrangement with one of the lodgers who didn't want to lose the room while she went abroad for a year. It's short-term, untraceable and perfect.

He whistles, his head craning back as he takes a stumbling step backwards.

'There's a pretty good view on the top floor,' I say without thinking. 'Do you want a tour?'

'Well, I came this far, I might as well.'

I let him in the main entrance, feeling like we're school-children sneaking around. We giggle and shush each other in the moonlit foyer. The champagne is still working its magic and tingling me from the inside.

'Follow me.' I grab his hand.

Time must have flown without me noticing, because it feels like the dead of night. Everyone's asleep. I hold a finger in front on my lips and pull him behind me.

'That's the living room,' I whisper with a show-hostess gesture.

He laughs, his shoulders shaking silently in the dark-ened reception area. We tiptoe to the next floor.

'And here is the Jacuzzi.'

I try to open the glass door but it's locked. It smells of chlorine. The machinery's quiet purr makes everything seem all the more silent and eerie somehow. I laugh at his amazed face and see it from his point of view. Water that just sits there, whirling all the time. When water is so precious, it must seem like the height of luxury.

I take his hand and pull him to the next floor. He lets me. His palm is dry and warm and my heart is beating fast as a giddy smile spreads across my lips. It feels like we're trespassing. Bubbles of excitement flow through me, and I let myself be carried away by silliness.

'And here's the ballroom.'

I push the swinging doors open, lightly pulling his hand. Behind me, I hear him suck in his breath. A vast room opens in front of us, mirrors reflecting our infinite silhouettes in the darkness. Shining wooden floors and chandeliers gleam in the moonlight. We pad over to the floor-to-ceiling window overlooking all of Central Park.

'Oh wow.'

'I thought you might like it,' I whisper.

He looks out of the window, still holding my hand although it's not strictly necessary anymore. Then he looks at me and lifts my hand up, pulling me closer.

We dance to the music of silence and the rhythm of our heartbeats. Our shadows dance as well, across the floorboards drenched in silver moonlight. Relaxing in his warm embrace, I glance up at him and his eyes soften. He leans in and his lips touch mine. They taste like hope and joy.

The kiss ends too soon. He's smiling and his glasses are fogged up as he wraps me in a bear hug. I snuggle close and we stay like that for a while.

When I look up, a small contented sigh escapes me and at the sound, his eyes fall to my lips again and his gaze changes. I reach up on tiptoes just as he leans in and our lips meet again, crashing this time, as the hunger consumes us.

Our tongues touch, tentatively at first, then we fall into each other, avidly searching, searching. It's as if I were starving and only he could fill me up. I'm shocked by the intensity of our desire. He pulls me nearer. My hips are so close to his that I can feel him harden against me as I melt into him. His hands get bolder, fumbling with my shirt, looking for a way in.

I come up for air and disentangle myself for a minute, feeling flushed and happy. He keeps me close and his comfortable body moulds to mine. I put both my hands on his chest and he slides his hands sensually around my hips as I lean back to look at him. We're so close.

'Michael,' I say, my voice hoarse.

'Mmmmh?' he says dreamily, looking like a sleepy bear, his hair mussed up, his glasses askew.

'Why did you kiss me?'

'It just felt like the right thing to do,' he says with that smile of his.

Then he looks out at the park again and pushes me against a nearby pillar to kiss me more thoroughly.

My shirt buttons come undone, my skirt inches up.

'If I'd known you kissed like that, I'd have done it a lot sooner,' he growls.

He tastes delicious. The heady liqueur of desire and infatuation coursing through my veins is starting to make me dizzy.

I wriggle free. And come up for air. 'You should go home.' I say, struggling to rearrange my clothes in a semblance of order.

'Mmmh. Can I stay? I'll be good, I promise.'

'No, no, no!' I laugh. 'You go and we'll see each other soon.'

'But I want to see you now,' he pleads.

What am I doing? I don't know anymore. What's reasonable and what isn't? What makes sense and what's nuts? I need to calm down and think about this carefully, I chide myself. I'm old enough to be his grandmother. I can't stay in 2082. I'm on the run. A relationship with me would endanger his life.

I push him back a little, feeling just as disappointed as him.

'Call me, OK?' I say, thinking the time off will help me do the right thing.

'If I call you, will you see me again?'

'Uh-huh,' I say noncommittally.

He makes a low groaning sound and unglues himself

from me. I already regret pushing him away. *Come back*, my heart pleads. *Don't give in*, my head admonishes.

He walks me to the door of my room, under the slanting attic, and as we start to say goodbye he leans in, pressing me against the wall and suddenly we're kissing again. My hands fly up of their own accord, and latch on to his curly brown hair as our lips press against each other's. His hand is cupping my breast, his mouth closing on my neck as his knee parts my thighs, when I shake myself free and push him away, laughing.

'No, no, no, mister. Call.'

He scatters little pecks all over my face as I summon the lift and a few seconds later he's in it and safely gone.

Five minutes later, as I'm getting ready for bed, humming to myself and smiling happily, my iMode rings. I pick up and have to laugh.

'See, I'm calling. Can I come back up now?'

I stay firm and promise him another date. We hang up and I go to sleep with a big grin on my face.

I haven't been this happy in years.

14

DEANN

S t. Louis, Missouri, USA, July 2082

THE LOW BRICK buildings around me are all boarded up with planks. They were never pretty to begin with, but now they look downright sinister.

Tightening my elbow against my purse, I hurry along the dark street, feeling sweaty and breathless. The heat is unbearable. This is the hottest summer on record. Ever. It's about 116°F.

A tall building, burnt and gutted, casts its long shadow across my path like a river of ink on the sidewalk, and for a moment I think of avoiding walking through it, but then I dismiss the uneasy feeling and forge on; I'm already late. I can't help but stare at the derelict structure as I dart past; it's obviously been standing here for years, half demolished. Remnants of living rooms where children played while mothers ironed, bedrooms where couples once made love and argued are gaping open, their walls crumbling away. Dog-eared wallpaper droops in long strips and steel rebars poke out of the decaying cement.

Evening is falling. Homeless people line the sidewalks; here an entire family shares a meager meal, while, a little further, others sleep on flattened cardboard, their unkempt hair protruding from sleeping bags that reek of urine. The street is littered with garbage, plastic bottles, syringes, beer cans and feces.

I could be walking in a war zone. But no, this is just downtown St. Louis. My neighborhood. Home sweet home.

I snort, thinking of the luxurious condo I used to own in Baltimore, a lifetime ago. These days, this dump is the only part of town where any landlord will rent to someone of my color. So I live here.

I'm nearly there. I stop to adjust my shoe and a frail elderly woman wrapped in a stars-and-stripes patterned blanket creeps out of the building's shadow. She approaches me cautiously, begging for money, her wrinkled white hand cupped and grimy. Over the last few months, we've been overrun with climate refugees from neighboring states. They lose their farms to the all-consuming desert and then they come to this city for help. They're mostly white. This woman's probably one of them. When she sees that I'm African American she spits on the ground and retreats into the darkness. Wiping my forehead, I hurry away. The streets aren't safe after sunset and I'm cutting it close tonight.

Finally I see it. A building in relatively good condition stands a few yards away. It's the only one that's lit on the block. I hurry along the darkening street, looking behind my shoulder, trying not to run. Never run when you're black.

Nearly there now. There's a queue of people snaking out of the entrance and wrapping around the corner. Ignoring the reproachful glares, I march into the building. A dust storm has been announced. I hope it won't last as we're only a couple of hours away from the curfew and I don't want to get stuck here for the night again. The military was already patrolling the streets before, but things have escalated this last month; there are riots practically every week now. Food is too scarce and people are starting to hoard it, fight over it and loot it.

This world is getting to me. What is wrong with us that we're unable to solve this extinction-level problem? The solution is so easy: just rein in our fertility and most environmental, food scarcity and civil unrest issues would go away within a generation. We wouldn't need to plow the earth so intensively if we didn't have so many people to feed. The plains would have a chance to recover, grass would grow back and capture the dust once more. The dust storms would end. But no, instead of considering the root cause, we prefer to bury our head in sand. Literally.

Inside, it's mayhem. There are crowds everywhere; in the hallways, the waiting rooms, at the reception desk pleading with the harassed nurses. The patients are gaunt, desperate, their skin hanging around their bodies loosely, like the cruel memory of happier, plentiful days.

Everyone here is black and as soon as I'm inside, my face relaxes of its own accord. I don't need to pretend and fake-smile anymore, for a while.

'Ah, Doctor Campbell, there you are,' the nurse says. I think that's a reproach.

Ignoring the rebuke, I'm rushing through to get changed when the sound of machine guns explodes outside and I freeze, remembering Kampala. But this is my country, my home. What is happening out there? People hunker down in the corridors, sitting on the floor, listening anxiously, as I resume walking. Might as well get ready and start my shift. If death comes to the clinic tonight, at least I'll be prepared.

Halfway through changing my clothes, my iMode rings. It's Olivia.

'Are you alright?' Olivia's face appears on the iBubble screen, looking rounder than when we left Africa. She seems to have healed completely.

'Yes, I'm alright. It's just... I'm so tired.'

I've been volunteering at the clinic most nights after work. I don't know why really. I shouldn't give a shit about these people. But I can't help myself. I care. Against my better judgment, I care.

'You're doing too much. You need to gather the evidence and come back as soon as possible. I don't think we should be apart. It's not safe. We need to look after each other.'

She's right, of course. But I don't want to go back to New York yet. There's more I can learn here.

'I need a few more months, Olivia.'

'Months?' Her face falls. 'But we need to come up with a plan to get back to 2017.'

'We're only in July and it's impossible to return before the thirty-first of October. We don't even know how we're going to make it back to Cambridge yet. So I might as well stay in St Louis and gather the information.'

'But don't you think you and I should—'

'I wouldn't be of any use at all in New York whereas if I keep working on finding out what the toxin does, at least when we make it back, we'll be able to stop the experiments from ever happening. And if we don't make it...'

'Don't say that!'

I pause, anxiety rising as I linger over the possibility. 'If we're stuck here for the rest of our lives, hopefully with the work I'm doing we'll have the kind of intel that the Resistance will want to trade for, in exchange for our protection.'

'And hopefully, we can prevent other test subjects' deaths.'

'That too.' I sigh. 'Anyway, are you making any progress on your end?'

'I'm gathering names, dates, trying to find out who's leading the project at GeneX, but it's not easy. The documents are restricted. The meetings aren't revealing as much as I'd like.'

'Maybe if there were a crisis...' I think aloud, 'that could push them to reveal more.'

'I have to run, DeAnn, sorry. I'll iMode you in a few days to keep you in the loop.'

'Same here.'

We've been catching up every few days since we arrived in the US and we're starting to develop a friendship of sorts. It's a work in progress.

A nurse barges into the locker room. 'Where the hell have you been? Shit's about to hit the fan out there, we need you!'

'Fine, fine, keep your panties on. Where do you want me?'

'You've got Consultation Room Five today. Your patients are already there.'

'OK, thanks,' I mutter.

This clinic looks like the French Doctors' outpost in Kampala, but it's different; I feel responsible somehow and ashamed that my own country has deteriorated so much that it would leave whole swathes of its own population without any medical coverage.

The familiar anger rises up. Why are we always the disposable ones? Why do things never change for us? Why can't my own country evolve a place for us to exist? It's like the American Dream is available for anyone who wants it, as long as their skin is white enough. You can come from Ukraine, Romania, Iceland and you'll be welcome. But if you've been here for 500 years and your skin is black, you're shit out of luck.

The irony, of course, is that none of us is really black or white. Five centuries of genetic blending will do that. The raping of slaves, illicit affairs and bi-racial marriages have made the melting pot a reality, in our genes at least. Most Caucasian Americans have at least 5 percent of African DNA in their veins. But all that is irrelevant in this instant. We're all in this clinic because of how we're perceived. Because we're unwanted. Because we're black.

Distracted by my somber thoughts, I slip on my coat and open the consultation room door. A black woman in a hospital gown is strapped to a gurney with two policemen on either side of her.

The woman's face is bathed in tears as she tries to attract the attention of her husband who is standing by the side of the bed, looking up at the TV.

Opposite them, the screen is turned on to a live conference call and a judge in black robes is questioning the husband: '...best of your knowledge, can you confirm what your wife was doing at eight o'clock on the...'

The policeman closest to the door marches over to me and pushes me out of the room, then taking in my name badge and my white coat, he asks, 'Are you a witness for the prosecution?'

'What? No. What's going on in there?'

His face closes up. 'Snap trial. Nothing to see. Get back to your day.' He pushes me out and slips back inside, closing the door behind him.

Frowning, I catch a nurse who's hurrying past in the crowded corridor. The woman tries to skirt past me but I grab her sleeve. 'What are the police doing here? Who called them?'

Fear glides over her features as she shakes free from my grip. 'Don't get involved, you can't do anything about it, Doctor Campbell. It's the law; just look the other way, it'll be over in a few minutes anyway.'

Unsure about what to do, I'm hesitating when an announcement rings out: 'Doctor Campbell to Consultation Room Five.'

Shit. My patients. They've been waiting for ages. I look at the door, it says Six. I should have gone next door, to Room Five. Glancing back, I go to the right examination room and push the door open.

'Come back here, Kevin!'

I nearly do a double take when I realize who's inside. A pregnant white woman is half-heartedly corralling about five children in the cramped space but it's pretty much impossible as the heat is making everyone restless, exhausted and irritable.

The oldest kid, a teenager, is sitting in the corner, looking miserable. The others are in various state of mayhem and the whale-sized woman seems on the verge of a nervous breakdown.

She looks up in surprise when I walk in. I see the thoughts unfold on her face. I'm black. I'm a woman. I'm her doctor. She opens her mouth and then closes it again. Good. I'm in no mood tonight. I'm already volunteering my time for free. She has a problem with me attending to her family, she can walk right out, see if I care.

They're the first white patients I've seen here. The situation out there must be dire for her to resort to coming here.

The heavily pregnant woman really is at the end of her rope. She regales me with the sad tale of her woes for five minutes before sticking the wriggling toddler in her teenage daughter's arms and stripping to the waist.

I examine her and diagnose gestational diabetes. Hardly surprising. The population's generalized overweight is jarring, especially after Uganda.

'What have you been eating?' I ask her.

'What I can find. What I can afford.'

'Carbs and sugar?'

'What do you think?' she asks sarcastically. 'I have a family to feed. I give them whatever will ensure that no one is hungry at the end of dinner.'

Seeing her size, I wouldn't be surprised if her diet consisted primarily of Twinkies. Then again, they're probably homeless. Shit. I hate this. This anger and powerlessness I feel all the time.

'You can get dressed.'

I grab one of her kids and prop him up the consultation table. Next door, some sort of commotion is happening. Screams and the sounds of a fight. What is going on in there? I glance at the wall. Maybe I should leave this family here for a few minutes and check on the patient in Room Six.

But all thoughts of walking out vanish when I see that the kid, Kevin, has sores and red blisters on his swollen feet. At first I thought there were burns and perhaps signs of mistreatment. I suck my breath in when I realize what it really is: kwashiorkor. Goddamn malnutrition. Here. In the US.

'Hey, my kids don't need treatment. We're here for me.'

'It won't cost extra.'

I push past the Mother of the Year and examine the rest

of her kids; it's as I suspected. The other children aren't faring any better. One of them is exhibiting the first symptoms of scurvy, his siblings have Keshan disease, rickets; these kids are not doing well.

Shaking my head, I start to put together a prescription for her. This is probably going to cost her more than she can afford. But there is one child in particular, seven years old or so, who needs to bring down his blood pressure or he's not going to make it to adulthood.

As screams erupt in the corridor, we all stop and look at the door. But just then, one of the kids misbehaves and the pregnant woman slaps the child in the face so I decide to focus on what is within my control: this consult, these patients.

The oldest kid, Britney, looks sullen and depressed. She's a teenager of the chunky variety; the kind who wishes she could disappear into the background. She's wearing baggy clothes and a cap, trying her best to hide her bulk under boyish clothes.

I'm 'borrowing' my work computer for the examinations here. The clinic's diagnostic instruments lag years behind what's available at GeneX. So after one hair-pulling consultation too many, I asked Lashelle to work around procurement and get my computer upgraded so I can now scan patients, take samples and diagnose with my work device. I wish I could take the device home if... when I leave this hellhole. It's the only thing that makes me happy about this godawful future. The tablet is a wonder to work with. I take a sample of the teenager's blood using a port on the side and mere seconds later, the modified processor pings with a diagnostic instantaneously.

The kid's anemic but otherwise OK. I noticed this a lot lately. Obese people who are in fact malnourished. I wonder if there's a part of the brain that encourages you to keep eating until a suitable amount of essential nutrients has been absorbed. Except that nowadays, food has nearly no protein, no vitamins, no selenium, no calcium. So people keep eating carbs and sugar but all that happens is that they get fatter and sicker.

I sigh, tap on my selected prescription and shake my head, glancing at the woman's enormous distended belly.

'What the fuck are you sighing about?' the woman says, getting her brood together, pulling their t-shirts sharply back in place, giving the ten-year-old a smack on the back of the head. Sensing the tension, the toddler's face crumples and we're engulfed in the shrill sound of his bellowing.

My skull reverberating and throbbing like a bell that's just been rung, I snap, 'Well, if you need to know, I'm sick and tired of seeing children in this condition, if you can't take care of the ones you already have then why the hell do you keep having them?'

'How dare you speak to me like this?' she hisses, radiating rage.

Oh here we go again, I groan inwardly. Another angry patient.

'You think I *want* to have five children and another on the way? Are you stupid? NO WOMAN WANTS TO HAVE SIX CHILDREN!' she screams. 'But what else can I do? The men can't take no for an answer and can't keep their fucking dicks in their pants, so you say yes; of course, you say yes. That's the only way to keep a guy around and you need a man and his salary to raise the kids you already have. So you say yes.'

'I'm sure you could have...'

'There's nothing to be done. I don't have enough money to buy the pill on the black market every fucking month. We have barely enough to eat even though I work two jobs. Their useless father abandoned us and the trailer park's already said that if I don't make rent this month, they'll evict us.' She turns, distracted. 'Stop that, Kevin! How many times?'

She slaps the four-year-old who was opening up a drawer full of medical material. The kid practically flies backward and starts to cry.

'Hey, stop that,' I say. 'He's not the one to blame here.'

I help the little guy to his swollen, blistered feet. His huge blue eyes are full of tears. I check him for injuries, then seeing none, reluctantly let Britney yank him back to her side. The little consultation room feels like a pressure cooker of anger and tension.

'Mom, we should go—'

'Shut up, Britney. I'm not going to let that stuck-up bitch tell me that I'm less than her. What does she know about our lives? Nothing.'

'I have other patients I need to...'

'I have other patients I need to...' she mimics me in a high-pitched voice and sneers. 'You fucking smug nigger. You think you're better than me, don't you? Us hardworking white folk don't get what's rightfully ours because of all of *you*! If you were all gone, there's be enough for us real Americans.'

It's not the first time, of course. But somehow every time, there's a part of me that's surprised at the violence of the hate.

'You're stealing money and jobs from us. Whose spot did you take to be here? Huh? You people shouldn't even be allowed to be doctors,' she spits, standing much too close to me for comfort.

'I'm going to have to ask you to leave. Now.'

'Go back to Africa, you fucking monkey!'

Grabbing a handful of children, she marches out.

I hold back the oldest before she follows her mother out of the room. 'Britney, right?'

She looks at me, mortified and apathetic, her body folded on itself, as if she were trying to disappear inside her t-shirt.

'Is there anything I can do?' I ask.

'Not unless you know how to abort a baby.'

'We don't do this here... it's illegal. And in any case, your mom is eight months in.'

She shakes herself free and leaves without a word.

I stare at her back, worry gnawing at me. I shouldn't have judged the pregnant woman. I should have tried to help. But lately, I've noticed anger and frenzy seeping through every interaction. St. Louis is electric with tension, it crackles in the air like lightning bolts before a storm, as despair mounts and food scarcity bites. Hunger, heat and a pervading sense of doom are unleashing the worst instincts in all of us.

Staring out the consultation room's window, my forehead pressed against the glass pane, I feel my chest tighten as a black cloud darkens the twilight sky.

A gunshot claps like thunder in the street. That one was really close.

I try to look through the window, to see if anyone got hurt, but all I can see is the black blizzard that's approaching. Extending for miles, the tsunami of sand closes in, leaping and bounding like a roiling wave until it crashes, whirling against my window.

I lift my hand and touch the glass and the storm responds with an enraged howl, shaking the building, screaming to be let in. Through every gap and slit, the dead dust seeps inside, as fine as talcum powder and as black as soot. It will get everywhere, in the food, in the water, in the creases of my eyelids, in my nostrils, my ears. It will seep into every interaction, sprinkling despair and hopelessness on the city like an evil fairy.

It will last for hours, well into the curfew.

I'm stuck here again for the night.

Unnatural darkness engulfs us all as light disappears from the world and every hardship, every obstacle becomes insurmountable.

I'll never make it back to 2017.

This is my life now.

I'm going to be stuck here until the day I die.

15

OLIVIA

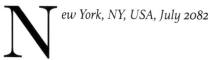 *ew York, NY, USA, July 2082*

'PENNY FOR YOUR THOUGHTS?' Michael is holding out a handful of tubes and smiling.

We're celebrating his birthday in a hipster street full of boutique shops and expensive micro-breweries. We're at an oxygen bar and a half a dozen of us are sitting in a circle. We were given weird machines that look a little like shisha pipes, a main body with a bendy tube snaking out and forming a loop at the end. I asked for mountain air, while the only other girl in the group of Michael's friends asked for sea air. The boys each selected a different flavour and we're going to share.

'Oh, sorry, this is my first time, I don't know how to put this on.'

'Ah, a virgin. My favourite.' Dmitry guffaws and Michael

elbows him in the ribs. 'So this is the girl you've been fanboying about, big guy?'

'Shut up, Dmitry.'

He's been talking about me, I lower my head and smile.

The other girl is Michael's sister, Rory. She's a little shy and nice enough with me. She reminds me of Mr Darcy's sister. The perfect young woman, accomplished, pretty, slender and reserved. I feel OTT next to her; too fat, too old, too curly. She's very sweet, though.

'You just insert the tiny nose piece there in your nostrils and loop the tube back around your ears. Then, just pull this tight and you're all set.'

This is preposterous, paying for clean air. Whatever will they think of next? I press a button on the side of the contraption and breathe in. Oh my God, this is wonderful. All griping forgotten, I press my nostrils together and concentrate on breathing in proper lungfuls of air for the first time in months. My shoulders come down and I relax.

Dmitry laughs, 'Someone get the tubes away from the virgin before she passes out.'

Rory smiles. 'Just take it easy or you'll get dizzy. Our bodies are not made to breathe one hundred per cent pure oxygen.'

I don't care. I just want to keep doing this and forget where I am and that I'm never going to breathe clean air ever again. And that I don't have a way back and that this world is bloody awful. I just want to forget for a while.

At length, our stomachs demanding to be filled, we push our way back into the street; an anthill full of people, milling around in the suffocating humidity. I hang back and Michael discreetly takes my hand. I got him a 1950s hat and he looked genuinely touched.

'I'm glad you came,' he whispers.

His warm breath tingles as he speaks in my ear. He presses my hand, then lets it go and walks ahead as I follow our small group into a busy restaurant with cosy booths and orange-coloured bottles lining the shelves from floor to ceiling.

A pleasant hubbub of conversations greets us in the semidarkness; young, well-off people are gathered at the cramped, narrow tables, laughing and drinking. This could be a normal Friday night in 2016.

Dmitry tries to sit by my side but Michael holds his friend back and makes a point of sitting next to me instead. Closer than is strictly necessary. His thigh touches mine and he sits back, possessively extending his arm along the back of my chair.

'So what's that place you've taken us to?' asks Chuck, Michael's childhood friend from the Midwest who's in town for the weekend.

That's strange, come to think of it: Michael seems like such a worldly guy, with his twentieth-century suits, his high-powered job and his knowledge about gourmet foods, I just assumed he came from a privileged background, but his friend Chuck looks like an all-American farm boy. Maybe Michael's sophistication is a veneer. It doesn't take anything away from him. It just casts a new light on his professional ambitions and social aspirations.

Michael orders for the whole table but I don't hear the menu, as Dmitry startles me, grabbing my left hand, twisting it to see better.

'You're not wearing a ring,' he states.

I pull my hand out of his and sit on it. 'No, I'm not.'

'So you're not married or a BoC nut, then. And you're obviously not a Beautiful One.'

I squirm on the uncomfortably trendy seat. 'Oh, well, I guess I'm not as pretty as—'

'No, no, a Beautiful One,' he says, pointing with his chin at an eerily quiet group of adolescents at a nearby table.

They're eating their food in deep concentration, ignoring each other. None of them can be much older than twenty. Yet they are wearing expensive clothes and they are groomed and surgically altered to look flawless. The young men are taut and muscular but their faces are strangely impassive. The girls look like evanescent sylphs, lithe, elegant, aloof. They eat in complete silence, their expressionless faces looking all the more pallid because of the white clothes they're all wearing.

'Erm, no. Clearly I'm not as beautiful as them,' I say.

Dmitry frowns and cocks his head slightly. I know that look. I made a mistake. There's something I should know and it's odd that I don't.

Eager to distract him from my *faux pas*, I ask: 'BoC nut?'

'A Bride of Christ. I guess that's an American thing. Vow of abstinence because of no contraception, yada yada yada,' he says too loudly. 'But let me tell you, from experience, the Brides have nothing against a bit of anal. Or blowjobs,' he guffaws. People from other tables glance at us and he continues at the same volume, enjoying the attention. 'They're not like those freaks over there.'

The unnerving young people turn their heads towards Dmitry, considering him for a few seconds, then look away.

'Dmitry...' Michael warns in his deep rumbling bass.

'I... So what was your question?' I say.

'Not married, not a Beautiful One, and not a Bride of Christ. So I guess you have no impediment against you know... fucking,' Dmitry chortles. 'Oh man, you're blushing. I can see why you like that one, big guy.'

'Fuck off, Dmitry.' Michael growls good naturedly.

'Well, you're in good hands, virgin – my man here is one of the good ones. We'll work on getting you drunk so he can pop your cherry tonight, then.'

Michael apologises for his friend but I get the sense that he probably wanted to know the answers.

'Ah, the food is ready,' Michael says, looking relieved. A red light is blinking on our table, so he and Dmitry go get our dishes and come back, arms laden with small plates.

There are little corn fritters lathered with a whipped paste, lobster in large slices drizzled artfully with dark brown sauce, a small basket full of crispy crackers with something like black olive chunks baked into them, a plate of little meatballs on sticks and a myriad of other delicacies. We all tuck in.

In the orange light it's hard to tell what any of it really is. It looks like Mexican maybe. I try a little tortilla with guacamole. There's a hint of nuttiness. The crackers have a vague bacon and peanuts flavour. It's interesting. But it doesn't taste like anything I recognise.

'What is it?'

'Fusion protein,' Chuck says as he keeps eating.

The menu is glowing on the screen-table so I push my plate aside and read the list of dishes. We're eating witchetty grubs in caramelised soy sauce. *Hormigas culonas* crispy crackers, cockroach meatballs and cricket tortillas. I start to retch and run to the bathroom.

Cradling the toilet bowl, I throw up everything I just ate and keep bringing up bile after that. A knock on my bathroom stall interrupts me as I come up for air.

'Olivia, are you alright?' It's Rory.

'Yes, yes, thank you.' I spit into the toilet bowl.

'Are you sick?'

'No, no, I just, I... I just didn't know it was insects.'

'Are you vegan?' she asks as I come out. 'Sorry, I didn't realise when I made the dinner reservations—'

'Oh no, no, don't worry, it's not your fault. It's just I never ate insects before.' I smile wretchedly.

'Really? That's so weird. Why not?'

I try to think of an excuse and remember an article by the environmental activist Paul Watson that stuck in my mind.

'It's just that... our planet is like a spaceship that's hurtling through space and the only thing standing between us and oblivion is a very thin layer of atmosphere. The crew that keeps the oxygen flowing on Spaceship Earth is mostly made up of insects. We're only passengers you see, humans, and yet we're killing off the crew that keeps us alive. Bees, worms,' I laugh weakly, 'and ants and whatever else was on our plate tonight, they're more useful to the Earth than we are. So...' I shrug, 'I can't bring myself to eat them.'

She's looking at me like I've sprouted antennas. 'Well, I'm really sorry if we killed off a few bugs, but humans need to feed themselves and if I have to choose who's going to live or die, I'd take a human kid over a cockroach any day. Humans can write symphonies, land on Mars and build particle accelerators – and you think these insignificant creatures are more important?'

'Well, not all of us are Mozart, Everett or Einstein, are we? The more pertinent question is how many of us can the spaceship hold? Once all the humans are fed and everything else is dead, do you really think life will be worth living for our descendants?'

'So what are you proposing? A good disease to wipe a few billion off?'

'No, no of course not,' I say, shocked. 'Just fertility

control. Prevent the growth from happening instead of dealing with the aftermath of unbridled fertility.'

She laughs. 'You Europeans. You're all so obsessed with controlling your fertility. You're dying off because of it, your population is sliding into old age and extinction while the rest of us thrive and grow. So sad.' She shakes her head.

I rinse my mouth and wash my hands, while she touches up her makeup.

'So if you feel this strongly about birth control, you must have one of these contraceptive implants they force every woman to wear in Europe, right?' she asks.

'No, no... implant-free.' I hold up my arm to show the tender part near my armpit. 'They're not mandatory in the KEW.' And certainly not in the UK in 2016, I add silently in my head.

A FEW HOURS LATER, we're all quite drunk. Michael loops an arm around my shoulders and kisses my neck as we zigzag along the night-soaked streets of Manhattan. Dmitry is talking earnestly to Rory, with a conspiratorial look on his face, leading a few strides ahead, while Chuck, unsteady on his feet, is relieving his bladder against a wall.

Michael says in a stage whisper, 'We're going on an adventure.' He chuckles, slurring his words.

'Okay, birthday boy.' I smile, running a hand through his hair. I can't get enough of him. All these possibilities, the desire, the glimmer of hope for a happy future. I'm intoxicated with him.

After a mile or so of drunken weaving through the gradually emptying streets, Chuck and Dmitry tinker with Michael's novelty vintage lighter; then they pass it to him to light up his expensive birthday present: a real cigar. Except they fail to tell him that they've boosted the lighter practically to flame-thrower level and they collapse with laughter when Michael turns it on and nearly singes his eyebrows.

How old are these men? They act like teenagers but they're all well into their thirties, aren't they? For the space of a night, I suspend my doubts and follow the immature group through the streets of New York. The simple joy of living in this moment lifts my spirits up and despite the horrors of this era, or maybe because of them, I indulge in my stupid fling and ignore the fact that I have to go back soon.

I'd forgotten what being carefree and sassy felt like. Maybe I don't need to make any decisions tonight. Maybe I don't need to assess Michael's suitability, maybe I don't need to be on my best behaviour to elicit a life-long commitment. Maybe I can just have fun.

We reach a large building on the river that looks like Battersea Power Station but smaller. Its four chimneys rise above us, high up into the navy blue sky.

'Ready for Twilight?' the young woman asks, pointing at the building in front of us.

'What is this place?'

'Oh, you'll see,' Michael answers with a mischievous smile. 'Rory wants to show you how we do things, in the US of A.'

'No, it was your idea, big guy,' Dmitry laughs, patting his back. 'Great idea too, I've never been to one before, can't wait to see it.'

'Are you sure, guys? I mean, I can probably get you in, but it's...' Rory begins, but the boys egg her on until finally she agrees to let them in.

She swipes her iMode and holds the door open for all of us. The building looks like a nineteenth-century factory on the outside, complete with red bricks and arched windows, but inside, it's pristine, sterile and modern.

A wide lobby with a three-storey-high ceiling opens up in front of us. The walls are white and glowing. There is no company brand, no indication of what the building could be. Gentle classical music plays diffusely and a pleasant but artificial scent pervades everything. Our steps echo in the cavernous place and a drunken hush interspersed with giggles descends on our group as we walk round the curved chrome reception desk.

The security guard looks up at us suspiciously. Rory gestures for us to stay put while she walks confidently over to him.

'Hi, Vince, how are you tonight?'

He relaxes as soon as he recognises her. 'Oh hi Miss Quisling, what brings you here so late?'

'It's my brother's birthday and he's promised his friends a tour of my workplace,' she simpers, 'I know it's not standard procedure but...'

He hesitates. 'OK, fine, Miss Quisling, that's alright, just this once and just because it's you. Take them in but make sure you stay behind the scenes. The last group has just started, so if you hurry, you should be able to catch up.'

'Yes, of course. Thank you, Vince, you're a star.'

I wonder if she always gets her way. She's very pretty.

She motions us through a door marked 'EMPLOYEES ONLY' and we find ourselves in a large space with desks and computer stations.

One of the walls is a two-way mirror and on the other side there's a typical waiting room. On our side of the room, things are decidedly more office-like. Rory logs into one of the work stations, then says excitedly, 'Oh, we're just on time, follow me.'

She hurries to the far end of the room, opens a door and lets us through. Now we're in a long corridor. It looks like the two-way mirror continues to run all the way through the facility, connecting room to room, behind the mirror.

My interest piqued, I follow Michael's friends as they walk along the hallway, running my left hand along the mirror, remembering my selection process with the Programme. Maybe a similar selection of candidates happens here and the judges observe from our side of the glass?

We emerge into the next monitoring office. On the clients' side, there's a softly lit locker room littered with clothes, some neatly folded, some strewn over chairs or hung in the metal lockers. A dozen suitcases are gathered in a corner. Shoes of all sizes are pushed under the benches, some removed in a hurry, some deliberately.

Rory holds a finger to her lips and opens the door at the far end of the corridor. Dmitry and Chuck are talking excitedly about seeing naked women and given the amount of discarded clothes, I guess this must be a gym of some sort or maybe a spa.

Rory slips through the door and whispers with someone on the other side. A few minutes later, gesturing for us to be quiet, she holds the door open and we file into another office equipped with monitoring stations.

An attendant is staring at us. He looks awkward and quite young, maybe in his mid-twenties. He doesn't exactly strike me as a high-achiever. More like a night guard with a student loan and bad acne. He keeps stealing glances towards Rory but she seems oblivious, laughing with Dmitry and playfully slapping his arm, saying, 'Shush, you idiot.'

Michael is looking sleepy now; I guess the amount of

alcohol he drunk today finally caught up with his tall frame. His arm is resting heavily on my shoulders and I like it.

'Michael?'

'Mmmh?' he replies, his sleepy eyes looking sensually at me, half closed.

'What are we doing here? I'm not a voyeur, I don't really want to watch naked people.'

'Even if it's an orgy?'

'Especially if it's an orgy.'

'Nothing to worry about, then,' he chuckles.

Rory asks the night guard a question, which I can't hear.

He answers, 'Yeah, sure', and presses a button.

The opaque glass becomes transparent revealing about twenty-five naked people, oblivious to our presence who are showering in stalls, lathering soap on their bodies, rinsing intimate parts or just shampooing their hair.

I avert my eyes, embarrassed, while Rory discusses something with the young night guard. As expected, Chuck and Dmitry start making lewd comments, standing close to a young curvy woman and mimicking what they'd do to her if there wasn't a glass window between them. The young night guard stares at them, looking distinctly uncomfortable. Michael's eyes slide over the woman, then come to rest on me and he kisses me hungrily.

The young night guard presses another button and we hear a loud beep and a pre-recorded announcement on the other side, muffled but audible: 'Attention please: you have thirty seconds left before your preparation ceremony begins. Please start making your way towards the next room.'

There is something vaguely wrong about the scene; there are older people here - as in aged eighty and up. Even more worrisome is the mother with her two young children.

She bends to explain something to her two little girls and smiles. Further away, a young man with Down's syndrome helps an old woman who's struggling to get into her bathrobe. He helps her knot her belt, and she smiles and pats him on the shoulder.

The lanky night guard lets us through into the next room on our side of the mirror. There is a lectern there with a dashboard and a small flotilla of steel machines that look like the restaurant robots. They have multiple arms and are fitted on rails.

'Ready?' the young man asks Rory.

She glances at all of us and the three boys nod. I don't know what I should be ready for, so I hang back and observe, feeling uneasy. The night guard presses another button, which opens the connecting door between the showers and the next area for the revellers. On their side, the room is now significantly smaller, just large enough for them to stand in two by two.

Again we hear a loud beep and a monotonous recorded voice intones: 'Please stand in pairs. You'll be called forwards shortly by your names and taken to your individual rooms for your personalised ritual. Each one of you will be accompanied by a dedicated attendant, who will arrive shortly. Please wait. Thank you for your patience. We appreciate your custom and wish you a wonderful and unforgettable experience. Thank you for choosing Twilight.'

Under the customers' slippered feet, the steel floor has a deep groove that runs along the length of the narrow room. The little girls are shivering and one of them has started to cry, holding on to her mother's thigh. The curvy girl is praying and the teenager with Down's syndrome is in a full-blown panic, trying to get back to the shower room. He's banging his fists against the door, crying, and it's so loud that even through the glass, we can hear it.

'Moooooooooom, Daaaaaaaaad, come back, come back. Moooooom!'

But the steel door is now closed.

Rory walks over to the young guard and smiling at us over her shoulder, she nods for him to proceed. The attendant presses a button on his console. The beep rings again, twice this time. I expect the voice to start calling names but no recording plays. The door to the following room doesn't open. Nothing occurs, really, for a few seconds.

Then something happens to the people wearing bathrobes a few inches away from us, on the other side of the glass. One by one, they start going limp and dropping. There is so little space in the narrow corridor that as they fall, some of them hit their heads on the glass, leaving stains of saliva or blood.

I jump, startled, as the sickening thuds and skidding sounds accelerate. The young man with Down's is hollering with fear now; incapable of making words, his shouts burst out, raw and feral, as he bangs on the steel door that leads back to the showers. The sound of his fists is like an odd beat to an even stranger song. The song of death.

I rush towards the glass and crouch, unable to tear my eyes away from the children. Their mother holds them close. I think she's singing but her daughters are holding up their hands to their ears, blocking out the screams as they cry. Finally, one of the little girls collapses and her mother falls to her knees, her face a hollow mask as she contemplates her daughter's small corpse. Her mouth opens for a scream that never comes. Instead, a drip of saliva dribbles out of her lips and her face sags.

The younger sister is clinging to her mother, her eyes

shut tight, and as the woman collapses, the child tips sideways too. Her arm stuck under the dead woman's inert form, the little girl is visibly panicking, her chest shaken by small pants as she tries simultaneously to wake her mom up and wriggle out from under her. For a split second it seems that she can see me as I reach for her, only a few inches away through the glass. But then her eyes widen and finally she goes still as well.

Then there is only silence.

The young night guard breaks the spell. He presses another button. Three beeps chime in the hollow silence. The floor parts in two, along the groove, dumping the white-robed bodies into the darkness below. Then the floor swivels back up and into place.

The automatons behind us buzz into life, making us all jump. Rory lets out a little startled cry and then giggles.

What I thought was a drain in the steel floor turns out to be rails; the four robots slot into place and start their dance, their octopus-like arms cleaning every surface. Light glints off their metal bodies as the detergent's foam slides down the glass walls and they hose the room.

'Do you want to go back to the locker room?' Rory says. 'Sometimes they leave good stuff behind.'

'Yeah sure, let's go see,' Dmitry replies.

Chuck says he'll go smoke outside and wait for us. The young night guard, his eyes too old for his age, says good night and leaves as well. I stay back, still kneeling by the spot where the girls died, watching the foam sluice down the mirror. Michael helps me up.

'Michael, what is this place? I don't understand why these people were killed.'

'Well, they're useless people. People who, in other times, would have been allowed to go on being a burden to society:

drug-addicts, single mothers, retards. Old folks who are too decrepit to contribute anything to the economy, you know...'

'That's not a reason to murder them.'

He frowns, puzzled. 'Nobody's murdering them. They're committing assisted suicide. They do it to themselves. They sign the papers in the reception room. They get compensated for it.'

'What do you mean, compensated? They're dead.' My voice is rising and hysteria creeps beneath the surface.

He shrugs. 'They come here of their own volition, or their loved ones send them here, to end it, when they can no longer contribute to their family's survival. It's alright, the people they nominate in their wills get an indemnity; it's all above board.'

I throw my arms up, frustrated at not getting through to him. 'But they didn't know, Michael. They thought they were going to another room.'

'Listen. About that. You can't tell anyone, you hear? Rory did us a huge favour to bring us behind the scenes. She did it to please you, she told me you had a conversation in the bathroom and that you'd find her work interesting.'

'Interesting?' There's a sob somewhere inside my chuckle.

'They used to give them massages, bring in spiritual advisors and all that crap. But the Twighlighters were expecting death as soon as they lay down on those tables. Rory told me that they used to change their minds, plead, shit themselves and puke. So the management company decided to change the method. Poison gas. Much more economical and clean. It's a win–win, you see? They're relaxed and anticipating the next step. It's more humane that way. Twighlight hasn't revealed this to anyone, so the surprise works.' He laughs. 'And well... it's not like the clients live to tell the tale. So as long as you don't say anyth—'

'It's so wrong,' I say, aghast.

'It's just reality. You said it yourself. There isn't enough for all of us. Those who are ready to make the ultimate sacrifice for our country are heroes. I think they're really brave and generous. This method saves them from suffering and having second thoughts. I don't see the problem.'

It's logical. But my soul bucks against it.

'You think this,' I gesture towards the glass panel, '*this*, is better than fertility control?'

'Well, yeah.' He frowns. 'That way, people like you and me get to have children who grow up to be contributing members of society, maybe even CEOs, geniuses or artists. You can't tell before someone's born what kind of value they'll bring to society. And if after a few years, the person's not worth the effort, we scrap them and start over. Look that retard, for example—'

'I can't, I can't,' I interrupt him, holding a hand up.

His hand slides on my shoulder, pressing solicitously. 'Anyway, let's meet up with the others. OK?'

'Sure,' I say, lost in my thoughts.

We start back, seeing the shower room through the mirror, then the locker room. In the locker room, the light is dim but something is moving in the far right corner. My heart leaps for a second, thinking someone's escaped the slaughter. But I realise that it's Dmitry and Rory. They did say that they'd go through the dead's possessions. How horrible.

They seem to be... Oh my God. They're having sex standing against one of the lockers. Dmitry is holding Rory's wrists above her head with one hand and ramming her against the locker door.

'Death is the ultimate aphrodisiac, you know.' Michael's hand find its way under my shirt and his fingers slide along the small of my back. I shiver.

He leans in to kiss me but his lips are too wet, the air is too close. I can't. 'I'm really sorry. I have to go home, Michael. Sorry. Sorry.'

I run out of the building as fast as I can, taking in big gulps of air to get my heart back under control and then hail a cab. Just as my car drives off, Michael comes out of the building, calling my name. I look at him through the back window as his silhouette recedes and fades against the dark street's shadows.

Maybe this was too good to be true. I need to put him out of my mind and focus on finding a way back to 2017.

16

DEANN

S*t. Louis, Missouri, USA, July 2082*

MY BREATH SOUNDS so loud in the facemask. I scratch the back of my head through the disposable cap with the knuckles of my gloved hand and sigh.

'Why can't I figure this out?'

'You're asking me or is this a rhetorical question?'

'Smart ass.'

'Half an hour, and this time, stick to it or I'll leave you behind, you hear me?' Jada says over her shoulder as she pores over the samples, next to me.

'Hmh.'

'OK, walk me through it. You can do this, DeAnn.'

Sighing, I take a moment to gather my thoughts and summarize what I've got so far: 'The data clearly shows that GeneX is conducting the tests on two distinct groups of subjects.' I point to the screen. 'See here?' She leans in and glances at the image I'm showing her. 'There's just a few alleles of difference in their genetic profile, look.'

'What's the difference between the two groups?'

I groan, 'That's what I can't figure out.'

She mulls it over. 'If we can't figure out what makes the groups different, maybe we should try and figure out why they have two groups to begin with. Tell me what you've deduced so far.'

'One group contains ninety-nine percent of the test subjects and the other group constitutes just one percent of the sample.'

'Huh. Well, I do that with my plants sometimes to check my genetic modifications against a normal sample.'

'What are you thinking? That this one percent is the control group?' I drum my gloved fingers on the work surface. 'You're right, it must be extremely hard to ensure the correct combination of genetic traits is targeted. It's never been done before. It must be even harder to ensure that the toxin delivers its payload only if that particular set of chromosomal variables are present. So maybe they are trying to ensure that the one percent who don't display these specific genetic markers are not affected by the toxin.'

It's a bit far-fetched but I suppose medicine has had a 65-year head start on me. Who knows what's considered realistic these days in a lab at the cutting edge of science, like this one is?

Jada's looking nonplussed. 'Erm... English please?'

'Ah, yes,' I laugh, heartened by the breakthrough. 'So, imagine that the toxin is like a small locked box with three padlocks on it. If I pass the box round a roomful of people, some will have one key but they won't be able to open the box, because two of the padlocks will still be locked.'

'OK, I get it. So the box will only open for people who have three keys?'

'Yes, exactly and it has to be the correct three keys to open these specific three padlocks.'

Understanding illuminates her features. 'And what does the box contain? Probably nothing good, right?'

'Uh-huh, the box contains a toxin that disrupts your body's protein expression. So if you open it, basically you're fucked. Ah! That's why they're using western blots.'

'The blotchy watercolor things?'

'Yes, they probably use them to check if the toxin managed to contaminate the correct people while leaving the control group untouched.'

I grab my computer and scroll through the files to show her, but at that precise moment there's a loud noise. Startled, I let the tablet slip and it falls on the bench, breaking a pipette into slivers of glass.

Jada freezes and looks beyond me at the darkened corridor, worry etched on her face.

Heart beating, I glance around the lab but nothing stirs. The noise was just one of the lab robots pinging to announce the end of an analysis. Cursing under my breath, I'm picking up the broken shards when a sharp pain slices through my anxious thoughts.

Jada sucks her breath in.

I follow her gaze and look down at my gloved finger. Blood.

'Are you infected?' She looks stricken.

'No, I should be OK—'

'What do you mean *should*?'

Panic's seeping in, but I push it away. 'I haven't handled the toxin today, I've only looked at the test subjects' analyses on screen, so I probably haven't contaminated myself.'

'Probably? Shit DeAnn how can you stay so calm?'

Getting my heartbeat under control, I gather the rest of the glass and throw it away. We can't leave any trace of our presence.

Jada's looking pale. 'We've been here way too long already, we need to go.'

'You're right, let me just...' I'm turning off my tablet, when I notice a pop-up message blink on the upper-right quadrant of the screen. A drop of my blood has touched the port I installed for my work at the clinic and the tablet's analyzed it.

My hand hovers above the touch screen, ready to close the unrequested window, when I spot something. Something... Oh my God.

The mishap has launched a DNA analysis of a handful of backlogged samples, among which is my own drop of blood.

'DeAnn?' Jada says over her shoulder, as she approaches the exit.

'Wait. Jada, come see this.'

Jada's at the door now. 'Someone could have heard us, we've been really loud.' She's checking the corridor for signs of movement. But when she glances back and sees my face, she doubles back.

'What have you found?'

'I know it's wrong, but I've started analyzing the genetic samples of my patients, at the clinic.'

'You did *what*?' She looks shocked.

'I was just trying to solve the toxin's mystery.' The words tumble out, as I wave away the moral quandary and focus on the idea that is burgeoning at the back of my mind. 'The problem was that sample after sample was just the same. For weeks, I never found anyone who presented the control group's alleles. Every single sample I took belonged to the ninety-nine percent. Until Britney.'

'Who?'

'Just an anemic teenager who came to the clinic with her family the other day.'

What makes her different than all the other people who came to the clinic in the weeks since I started testing? For that matter, what makes her different than me?

'Do I know them?'

'No, no, they'd never been to the clinic before. Anyhow, you wouldn't know them, they're—'

Wait a second.

No.

That's not possible.

I yank the rubber glove off my hand and express a drop of my blood into an Eppendorf tube; then, while I pull a new glove on, I run to the fridge and grab a blood vial from the uncontaminated control group samples. Next, extracting the powder that Kitsa gathered, I add a few particles of the toxin to both samples.

Jada looks bewildered. 'What's going on?'

'I'll explain, give me a sec.'

While the lab tech robot purifies the two samples of contaminated proteins. Then, hands shaking badly, I extract minute drops of each sample's proteins and place them on small cover slips. Holding my right hand with my left, to stop the tremor, I carefully lift the flimsy cover slips with tweezers and place them in the machine, programming both samples for crystallization.

Every noise makes me jump as I wait, leg bouncing up and down.

'DeAnn?'

'Come on, come on.' I mutter.

'We need to wrap up and leave.'

The robot completes the purification and I check the crystals. 'When's the next patrol?' I ask, nose in the scope.

'Ten minutes.' I don't look up but I hear the panic in her voice.

The hair is rising on the back of my neck. Come on. Come on. There! A single crystal and it's birefringent. I look for another crystal in the second sample and when I find it, I select it carefully and place the two syringes in liquid nitrogen. Hurrying to the X-ray room, I place the two crystals on the holder and dart back out of the room and, looking over my shoulder, start the X-ray defraction.

'What's going on?' Jada's left her lookout post and hurried over.

'I think I figured out what differentiates the two sample groups.'

'Can you do your figuring out faster?' Her eyes slide to the door.

'Remember how I told you that the only people with three keys can open the toxin box?'

'Yeah and if they open it, their proteins die or something?'

'Exactly – I've just exposed my blood to the toxin and someone else's as well, to check a theory.'

Every clanging noise makes us flinch, but finally the results appear on my screen and the air escapes my lungs.

'It can't be...'

My crystallized molecules have the same characteristics as 99 percent of the test subjects. And on the screen, it's as clear as day: my proteins have deteriorated following exposure to the toxin.

'DeAnn, we have. To. Go. Now.'

Ignoring her, I quickly swipe my screen to review the

control group's crystal, the one that's identical to Britney's. The proteins are intact. Goosebumps erupt on my skin as the ramifications of this discovery become clear.

'But... it's just an urban myth. It's not scientifically possible to target a combination of inheritance markers,' I whisper.

Or at least it wasn't possible sixty-five years ago. I rub my temples, feeling a massive headache gathering there.

'What is it? What have you found?'

'GeneX has managed to isolate the eleven out of twenty thousand human protein-coding genes, which determine skin color, hair color and texture.'

'What do you mean?' she asks, but I can already see realization dawning on her.

'It means that the bastards have identified what makes an African-descent person black, and not only that but they've engineered a toxin that targets *only* the people who bear that specific repetitive DNA combination.'

'The toxin targets black people? We're the ones with the three keys who can open the box from hell?'

'Yeah. Once the target is identified, the molecule of MSA8742 binds itself irreversibly to the gene sequence and prevents the expression of the targeted protein.'

'But what does it do?' Her face is the picture of horror. 'What does it do to us once it's open?'

I stare at the beautiful ribbon of the protein swirling endlessly on the screen, as a shiver of foreboding slithers down my spine.

'I have no fucking idea, Jada.'

17

OLIVIA

ew York, USA, August 2082

I STARE RESOLUTELY in front of me, ignoring the screens positioned all around in the office. Some of my colleagues have gathered around the screen, pointing.

Lifeless bodies lie on the beaten earth, their glassy eyes staring at the sky. Or maybe looking at something I can't see, something beyond this world. Their mouths are stained with foam and vomit.

Somebody's filming this as they walk, trying to avoid stepping on the bodies, and crying.

It's a woman.

And the woman is me.

'There you are. Come on quickly, emergency meeting.'

Michael is in work mode, carefully pretending that he never kissed me and that we barely know each other. I follow him, glancing back at the TV screens, wanting to see the whole sequence. So my plan worked.

Well, to be fair, it was DeAnn's idea. I'm so lucky that she's here with me. I shudder to think what this mission would have been like if I'd jumped forwards with Frank or any of the other candidates. Since we came back from Uganda, our partnership has strengthened. When we spoke a few weeks ago she had a brilliant idea: to provoke a crisis; shake the tree and see what falls out. So I did. And here we are.

Michael motions me to come into the packed lift. All eyes are on the screen above our heads, people crane their necks to get a better view. A journalist in voice over is saying: 'This video was sent this morning to all the news organisations in the world with a memo graphically describing the human experiments that have been conducted in Uganda....'

My anonymous contact released the video, as agreed. This has got to make a difference. People will be outraged and the tests will come to an end.

The lift doors open and Michael hurries out, completely ignoring me. He's behaving oddly. Is my cover blown? Has the firm finally figured out that I'm not who I say I am? My breath catches in my chest when another idea occurs to me. Maybe somehow, they figured out that I'm the source of the leak. I reluctantly follow him, not knowing whether I should run instead. But where to?

Something is different in the top-floor boardroom; instead of our usual senior GeneX counterparts, this morning the room is filled with a contingent of grey-suited people who look self-important and grim. I notice idly that, apart from me, there are only white men here.

I slink to my usual seat in the corner and pull out my

tablet, ready to take notes. When the entire firm's board has finally arrived, the door closes and all eyes focus on a man at the head of the long conference table.

One of the partners gets up, and uncharacteristically ill at ease, he gestures for the room to settle down, then addresses the man at the top of the table. 'Secretary Matthews, welcome. We at Carapadre and Dergrin are hon—'

The leader of the group of new comers waves his hand in a very slight gesture, which I can see from my vantage point but the partner can't, and a grey-suited man gets up.

'Thank you,' he interrupts. Shaken, the partner sits down, unsure how to process the snub. The man at the head of the table half closes his eyes, hands crossed over his bulky stomach. I catch a glimpse of gold around his wrist and an air of contempt on his toad-like face.

The aide in grey continues, 'Mr Viles, can you please explain the situation to the lawyers?'

On the far wall, the GeneX CEO's leonine face appears on a screen; he looks like he's just had more collagen injected. His over-puffy lips move disturbingly like slimy red slugs on the giant screen.

'You have all seen the videos...'

A chorus of whispers and uncomfortable rustling greets the remark.

'This is not the first leak, but all the previous ones were contained and this is by far the closest we've ever come to the project being brought to light.'

Viles licks his bulbous lips. 'Last month, our field tests had to be scrapped at the last minute, as our facility was about to be discovered.'

What can he be talking about? Surely Camp Askaris was evacuated back in February?

'Our scientists were able to destroy the physical evidence and fly the proprietary data out of the country. So nothing was discovered. We're working on finding the culprits who leaked the information about our activities to the local authorities.'

Viles throws an uncertain look at the man I now recognise from TV; it's the Secretary of Defence. When the large man doesn't move, his eyes slide to the grey-suited man who's still standing near him. Neither one interrupts, so the GeneX CEO continues: 'In the wake of these close calls, we realised that we needed to inform you of the DoD's upcoming plans to... erm... go live.' He falters. 'Just in case any of our other facilities were breached and the exact nature of our project was divulged to a foreign government or to the press ahead of the... main event.'

The Secretary's aide nods and adds, 'Of course, the recent incidents could be coincidences. But we're erring on the side of caution and assuming that these various setbacks are the work of a terrorist group known as the Cassandra Resistance.'

Palms tingling, I continue typing on the tablet, nose down.

'At the moment, we're fairly confident that no one has grasped the exact nature of our project. No one seems to have uncovered either the fact that the DoD has commissioned GeneX to reverse engineer the chemical in question. But given the acceleration of the leaks, it is only a matter of time before a smart reporter puts two and two together.'

The DoD aide holds a hand up to interrupt the GeneX CEO who stops speaking immediately, looking anxious. 'Our game theorists extrapolate that our window of opportunity for a surprise tactical deployment is closing down fast. That's why we may have to bring the legal arm of the operation into play faster than anticipated.'

The Secretary's aide continues, 'We need to have a legal strategy in place for that eventuality. We can't allow the public to understand what this chemical compound does before we're ready to... distribute it. We may have to silence anyone who might reveal it ahead of our deadline.'

Silence people? As in subpoena or assassination?

A senior partner of our firm speaks up, his fingers in a steeple. 'Mr Secretary, we can deal, of course, with information breaches, but it's unlikely we'll be able to manage the backlash that we can expect from the countries outside of the Coalition once you deploy... especially on the scale you're intending.'

Michael winces. Tanner isn't the most judicious man and often puts his foot in it. Today is no exception.

Oblivious to the ripples that are shaking around the room, Tanner continues, 'We're talking about massive repercussions for the US here, political and even maybe military repercussions that we'd be unable to prevent. I can't imagine that the UN is going to sit idly by as—'

The Secretary speaks up for the first time. His hands, clasped on his paunch, rise and fall with every breath, yet the man's face barely moves. 'You let me worry about the UN. At the moment, your job is to contain any breaches of information about GeneX's tests and preparations, pre-deployment. Can you do it, yes or no?'

'Of course, I didn't mean to imply...'

The Secretary of Defence interrupts Tanner again, looking around the table and blocking the man out. 'Any ideas?'

The lawyers look at each other and I hear a few mumbles.

'Doctrine of inevitable disclosure?'

'We can couch it as intellectual property infringement.'

'Pursue damages from breach of NDA?'

Michael whispers something in his manager's ear. John Bartlett nods and speaks up: 'We should be able to have this back under wraps by end of week, Mr Secretary. We can't remediate the leak but we can divert the public's attention, pressure the media with threats of libel and deny that it had anything to do with GeneX. We'll work with your department and Mr. Viles's team to make sure that no further information is divulged and that the man responsible is apprehended and stopped.'

What? No, no, no, that won't do at all. I mouth a quick message to Michael, volunteering to be part of the team, so I can sabotage their efforts from the inside and make sure the video continues to raise awareness.

His lips move silently and a second later I hear his voice say, 'OK, you're on, Sinclair.'

18

DEANN

St. Louis, Missouri, USA, August 2082

HOWELL ISLAND MUST HAVE BEEN beautiful, once upon a time. But the swarm of humanity has reduced it to little more than a desert. The weather is nice today, no dust storms announced. Jada and I are out walking with her two kids.

I still don't like kids but hers are OK. Imani and Dion are quiet and well behaved. Jada's daughter especially, she's whip smart and reminds me of Kitsa. I try not to see the girl too often, it makes my heart ache too much.

'Kids, don't stray too far, OK?' Jada calls out as the children run ahead of us.

They crouch in the mud by the pathetic little stream that trickles there; the ghost of the Missouri River.

At first I found Jada irritating; she's young and angry and still has the fire I lost somewhere along the way. I'm more of a cynic nowadays, but she still gets outraged. She reminds me of myself at her age. Abrasive, authentic, rebellious; she's grown on me.

Jada's stomach growls. 'Dang, I'm hungry.' She doesn't really expect an answer.

'I know, we all struggle with the food shortages.'

'No, DeAnn. You don't get it. You live alone on the salary they give you at the R and D facility. I feed three people with mine. We're *struggling*.'

Each lost in our thoughts, we walk for a while in the desolate conservation area. 'Why three? Where is your boyfriend? Doesn't he participate?'

'He just bailed.'

'What? When? Why?'

'Last week. Because I told him I'm pregnant.'

My breath catches. I glance at her as she bites her nails, with that faraway gaze that pregnant women get. Her stress is seeping into me. How will she cope?

'Oh.' That's all I can manage.

'The thing is, I didn't even want this kid. It's an accident. But Darnell's acting like I did it on purpose; all high and mighty and offended. Asshole. I don't know what to do now.'

'Do you think he'll come back?'

She looks off into the distance at her kids. The girl is twelve and the boy is ten or so. This news was really unexpected, I guess.

'No. I don't think I'd want him back either.'

'Once the child is born, can you make it with what you earn?'

'No, DeAnn, I can't. Darnell left without a word and I have no address, nothing. I won't get alimony. We aren't married. Not that the court would have looked for him or forced him to pay me anything, anyway, if we had been married. Deadbeat fathers are a dime a dozen.' She shrugs.

A familiar pang of anger rises up. Why do men so seldom rise up to the occasion? I bottle up my irritation and focus on my friend. Her anguish is catching; I'm starting to feel its frantic itch nibbling inside my gut. I glance at her slender form, her flat belly. She's probably barely started her first trimester.

'Mmh. So what will you do?' Neither of us spells it out. But she knows what I mean.

'What *can* I do?' she exclaims. 'There are no options.' She throws her arms up in frustration. 'There is nothing *to* do. I'll just have to bring this baby into the world and watch it starve. Or maybe reduce all of our rations to feed it. I don't know, I just don't know.'

She wrings her hands and looks away again. I'm so accustomed to her feistiness that I'm not sure how to react to this. What can I do for her anyway? Nothing. The drugs that would allow it to pass on its own aren't available anymore and we aren't allowed to perform abortions at the clinic either. The last thing I need is to be thrown in jail. Maybe there are other ways I could help her. I fall silent, thinking things over.

Jada is also lost in her thoughts so we walk in silence for a while in the desolate conservation area. There's nothing much left to conserve, unfortunately. Withered trees stand bare, guarding over an expanse of parched soil interspersed with tufts of yellow grass. The silence is eerie. I frown then realize: there are no birds.

'So,' she rallies with a smile, 'have you figured it out yet?'

'No, I'm stumped.' I sigh.

'Walk me through what you do know.'

I smile, grateful for the change of topic and start

enumerating on my fingers, 'This is what we've found so far: MSA8742 is a toxin. It binds itself to a combination of genetic markers to modify the protein expression of the subject. And it only affects the target group, leaving the control group unharmed.'

'Sometimes, I'm really glad I work with plants,' she says.

'What I can't figure out is what the deterioration of the protein chain does to the subjects. It's not skin related. I've checked. It's not killing the subjects, I checked that too. It's doing something, but what?'

'Have you checked—' she starts but is interrupted by the kids running back toward us, very excited.

'Mom, Mom! A rabbit drive, can we go watch, please? We've never seen one.'

Jada is conflicted and looks back at me. I stare back blankly, as I don't know what a rabbit drive is.

'Fine, but we only look, we don't participate, OK?'

The kids whoop with joy and start to run. We follow them at a more measured pace as I ask Jada what this is but she tells me she's only ever heard about these drives. Soon we pass the crest of a small hill and dozens of men come into view, marching in the distance, holding hunting rifles and clubs.

I tense up, but Jada doesn't seem to find the sight strange. She calls her kids and the four of us catch up with the wall of men, who are walking arm in arm, forming a line. We walk for a while alongside them, listening to their banter and trying to keep up with their strides. Now, in the distance, a similar group of white farmers and climate refugees approaches, exactly opposite us. After a moment, two other lines of armed men appear, closing in from the left and the right.

There's a hundred of us at least now, forming a square

that's getting smaller and smaller as we get closer to each other. In the middle of this dwindling square, the ground is moving. Unsure why, I squint and realize that the plain between us is swarming with thousands of jackrabbits. Their taut bodies twitch as they sense our approach, their jerky movements unsettling.

Some of the men start running but most keep walking in line. Now I understand what they're trying to do. They're corralling the animals into a huge wire pen in the middle. There are only two entrances and the small creatures are being pushed inside the enclosure from both sides. The rabbits try frantically to escape and run between our feet, but the men stop them and kick them back toward the pen.

I didn't know that rabbits could make a sound. But as the clubs start falling, the animals begin to squeal in terror and pain. Their cries are heart wrenching. Unbearable. Palms on my ears, I try to block the shrieks. They sound like human infants being killed and crying for help.

The smell of blood, metallic and syrupy, mixes with the men's sweat and the stench of the rabbits' bowels emptying. I try to look away but I can't. The rabbits are jumping up the pen's wall. Frantically trying to escape. Paws entangled in the chicken wire as they kick and buck. Struggling to get free. Squealing. The men are clubbing them and calling to each other, yelling, swearing.

One of the rabbits escapes its executioner and darts past me, one eye out of its socket, the slimy globe bouncing as it hops desperately away. Others caught by the ears, or trapped in the fence, scream for deliverance, kicking in vain. The enclosure is full of small cadavers, their fur bloody.

Imani turns to her mother in tears, her hands on her ears. 'Mom? Mom!'

Jada is livid, a hand on her belly, as she looks at a man

clubbing a rabbit to death. He's grunting with the effort, as droplets of blood and brain splatter on his bent face. He gets up and grins, grabbing a handful of rabbits by the ears.

'Guess what's for dinner?'

I look away, repulsed.

Dion is running around the pen, darting in and out to stay out of the men's reach as he stares at all the rabbits excitedly. Jada calls her son back but he can't hear over the sounds of the animals' agony, so she starts to run toward him. When she's nearly within reach of her son, Jada trips on a pile of rabbit corpses and stumbles, extending her arms to break her fall. Even though I'm too far away to do anything, I rush toward her. Dion and Imani, who are small and fast, have already reached her and are trying to help. She's on all fours, trying to get up, her arms deep in the pile of furry bodies as she retches.

'Hey, you fucking chimp, go puke somewhere else and don't ruin my meal.'

Dion turns his innocent face toward the man, just as the club descends toward Jada. The grimy baseball bat smashes into Dion's shoulder, lifting him for a suspended second before he falls whimpering to the ground. With a scream, Imani stands up to face the man, her frail, slender body so fragile and small. I rush over to them, my stomach dropping.

'My friend's pregnant, you animal,' I shout at the guy, as I run.

'Well, move out of the way, so I can finish her off, then,' he says to the child. 'You fucking niggers reproduce like rabbits and I say it's about time we had a culling of a different kind!'

Other men roar with laughter but it's a dangerous sound.

The man who spoke is laughing, as he clutches his bloodstained bat, rolling it in his hand, cocking his head to the side as he considers Imani. I imagine the sound it would make as the wood hit her skull and smashed it. Would she sound like a squeaking rabbit? Kitsa didn't make a sound. The men are waiting, as if suspended. The little girl stares the man down, hands raised in front of her as she protects her mother and brother. Time slows down.

And then Jada gets up, breaking the spell.

Her hands are stained with bright red blood and her face is ashen. She looks up at the sneering man's puce-colored face and wipes her mouth with her hand, not realizing or caring that she's staining her face with blood.

For a moment, I stand frozen as the image of Jada standing in front of the attacker sears itself in my mind. She stands tall, a swipe of blood across her face, her two children by her side, knee deep in cadavers, looking like a queen. Without a word, she grabs Imani and Dion and walks away.

Oh my God.

I know what they're testing.

I know what the toxin does.

They're sterilizing People of Color.

19

OLIVIA

N *ew York, NY, USA, August 2082*

MICHAEL and I are standing on the square outside the UN, the building rising above us against the deep blue sky as a myriad flags wave in the wind, their bright colours flapping from side to side with a frantic metallic clinking.

The team I'm now part of spent the rest of the week essentially pressuring the media to stop divulging national security footage and, in parallel, putting a fake news spin on the video, so they can threaten the news organisation with defamation law suits if they say 'GeneX' when showing the footage. I feel soiled simply by working on these smear tactics.

While the team has been busy burying the video, I have come up with a counter-measure with the Resistance and my anonymous whistle-blower has agreed to take the plan forwards. So when Viles called an urgent meeting this morning, I was sure I'd been found out. The GeneX CEO's face appeared abruptly on screen, his cheekbones poking through his skin like the corners of a sharp frame through white canvas.

Startled, Michael stopped the team's work and turned to the screen. 'Good morning, Mr Viles, thank you for—'

'There is no time for pleasantries,' the CEO interrupted. 'The source of the leak has been identified.' My heart stopped. 'It's one of the Under-Secretaries-General to the UN.'

Colour returned to my cheeks as I realised that they still had no idea I was the source. But now I knew who the anonymous Resistance contact was. Unfortunately, so did GeneX.

'I'm sending you his details now. Contain the situation immediately.' He hung up.

We spent the rest of the morning preparing a subpoena and pulling in a lot of favours. When everything was ready, Michael announced that he was going to the UN to serve the papers and I managed to tag along. This was my first opportunity to talk face to face with the Resistance since London and I wasn't going to let it slip through my fingers.

A MOVEMENT through the crowd pulls me out of my thoughts and I focus on the UN square. That's when I spot him, the Under-Secretary-General who's causing all the commotion. The old man still looks formidable, his body like a cannon ball barrelling through the mob of reporters and gawkers. His bodyguards stand in front and behind him, scanning the mass of people anxiously. Flashes light up the scene, journalists holding out their iModes for him to make a statement. But he parts through them unperturbed and disappears inside the building.

'Follow me, we might still be able to stop him if we hurry.'

Michael grabs my hand and pulls me through the crowd, waving his ID in front of him at the gate.

The guards stop us and inspect us from head to toe; then, after a good fifteen minutes of arguments and threats, they wave us in.

Inside, the cathedral-like lobby greets us with its arches and curves and its milling crowds of UN personnel. Michael cranes his neck, looking for the old Nigerian man everywhere and I can't help but notice that he's still holding my hand although it's no longer strictly necessary.

'There.' I point.

The Under-Secretary-General is talking to a group of people on the curved staircase. One of them is shaking his hand and tapping him on the shoulder. Another one is speaking intently to the old man and then they both go into a room and disappear from view.

Michael seems to realise that he's still holding my hand and drops it. 'Ready?'

I nod, butterflies in my stomach.

We follow the old man up the stairs and when we open the door behind which he's just disappeared, the General Assembly Hall opens up in front of us. I stop, awestruck; it's so much bigger than I thought it would be. Light green carpet rolls under our feet, leading the way towards an impressive golden podium. The ceiling is dotted with pinpoint lights like a night sky. The effect is oddly futuristic and uplifting.

But no one is here; the benches are all empty, country nameplates are propped row after row with the representatives' names, but the chairs are vacant. A sound makes me look to the right. There he is.

Michael motions me to come with him and we get closer to the Nigerian diplomat who is deep in conversation with an old Asian man. They consider us suspiciously as we approach and one of his bodyguards holds out a hand blocking our path.

'What are you doing here? You're not allowed in.'

'Mr Chukwudi Ejiofor, you have been served.' Michael hands him the subpoena and the old man, glaring at us with thinly disguised contempt, shakes a pair of reading glasses out of his breast pocket and slowly grabs the tablet that is being proffered. He perches the glasses on his nose and reads, his eyebrows knitting.

'Ah, our friends at GeneX don't think I have the right to make a statement today, to reveal their latest *technology* to the world, do they? Industrial espionage.' He shakes his head in disgust and then focuses on Michael. 'Why do you work for these people, son? Can't you see that they're evil? Where is your soul?'

Michael's maintains a straight face but he seems jarred by the old man's rebuke. Maybe he remembers our argument as well.

'And you, miss?' The Under-Secretary-General turns his intense gaze on me 'Don't you know that—'

He narrows his eyes and falls silent, staring at me. Oh no. A. specifically said she wouldn't reveal my identity when she sent him the video. Does he know it was me? How?

The two bodyguards, the Asian man and Michael all look at him curiously, then at me.

I try to keep a straight face.

Fuckety fuck fuck fuck, the old man is about to blow my cover.

'Leave us.'

'Mr Ejiofor, I must protest,' the Asian man starts.

'Leave us, all of you now.'

I start to leave too but the old man grabs my wrist and looks intently at me. Michael frowns, but I nod and finally they all leave.

The UN diplomat is still holding me by the wrist when the last one of them exits the amphitheatre.

'Follow me,' he says.

He must be at least ninety but his grip is hard as iron and he's determined. He pulls me into a small glass booth overlooking the auditorium and closes the door behind us. Then for a few seconds, an awkward silence falls on the small, enclosed space, as he details my face quite unabashedly.

'Olivia Sagewright,' he says, his eyes full of wonder.

I can't be sure he's the Resistance's anonymous contact. A. didn't reveal his identity, so why on earth did she trust him with mine? Unless he's not Resistance at all and this is all an elaborate trap. I should never have come. There's a reason we never know the other Resistance members' identities. This was a huge mistake. I start to scramble backwards towards the door, but he says, 'It's you isn't it? You haven't aged a day.'

That stops me in my tracks. I look carefully at his face as recognition dawns. Woody.

My mind struggles to associate his wrinkled face with the young candidate who trained with me to get into the Cassandra Programme sixty-five years ago. I didn't think he was a very trustworthy man then, but he leaked my video to the press, so could I trust him today? What will he do with the information he now has? My life is in his hands and that's much too dangerous.

'Oh, you mean my grandmother, I've been told before that I look like her.'

'Olivia, I'm an old man, I don't have time for this. Let us not play games, please.'

I hesitate.

'I'd know you anywhere, there's no point denying who you are.' He adds, 'I will not betray your secret. I know that you have no reason to trust me, but I looked for you, a few years later, to apologise for the things I said when you were selected and I wasn't.' He looks bemused. 'I was told you went missing.'

Not knowing what to say, I stay silent.

'Over the years, I have pieced it together, what the Programme does. I know about time travel.'

'How did you...?'

'There's no time,' he says, batting away my question. 'There are things we must discuss, Olivia, things I want you to bring back. But I'm worried now, because if you're in my timeline and you went missing in 2016, that means you never made it back to your present.'

Well, bugger. I hadn't thought of that. I lean on the glass wall when my knees start to shake.

'You think I died here?'

'Maybe, who knows.' He frowns when he sees my worried face. 'But listen, events can be changed. This is the whole point of the Programme. If they believed that the future was immutable, they wouldn't bother sending agents forwards to learn what should be changed. So we've got to believe that what we do now will allow you to go back to 2017 unharmed. Maybe this meeting has never happened before. Maybe that's why you didn't go back before?'

He seems to make up his mind and adds. 'Yes, that's got to be it. This meeting wasn't supposed to happen and I just have to believe that it will make all the difference.' A smile blossoms on his face. 'Maybe I can change history after all.'

'Woody...'

'Ha. I haven't heard that name in a long time. I go by Chukwudi nowadays, more dignified.' He chuckles. 'Call me Woody, I love it. It reminds me of my youth.' The old man's laughter turns into a coughing fit.

'Are you alright?'

'Well, I'm very old, you know. Although you...' he looks at me with amazement, 'you're just as pretty as I remember. How long has it been for you?'

'I last saw you about ten months ago, give or take.'

He whistles.

'If only I could go back. But those are young men's dreams. Let us talk seriously. You've seen the video, right?'

'Actually I filmed it. I'm the one who sent it to you.'

His eyebrows lift. 'Really? My, my, you *have* been busy.' He pauses. 'So you know about the medical tests that GeneX conducted in Kampala?' I nod and he continues, 'I thought I was going to give you information, but it looks like you may know more than me. I've called a press conference, just like our mutual friend asked. Do you have any more information, anything new? Why did you risk coming here today?'

I tell him quickly everything I've learned about Carapadre & Dergrin's legal strategy to silence him, explain that the DoD is behind the pharmaceutical giant and then, biting my lip, decide to add the last bit of information that DeAnn just discovered, even though she hasn't been able to prove it yet.

'Woody, you believe in overpopulation, don't you? That it's the root cause for the lack of food and water, the violence, the extreme pollution...'

'Yes, of course, we're aware of this at the UN. That's why

we're working on the Beijing Agreement. The only way for humanity to survive is to impose restrictions on fertility. We've worked really hard, we're so close to a worldwide ratification. Every country is committed to sign the treaty except the four Coalition countries. We've even managed to convince US to sign it in exchange for lifting their sanctions...'

I interrupt, 'Woody, I'm so sorry but it's a diversion. While they pretend to negotiate in good faith, the Department of Defense is working covertly with GeneX to test a toxin in Uganda.'

'You mean GeneX isn't conducting medical drug experiments? They're testing a weapon?'

'I'm afraid so, the video I sent you was a cover-up. They massacred a whole village to hide the effects of their tests.'

He looks shaken. 'What does the toxin do?'

'My partner and I can't prove it yet, but we think the chemical sterilises people based on their ethnicity.'

Woody's eyes widen and his face takes on a grey tinge. 'What? That's impossible.'

'I'll send you the evidence as soon as my partner has it. But there's more.' I forge on. 'From the discussions I overheard at the law firm, it sounds like deployment is imminent. Maybe in a few months, at the most.'

Woody looks pensive. 'And you say that they're developing this chemical to target Ugandans?'

'Yes, as far as I'm aware. But it might also work on other populations that present the same genetic characteristics.'

Woody goes very quiet for a moment. 'If, like you say, the Coalition is prepared to deploy this weapon in the field, then they will likely make a big statement in Uganda. The media will spin all they want but the Security Council will know what really happened.'

'We can't let it progress that far, they must be stopped—' I start, but he holds up a hand, deep in thought, as his political mind unravels the ramifications.

'Then the Coalition will probably blackmail us. They'll use the Sterilisation Agent as a deterrent, to put pressure on all of us. There will be no way for the remaining UN countries to know which genetic markers the Coalition is really able to target, so they'll use it to extract anything they want from us.'

'We've got to prevent them from using it at all, on anyone. Do you think that some countries in the UN will stand up to the Coalition? Surely at least African countries will—'

'If any country moves against them at the UN, the Coalition will threaten to deploy the toxin on their population as well. The Security Council will back down and sanctions will be lifted. The Coalition will have unlimited power...'

He looks ashen, as he works out the consequences aloud. 'The Coalition sees race literally as a black and white thing. Pun intended,' he smiles sadly. 'But in truth, race has become a spectrum. The Coalition countries are the only ones who have maintained a really low percentage of interracial mixing. Whereas the United States of Europe, for example, are truly assimilated now, so there is no telling what this toxin would do when used against their mixed-race populations. They won't dare lift a finger...'

'Do you think you'll be able to convince anyone to help?'

'Unfortunately most of the Security Council is still made up of Coalition countries, the US, Russia, the KEW... I don't know, Olivia... I need to start talking to my network as soon as possible.'

'Is there anything I can do to help?'

He ponders that for a while. 'Actually, yes. In fact, Olivia, you may be our only hope. Once a weapon exists, mankind is doomed to use it. All my efforts will probably be in vain. You must survive, do you hear me?' He grabs my shoulder and his eyes bore into mine. 'You must go back to a time when this horror had not yet been invented and prevent it from ever seeing the light of day.'

'Will that be enough to prevent this timeline, Woody? There will still be the overpopulation issue, won't there?'

'Yes – yes, you're right, of course.'

'I've been thinking about what we could do. The massive surge happened in Africa, where the population quadrupled in the last sixty-five years. But as you know, once a country reaches a certain level of development, fertility decreases naturally to less than two children per woman.'

'Yes, the demographic transition, I know.'

I lean forwards, willing the ideas to convince him as I warm up to the solution I'm hoping for. 'We should support African countries to develop sustainably, as fast as they can. We could provide aid in the form of loans, education, sanitation and urbanisation programmes, which might make imposed measures to reduce fertility unnecessary. If developed countries help—'

Woody's shaking his head and I stop, puzzled.

'We don't want to be helped,' he say, irritated. 'Every time you white saviours meddle in our countries, we end up worse off. We don't want to be colonised again.'

'I'm not suggesting colonisation,' I say, shocked. 'I'm just suggesting that we could do a sort of Marshall Plan for African countries, to help them.'

'Helping, helping, helping. That's the problem. African nations can't change for the better through the intervention of any other country. We need to be left to our own devices.

We need to lead ourselves. We need to achieve our development on our own, like Europeans did.'

'But that took us centuries and we wrecked the environment to do it.'

'Well, maybe we'll also take centuries and that's just the way it's got to be.'

'Woody, you know very well that the Earth can't wait centuries for your continent to lower its birth rates. Developed countries need to help you grow sustainably, with renewable energies, with micro-credits and by providing education.'

'That's all very well and—'

'Mr Under-Secretary-General?' One of his bodyguards has opened the door and interrupts us, an apologetic look on his face.

'Yes, Charlem,' Woody says, looking tired, old and small all of a sudden.

'The press are ready for your statement, sir. We've stalled them as long as we could,' the bodyguard says, giving me a curious glance.

'We'll have to finish this conversation another day,' the old diplomat smiles tightly. 'Olivia, you have no idea of how happy I am to see you again.' He holds me by the shoulders and looks straight into my eyes. 'Survive this,' he says earnestly. 'Your mission is the chance this world was waiting for. You've given hope to an old man.'

Then, he hugs me. I'm surprised at first and then I mellow in his arms.

'I was wrong about you all along, you know, Agent Sagewright,' he whispers in my ear.

Tears prickle in my eyes as I take a step back.

He smiles and follows his bodyguard out with a wave.

I watch him go and take a few minutes to regain my composure and slip into my role again.

Outside, Michael is having a staring contest with the second bodyguard and he relaxes when I come out.

'Come on,' I say, as I follow Woody, anxious to hear the press conference.

'What was that all about?'

'Oh nothing, he knew my grandmother.'

'What? Do you expect me to believe—'

'Michael, let's hurry, I want to hear what he has to say.'

On the square outside the building, an enormous crowd has formed. Now that the leaked video has gone viral, the speculation about the announced press conference has reached fever pitch and the press conference is going to be broadcast live, all around the world.

When Michael and I step out, we find Woody already on a podium, preparing to make his speech. Journalists lean forwards, asking a frenzy of questions, while cameramen film him.

'Mr Under-Secretary-General, where was the footage taken?'

'Is this a disease outbreak and should we be concerned about contamination?'

'Who's your source?'

A lightning storm of flashes crackles as the old diplomat adjusts his microphone.

'Who are the perpetrators, Mr Ejiofor?'

'Do you have any additional information about the reason for the massacre?'

Behind the journalists, people are edging closer to hear the speech.

'Mr Ejiofor, there are rumours that this is all a hoax. Have you come here to deny that you leaked this fake news?'

'Mr Under-Secretary-General, what do you feel about the statements of the victims' families, who have come forwards, requesting that you apologise for publicising footage of their personal decision to commit mass suicide?'

Woody's two bodyguards stand on either side of him, looking intently at the mass of people, hands clasped in front of them as the journalists continue clamouring for attention.

'Is this thing on?' Woody motions for silence.

'Esteemed members of the press...' he starts.

His voice is booming, amplified by the microphone. A moment ago he was just an old man, just Woody. Now I see him as the world sees him: a statesman, a force for change, a maverick who dared to release the video and reveal the conspiracy. His charisma, his lifetime of achievements, his position at the UN, all of it comes together to lend a reach and a weight to the revelations he's about to make that they couldn't achieve otherwise. The crowd falls silent as he takes a breath.

'Ladies and gentlemen, thank you all for coming here this morning. I have revelations to make about the video, which I streamed a few days ago. It is crucial for the world to know what has been going on behind the scenes and who is responsible for these heinous acts—'

A shot explodes, reverberating throughout the silent square like a clap of thunder. Red mist blooms behind Woody's head like a halo and he falls.

20

DEANN

S t. Louis, Missouri, August 2082

A DROP of sweat rolls from under my breast all the way to my waist. I rub my t-shirt against my skin, uncomfortable. There's not much point in being embarrassed. Everyone is drenched in sweat here.

The AC is on, but it barely makes a dent. I can hear it straining somewhere nearby; the permanent whirring noise doesn't even register anymore. Nor do the incessant beeps of the medical machinery, the rustle of blue curtains around sick beds, the incessant to and fro of attendants or the fluorescent bulbs flickering overhead.

To my shame, I've also become immune to the sounds of crying, arguing and pleading, which have just become background noise at the clinic. The place is packed, as usual. Patients are crammed in the waiting-room, hanging around for hours to be seen, sometimes resigned, sometimes angry. Always waiting.

The hallway smells like vomit; a previous patient's unfortunate offering. I walk down the corridor to my next consultation and relax when I push open the examination room door and see an old black woman and her grandson, a beautiful toddler with a curly afro.

She tells me the usual story; they left all they had behind. Their farm is under several feet of sand and nothing grows there anymore. Their situation got so desperate that even coming here to live on the streets of St. Louis seemed preferable to dying of hunger and thirst where they came from. So now they wait here at the clinic. For me, for salvation, for someone to care. Who knows?

I unwrap a tongue depressor and turn to the old woman. Her skeleton presses against her papery skin as if it cannot wait to burst free of its cocoon. She coughs, as I open a bottle of orange soda and give it to the little boy with a smile. Soda's not usually great for cavities and obesity, but under the circumstances...

For once, the state has come through for this neighborhood with surprising generosity, sending energy drinks and sodas to the clinic by the pallet-full, together with rations for the refugees. I arrived at the end of my workday to find a festive atmosphere at the clinic. Volunteer nurses are giving out the food and fizzy drinks to the patients and everyone is feeling more hopeful.

The gorgeous boy grabs the sugary drink and guzzles it down, both of his small brown hands clasped around the unexpected treat. While he's busy, I go behind his grandmother, lift her shirt and listen to her lungs through my medical tablet's ear bud. She sounds really clogged up. I'm reminded of the animal carcasses that litter the roads all around the city. Their stomachs split open sometimes and they're always lined with several inches of sand.

Walking round to face the old woman, I offer her a cardboard pan and encourage her to cough. But she doesn't take the bowl; instead she raises her hand to my face and cups my cheek gently. Her eyes are soft and milky around the edges. Her touch is brittle but soothing and I feel like leaning into her shoulder. But I hold myself upright and smile encouragingly. 'Go ahead, Auntie. It's alright.' She pats my cheek gently. A world of words in that small gesture. My eyes well up. These are my people dying out there. My people.

The boy lets out a loud burp and we're both startled. I laugh and she smiles, holding her wizened hand in front of her mouth to hide the missing teeth. We look at each other fondly, then at him, and I find myself running my hand in his hair and looking into his bottomless, shiny black eyes. So innocent, so beautiful. Two liquid pools of trust and naiveté.

The moment is broken when the old woman starts to cough into the pan and although I've seen it countless times by now, I still can't help but shudder. Out of her mouth comes a long string of gray gunk, like a cat hairball. It's the length of my forearm and the width of my finger. She half chokes as it comes out. A mix of undigested food, dust and hair. Everybody who's come from the heart of the dust bowl coughs these up when they're near the end.

I started coughing too a couple of weeks ago. Black slime comes out, like tobacco juice. The old woman is far more advanced and I can't imagine what it must be like to feel that thing come up.

I scoop the little boy up in my arms and turn his face away as I wipe it carefully to remove the dust. He lets me do it, playing with my curls, wrapping them around his fingers and letting them spring back. My hair is free now, since I came home. It's curly and willful and I won't ever tame it again.

I rummage in my white coat pocket, looking for the handful of sweets I pinched from the office earlier today and when I give the boy one, his eyes light up.

His face shiny and clean, I plop him down and take the disposable pan from the old lady, patting her shoulder. I prescribe a few drugs for the pain and to clear the obstruction in her lungs but I don't think it's worth it. She won't last the month.

Well, it's probably worth it to him, I guess. She might find him a new home in that extra month of life that I'm buying her. My throat constricts as I shoo them out of my examination room and call in the next sorry lot of refugees.

Why was I so happy again when I started my shift? Oh yes, I brighten up as I wait for the next patients to come in. Dick got arrested by company security this morning. The wicked smile stretches on my lips again, unbidden.

Apparently they found the email I sent to my dummy account from his computer with the material about MSA8742 all wrapped up in a nice little bow. I've long since forwarded the information to A. and I've been browsing through the data myself, every evening when I'm not here at the clinic.

Two months had gone by, so I thought the incident had gone unnoticed. But this morning they came for him. That nitwit got his comeuppance and the memory of his face as he left the lab sends an evil jolt of satisfaction through me. I should be a better person, really. But petty revenge is so much fun sometimes.

I keep seeing patients well into the evening, then take a break with Jada. She's come to volunteer as well tonight. She doesn't have any medical knowledge but she still helps out when she can. Today she's been giving out the rations and she feels the boost as well, I can tell from the big grin on her face, as we have tea in the staff break room.

'You OK?' I ask her, discreetly looking downward.

She catches my meaning and places a hand lightly on her belly, her face darkening.

'Yeah. Yeah. Nothing new. Still no progress.'

I've been trying to source a drug for her that could terminate the pregnancy. Just a pill, painless for both of them. It existed in 2016 and was fairly simple to procure but it's practically impossible to find nowadays. I still have one contact I can try this weekend.

'What time is it?' I ask.

'It's alright, just eight o'clock. We still have an hour and a half until sundown and the curfew.'

'Did you see the pallets? All that food.' I smile.

'Yeah, the city usually sends us healthier rations, but this year, it looks like it's all they can afford to—'

Anguished cries ring out and the staff room door bangs open.

That white teenage kid, Britney, is there, her baggy white t-shirt gory with blood, a wild look in her eyes.

'Help!' She looks straight at me and recognizes me. 'Help,' she pleads, her voice fizzling out.

Jada and I rush to help her but she turns and runs. We follow her as people jump out of her path. We run behind her and she leads us to the front of the clinic. The street's heat envelops us, hot and dry like an oven door opening. As usual, lines of people loop around the building, emitting a strong odor of urine and unwashed bodies.

A cluster of people have gathered a few yards away from the entrance and Britney makes a beeline for them, pushing people roughly out of her way, until a red pull-along wagon appears, loaded with small bodies. Jada sucks her breath in and holds Britney back as I kneel next to the curb and check for vitals on one small form after another. Finding no pulse.

A moan. A small arm moves. There, at the bottom, crumpled in a pool of blood. It's Kevin, her four-year-old brother who played with my equipment the other day.

His throat has been slit and blood is gurgling out of the gaping wound. The arteries aren't cut or he'd have bled to death by now.

'There's one still alive! Jada help me!'

I press my hand as hard as I can on the wound, as Jada helps me carry the boy inside and Britney runs beside us, panicked.

'Make way! Make way!' I shout, as we run to the nearest consultation room. We're not equipped for this sort of emergency here and I'm not a surgeon. What the fuck can I do?

I try to think while Jada carefully lays the boy on the table, my hand still pressed against the child's throat.

'Britney! Put your hand on the wound,' I say, taking in the teenager's distressed face as she cries silently, staring at her younger brother. 'Jada, do we have the equipment for endotracheal intubation?' I yell.

Her eyes widen and she shakes her head, staring at the young boy.

'I don't think so... I...'

Clamping her mouth shut, she rushes to the cupboards

while I quickly put on gloves and try to find suture material in the drawers.

'That's all I could find. Is this it?' Jada holds a transparent bag with a cricothyrotomy kit. Close enough. Groaning with frustration, I rip it open and empty the bag on the equipment tray. Shit, it's an adult tube, I'm going to have to dilate. Just as I'm wondering how to manage this on my own, a nurse barges in.

'Where were you?' I shout. 'Saline, quick!' The nurse nods, looking grim. She pushes Jada out of the way and comes back with a pouch of saline solution. Once it's hooked on a pole, she grabs the boy's arm.

Britney is looking from the nurse to me, her hand pressed on Kevin's throat. I push her hand gently aside to have a look at the wound and blood starts to pour into the windpipe hole.

I am so close to the little boy's face. His eyes are wide, whites showing all around and his pupils are completely dilated. They jerk from side to side, looking at me then at his arm where a sharp needle just broke through his skin. Shit, there's nothing to strap him down with.

'Jada, hold him! He can't move for what I'm about to do.' My friend hesitates, hovering.

'Now!'

Jada grabs his small legs and holds them down, looking away.

The child is panicking, his heartbeat is erratic, his breathing labored. His windpipe is punctured and a blood vessel is leaking into it. He's drowning in his own blood. Fingers slipping with slick blood, I try to stabilize his larynx and taking a deep breath, I slice the skin open and make my incision in the crichothyroid membrane. Throwing the scalpel on the tray, I grab the tracheal hook, lift the flap and part the lips of the wound with the dilator.

'Nurse. The airway, quick!'

The child's eyes are rolling wildly from side to side, panicking. His mouth is wide open but only gurgling sounds are coming out.

His sister's shuffling from foot to foot, unsure what to do, wringing her hands a few feet away.

'Hold his arms, Britney!'

Holding the dilator in one hand and the hook in the other, I check on the nurse, who is struggling with the airway; he's moving too much and blood's spurting and bubbling too close to the incision point.

I try to get the child to hold still. 'Kevin, Kevin, look at me. Everything is going to be alright. Do you hear? Everything is going to be OK, sweetie.'

His blue eyes are so big. Just like the boy a few hours ago. He doesn't deserve this. None of us deserves any of this. 'Try to hold still, OK?'

His panicked wet breathing is the only sound in the room now. 'I've got you Kevin, you're going to be OK, just hold still.'

Pink bubbles froth at the entrance of the gaping hole in his throat.

Without breaking eye contact with the small boy, I gesture for Britney to come next to me.

His tiny hand latches on to hers and she grabs back fiercely.

'Hey, baby boy,' she smiles, tears in her voice. 'Don't you worry, you hear me? The nice doctors are taking care of you. You'll be OK.'

He takes a big rattling breath and his hand lets go of hers.

'No! No, no, no! Kevin!' Britney grabs the boy's hand, kissing it, shaking it, as if to wake him up. His huge blue eyes still open, stare at nothing, as his jaw goes slack.

The tools are still in my hands. The nurse looks up, a distressed expression on her face. I notice absently that there's a smear of blood on her forehead and the airway's still in her hand.

There was too much blood, the view was too obstructed, she didn't get it in. But even as I think that, a surge of guilt and anger submerges me. I'm sure *I* could have inserted the tube. I avert my eyes; there's no point in laying this at the nurse's door. It's my fault, I was in charge. My fingers stiff, I remove the dilator and the hook, straighten up and motion to Jada and the nurse to back away.

But Jada doesn't step back, instead, she puts a hand on Britney's arm as the young girl clutches her brother's limp body, rocking him back and forth.

A long time passes. A lump in my throat, I thank the nurse. She leaves, shoulders hunched and Jada and I stay with the girl until her sobs die down.

'What happened, Britney?' I ask softly.

'My mom, my mom. She gave birth during the night. It was twins,' she sobs, shaking her head at the terrible bad luck. 'Twins.' Jada strokes the teenager's shoulder kindly. 'Mom killed them all. Everyone of them. Then she killed herself. Slit her own throat.'

I suck my breath in. She did this to her own kids? She seemed at the end of her rope the other day, but this...

Jada doesn't look surprised. She just looks sad. I can't even imagine what I'd do if I had children in a world like this. Maybe I'd want out as well. Who knows? Perhaps she thought they'd be better off dead than starving slowly. It's still despicable, but looking at Jada's thoughtful face, I understand the woman's desperation as well.

'Where were you?' I ask Britney.

'I was at my friend's, because of the curfew. I should have been there. I could have stopped her.' she sobs, holding her brother's little body against hers.

'If you'd been home she'd have killed you too.' I pat her back gently. 'I'm so sorry, Britney.'

21

OLIVIA

ew York, NY, USA, August 2082

THE CROWD in front of the UN screams with terror and people scatter in all directions. I start towards the platform instinctively to help Woody, but Michael yanks me back and holds me against him.

'Run!'

He pulls me with him, away from the podium, as we flee. My heart is pounding, I swivel my head in all directions, trying to guess where the next shot is going to come from. We run, we run, my legs are on fire but we can't stop.

Claps of gunshots explode, echoing through the square in close succession, and people fall, all around us, stumbling while they run, their bodies trampled by the crowd. A small group to our left erupts in screams of panic. I don't have time to see why. We run. We run. We run. My lungs burning.

The sound of my heart beating a tattoo against my ear drums. People collapsing. My throat raw.

A woman sprints in front of me, her pumps slapping against her stockinged heels. She falls and I bend down to help her up, but she's dead, her face a mangled mess of flesh and bone.

'We've got to keep going, Olivia,' Michael pants over his shoulder, pulling me behind him.

Panic is like a catching fever, spreading from person to person as we flail and shriek. We're all trying to escape the sniper but we don't know whether we're running away or towards danger and the uncertainty is like a madness that sets our minds on fire. The only constant is Michael's hand pulling me forwards. I stumble. He catches me and we keep going, the thunderclap of bullets spurring us on. There's a sharp pain in my side. My back feels like a target and I wish I could just lie down and hide, but he won't let me.

His brown leather satchel is flapping against his back, I try to slip my hand free to push my hair away from my face, but he's pulling me and not letting go of my hand. He drags me into the nearest subway entrance. There, finally he stops, panting, his hands on his knees, his curls wet against his forehead.

My breathing ragged, I lean against a wall, sweat pearling my forehead. Some commuters stare but most are oblivious, absorbed in their iModes.

'Are you OK?' Anxiety is seeping through his deep voice, as he moves my face from side to side, checking that I'm not wounded, gently pushing my hair aside to check my forehead. He's so close that I can see little specks of blood on his cheeks and on his horn-rimmed glasses as he focuses on me, trying to figure out if I'm hurt.

'I'm fine, I'm fine. Are you OK?'

'Yeah, I think so,' he says, out of breath and then, reassured, he taps his collar and the iBubble snaps on. Through the curved glass I can see him speaking animatedly, probably reporting to the office that the main target in our lawsuit is now dead and that we don't have to worry about leaks anymore. Poor Woody. My throat constricts as I think of his wrinkly smile and his last hug. He tried to do something right, something good.

I sit down on a moulded plastic seat and hunch forwards. How could I think that I would make a difference? I'm so stupid. It's all my fault and now Woody's dead because of me. This is too big for me. I'm in way over my head.

A few moments later, Michael emerges from his iBubble.

'I don't know who else saw you talk to him before he died. They could be coming after you. You can't go back to your place until we figure out if you're in danger too. They won't find you where we're going.'

A chill runs down my spine as I imagine the sniper breaking into my flat in the middle of the night to finish the job. I feel the colour drain from my face. Oh my God, what have I done?

Michael is wasting no time; when the next train arrives, he pulls me to my feet and we jump in the carriage as the doors close.

'Where are we going?'

'It's safer if you stay with me tonight,' he says as we both collapse on the grimy seats.

His place is in an industrial part of town, a small open-plan loft with a mezzanine overlooking the living room. As soon as we're inside, he strides over to his brushed steel desk, removes his satchel and moves a few sliding glass panels to create an office space. Now enclosed in a hermetic glass cubicle, I watch him continue his silent conversation, moving his hands and pacing up and down. Then he glances at me and flicks a switch, instantly turning the glass opaque.

Startled, I avert my eyes and take in the grey concrete walls covered in old-fashioned maps of various American cities, the old Chesterfield sofa that's scratched and stained yet still manages to have aged stylishly, the chrome and steel appliances on the kitchen counter.

My teeth are chattering so I grab the sofa throw and wrap myself in it, then make myself a tea. Images of people panicking and screaming, as they dart in all directions, flash in front of me as I try to grab the teapot. My hands are trembling so much that I drop the lid, jumping at the clang.

The room blurs. I wipe my eyes as the kettle spews a cloud of vapour. Woody's head explodes. The kettle starts to whistle. Screams in the square... All these poor people, should I have done something more? A hand clasps my shoulder and I jump with a shriek.

'Sorry, sorry. I startled you.' He looks at me, concerned. 'You should clean up, you're covered in blood.' He hands me a folded towel.

'Where's the— '

'First right.'

I remove my iMode collar, bracelet and ear bud, leave them on the countertop near my handbag and take the towel gratefully.

The bathroom is small and obviously occupied by a man. At least he hasn't got any flatmates. This loft is little more than a studio but it is probably what wealthy professionals can afford in Manhattan nowadays.

A glimpse of myself in the mirror makes me pause, startled. Freckles of dried blood dot my entire face and there's a bleeding gash on my forehead. The screams echo in my head as fatigue and relief wash over me. My teeth are still chattering and I'm frozen. Chasing away the images of the dead, I catch myself on the sink before my knees buckle.

I strip down quickly and take a long, hot shower, thinking fleetingly about the amount of water this entails and shrugging it off. The hot water pounds my shoulders, running down my back. Arching my head back to let the warm water wash the blood off my face, I start to relax.

At length, feeling better, I'm starting to dry myself when Michael barges into the bathroom, his face serious. I squeak, wrapping myself in the towel.

'Hey! What do you think you're—'

'Come.' His face is closed, his brow furrowed.

He grabs my hand and pulls me roughly in his wake.

Shit, shit, shit. What if his superiors have found out that I'm responsible for the leaked video and that's what he was just discussing with them over the phone? Is that why he brought me to his place? To remove me quietly? No one knows I'm here. I try to yank my fingers out of his but he's too strong.

I follow as best I can, tripping and grabbing the towel with my free hand, climbing the stairs behind him, as he pulls me, hurting my wrist and I flash back to Burke breaking it.

'Michael?'

He doesn't answer and pulls me to the mezzanine's edge.

Oh God, he's probably found my iMode. It was careless to leave it on the kitchen counter unattended. He probably read my exchanges with the Resistance. What should I do? I'm trapped here. I don't even have my Swiss Army knife with me.

'What the fuck is going on, Olivia? Who are you? Did you do this?'

I look at him uncomprehendingly. 'What are you talking about?'

He grabs a remote control on the bed and turns up the volume on the TV that takes up the whole wall.

I hear the presenter say: 'Witnesses say that the Under-Secretary-General had a conversation with a mysterious woman moments before his death.' Crystal-clear, colour, HD CCTV images show me walking out of the General Assembly Hall with Woody. What the ...? Oh my God, this is national TV. Thankfully, it's filmed from very far away and my face is cast down.

Michael turns me around and grabs my shoulders, shaking me. 'Olivia, this is serious. Answer me. What happened between you and Under-Secretary-General Ejiofor? How are you involved in this? Talk to me damn it!'

His hands are not kind, not soft on me and that snaps me out of the haze that has enveloped everything since the assassination.

'I told him everything, Michael. I'm the leak!'

'What? Are you crazy? You saw what they do to people who divulge their secrets. How could you be so stupid—'

'I'm not stupid! You don't understand what's really going on, Michael. I'm trying to do the right thing. I'm trying to save people.'

'What do you mean? This is a simple case of industrial espionage and intellectual property being—'

'No, it isn't! GeneX is not just testing a proprietary drug to cure malaria or whatever; it's poison...'

'Do you have any proof of this?'

I hesitate. I can't tell him about DeAnn; that would put her in danger as well.

'No. Not yet.' I hoist up the towel and glance at the staircase. I need to get dressed and get out of here.

Michael's shouting something '... if you don't have any evidence, you can't go around telling people outrageous things like that—'

'The UN Under-Secretary believed me—'

'Yeah and look where that got him!' he snorts.

'Don't you understand? GeneX is preparing to harm more people. They said they're preparing for field deployment of the toxin, you heard them! And our firm is helping. We're cogs in this machine, you and me, Michael. We have a moral obligation to do something about it.'

'*Do something*? Oh get real, Olivia – even if this were true, which you can't even confirm at the moment' – I start to protest but he forges on – 'this is so far above our heads, there is nothing you or I can do. A single person cannot change the course of history and you're playing with fire. I want *you* to survive. If the firm finds out you're the leak, you're dead.'

'I won't be able to live with myself if I sit on my hands while they harm thousands of people. I have to blow the whistle, Michael.'

'I can't let you do that.'

'*Let* me? What are you going to do? Report me to the firm to save your precious career?' I spit out, furious.

He looks really angry. His hands are shaking, gripping my shoulders way too hard. Memories of Burke float to the surface of my consciousness and my courage and strength surge. I try to shake his hands off my shoulders and my towel falls in a pool at my feet, but I don't care. I take a step back, feet shoulder-length apart and make two fists, scanning the room for something I can use as a weapon.

Michael opens his mouth to say something else, frowning, but as my towel falls to the ground his eyes involuntarily follow it down.

'Damn, you're beautiful.' He swallows.

'Let me go!' I hiss.

My wet hair skims the top of my naked shoulders as I look for ways to escape.

'What?' His eyes travel back up to my face and he says quietly, 'I'd never hurt you, Olivia. I'm trying to stop you, so you don't get killed.'

'Let me go, then.'

His hands drop to his side. I retreat another step, feeling the mezzanine's glass banister behind my bare back. As the TV continues its mindless droning in the background, I dart a glance at the staircase; I think I can escape.

Michael takes a step back and holds his hands up in front of him, placating me.

'Sorry, sorry,' he says, probably sensing that he's up against irrational fear. 'I freaked out, I don't want you to get caught or hurt. I won't tell the firm it was you.'

I ignore him and start to sidestep him. He moves to the top of the staircase, barring the exit.

'Olivia, look at me, *it's me.*'

He takes a tentative step forwards and I raise my fists. Still holding his hands open in front of him, he takes another step towards me, I can't escape; I'm pinned against the handrail. As the TV continues to display images of the mass shooting, very slowly, he lowers his hands on either side of me. I hesitate. His hands run along my arms, softly, from my shoulders to my wrists and goosebumps erupt on my skin all along their path.

His hands float around me and alight on my breasts, barely touching them, yet it's enough for the soft pink tip of my nipples to harden and I realise that it's quite cold and I'm quite naked. He doesn't seem to mind. His left hand travels to the back of my waist, pressing me against him; then he leans in and kisses me hungrily.

We come up for air and he says in a low rumble, 'I'm sorry, I'm so sorry. I love you, Olivia. I love you.'

I look up in surprise but he's already kissing me again, eyes closed, his long brown lashes lightly touching his blood-freckled cheeks. He holds me close, as he grabs the handrail, pushing me against it with his hips. He's still dressed in his suit and tie but I don't care. His kisses are deep and voracious and I give in to them, opening up to his desire.

He drops to his knees in front of me and holding my gaze, caresses the inside of my thigh. His hand goes up, stroking my leg; then he lifts my thigh gently and puts my knee on his shoulder. I grab the handrail behind me and close my eyes, throwing my head back as his soft lips close around my clitoris.

Moaning with desire, I move my hips involuntarily, trembling as he starts to suck until finally I inhale sharply and light blooms behind my eyelids like my own personal fireworks, erasing all thought.

His fingers find their way into me as he holds me captive. I dissolve with pleasure under his touch. His fingers impress a faster rhythm and I grip the bannister for support, knuckles white. My knees buckle and pleasure trickles out of me, rolling down along my inner thighs.

His fingers, slippery with my orgasm, slide out of me and I grab him by the tie, pulling him up so I can kiss him.

Without warning, my heart expands inside my chest like a sail taking wind, propelling me forwards into love.

I loosen his tie and he fumbles with his belt, I try to unbutton his shirt but he just pulls it above his head. Walking backward, I stumble against his unmade bed as he looms over me, surrounded by the strange halo of the gigantic TV, displaying images of terror and bloodshed. He looks at me, head tilted to the side, devouring me with hungry eyes. I try to straighten up to touch the curly brown hair on his chest but he pushes me back on the bed as his cock springs out of his trousers. He lays on top of me, his weight crushing me but in a good way.

Holding himself, he plays with me, entering me slowly and then removing himself when I moan. Until, at last, I can't take anymore teasing and I move my hips upward. He penetrates me with a hard thrust, sliding in the whole length of his cock and I explode with watery pleasure.

I wrap my legs around him and he grinds into me, kissing me ravenously as we hold on to each other, locked in the primordial dance of life.

22

DEANN

S *t. Louis, Missouri, USA, September 2082*

A STEEL GIANT IS DROWNING, swallowed by the Earth. His ugly, hairy face is screaming silently for help as fat white tourists swarm around the famous sculpture, completely oblivious to the pain and anguish of the statue's half-submerged face. They laugh and take silly pictures of themselves inside his mouth and his fist. Idiots. This isn't even the original. But in a way it's the perfect metaphor for this pale copy of my world drowning in sand.

All around the landmark, the desert ripples as far as the eye can see; this man-made cancer is spreading to healthy organs all around it. The sand storms started out in the northern tip of Texas, where Oklahoma, Kansas, Colorado and New Mexico meet. But this was eight years ago. With every blizzard, more plants and animals die, killed by the clouds' static electricity. Now, the desert is growing, reaching all the way up to North Dakota. It's even swallowed Wyoming and devastated parts of Montana, Iowa, and, of course, Missouri. I look anxiously around for signs of the next storm but all appears peaceful for now.

Leaning against the back of the bench, I continue browsing the data on my tablet. The scale of the study is astounding. I simply had no idea. Thanks to the records I stole from Dick's computer, I've been combing through the results of every field test currently in operation for the MSA toxin. I was right, MSA stands for Mass Sterilization Agent and it turns out that 8742 is only the code that applies to the Ugandan tests. There are dozens of variants.

A small noise makes me look up in alarm, but none of the tourists in pastel cycling shorts is paying me any attention. I breathe in and continue perusing the results of the tests on Chinese minorities in Madagascar. I didn't even realize there were people of Chinese descent there. But I guess it makes sense. GeneX can hardly waltz into the first economic power in the world and conduct experiments there with impunity. There are tests in Bangladesh and Bolivia, Uganda of course, but also Finland, Japan and Australia.

Why these places? Scrolling rapidly through the documents I come back to the test map and click on the southern half of the American continent. Then I get it. Of course. It all makes sense; in countries where populations have mixed with each other and integration has taken place, GeneX are having trouble with the MSA tests. I guess the toxin needs specific genetic markers to latch on to. So they choose countries with distinctive ethnicities. Like Aboriginals, Sámi people.

I zoom in on the tests in Bolivia: 62 percent of the population there is Native American, which makes it a lot easier for the Mass Sterilization Agent to single out inheritance markers. And as an added bonus, it's the poorest country in the sub-continent, so there's little chance of discovery there. I've got to hand it to GeneX, they're logical. Cold and ruthless. But also astute.

This is huge.

Someone taps me on the shoulder, startling me.

'Hey, D. What's up? Why are we having lunch here with the tourists?'

I scoot over so Jada can sit next to me on the bench and hand her a sandwich.

'What's all the mystery about?' she asks, rubbing her nascent bump as she unwraps the impromptu picnic.

'I needed a place to chat. Away from the office. I... I'd like your help deciding on something, but it's really confidential.' A year ago I would never have admitted that I needed help to anyone. I guess this trip has changed me more than I realized.

'Is it related to your... pet project?' she asks.

'Yes. It could be dangerous to know this.'

'But you need me, right? You need my advice?'

'Yes.'

'OK, shoot, then.'

So, at last, I tell her everything I know and it feels good.

'My partner, she's...' I stop myself before I reveal Olivia's location. 'She's trustworthy. She can leak this information to the press.'

'Are you guys undercover reporters or something?'

I pause, trying to gauge how much I can trust her. 'Something like that, yes. We're thinking of revealing the fact that GeneX is doing tests on Latinos...'

'So what if they're also doing tests on Latinos? It isn't worse than doing tests on Africans or Aboriginals,' she says.

'No, of course, it's the exact same fucked-up repulsive process. My partner just thought...'

I don't want to finish that sentence.

She has no such compunction and, in her usual abrasive manner, she says, 'Basically, you're saying that people don't give a shit about lots of Africans being sterilized against their will, but maybe if you went public with something closer to home, like Latinos, we might manage to make someone care?'

'Well, yes,' I admit. 'That's exactly it.'

'You know, DeAnn, I hate to break it to you, but people won't care about Latinos either. Migrants are responsible for most of the population increase these last fifty years. If it wasn't for them, we'd be below the generation replacement threshold by now.'

'So there'll be no empathy for Latinos then?' I sigh.

'Fuck no!' Jada says, surprising me with her vehemence. 'It's their fault that we're in this situation. My kids need food, they need water. I work two jobs and barely earn enough to take care of them. We already eat instant noodles more often than I'd like.' Her voice wobbles. 'So the wet backs can get the fuck back to Mexico or wherever the hell they came from, they'll get no sympathy from me.'

Taken aback by her violent outburst, I take a minute to adjust.

We should have brought the world's population under control while there was still time. I think of Imani and Dion, her kids; they're so accomplished, so smart and well behaved. I understand what she means; if I were her and I had to choose, I too would rather see her kids grow up having enough, rather than feeding countless additional Latino or Asian kids whom I've never met. It's just because

I've actually met hers and it's completely irrational. It's a horrible thought, but still, I get it.

She stays silent, absentmindedly looking at the metal fingers of the statue as they protrude out of the vast sandy expanse. Tourists wriggle under the massive phalanges like fat white maggots exposed by the lifting of the giant's palm. Even here in the middle of nowhere, there are people swarming around us. Laughing, arguing, shouting, eating.

Greasy papers float away and a mountain of plastic bottles grows by the public garbage bin.

I glance at her sideways, willing her to live up to a higher moral standard, just as I struggle to raise mine.

'I don't think you understand, Jada – GeneX is not in charge anymore. We're not just talking about the few hundreds of subjects who took part in the experiments. In the next few months, we have reason to believe that the Department of Defense will deploy the toxin and sterilize millions of Ugandans.'

'Are they? Well, I don't see what your problem is. You're the one who keeps saying we've got a worldwide overpopulation issue. So that's the solution.'

'But that's not the way to go about solving the problem. There are still options, the Beijing—'

'Oh get real, DeAnn, for God's sake. The Beijing Treaty's too little too late. It's not even binding and none of the Coalition countries have signed it. No more talking, we need action.'

'What – and you're happy to just throw the Ugandans under the bus? Don't you see? If we let GeneX and the DoD decide who can have children and who can't, we're opening the door to gross human rights violations. We can still stop them. Warn the press, get the information out there.'

'Why would you take such a risk? For people you've never even met before. That's ridiculous.'

'I *do* know people in Uganda. But that's not the point. Even if I knew no one there, I couldn't let millions be sterilized just because they were born in the wrong country. What if you had been born Ugandan? Would you want to be wiped out off the face of the Earth within the next two generations?'

She shrugs. 'If we don't do something soon, we're all going to die of famine and thirst, no matter what our passport says on the cover. Maybe it's the kinder, more humane solution, have you thought of that? They're not being killed, are they?'

'No, but—'

'Well, then I don't see what the problem is, DeAnn. I mean, for once, my country is doing something for me, for my children. Frankly, I can't think of a good reason why we shouldn't unleash the toxin. I don't think you should leak this information to the press at all.'

'But don't you understand? These people, Ugandans, they're like you and me, they don't deserve this. Once the toxin has modified their genetic makeup, it's irreversible. This is monstrous. They won't ever be able to have children anymore.'

'So what if they don't?' Jada says. 'There're too many Africans. They've reproduced so much that my kids don't have anything to eat anymore. It's us or them at this point.'

'We should never have let overpopulation get to this point in the first place.' I shake my head.

'Yeah, well. It is what it is. Not much we can do about it now.'

Sometimes it's really hard not to tell her who I really am. I can still do something about it… if I ever make it back.

'The funny thing is that in the 1960s everyone knew about the overpopulation issue,' I say. 'Martin Luther King even said that it was a catastrophe that was within our power to actively prevent. Or something to that effect.'

'Really?' Jada answers pensively. 'That's stupid. If we knew about overpopulation back then, how come we forgot?

'We didn't forget – politicians just stopped mentioning it because it wasn't palatable. The US fertility pattern might have naturally gone down because of wealth and economic growth, but instead the US population nearly doubled over the last sixty-five years.'

'So I'm not wrong about immigrants, then?'

I'm disappointed in her but don't see any point in mentioning it, so I reluctantly concede. 'I suppose that it's because overpopulation is mainly down to immigration and underdeveloped countries that the Democrats never mention it as an environmental and social issue to be dealt with. They'd have to speak up against immigration or propose a solution to control fertility rates of immigrants and that would be completely at odds with their ethos.'

'Don't environmentalists care, at least? Overpopulation is directly responsible for the animal extinctions and most of our environmental issues we face, isn't it?' Finishing up her sandwich, she stares despondently at the arid landscape. I wonder if she still thinks she'll be able to engineer a plant to counteract the drought and the Dust Bowl. I don't know how she still musters the energy for faith and hope.

I shrug. 'The Greens are all traditionally on the left of the political spectrum, so none of them want to mention it either. I suppose it's easier for them to focus the public's attention on energy-efficient light bulbs and recycling.'

'And Republicans are roped in with religious groups and

get most of their base from supporting pro-life lobbies,' she says, rubbing her bump.

'Yes, and don't forget that more bodies is always good for wars and consumerism, so Conservatives are always pro-natalists by default,' I say.

'So in the end, it was easier for everyone to just sweep it under the rug for political reasons?' she asks, looking demoralized. 'I wish politicians had done something in the twenties, before it was too late.'

'Politicians.' I sigh, glancing at my watch. 'We'd better get back.'

We ride back in silence through the vast red expanse. Shaken by our conversation, my thoughts take a somber hue; perhaps Jada's right. I could just let it happen. After all, it's not like humanity is going to suddenly exhibit rationality and self-restraint after centuries of selfishness and greed. I understand Omony now. You can plead and reason and explain for so long. But after that avenue is exhausted, and free will fails... maybe a person who knows best and who has the greater good at heart is duty-bound to do something. Anything.

Pretty much any action is better than inertia. Because inertia leads to this future. I mean, I feel for the African test subjects, of course, and I don't condone what this pharma-ceutical company has done to get this drug ready. But now that it's ready...

OLIVIA

N*ew Jersey, USA, September 2082*

THE BABY WAILS, its heart-wrenching cries tearing through the hubbub, unbearable. The itch devours me and a grimace of a smile etches itself on my lips as I will my legs to stay put, my body to stay seated.

Guests are agglutinated around the pastel cake like cockroaches on a rotting wedge of cheese. A bright sign screams 'Congratulations!' and pink and blue balloons are strewn about the room.

How can they be so oblivious? So happy? The screams of terror as the shooter aimed at the crowd startle me anew as a champagne cork pops and people cheer. I jump and clench a cushion, cold sweat on my forehead.

After the UN debacle, DeAnn wasn't best pleased with me.

'What? Why would you do that?' she said when I

explained about the leaked information and what happened to Woody.

'I had to do something. I couldn't just sit idly by as they deployed the Mass Sterilisation Agent on all these people.'

'But that's idiotic. Our mission is to gather facts, not to try and stop anything.'

That got my goat. I said a tad too heatedly perhaps, 'Well, you said yourself, last time we talked, that if there were a crisis, they might reveal more – and it worked, for Pete's sake.'

DeAnn and I aren't exactly BFFs. I mean, we're way better than before, but sometimes, she's so cold and dismissive.

I added, 'I'm not an idiot. I know what's at stake. GeneX and the Department of Defense people have been sending Carapadre and Dergrin more information about their project, so we can protect it with patents and look into who might have leaked what to the UN Under-Secretary. I now have dozens of names of scientists, politicians and military officers to put on a watch list when we get back to 2017."

'OK, fine, but don't take any more risks. You know the drill, Snow White: stay out of trouble, make it back alive, try not to care.'

'But I can't do it, DeAnn. I do care.'

I care about baby Jonathan and all the Adroa orphans, about Edigold and her children, about Father Opok and Edmand, the kind shuttle driver.

I look around me at the obscene display of food and think of my friends with a heavy heart. I got word to all of them that they needed to flee Uganda and escape the large-scale deployment of the Mass Sterilisation Agent. I hope they got my message. It's imminent now.

I know that DeAnn cares as well, even if she claims

otherwise. I want to do more. It's not enough to get the word out to a handful of my friends. But what else can I do? I tried to blow the whistle and it failed. I could try contacting the press directly. But who would believe me and how could I trust any of the journalists? I need to keep thinking about how to prevent this.

She sensed that I was annoyed and backed down. 'You were lucky. If they'd known you were the leak, they'd have had another sniper trained on you when they assassinated Woody.'

I shuddered. 'You think? Nobody's seems to know it's me.'

'Yet. But you've got to stop. This is not our mission.'

'But these poor people—'

She interrupted me, her face serious: 'Listen, Olivia, I understand what you tried to do. I really do. But these people haven't been born yet and if we succeed in curbing fertility, most of them may never be born at all. You can't care about all of them, it's useless.'

'Well, that's a bit rich coming from you,' I snorted.

'What the hell do you mean?'

Was it my imagination or did she sound emotional?

'You're spending all your free time tending to patients who may never be born either,' I said.

'That's different...' she hesitated, 'that's research.'

'Right, you keep telling yourself that, DeAnn. Keep pretending that you don't care about any of them. But I know better. And so do you.'

A shadow passed over her face and she looked down. Already regretting my harsh words, I said, more softly, 'Listen. Come home. It's time. There's nothing else you can do now.'

'There's nothing you can do either, Olivia. You tried.

Don't push your luck. Keep your head down. The most important thing is the mission. If we get back, we'll be able to prevent all this. Just stay out of the limelight for a few more weeks, OK? No more heroics.'

'Don't say "if".'

'Huh?'

'Say "*when* we get back", please.'

She rolled her eyes and hung up.

'YOU ALRIGHT?' Michael brings over two sizeable portions of cake and hands me the one with pink icing.

'Headache,' I say, as I wince a smile for his benefit.

'Come on, eat some. Cake makes everything better.' He crams in a mouthful of the blue sponge and sighs with relish, a big goofy smile on his face. I smile at him fondly, feeling inexplicably dejected as he stuffs his face, the blue icing smearing on his nose. Can't these people see that their world is dying? And no amount of cake can make this better. I give him my slice and he breaks into a grin and eats it too, all his focus on the sugary treat.

Food is displayed with abandon here: cupcakes are adorned with garish colours that look so sweet my teeth are hurting just to look at them, flaky tartlets piled high on trays shed their crumbs like dandruff on the table cloth, and fake chocolate ice cream melts away despondently in a nest of toxic-looking fog.

'So, I heard Travis just got the Hong Kong account?' Michael asks Imogen, who beams back.

She's wearing pink from head to toe, a plastic smile plastered on her plastic face. The swell of her enormous belly is gone now, replaced by a flat stomach and the two prizes upstairs, who are tended by her staff 24/7. She looks well rested, smug, and today her blonde hair seems obscenely long, reaching past the small of her back. It's ostentatious. Just like the rest of this party.

'Yes,' she says, 'we're thrilled, as you can imagine, we're going to...'

The baby's scream pierces through the fog of polite conversation and punctures right through me again. I can't do this.

'I need to go to the loo.'

I spring to my feet, pushing off Michael's knee without thinking. He looks unhappy at the near reveal of our intimacy, but I don't care.

The infant's cries pull me forward like a homing beacon as I sneak upstairs, feeling like a trespasser. The thick cream carpet swallowing my stockinged feet, I tiptoe down the corridor, trying a few doors until I push the right one open and find little Isla. She's screaming her lungs out and her face is scrunched up in flushed anguish.

Nearby, in his blue crib, her twin brother's face is starting to crumple up as well, so I grab the infant and rock her in my arms, as the yearning opens in me like a gaping chasm. Twirling my hand in front of her dark blue eyes, I help the baby girl quiet down. Her tiny fingers scratch, as they open and close around my neck, her body moulding easily into my arms.

'Shhh, baby, shhh.' I sway, blowing gently on her long blonde lashes.

Her brother, Asher, gurgles in his crib, reaching up for us, as Isla falls asleep, her mouth making small wet movements. The sun shines through the nursery window, bathing her face in light, and for a moment I allow myself to imagine that she's mine, that this is my house, my life, my happiness, tricking my heart into swelling with joy. She lets out a heart-felt sigh and I kiss the top of her silky head, careful not to wake her as I breathe in her vanilla scent.

'Ah, there you are, Olivia.' Imogen barges in, a suspicious look on her face.

'Imogen, oh yes, sorry, she was crying. I...erm...' I stammer, feeling ludicrous.

'That's fine, you can just leave her there.' An unpleasant smile etches itself on her lips. 'Not everyone is made for motherhood. Better leave it to the ones who know what they're doing.'

She snaps her fingers and I let go reluctantly, my fingers still feeling the terrycloth's softness as I entrust the baby to her mother's arms. She sticks baby Isla in her crib, throws a cursory glance at Asher and walks out. On our way back downstairs, she stops and opens two doors, irritated. Behind the second one, the rest of her brood is playing noisily.

'Where is that damn woman?' Imogen mumbles as she goes in search of the nanny.

Back downstairs, the power display of food littered on every horizontal surface is starting to sour and the smell is nauseating, dog-eared sandwiches reek of mayonnaise, cupcake bouquets are wilting and the heat is suffocating. My colleagues are gathered around the buffet, heads bent, teeth gnashing, their cellulitis encased in glossy spandex. Here a glob of icing has dripped disturbingly green on Aubyn's chin. The smell of artificial sweets fills the warm sticky air, beads of sweat pearl on upper lips, too-orange concealer melts over creased eyes, double chins wobble under wagging jaws.

I put my plastic plate down on the coffee table, nauseated, as the wasteful display and smell of greed threaten to bring my stomach to my lips.

'Well, now that you have two sets of each, you'll be just like Mandy and Chad,' Cressida says, a bitter slant on her mouth.

Imogen giggles, accepting her friend's allegiance.

'Oh. My. God.' Blythe claps her hands, squealing like a seal. 'I hadn't thought of that. Have you heard? They're pregnant with another set of twins. That'll make six. Have you seen their latest movie? They're so galactic.'

'No, we haven't had the time to go to the cinema, you'll see why... I saved the best for last.' Imogen brays a fake laugh and excuses herself, gesturing to her domestics as she walks over to her husband.

The nanny brings the twins and the rest of the children to stand all and around the immaculate couple in a perfect tableau of domestic bliss while her staff corrals the guests and soon we're all focusing on Imogen, just as it should be. Little by little, silence descends on the room, interrupted by occasional bursts of murmured speculation and excited gossip.

Michael comes to stand next to me and inconspicuously sneaks his hand on the small of my back. It's just for a moment, but it's enough to loosen the tightness in my chest a bit.

'What now?' he whispers.

I shrug. 'I don't know. Fireworks? A knighthood? Maybe Travis got another promotion and they're going to pop out a few more?'

He snorts and I feel the onset of a nervous laughter, as he pinches my side, tickling me.

Meanwhile, Imogen has started her announcement, 'my friends, we are so happy to have you here with us today, to celebrate our successes. As you know, with young Asher and little Isla, we've now reached a half a dozen children.'

Laughter breaks out, tinged with envy. 'But Travis wasn't content to stop there...'

She looks up and beams at her husband, who struts to the door and places his hand on the knob.

The tall blonde continues, 'So my friends, I would like you all to meet the latest addition to our family.' Imogen's husband opens the door and the whole room gasps as a Golden Retriever puppy ambles into the room, shaking his tail and happily trotting up to everyone to lick their hands.

The power couple's older children start to scream, as they jump up and down in theatrical joy. The men walk over to the husband and clap him on the shoulder. The women crouch and try to coax the dog towards them with cooing sounds.

Michael whistles as we approach Imogen to congratulate her. 'A dog! A *dog*. Oh wow, Imogen. You're... unbelievable.'

Cressida looks far from happy for her friend. A few metres away, her husband helps himself to champagne and wraps four cupcakes in a napkin, slipping them in his wife's bag. Crouching to pet the puppy, I sneak a glance back at the couple.

'What on earth are you doing?' Cressida hisses, yanking the bag out of his hands.

'It's for the kids,' he says, looking sheepish.

'Instead of stealing cupcakes, why don't you go and find out from Travis how he made all his money, you useless lump. I want a third baby, William, do you hear me? Travis and Imogen already have six and a fucking dog. A *dog*, William.' Her voice is shaking and her eyes fill up.

The puppy nips my hand playfully and I scratch him behind the ears, smiling. Neither one of them is paying me any attention, as they continue their whispered argument.

'You know they probably finance it all through credit card debt. I'm not going to do it, Cressida. I love you but we just can't afford it. Let Imogen and Travis pay for their flashy lifestyle, their six kids and their *dog* while they dig themselves into debt.' His voice is dripping sarcasm. 'When they go bankrupt our children will still have enough to eat. Theirs won't.'

Unfortunately Imogen has heard him, and she slithers over to us, narrowing her eyes.

'Travis and I are *not* paying for all this on credit cards. We can afford ours, unlike some.' Imogen glares at the cupcakes in William's hand as he turns beetroot red.

They're all starting to get on my nerves, so I try to change the topic to something less personal. 'Are you saying poor people shouldn't have children?'

The blonde laughs, a girly, high-pitched tinkle. 'Nobody's telling them not to, but they'll probably have trouble feeding them and won't be able to afford school, so hopefully they'll start making fewer.'

'What about you? Why aren't you restricting your fertility as well?' I ask her.

'We can afford our children, so what's the problem?' Imogen shrugs. 'How many we choose to have just becomes a personal preference at our level of wealth.'

Thinking of the MSA toxin, I push, 'How can you say that it's a personal preference? Your individual choices have global ramifications.'

'That's ridiculous, we're just exercising a personal liberty to—'

'Can't you see that restraining our fertility in this country is even more important than in poor countries? Every single one of your children here is going to have practically a fifty-fold higher impact on the environment than a child born in an underdeveloped country.'

'The environment?' Imogen looks at me as if I'd just said that I'd been abducted by aliens last week. 'What are you talking about?' she laughs. 'Everyone knows that global warming is a scam. It's not real.'

She exchanges a meaningful look with the others, eyebrows raised, and they sneer, happy to find common ground from which to despise the stranger in their midst.

'Anybody wants a top-up?' Michael arrives holding a champagne bottle, careful not to touch me, now that we're in plain view of our colleagues.

He's starting to annoy me too. He's happy enough to make love to me but he won't tell anyone that we're together. The lack of respect is starting to get to me. He's so affectionate when we're alone, yet so cold and distant when we're in public. It makes me sad. Maybe he's ashamed to be with me. I'm older than him, not exactly thin. Maybe dating the paralegal isn't the done thing. I don't know, I don't understand it. I'm proud to date him.

Shaking my head, I walk away.

'Olivia?' Todd, one of my colleagues who's a halfway decent human being, comes over. 'You want a ride? We're going back to the city.'

I exhale with relief. 'Yes, please.'

Michael isn't even looking at me. Completely ignoring me, like we're strangers and it's no concern of his how I get back to Manhattan. A solitary eel of unease burrows through my gut as I accept Todd's invitation and say my goodbyes.

Todd and Brad like to pretend they hate Imogen but once in their car, they start to gush about the pink phoniness of it all while their daughter sleeps in her car seat, next to me. I tune them out, feeling like a sullen teenager as I wonder yet again why my life never seems to start in earnest. Why I'm never in the front seat with my husband, why I'm always in the back seat feeling like a failure?

Outside, the neighbourhood scrolls past our car, the soul-sucking sameness feeling suddenly engineered. Is there a grand design at work here? A will behind the cookie-cutter hopes and dreams we're all encouraged to feel? The perfect manicured lawns and identical pastel houses of deep suburbia begin to look not so much like a fifties dream neighbourhood and more like the stables of battery cattle. Are we all being lied to and manipulated into breeding without restraint, our desirable white genes and wealthy profiles nudged towards procreation, like so many cows?

The blonde toddler sighs and her dreaming face scrunches up then relaxes, and all thought of political manipulation flutters away as my hand flies of its own accord to move a strand of golden hair away from her forehead.

24

DEANN

*S*t. *Louis, Missouri, USA, September 2082*

IT'S NEARLY CURFEW, time to go home. I should leave but instead I'm still at work, pondering the delivery medium, jotting down ideas in my leather notebook. The toxin must be odorless, colorless and tasteless if it can be added to water without people noticing. That being said, the people in Kampala might not have been so picky.

Well, anyway, the medium doesn't really matter. I don't need to bring back that information. But I do need to understand how the drug withers the subjects' reproductive organs. MSA8742 works in two interconnected stages. In the first stage, the toxin targets the correct subject – for example, women with Aboriginal genetic characteristics – then, if the markers are present, it triggers the second stage and inhibits reproduction.

I get up and go make myself tea. I'd kill for a coffee right now. In the last few weeks, I've been able to surmise that the toxin targets women. Basically if anyone but an Aboriginal woman with the correct genetic profile came into contact with the toxin, it would have no effect on them. A man's testicles would remain whole, a white woman's ovaries would continue to function. But if an Aboriginal woman ingests it, the toxin will latch on to her DNA and deliver its payload. The woman's ovaries will go from grape to raisin within twenty-four hours – and it's irreversible.

How ironic. The scientists who came up with that must have been men. They invent Viagra for themselves, but the only thing they can think to do for women is to maim us. I guess ultimately if all men are still fertile but women aren't, the overpopulation problem will be taken care of. And fragile male egos will remain intact. Win–win from their perspective. I sigh and rub my eyes, finish the tea and review the research one more time.

A conversation I had with Jada a few days ago, in the gym, springs back in my mind, laced with a twinge of guilt.

'Maybe we could reverse the compound's genetic programming to target blondes with blue eyes? I bet people would care then,' Jada laughed.

'Shh, keep your voice down.'

She rolled her eyes and continued pedaling.

'I might be able to pull that off, actually,' I said pensively.

She looked at me and whistled. 'Well, I'll be damned! DeAnn Campbell,' she said, 'maybe it wasn't such a bad idea to save your life after all.'

I had to laugh.

'Jokes aside,' she continued, as she wiped her neck with a towel and got off the bike, 'I know you'll crack that nut. You're one of the smartest people I know...' she hesitated, '... and your heart's in the right place, girl.'

I smile now, as my mind returns to the deserted office plunged in darkness.

Actually, she had a really good idea. In theory, it should be possible to decouple the DNA-targeting stage from the sterilizing stage of the toxin. But for now, I need to find out how the drug goes from hindering protein expression to withering major organs. And when that's done, I need to find the delivery medium, so I can tell the media what to look out for.

Everyone else has gone home. I'm the last one here, as usual. I've sent everything I found out to A. but she hasn't replied with new instructions. After the UN Under-Secretary was killed, the media spun his assassination as if it were a random mass shooting, as people in the audience were killed as well.

Soon, Olivia's recording of the dead Ugandan village became old news, superseded by some other bloody massacre, somewhere else in the world. A few weeks onwards, it's exactly as Jada and I suspected: nobody cares about a few dead Africans and all of it is already forgotten. Mandy and Chad, some celebrity couple, have broken up and the press is aflutter about that. They're so pretty and white; much better ratings to cover that.

I try Jada's number for the umpteenth time and sigh with frustration. She's called in sick for the last two days. I try her again and still no answer. She's supposed to join me tonight for one of our lab break-ins. I glance over my shoulder at the dark office. Maybe I could risk doing it on my own tonight? Tapping my fingers on the table, I mull it over and decide against it. Too risky.

I really should go check on her this evening, so I turn off my tablet, put the leather notebook in my locker and go catch the bus back to our neighborhood.

While the bus idles at the red light, I glance at an entire family sitting cross-legged around an emergency box provided by the city, rummaging in the package for their dinner. The gaunt mother distributes the small silver packs to her kids, then tightens the blonde pigtails of her daughter. An elderly man, probably her grandfather, clearly can't get up anymore; his pale skeletal limbs are stretched out on the sidewalk and he strains to open the ration. I'm shocked anew to see a white man so thin and poor. Yet a part of me always thinks of starving Africans and how there's no reason why whites shouldn't feel hunger as well.

I push the uncharitable thought away, as the driverless bus rounds the street corner. Maybe Jada's right, perhaps we could spark outrage after all, if the Mass Sterilization Agent affected whites as well.

I wish I could help that family but today I'm overwhelmed by the scale of the issues. What can one person do, really? The mass unemployment and near famine conditions were already an underlying problem when I arrived, but in the last few months, the record heat and mass exodus from the states worst affected by the droughts and dust storms has exacerbated St. Louis' downfall to fever point.

Thousands of people arrive every day in the city, homeless, completely destitute and in such dire straits that they'd rather leave their farms and come starve here. They line the streets now, sleeping in abandoned squats and cardboard boxes, as we wait for the next dust storm to take its lethal toll.

Thirty minutes later, I'm at Jada's place and Imani answers the door. The little girl usually looks perfectly put together. But today her hair is mussed and she's thrown on her clothes haphazardly; she looks lost and scared, she doesn't seem to have slept much either.

'What's wrong, Imani? Are you on your own?'

'Mom's not well,' she says to me through the half-closed front door. 'And Dion's at the neighbors' for a sleepover tonight. Sorry Auntie DeAnn, it's not a good time to visit.'

'What's wrong with her? Do you know? Is it that nasty cold that's doing the rounds lately? Let me in sweetie, I'll check how she's doing and help you.'

'I'm not supposed to let anyone inside.' She tries to close the door but I hold it open, push and barge in.

'No, I don't think... Auntie DeAnn, please...'

There are dirty dishes in the sink, all the windows are closed and a sickly smell is floating around the place.

Imani makes a beeline for her mother's room and I follow her in.

Jada is sleeping fitfully, her hair plastered to her forehead and a film of sweat clinging to her body. The tangled sheets are damp, wrapped around her legs. Her nightgown has hiked up because of her trashing. I step gingerly around the puddle of vomit on the carpet by her bed and touch her forehead; she feels too hot and her breathing is too fast. I try to wake her up but can't.

'That's not a cold... what happened?'

The girl is alone and this is too much responsibility for her; she's backed into the bedroom corner, sobbing. She looks helplessly at her mother, then switches her wet gaze to me. I'm being too harsh. I need to soften my tone.

'Imani, I want to help your mom but I need information, OK? Just tell me what happened. You're not in trouble.'

She sobs, hiccupping between long gulps of air, her nose and eyes puffy.

'She... she told me not to say.'

'It' alright, I won't tell anyone, Imani.'

'A woman came... two nights ago... they locked themselves in Mommy's bedroom. She cried... the yells...' The little girl chokes up and I put my hand on her shoulder.

'Did she do anything else?'

'I don't know. I don't know anything.' She sobs harder.

I lift up the tangled sheets and recoil at the smell. Vaginal discharge and pus stain Jada's inner thighs and her abdomen is distended. Fuck. *Clostridium sordellii*. She got a home abortion. Why didn't she come to me?

I take her pulse; her blood pressure's too low. She's probably septic by now. Toxic shock syndrome. She needs surgery but I can't take her to a mainstream hospital like this. She'll get arrested. I try to wake her up in vain.

'OK, Imani, I want you to call Auntie Lashelle. Can you do that for me?'

Imani nods and while I start to dress her mother, she runs to get her tablet. Jada comes to but she's incoherent. Her limbs are clammy and cold and she's completely limp. The girl darts back in the room and shows me an extended iMode with Lashelle's concerned face on it.

'Jada's in trouble. Can you come pick us up and take us to the clinic?'

'What's wrong?'

'She tried to do a backroom procedure,' I say cautiously, not knowing how much Imani is aware of.

'Fuck. Is she alright?'

'No. No, she's not. I need you. Now.'

By the time I'm done getting Jada ready and down into the street, Lashelle arrives and helps us walk our friend to the car under the curious stares of neighbors.

'Just a severe case of gastro,' I smile apologetically. They steer clear, wrinkling their noses.

'DeAnn?' Jada comes to and gazes at me, puzzled. 'Where are we?'

'Don't worry, OK? I've got you. Just lean on me and focus on walking.'

She frowns and concentrates on her feet. It takes all her energy.

We drive in silence, Imani in the back seat, her mother's head on her knees, stroking her hair and crying. They talk softly when Jada flits in and out of consciousness. Lashelle and I exchange a worried glance.

Fucking hell, Jada, what have you done?

I remember mine. I was in university, two years into Med school and doing well. When I first saw the pregnancy test my heart swelled with joy. It was not a rational thought, just a spontaneous feeling. As if a precious golden light had started radiating from my abdomen. I was the guardian of a treasure, a wonderful secret.

That evening, I hummed to myself as I dressed for my date with Jake. He took me to our favorite restaurant and I looked at his beloved face, his green eyes and chestnut hair, his lovely smile and I thought: *This is it; I'm going to be happy with him for the rest of my life.* Me, a doctor, him an engineer, and our child who'd have his easy charm and my grit.

When I told him, his face fell. I tried to explain how happy I was, how wonderful this felt. But he just said, 'This isn't funny, stop smiling.' He got up and left the restaurant. I just sat there, dumbfounded, looking at his back as he left. Later he texted that he'd pay for the abortion and that it was over between us.

I called my mother. Thinking she'd help. She'd understand what a wonderful gift this was. But she told me, 'I haven't worked all my life so you could drop out of college and be a disgrace to your father's name.' I went to the family planning clinic and the therapist there said to me, 'You just want to play doll. You're selfish. A child is the product of a man and a woman's love. You can't just have one like that, on your own. You need to abort.' I was flailing. That's when I started detaching. Instead of joy, I felt dread. How would I sustain this child? With what money?

Instead of connection with the fetus, I started to feel like it was inexorably growing inside me and there was nothing I could do to stop it from wrecking my life. Whether I had it or not, my life, as I knew it, was over.

My understanding of what kind of person I was and my self-worth were rocked to their foundation. Finally, sick at heart, I made my decision.

My mother flew in. She never visited on her own usually. She said, 'You're not having this baby, end of story.' She demanded to sleep in my bed that night. So I took the pill that the Family Planning Clinic had given me and went to bed on the sleeping cot.

The next morning, we went to the clinic. I lay on the table clutching the sides of it and cried as they removed him. I wondered if he suffered.

On the ride back, my mother didn't say a word. Jake wrote a text to say he'd wired the money. He never wrote again. In the afternoon, my mother said, 'I expect you to get back to class tomorrow morning.' And I did.

I haven't really been the same since. I didn't do it light-heartedly. But at least I survived the procedure. I throw a glance in the rearview mirror at Jada's unconscious form on the back seat.

No woman rejoices when she has to terminate a pregnancy. But to risk her life to make that choice shouldn't be part of the deal. What's the point of forcing women to have children they can't or don't want to raise? I'm reminded once again that it's men who make our laws. What do they know about a woman's ability to love her offspring? If she thinks she can't, then surely she shouldn't have to. And whose business is it but her own?

Finally, we skid to a halt in front of the clinic and a nurse helps us get Jada to the resident ob-gyn. We exchange a look. I can only hope that she won't report Jada. She knows her well.

We sit in the cafeteria with Imani and Lashelle. It's odd to be on the other side of the doctor–patient divide for once. I don't really know what to do with myself. So I get up and fetch a cola and a handful of sweets for Imani from one of the charity packs that are regularly delivered to the clinic for the dust bowl refugees.

Then, trying to distract myself from the agony of waiting, I grab my tablet reader and browse through the reports on our patients from the last few days as we wait..

Imani drinks the cola, looking anxiously over her shoulder every couple of minutes, toward the cafeteria entrance. I watch her small legs as they swing back and forth nervously. Her mother wouldn't approve of her drinking this stuff, Jada never drank soda.

I return to the reports. How does the chemical deliver its payload? What is the medium?

Imani finishes the drink, she screws the cap on and holds the bottle in her hands, spinning it. I watch the black liquid spin in the plastic bottle and suddenly it hits me.

That's the delivery medium.

The soda.

I'm sure of it.

The city of St. Louis has been delivering the bottles of soda to this clinic by the palletful for months.

They couldn't.

They wouldn't.

MSA8742 was just supposed to affect a handful of

strangers in remote areas of the world.

I grab the bottle from Imani's hands; there's some left at the bottom. Pulling the girl behind me, I hurry down the corridor, in search of an empty consultation room.

Lashelle calls after us, 'DeAnn? Everything OK?'

Absorbed in my apprehension, I raise a distracted hand and keep dragging the child behind me.

'What's going on, Auntie DeAnn?' she asks, worried.

I make a conscious effort to smile and manage it with difficulty. 'Nothing, sweetie, nothing. I just want to take advantage while we're here to have a look at you and make sure you're alright.'

Finally, I find an empty consultation room, grab her by the waist and hoist her on an examination table, motioning for her to just sit there for a minute.

I absorb a drop of the black liquid with my tablet's port and anxiously tap my fingers against the back of the clear plastic device as I wait for it to process the results.

A ping.

And the results appear.

No. Please no.

The familiar shape of MSA8742 materializes on the screen, as if blooming behind my eyelids; I've stared at it so many times, in so many test results that I would recognize it anywhere.

It can't be, they haven't.

I check the provenance, the sample, the time and date. It's really the drop I just uploaded. Not some old test results from Uganda.

The toxin that occupies my every thought and my every nightmare has arrived here.

At home.

I can't believe my own eyes. Frantically, I tap the reader

and make sure it's able to scan.

'Imani, just lie down on the table for me please, I'm going to scan you, OK sweetie?' She hears the alarm in my voice and lies down, looking scared, as I scan her abdomen.

Her ovaries have shrunk so much that they're nearly gone. My hand drops to my side, the scanning tablet hitting my thigh softly.

THERE'S a knock on the door and the nurse's head appears. 'Doctor Campbell, you should come immediately.'

I can see on her face that the news is serious.

I help Imani off the examination table and walk her back toward the ER, worry clutching my heart as I squeeze her small hand in mine.

We're nearly there, when the ob-gyn runs into us, out of breath, looking distraught.

'Did the nurse tell you? I'm really sorry, I couldn't do anything, I'm so sorry.'

'What? Is she dead?'

'No, I...'

We run to the ER and arrive just as two white policemen wearing combat gear pull back the curtains around Jada's bed. Seeing them, the ob-gyn gestures for us to stay back.

'They knew, DeAnn, I'm so sorry,' she whispers, 'The snap trial already took place while you were in the cafeteria.'

'What are you talking about? We were gone less than an hour. You were treating her.'

'At first yes, but they barged in and I couldn't send word. They subpoenaed my medical records and I was forced to bear witness... that young woman too.'

Britney, the teenage kid, emerges from behind the blue curtain, looking deeply uncomfortable. Her eyes meet mine, she lowers her gaze then skulks out of the clinic really fast.

The ob-gyn clasps her hands, looking remorseful. 'You know what the sentence is for doctors who perform it, I had to save myself, I had to tell them. There was really nothing I could do. I'm so sorry—'

The two cops are already off, dragging Jada between them. She's barely conscious, her head lolling back on her shoulders, her mouth open.

'Mom? Mom?'

I pull Imani back and my eyes meet the ob-gyn's. She shakes her head discreetly as she steps out of their way. But I can't just let my friend get arrested. I catch up and stand in the policemen's path.

'What are you doing? Where are you taking her?'

'Step away, ma'am. Now.'

Jada's bare legs are dragging behind her, her hospital gown gaping open behind her, revealing her naked body. A smear of dried blood is visible along her thigh. She struggles to wake up and shake the drugs off.

The two men drag her along the corridor, toward the back of the hospital. Only a few people are here, at this time of night, but the ones who cross our path jump out of the way and whisper to each other, pointing at Jada.

I run behind them. 'She can't be moved right now. Just come back and arrest her later. Where's she going to go? Have you seen the state she's in?'

'She's been tried and found guilty of murder. Now move away or we'll arrest you for obstruction.'

Imani darts after me in the deserted hallway, as fast as her small legs can carry her, her sneakers making squeaking noises on the linoleum. Just as the girl catches up with me, one of the policemen bangs the back doors open and we emerge into the scorching night air behind the hospital. The other cop drops her mother next to a large blue metal trash container.

Jada crumples, her vulnerable pubis on the filthy pavement, her knees scratched and bleeding. I rush to help her up but one of the policemen holds me back, twisting my arm behind my back and grabbing Imani by the neck.

I freeze as Kitsa's frail graceful memory grips my soul.

No.

Not again.

Don't move.

Don't make a sound or he could break Imani's neck.

The other cop reads something on his iMode bracelet to Jada: 'You have the duty to remain silent. Anything you have done to the unborn citizen will be done against you, as mandated by the court of law.'

Jada's still trying to shake off the drugs but her gaze is latched onto her daughter, then it travels up to me. Our eyes meet and in that minute, the silent message that passes between us brands itself into my soul.

The moment ends and I stop fighting the policeman and gather the girl to me, with my free arm, carefully. His vise-like grip on my arm tightens.

'Given your crime, your right to an attorney is forfeit. We are appointed by the court of law to carry out your sentence.'

A tear falls down Jada's cheek. She tugs on the hospital gown and folds her knees under her.

'Do you wish to deny the murder charges raised against you?'

My friend just shakes her head and straightens up.

The policeman swipes away the text. Imani shakes

against me, the other cop's large white hand still around her throat.

I'm about to ask why they're not taking her away to the patrol car, when the gunshot explodes in the silent night.

Jada's head jolts away from the muzzle as the bullet continues its trajectory through her skull and out in a spray of blood.

My brain refuses to process what I see; my friend's dead body, lying sprawled next to the garbage dumpster on the filthy pavement.

The policeman's grip slackens.

Imani shakes her head 'no' and falls to her knees as her small hand slides out of mine.

I'm numb.

I stare at this little girl, this proud, beautiful daughter of my people, and I remember the way she looked up at her mother, that day in the plain, dead rabbits everywhere, and Jada, undaunted and beautiful, holding her children tightly against her.

What has been done to this girl? What has been done to Jada's legacy? What has been done to the next generation of proud and fierce women to succeed us? A tear rolls down my cheek, as I mourn Imani's mother and her own shriveled future.

The two cops leave, chatting between themselves casually.

'Two birds, one stone.'

'Don't joke, Chip. We're doing God's work.'

'Hey, don't get all fucking prissy on me, man. I'm just sayin' two less chimps in the world. Not a bad day's work.'

'I don't know. Even with the snap trial and Judge Matthews's orders, it don't feel right. We should at least bring them in or something.'

'What for? Waste of tax payers' money if you ask me.' The other one shrugs and orders a garbage collection as they get into the patrol car and drive off.

Imani approaches the limp form of her mother and tentatively touches her cheek. I suppress a sob and sit next to them as the child cries, hunched over Jada's body.

Rage grips my belly and clenches my teeth as a long, painful scream builds up in me and, like a kettle's whine, it bursts out of my mouth of its own volition.

How dare they kill my own? My sisters? My daughters? The toxin isn't the solution I thought it was. It's not an elegant answer to the overpopulation issue, it's a weapon in the white man's hand and as with all other weapons, they'll use this one to oppress us and enslave us to their wills.

Jake's face appears in my mind's eye. He said he loved me, until I said I was pregnant and then I was just an inconvenience to get rid of. He never intended to have a half-black child. They hate us all. They always have and always will.

Lashelle pads over to us. She lifts up Imani and folds the child under her wing, trying to bring us both back inside with soft words of comfort and practical advice. I listen with one ear but my focus is already on revenge.

'Let's go get your brother and I'll take you both to my place, OK? You're going to stay with me for a while until we sort out a more permanent arrangement.' Lashelle says.

Imani doesn't answer anything. She rubs her hand on the leg of her trousers. There is a small drop of blood on her palm. She rubs but it doesn't go away. Her skinny elbows are protruding out of her pink t-shirt, she looks so small and lost. Kitsa looked just like her. All lanky limbs and puppy eyes.

Kitsa.

Anger submerges me and I let myself drown in it. MSA8742 is a weapon. A long-term one that will kill us over generations. But we'll all die in the end, just as surely as if they'd shot us. I can't let that happen. People have a right to choose.

Maybe humanity *has* made the wrong choices up to now. But at least where we've gotten to was our decision. I thought the toxin was science, coming to the aid of humankind to solve an issue but I was looking at it the wrong way; the toxin is a hideous shortcut that's bypassing the necessary moral debate that our species must face sooner or later. We can't hide behind science to rob ourselves of free will and sidestep our responsibilities to this planet.

Whites are not restraining their own fertility, they're just making sure instead that People of Color all go extinct, so they can keep the Earth to themselves. Like they've always done. They're making us bear the brunt of the world's collective bad choices. We're the sacrificial victims that allow humanity to continue business as usual.

I need to go back to 2017 and raise awareness of the consequences of overpopulation. Fight for American women's right to contraception, our right to choose. I need to educate young women about the duties that come with the privilege of choice. Choose smartly. Don't make so many children that you remain mired in poverty forever. Get education. Fight for our future, for our right to live with dignity. Nothing is more important.

I must find a way to go back and change this future. The year 2017 is still on the brink. If I can go back, I can change this fate for Imani and for countless other daughters of my blood.

25

OLIVIA

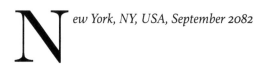ew York, NY, USA, September 2082

MICHAEL IS BEHIND THE COUNTER, rinsing some vegetables with a look of concentration on his dimply features.

The fact that he can cook must be a subject of admiration for his other conquests, as nobody seems to know how to cook anymore. I've failed to mention that I can cook quite well myself and he's never thought to ask. Michael's borrowed Dmitry's bar for the night; his loud-mouthed Russian friend lends him the professional kitchen sometimes, when the place is closed. I wonder whether I'm the first date Michael's brought here. Probably not.

The cooking robot is pushed to one side, its six arms limp. It looks oddly forlorn and the alcohol must be getting to my head because I feel like consoling it. Instead, I sit on a bar stool and watch as Michael hacks mushrooms into thin slices. I've offered to help a couple of times but he dismissed me out of hand. As in 'I can't trust you to do it well enough, go away'. He didn't say it but it's plain from the way he carefully handles the precious produce with the huge knife.

The bar is plunged in darkness but there are lit candles everywhere – on the bar, on a few tables, on the floor – and it feels magical, a stolen moment that belongs only to the two of us.

'That's Jerusalem artichoke.' He holds up a misshapen little root that looks nothing like an artichoke. 'Have you ever had it before?'

'Nope.'

'Well, tonight's the night, then.' He looks at me mischievously.

The caipirinha burns a warm sweet path through me, branching out and warming me everywhere from the inside out. I sigh contentedly. I don't want to think about difficult things tonight. I just want to enjoy this moment alone with him and forget about the world, about the toxin, about ethical choices and most of all I want to forget that there's only one month left.

I've had an idea about how to get back. I think it could work. I look at his adorable face and my heart crumples.

'What's wrong?' he asks, tilting his head.

'Nothing.' I try to change the subject, to think of happier things. 'Tell me Michael... what do you want to do with the rest of your life on this Earth.'

'Ah. Diving straight in,' he smiles, 'not even bothering with the small talk, are we?'

'Yes, well, it was either that or discussing whether it's true that some people today live to be one hundred and twenty.' I take a sip of my cocktail and push away my disquiet.

'The answer to that is yes, of course – and I fully intend

to live that long. Let's see...what I want to do with my life... I want to cook for a living,' he knocks on the robot with the butt of his knife, 'but Tin Man here has made that impossible.'

He drizzles oil in a pan and throws the mushrooms and artichokes in.

'Well, at least you have a heart,' I quip and then the thought comes to me unbidden, 'Does he?'

'Ha, ha. Heart or no heart, I can't be a chef. Instead, I'm gonna need to make a shitload of money, so I can continue buying enough gourmet food. So it looks like it's going to be a career in law for me.' He sighs as he throws some brown pasta into boiling water.

'Is that it? That's all you want out of life?'

'Well, yeah. Eventually I'd also like to marry and have kids. When I find the right person.' He looks assiduously down at his chopping board, while he chops some coriander.

He doesn't ask me what I want to do with my life. Men so rarely think of mirroring. To be fair, I'm glad he didn't. I have no idea what I want anymore. Uganda and this trip forwards have changed me more than I thought possible and I can feel myself changing still, although I'm not sure about where I'm heading yet.

Until I figure it out, I might as well let this Michael thing go wherever it wants to go. It's not like it can amount to anything anyway. It's just a fling. That's all.

My idea to get back to 2017 shimmers in my mind's eye. Possible. Feasible. Within reach. I haven't told DeAnn yet. Yes, I'm sure we can go back home.

Michael places the fried slivers on the plates of whole-grain pasta, sprinkles the coriander on top and drizzles everything with truffle oil, then he picks up the plates and looks up proudly, announcing, 'Dinner is served,' in his deep bass voice.

'Oh wow, you're brilliant!' I beam at him.

'Thank you odd duck. I think you mean galactic. Or maybe at a stretch I'll take soop.'

I blush. Another mistake. 'Yes, you're soop Michael,' I say, with a light peck on his lips.

We sit in one of the empty booths, and he slides close to me. The little candle lights flicker all around us like stars against the night sky. He asks me a bit more about my family. We talk about our siblings, our parents, our child-hoods. The night is calm and for a moment, enveloped in this quiet bubble, it's easy to believe that we're alone in the world.

I tell him about my mother and my cat, left behind in London. I tell him about the dead, my father, my brother. He tells me about the compromises he's had to make to get this far at the firm. He tells me why he likes the past more than the present and that he feels like everything that was once beautiful and good in this word died before he was born. He looks sad. My arms ache with the longing to hug him.

At last, the food is eaten and several caipirinhas have been drunk. The dishes are washed and we can think of no reason to linger anymore.

'Pudding?' I ask, hoping to stay in this cocoon a little longer.

'I know a great place.' He smiles and dimples prick his cheeks for a second.

So we put our coats on, blow out the candles and step into the cold dark night. It's only the end of September but snow is already falling. Only four weeks and two days to go before my chip activates.

Michael opens a large golf umbrella and I loop my arm

in his without thinking. It feels natural to be so close to him. Our shoes crunch on the new snow, the only sound all around as we watch the snowfall in companionable silence. I love the quiet that drops over cities when it snows at night. The fat snowflakes dance in the dark and the street is empty for once. The crowds of people are gone. Being nearly alone feels like an incredible luxury. It must be late.

On an impulse, I wander away from him playfully. I spread my arms wide and turn, opening my mouth, throat thrown back to catch snowflakes. He laughs and looks at me with shining eyes. Then, he runs his fingers through the layer of snow that has accumulated on a car and starts making a ball.

'Oh no, no, no you don't!' I giggle.

He throws the snowball and it catches me square on the chest. I splutter in mock outrage and burst out laughing, then hurry to make a ball of my own. He's already making the next one. I throw mine and can't believe it when it hits him on the cheek. Squeaking with mock terror, I run away as he comes for me and we play like children, cheeks flushed, out of breath, pelting each other with snow and running away screaming and laughing.

Half an hour later, I'm pinned against a car, panting, as he holds a snowball in front of my nose, his whole body enveloping me in a bear hug.

'Surrender!' he growls playfully.

I wriggle and laugh but then panic stirs in my chest. Flashes of Anthony derail the moment and I start to choke. I push him away and start to struggle for real.

Michael senses my change of mood and steps back. 'You OK?' He touches my neck.

I flinch and brush away his hand, taking a big gulp of air. 'Yes, yes, sorry. I just need some space to breathe.'

He reluctantly takes another step away and I feel a twinge of remorse. Michael would never hurt me. He's not the same man as Burke was. Michael's kind. A bit short-sighted perhaps and an epicurean for sure. He's too trusting in the system and sometimes his ambition gets the better of him, but he's fundamentally good, I think.

Subdued now, we walk on and stop at a tiny shop where he purchases a small box of designer delicacies to go and then we walk back in the eerie, frozen silence, contemplating the city by night.

As he offers me a miniature doughnut, I kiss his snowy bearded cheek, grateful for his love, for his unquestioning patience with my moods, his fundamental decency.

Looking quizzical, Michael smiles down at me, his deep brown eyes earnest and loving, and he kisses me on the tip of my frozen nose, as snow falls from the night sky and deposits itself delicately on our lashes and our hair. He licks sugar off my lips and his hands find their way under my coat, sensually pulling me against his warm solid body, as his kiss deepens.

We start walking again, my arm looped in his and I wonder how this all happened. I'm usually the smitten one. I'm the one who gets excited and says 'I love you' first, but not this time. How did I get so lucky? I have no idea.

Abruptly overcome with gratitude, I hug him from the side. He makes a surprised sound as the air escapes his lungs and then loops his arm around my shoulders.

'You OK, gorgeous?'

I should tell him.

I must tell him.

I'm leaving in less than five weeks to go back to 2017 and we'll never see each other again because we belong to different time-

lines and I'm seventy-two years older than you. The words are stuck in my throat. Impossible to say.

'Everything's just fine.' I press my face against the side of his chest, squeezing him tightly. 'I love you, Michael.'

'Ow, ow, ribs being crushed.'

I ignore his mock protests and inhale the delicious smell of him, smiling inside his coat.

Finally, we get to his flat. Michael goes to the kitchen to pour us a drink while I run a finger along his music and his books. He's so adorable. Everybody else has done away with paper, but a bookshelf full of paperbacks has pride of place in his flat. I trail a hand along his vintage wood turntable and choose a vinyl Rat Pack record.

Dean Martin's honeyed voice pours out, crackling through the ages, soothingly familiar. I straighten up and nearly bump into Michael.

'Ah. A woman after my own heart. You know how to work the turntable.' He smiles.

He opens the sliding door to his winter garden and we sit in the Adirondack chairs to watch Manhattan, covered in a white blanket of snow. Tiny lights twinkle like fireflies against the night.

'Olivia?'

'Mmmh.'

'There's something I'd like to say.'

He's been acting odd all evening. I glance at him sideways, wondering what's wrong. He's looking into the distance, a tumbler of whisky in his hand. He takes a gulp, puts the glass down, and gets down on one knee.

'Olivia Sinclair.' He pulls out a small box from his pocket.

'Oh my God, Michael.' My hands fly to my mouth.

'You are the woman of my dreams. You are kind, funny, generous, smart and fierce. You inspire me to be a better man and I've been happier with you these past few months than ever before in my life. Will you do me the honour of becoming my wife?'

DEANN

*S*t. Louis, Missouri, USA, September 2082

I PULLED Imani away before the garbage collection came for her mother. She didn't need to see that.

And then we waited, all our words spent, all our energy exhausted. Another night spent at the clinic, stuck after curfew. Another morning, escaping at the break of dawn, painful scenes seared on our retinas.

Lashelle will take good care of Jada's children, I'm sure. I'm telling myself that I'm leaving so I can do something to change their fate, but really I'm running away from the pain and the powerlessness I feel around Jada's children.

I didn't say goodbye. I just dropped by my apartment, showered, packed my clothes and left. And now, I'm on my way back to the office through the streets of St. Louis. I can't leave without my leather notebook and I left it at the office last night.

The bus takes me through streets that no human driver would choose. Outside, the aftermath of yesterday's post-curfew violence has left its mark on a landscape suffering from years of dereliction. The husks of buildings loom over deserted streets, their boarded-up windows like eyelids stapled shut.

Fires burn here and there, graffiti covers every vertical surface, garbage and corpses litter the street. It's clear from the automatic assault weapons clutched in the dead's hands that there was yet another gang war last night.

The lack of water, dead crops, rising prices for basic food, masses of refugees; all of it is colliding with an already desperate situation for the young men who live in the impoverished inner city. The state's given up on my neighborhood and instead of trying to help, they're sterilizing us, slowly killing us, so they don't have to take care of us at all in a few generations' time.

Where has the spirit of the 1960s gone? Why aren't we demanding better from our politicians, organizing ourselves into activist groups or working to pull ourselves out of this ghetto? We've all just given up. Instead of looking for a goal outside these sordid neighborhoods, we've turned against each other and made each other the enemy. There are too many young gang members with not enough left to do, not enough left to look forward to, and, above all, not enough left to eat.

A small group of thugs marches toward the corpses, their stringy arms and emaciated torsos an unhealthy shade of graying brown, visible through their wide sleeveless shirts. Danger could erupt at any second, as my morning collides with the end of their night, so I slide down on the back seat of the empty bus, hoping they haven't seen me. They tug the automatic weapons out of the dead men's hands as the bus rides by calmly, its computer brain not realizing the danger I'm in. I swivel in my seat to peer through the back window and my eyes meet with one of the young men. He raises his rifle to shoot me, but someone calls him just then and he runs to catch up with his gang. I watch them go, my heart pounding.

I can't face spending another minute in this neighborhood. The grittiness, the violence, the hostility are getting to me. The fact that I'm forty-three and childless is exceptional here and they envy me and resent me in equal measure. That's not even mentioning the fact that I have a job in the white, privileged neighborhood, outside the squalor of downtown St. Louis. None of them like me much. None of them except Jada, but she's dead now.

I'm leaving today, I reason, I won't have to bear this much longer.

And what if I am on a plane out of St. Louis in three hours' time?

I'll still be stuck in 2082.

I looked up my future as soon as I arrived in 2081 but I couldn't find any traces of myself in Baltimore in 2017. No DeAnn Carpenter received any awards for genetic research, there's no millionaire by that name who made it through a long string of stock market wins. No one by that name owns property in the Baltimore area. It's worrisome.

But we'll find a way to go back. We must. I am *not* spending the rest of my life in this fucking horrible future. So I have to pull myself together and find out everything I can about the Mass Sterilization Agent. If I can't prevent it from being deployed in 2082, I will have to go back to 2017 and prevent it from ever being invented.

I get to my lab at 5.17 a.m.

I'm the first one here.

Olivia's stint at the UN has at least produced some results. It was a stupid risk to take, but at least it shook the tree. Poor Woody. GeneX has been scrambling since the near-miss with the UN leak.

They're gathering all the data about the Mass Sterilization Agent and tying up loose ends, making sure that all the information about the experiments is centralized in one place: my lab. I've taken advantage of the fact to gather a file of my own with all the information we'll need.

I hurry to my workstation and download all of the information from the network cache where I've hidden it. I don't think I can find out anything more than I already have. Dick has been gone for weeks now. I wonder what happened to him. I empty my locker, retrieve the precious leather notebook and go back to sit at my cubicle. The progress bar on my screen is moving excruciatingly slowly.

While I wait for the data to download, with my finger I trace Enok's painting in the journal, remembering Kitsa, Dr. Eskelin and Rosebell. Maybe their sacrifices will not be in vain, if I can bring this information back to 2017. Perhaps I can even save their lives, even if I will never see them again.

Only 80 percent of the download done; just a few minutes more. My leg twitches anxiously. Come on, come on. I have a plane to catch.

The office feels eerie. Lights keep turning on when I move, then turning off when I stay immobile for too long. My foot taps up and down. I check my backpack. I've put everything I own in it. It's not much but at least it's more than what I had when we fled Uganda.

A noise.

I stop and hold my breath.

Silence.

There's no one there.

My breath flutters out and I resume my anxious watch. 90 percent complete. I need to talk to Olivia about her plan. How are we going to get back to London and when? She's being very vague. She's thought of something but can't talk about it over the phone. I hope it's a real plan.

Finally, the download is done. I put my backpack on my shoulders, wipe my prints off my desk and armrests and check that I'm not forgetting anything. I can't hide my face from the cameras, but at least I can make sure I don't leave any additional clues. My cover will probably be blown after today but I'll never come back here anyway.

I hurry toward the exit and, on a hunch, take the back stairs down. As I arrive on the ground floor, I start to open the door and prepare my badge when I hear movement by the elevators. 5.45 a.m.; it's still way too early to be my colleagues. I freeze, push the fire door ajar and peer through the gap.

A dozen soldiers wearing black combat gear, guns strapped to the side of their thighs, are in the elevator lobby. They surround two men; one of them has his back to me but I recognize Dick's obese form and his greasy comb-over.

Dick seems to have shrunken somehow. He was gone for months. What did he say to them that made them release him? I risk a peek at the uniforms. Police? GeneX internal security? They look military to me. Whoever they are, it seems they've wiped the smugness off—

Any small pleasure I felt at teaching Dick a lesson ebbs away when he turns around. His face is unrecognizable; part of it has been melted.

'I swear to you, I swear to you!' he pleads, unable to wipe the snot from his face because of his bound hands. The hideous folds of liquefied flesh are flushed red. One of his eyes is trapped in swirls of burnt skin, pulled downward by the disfigurement. For the first time, I feel a twinge of remorse for what I did. I shouldn't have sent the data from his computer. He wasn't supposed to get hurt.

The armed men shove him forward, maneuvering him by the scruff of his neck as my former manager whimpers and flinches.

The leader is hidden by Dick's massive shape. He speaks in a low deep voice. I can't hear what he says.

'I had no idea, I swear to you!' Dick replies. 'How could I have known? I'll show you where she sits. She usually comes in early. You'll be able to catch her. I swear to you I didn't know.' He recoils when the slap connects with his maimed cheek and I feel another stab of guilt.

The elevator doors ping open and the armed unit walks in. The soldiers' leader comes gradually into view, bringing up the rear.

When I see his face, I inhale sharply and throw myself against the wall, in the darkness of the emergency staircase.

It's Colonel Groebler.

The Programme has found me.

OLIVIA

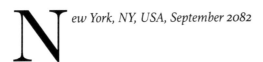

New York, NY, USA, September 2082

MICHAEL OPENS the box and inside it is a diamond engagement ring.

In a flash, I remember Martin and how unhappy I felt back then; it seems like a lifetime has passed since those miserable days, but it was only a year ago. Martin and I had nothing in common, nothing to talk about. He took pride in the fact that he never read books, never watched the news, never understood anything. How can one value wilful ignorance? The only things he cared about were his appearance, his comfort and his entertainment. Why did I even want to be with him? Maybe I didn't love him after all. Maybe I was just afraid of being alone.

But then is this any different? Maybe I'm just afraid of going back to 2017 and being alone for the rest of my life. Maybe this isn't love either, just infatuation and desperation mixed together in a dangerous cocktail that could lead to bad decisions. How does one know the difference?

All my married friends make it look so easy. They don't seem to ask themselves the same endless questions that I do. They just picked a guy in their twenties and never looked back. Now they're all in their forties, married, with children, houses and sensible jobs. Normal.

I too wanted to move to the next stage. I too wanted just to pick a guy and build something. But somehow, for a reason I can't understand, I was stuck. Always stuck. Always at the stage of 'will he like me as much as I like him'? Eternally in high school, waiting to be seen, waiting to be chosen.

Now, at last, someone sees me, someone has chosen me.

Hands still clasped over my mouth, I'm not looking at the ring, I'm watching Michael, this wonderful man who is giving me everything I've ever dreamed of.

He deserves to know.

He's looking expectantly at me, a worried look replacing hope on his lovely face.

'Michael,' I say, gathering my resolve.

'Oh God. You're going to say no, aren't you?' He looks crestfallen.

I slide to my knees next to him and kiss his beautiful lips. Loving him at this moment more than I've ever loved anyone.

'Michael, you remember I told you that I have to leave in one month, right?'

The hand that holds the ring box falls at his side, as he stares at me, horrified. 'Yes, you said. End of October. I thought... I thought.'

I hesitate. 'There's something I need to tell you.'

'You have a boyfriend.'

I shake my head.

'A husband?' He lowers his head, looking dejected.

'No, no.' My fingers alight on his bearded cheek, careful and gentle.

'So why do you have to go back to England? Stay with me, Sinclair.'

He doesn't even know my real name. This isn't fair to him.

'I can't.' I bite my lower lip. As I look at his kind face I know have to come clean. 'Do you know about the Programme, Michael?'

'What does this have to do with—'

'Just humour me, please.'

'Yes. I've heard far-fetched rumours, absurd stuff,' he says, deep in thought, 'that GeneX are using a technology that was procured by the Programme on a trip to the future. But that's just an urban legend. Everyone knows that time travel is not scientifically possible.'

'It is possible.' I take a big breath and dive in. 'Michael... I'm not just going back to England in October. I'm going back to my own time.'

He chuckles and looks up, meeting my eyes. When he sees that I'm dead serious his smile falters. 'What the fuck—'

'I'm a Programme agent.'

Seeing that I'm not joking, he gets up and starts pacing, running his hand in his curly hair repeatedly, looking at me, as I get up too.

'Is this a joke? What are you talking about? Because if it is, I have to say—'

I cut across him. 'It's not a joke, I'm very serious, Michael. I want you to know the truth, so that you'll understand that I'm leaving because I must, not because I—'

I don't get a chance to finish, he's already asking the next question. 'Did you come from the future?'

'No, no.'

'But where...' he falters, '...when are you from?'

'In October, I'll go back to the year 2017.'

He stops pacing and looks at me, eyes wide. 'Are you for real, Sinclair?'

'I swear to you, Michael. It's true. I was born in 1974.'

'Wow.' He sits down hard on the armchair, shaking his head, which he holds between his hands. 'My fiancée is a time traveller.'

I can't help but smile.

I know it's silly, but he said fiancée.

He sits back and looks up at me curiously. Then he pulls me down on his lap and cups my cheek.

'So you're a hundred and eight years old. You look pretty good for an old lady.'

'You're OK with this?'

'Are you kidding? You're my dream come true, Olivia. I have a thousand questions.'

I sigh with relief and laugh. 'I can't answer anything confidential—'

He interrupts: 'Oh no, no, not about the Programme. Tell me, what did lobster taste like?'

I laugh, it's such a Michael question; I start to answer but he's already moved to the next questions.

'Where did you live? What was it like to breathe clean air? Did you ever see a penguin? What did peach skin feel like, was it really fuzzy? Did you ever ride the Orient Express? Which president was in power when you left?'

I laugh and hug him fiercely, loving the comfortable, broad-shouldered presence of him. He kisses me and starts another round of excited questions.

28

DEANN

*S*t. Louis, Missouri, USA, September 2082

AS SOON AS the elevator doors close, I run across the lobby, the heavy pack bouncing against my back, palms tingling. I skid to a halt in front of the entrance and hesitate. Maybe they've disabled my badge.

I don't know any other way out of the building and in the time it might take me to find another, they could catch me. If my badge still works, I'll be out of the building and on my way to the airport in a few minutes. It's worth the risk.

I need to make a decision, right now.

Holding my breath, I swipe my iMode. For what seems like an eternity, nothing happens. Heart pounding, I dance from one foot to the other and start to fumble with my bracelet. It didn't work.

I'm backing away from the revolving glass doors when all of a sudden an alarm starts to blare. Shit.

Red lights flood the lobby, pulsating angrily as the siren tears through the morning's silence.

Adrenaline courses in my veins as my legs snap into motion and I sprint to the side entrance.

Locked as well.

I try to push my way through, my shoulder pressed against the gate, in vain. Panicking, I step away and look for another exit. I can't see any.

The siren shrieks, reverberating inside my skull as I throw myself against the door, getting increasingly desperate and succeeding only in bruising my shoulder.

I run back to the elevators.

Maybe I could... All thoughts fly out of my head as I notice, horrified, the numbers scrolling rapidly downwards. Shit. They're coming back. I'm trapped.

Pressing the elevator button repeatedly, I glance over at the reception lobby, as fear and indecision rise and panic robs me of my faculties. Should I try to break the revolving glass doors? Should I stay here and attempt to catch the elevator to another floor? They'll catch me if I stay here any longer. There's nowhere to hide in the lobby.

Dread soars in my chest as I throw anxious glances over my shoulder, imagining I hear footsteps. OK, fuck this.

I run to the fire escape and barge onto the cement stairwell, nearly slamming the door against the wall in my hurry.

I didn't imagine the sound of footsteps. They're here!

I run downstairs, jumping the stairs two by two, the rucksack slapping on my back with every panicked step. Half falling, I catch myself on the bannister and keep going, panting, my breath burning in my throat.

The only thing I can hear, the only thing that matters is the sound of boots thumping against the stairs a few floors above my head.

Yells erupt in the staircase, echoing along the cement walls.

'Find her!'

'Unit one, with me! Unit two, cover all exits!'

I hurtle down the steps, nearly twist my ankle and fall to my knees on the landing.

The door says LOWER GROUND 5.

I don't think my badge allows me to enter or exit this floor. Fuck. I'll be stuck in there like a rat in a box. Once I go in, my badge won't allow me out. But I'm about to run out of stairs.

I hesitate for a beat, then open the door as quietly as possible and slink inside the dark parking lot, losing a few precious seconds to close the door soundlessly behind me.

My breath seems impossibly loud. The parking lot smells of rubber and oil. Dark puddles spread across my path so I step carefully around to avoid them; I can't leave any trace.

The door slams open.

'Search this floor. I'll go to the next one.'

Bent at the waist, I run as quietly as possible. Hiding behind the parked cars, as I try to near an exit, knowing that it's pointless, as I won't be able to open the gate.

Maybe I should hide in a car. Although they'll find me sooner or later. My instinct is telling me to keep running.

Someone else is breathing in here. A set of boots is running on the asphalt, the rattle of a machine gun rhythmically punctuating the man's run.

Finally I see it. The exit. There's a badge reader on a pedestal next to the main car gate and a smaller one a few lanes down, near the pedestrian door. Creeping in the shadows, I crouch behind the closest parked van and turn around to try and locate my pursuer. I can't hear him anymore. Shit.

The gate is so close. I force myself to look behind me, to scan the shadows in search of my pursuer, but my eyes keep snapping back to the exit. So close and yet completely out of reach. I need to try at least. I can't just let them catch me.

I'm playing nervously with my iMode when the idea comes.

Of course.

Shanice's badge.

Creeping round the GeneX van, I swipe her badge and try the trunk's handle. It clicks open.

Searching for anything that could help, I retrieve a lug wrench and close the trunk, wincing at the muted sound.

My heart is pounding so hard that I'm certain my pursuer must be able to hear its beat. Moving slowly, I pad around the vehicle, running my hand along the van door and slide my fingers in the handle. It opens as well, so holding my breath, I get in and lying down on the front seat, I push the start button. It starts noiselessly. Electric.

Releasing my breath, I swipe Shanice's badge and program the GPS to drive to the first location that comes to mind. The *Awakening,* the statue in Chesterfield where I once met with Jada pops in my mind, it's out of the way and random. Perfect.

I let the door close and, clutching the lug wrench tightly against my chest, I lie low and try my best to stay hidden. The van rides out of the parking spot and approaches the gate.

As my van approaches the barrier, a short burst of thunderclaps explodes in the cavernous underground space and the driver's door is riddled with bullets, the metal shrieking as the projectiles shred through it.

By all rights, I should be dead.

But I wasn't in the van.

Hidden in the dark behind the row of other company vehicles, I observe the telltale flare of the gun and I wait, quiet as a shadow, for the man to leave his hiding spot.

While he runs to the van, yelling for back up in his iMode collar, I move with deliberate slowness, leaving the backpack leaning against a column as I approach him from behind, gripping the lug wrench tightly in my hand.

My attacker rounds the side of the idling vehicle. He opens the door and jumps back to take aim with one hand on his Glock. When he steps away from the van, I run at him from behind and just as he turns toward the sound of my footsteps, I hit him on his right temple my improvised weapon. The metal rod connects with a dull crack and I waver for a fraction of a second.

My moment of hesitation is all the man needs to recover, his gun arm swings toward me and he aims. But before I have time to form a thought, my hand tightens on the lug wrench and I hit his wrist as hard as I can. He bellows as his hand goes limp and he drops his firearm.

The gun skitters away and as the assassin scrambles to pick it up, I swing the lug wrench down, whacking him on the back of the head. He falls down and stops moving.

Hoping that I haven't killed him, I pick up the Glock that's lying, near his bloody face. It's fingerprint locked. Disgusted, I pop the magazine, remove the chambered round and throw it all as far as I can. I hear the pieces skid in the dark as I grab my backpack and run to the pedestrian door and use my assailant's pass to open the door.

Outside, police cars are skidding to a halt in front of the building, their red and blue lights mixing with the red lobby alarm. A crowd of onlookers is gawping at the reception lobby and I catch a glimpse of the soldiers in black, running out to meet the cops. I tug a cap out of my pack and pulling it low over my face, walk calmly away, hoping that if anyone checks my badge they will mistake me for Shanice.

29

DEANN

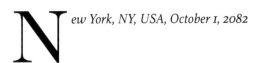 *ew York, NY, USA, October 1, 2082*

I DIDN'T USE my plane ticket and instead managed to get a bus out of St. Louis, then hitch-hiked part of the way, walked some of it and at last made it back to Manhattan days later, exhausted and grimy but alive.

When I finally arrive in front of Olivia's building, hesitation and fear grip me as I stand in the cold night. Observing the entrance from across the street, I ponder what to do and bite the inside of my cheek.

Once all my research was sent to the untraceable Resistance cloud, I had to ditch the iMode. I feel vulnerable without the device and more importantly, I haven't been able to send Olivia word and I haven't had any news from her since Saturday. For all I know, she's dead and the Programme is waiting to jump me as soon as I step into her room.

Pushing aside any questions, I pick the lock on the back door that leads to the servants' quarters and let myself into the silent building, flinching at every sound.

My feet sink into the thick red carpet, as I ascend the creaky stairs under cover of darkness. Everybody's asleep. She said she had a small room under the eaves of a Manhattan building. I didn't realize it was a freaking lime-stone townhouse.

This place looks like it's frozen in time, cocooned in a bubble of luxury and contentment. It's surreal to be here after what I've witnessed on the road. Mass exodus, entire homeless families starving by the roadside. Water scarcity starting to bite. People on the verge of rioting.

Wishing I had a gun, I hold my flashlight in front of me, as I reach the landing. In the narrow cylinder of light, a few doors appear and I tiptoe along the threadbare runner, looking for number five.

There.

I rap gently on the door, under the brass number.

There's movement inside.

Heavy footsteps on the creaky floorboards.

A man's voice whispering something.

Shit. I'm too late. They got to her.

I grab the flashlight tightly, lifting it above my head like a club and wait, my back pressed against the wall.

The door inches open and a male hand holding a knife comes into view. I swing down the torchlight and when the man yelps and drops the weapon, I jump inside and on top of him, lifting the torchlight again to bash his head in.

Just at that moment, light floods the room and a familiar voice exclaims, 'DeAnn! Oh my God! You're back.'

In the stark light, the situation takes on a completely new meaning. The man I'm straddling is chubby, his horn-rimmed glasses have been knocked askew by our tussle and he's wearing nothing but his boxer shorts. His hairy chest is heaving with fright as he stares at me, speechless.

Abruptly conscious of my appearance, I scramble off his naked thighs and stand up awkwardly. Feeling like an intruder, I'm rooted to the spot, not sure what to do with my flashlight, when Olivia falls into my arms and hugs me fiercely.

I hate hugs. But I just let her embrace me and midway through, I realize that I needed that one badly.

She dispatches Pudgy and in the end he agrees to leave, still looking unsure and protective. Olivia seems delighted that I'm back. She gives me her iMode, so I can access the bathroom on the landing and I take the mother of all showers, probably costing her a huge chunk of her weekly budget. When I come back, she's laid out some clothes and as I emerge from her tiny bedroom my jaw drops when I see what she's holding: a bottle of red wine and some chocolate.

'How? How did you...'

'Not saying,' she beams. Her silly mood is contagious; I smile, feeling unaccountably happy to see her.

A few moments later, we settle down on the small sofa and as I wrap myself in the unfamiliar cardigan, she uncorks the bottle. The beautiful sound it makes, as it pops out, lifts my spirits already. This is an incredible treat. I haven't had wine in nearly a year. There are no grapes anymore, so the only wine left is very old. Very rare. Very expensive.

'To life's little twists,' she says, lifting her glass as a relieved smile spreads on her face. She always looks like that when she's happy – a big grin and dimpled full cheeks.

I drink my first swallow with relish, savoring the deep taste of tannin and allowing myself to relax as she brings me up to date on her progress.

We catch up until the small hours of the morning. I tell her about the medical tests on the Chinese, the Sámi, the Bolivians. I tell her about the women I met in St. Louis and the desperation there. I tell her what I saw on the road: the drought, the civil unrest, the mass exodus. And Groebler.

'How did he find you?'

'I don't think he was looking for me, actually. I've had time to puzzle it out on my way back.'

I gather my thoughts and share my deductions with her. 'The R and D facility I worked for was experimenting with technology brought back by Programme agents. They must have had automated alerts in place, which were triggered when the data was sent outside the firewalls.'

'So they thought Dick was a corporate spy or something?'

'Probably. But if they didn't know I was there when they first arrived in St. Louis, they sure know now. My face is all over the CCTV cameras.'

'Oh bugger.'

She tells me about the leak, about Woody, about the government pulling the strings of GeneX. We try to make sense of it all.

'What I don't understand,' she says, after we'd brought each other up to speed, 'is why the US let it get to this point, instead of simply encouraging populations to slow down their fertility. How is deploying the toxin even compatible with their Christian views?'

I shrug. 'They never had much issue with the concept of protecting fetuses while massacring adults in their droves through police brutality, mass incarceration and the death penalty.'

'But why even go to those lengths? Wouldn't it have been easier and more painless simply to offer birth control and family planning to everyone? I remember reading about Iran, where between 1988 and 2009 they managed to reduce fertility from 5.5 to 1.7 children per woman just by making it their political, economic, social and cultural top priority. And, I mean, Iran is hardly a Scandinavian country, they're not exactly famous for their progressive mentality when it comes to women. Yet they managed. So surely others could as well.'

'You're a foreigner, you just don't get it, Olivia. It's a race thing. The government doesn't want to reduce Americans' fertility. They just want to get rid of my people.'

'Oh.' She pauses as pity spreads across her face.

We stay silent for a while. She pours us more wine.

'It no longer matters anyway,' I say, feeling dejected. 'I don't think anything can stop the downfall of humanity at this point. There's just not enough food and water to sustain us all, and even if by some miracle our species makes it, we'll have decimated the environment in the process. It's just too late to do anything.' I swallow the rest of my glass to fend off the hopelessness that's creeping through me. We have less than four weeks left before our chips activate and we have to be inside the Pyramid. It's impossible.

'Well, maybe it's not too late...' Olivia says, taking a small sip of her drink.

'Do you know something I don't? Because last I checked, the Pyramid was still in Cambridge, deep in the Programme's bowels. They're trying to kill us, in case you haven't noticed, so it's slightly unlikely they'll let us use their device and send us merrily on our way.'

She gets a faraway look in her eyes. 'I've been thinking of something. Something I saw a long time ago.'

Then she tells me her plan.

I sit back and stare at her.

Damn. This could actually work.

We stay silent for a long time, each one lost in our own dreams.

The night is dark and silent, and it feels like we're in an island of golden light and warmth in the middle of a nightmarish world. Maybe we can go home after all. The tantalizing thought spreads its tendrils of hope all through me as I glance at her fondly. Olivia Sagewright. Who could have predicted she'd be so full of surprises.

'So who's the nerdy beefcake?' I ask.

'Mmmh?'

She blushes. Seriously. No poker face whatsoever. Some things never change. I roll my eyes and smile.

'The guy who's obviously putting a spring in your step, a smile on your lips. You know – chubby, naked, knockout guy. And when I say knockout, I don't mean—'

'OK, OK, OK.' She chuckles, holding up her hands. 'That's Michael.'

Her eyes dart to a small case on the coffee table. I follow her gaze and raise my eyebrows. Before she can spirit it away, I snatch the box and open it. An engagement ring sits ensconced in a puffy red velvet cushion. It's a retro setting. A simple platinum band with a princess cut. Simple but a good carat size.

Wow. I didn't expect that. She's gone and gotten herself a freaking fiancé. I should probably exercise some caution. Reigning in my usually blunt self, I try to find the positive in this madness.

'It's nice. Not one of those sky diamonds made from CO_2 pollution that they wear nowadays.'

'Yes,' she smiles. 'Michael likes vintage stuff.'

'So, you've been busy...' I prompt, tentatively.

I just don't want her to get hurt again. I wished her harm

when we were in Uganda. I wished Burke would hurt her, so she'd toughen up and learn. Now I just want her to stay safe and be happy and this seems like a spectacularly bad idea.

'It just sort of happened—'

'You know, I get it, Olivia – that you want a man.' With deliberate care, I try to find the right words. 'But maybe this particular one... you know, it could get complicated... with the time travel and the fact that we're leaving in less than a month and all.'

She bites her lower lip, looking miserable. 'I know. It's just... I really like him. He's a good person.'

'Yeah, OK, but being nice is a basic requirement. It's not a plus, it's a must-have. Why this guy? I know you want love and babies and a white picket fence, but you can find someone else and do it in 2017. I mean, it's a terrible idea and there are already enough of us as it is. But if you absolutely have to, do it back home.'

'But it's not that easy!' she exclaims. 'It's so frustrating when you can do everything you set out to do, you know? Get a job, buy a house, take a trip. Easy. You just decide to do it and make it happen. But when you want love, companionship, you need someone else to agree to give it to you. You need someone else to want you.'

'You can find another guy. You're smart, you're self-sufficient...'

'Michael isn't interchangeable. I can't just switch off my feelings and find another. I love *him*. And for once, I've found someone who is worth it and who actually wants me; not someone thinner or smarter or younger. He wants *me*.'

'You can't be serious. You're going to say yes?'

'I haven't answered him yet.'

'You can't do this, Olivia. It's madness. Why would you even want to stay in this dreadful future?'

'You could go back on your own. You've got this. I can give you all the information I've gathered at the law firm. You're the one who understands the scientific stakes of the toxin and that's what matters the most, isn't it? I'll help you to get back. I'll go there with you to see you off.'

'OK, fine – thanks and all. But who knows what could happen to you if you stay? This is irrational. What if I go back and change this future? What-his-face's parents might never meet. He might never be born.'

'I know. Huge risks. I know,' she says. 'But I need to try. This is everything to me. If I'm never going to have a husband and children, then what am I for? Why would I go back to 2017? Nobody loves me there. My existence is hollow and meaningless. I want to be a wife and a mother, and if I can achieve that in 2082, then I must try.'

I'm shocked. 'How can you define yourself only by what you are to others? A wife and a mother? That's not enough. Don't you want more?'

'I had a career, a house, money. I had "more" but it's all meaningless to me without love. Don't you get it?'

Jordan's kind face flickers in my mind's eye. I've always thought of him as a friend, but for some reason I remember now the time he came to visit me, years ago, when I had the flu. I'd been bedridden for days, my temperature flirting with 105°F. I'd run out of food by that point and as I got worse, I started to worry about not being able to visit a doctor and having no one to call for help.

He'd been the only one who cared. The only one to come over with chicken soup and oranges, the only one who I allowed to see me weak. He was a good man and I missed my chance with him. Back in 2016, I had everything I could ever want; success, material comfort, professional recognition and yet sometimes I felt it too, the emptiness she describes.

I empty the bottle into our glasses and open the chocolate. Perhaps if Jordan and I... Maybe I can understand Olivia after all.

'Well, more power to you,' I say, pensively. 'But what about the kid? Let's say everything goes well, and you and Chubby live happily ever after and have children. What will happen to them? It's a really terrible world here, Olivia. Do you want your kids to grow up in this awful place?'

'It won't be so bad. As long as you have money in this country, you can still get decent food and space enough.'

'But the planet can't take any more people. You've got to think about the bigger picture too.'

'A few more won't change anything.'

'You're part of the problem if you think you can get a pass because you're white and you're wealthy.'

That gives her pause. 'But we can't all just stop having children. We also need to raise the people who are going to make a difference and change the world. What if I can have a positive impact here? Maybe it's not too late. Look, most countries are signing the Beijing Treaty and starting to adopt one-child policies – maybe things will go back to normal in a generation or two.'

How can she be so deluded? I wonder if she'd feel quite so lenient if I'd decided to stay and have babies. Then again, maybe this isn't about the big picture or about race. Maybe this is what hope and faith look like. I wouldn't know. I rely mostly on rationality and logic.

'I just want to grab my chance at happiness. I think he's The One, DeAnn.'

Oh, for God's sake. We're not fifteen anymore. The One. Seriously.

30

OLIVIA

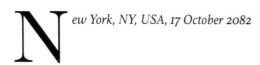

ew York, NY, USA, 17 October 2082

I WAKE UP, with sunlight playing on my face and watch sparkling motes of dust float in a shaft of light. The window is open and a draught of air makes the curtains billow. Michael's arm is draped around me, possessively claiming me in his sleep.

Wonder grips me anew as the jigsaw pieces of the last few days assemble gently in my foggy brain.

Since DeAnn's return, I've been planning and preparing with her every evening at my flat and then joining Michael late into the night at his loft. Our clothes are lying discarded at the foot of the bed and we're naked under a light bed sheet. We had snow last month but now it's 25°C outside and the weekend promises to be glorious. I smile to myself, relishing the softness of his curly chest hair against my naked back, his limbs tangled with mine, his reassuring warmth radiating against my skin.

I always wake up before him and I love these moments before life starts again in earnest. I need the time to think. There are only two weeks left and things are moving fast now. Maybe too fast.

Admitting to Michael's proposal a fortnight ago made it real, but under DeAnn's judgemental eyes I felt like a sentimental idiot. I avoided Michael for a few days after her arrival until he decided to walk me home, his fingers looped in mine, making no comment about the fact that my hands were bare. Still no ring. Still no answer.

We sat on a bench in Central Park, watching the wind rustle in the yellowing leaves, as the trees struggled to decide what season it was. After a long spell of silence, Michael turned to me and tucked a strand of my hair behind my ear, stroking my cheek gently.

'I know you're worried about the fact that you went missing in 2017, Sinclair and I know that you think it means you're probably going to die.'

'Way to ruin the mood, Michael,' I chuckled weakly.

But he looked serious. 'What if there was another reason?'

I had no idea what he was getting at. I'd already discussed all the possible angles with DeAnn. We both seemed to have disappeared without a trace. In all likelihood, it meant that neither of us found our way back, or that we died trying.

'What are you thinking?' I asked, puzzled.

'What if you didn't die? What if you disappeared in 2017 because you never went back?'

'Well yes, that's exactly what I'm afraid of...'

'Hear me out.' He forged on, an earnest look in his eyes.

'What if the reason you never went back was that you'd already accepted my proposal, Olivia... Quisling?'

Maybe I'd already made this decision and there was nothing left to ponder. I just didn't know it yet. Urgh, time travel was doing my head in. Was this all fate? Was everything already written? Hope fluttered in my chest as I tried to make sense of it all. Maybe I'd never come across the right man before because The One was waiting for me here in 2082. Maybe God really did have a plan.

I turned to Michael. This was it. Now or never. My last chance at love, my last chance at a husband, children. Everything I'd ever wanted in my life. Happiness was there at the tip of my fingers if only I summoned to courage to grab for it.

'Oh, Michael...' I flew into his arms and through a haze of happy tears, whispered in his ear, 'Yes! Yes, yes, I'll marry you.'

THE CURTAIN SWELLS like a sail and the movement brings me back to the bed and Michael's soft embrace. I'm really doing this, I'm really staying. I raise my left hand for the hundredth time this week. The sun plays with the diamond, throwing sharp rainbows across the room as yesterday's news comes into focus in my sleepy brain.

I'd been waiting for a week for the results, so when I picked up my Mode yesterday evening, I'd been checking my inbox obsessively every few minutes for days, by that point, waiting for the verdict. And finally late last night, the email appeared. My palms started to sweat and my stomach dropped as I opened the message. My eyes skipped over the paragraphs as I tried to read the words faster, tried to guess what it would say.

Healthy. Fertile.

Relief and excitement burst like a thousand champagne bubbles in my chest. I re-read that small sentence: '85 percent chance of success'. The email went on: there was apparently just one treatable issue that a small operation could fix.

The condition was discovered only ten years ago and there are very few places where you can get the operation, as most countries don't facilitate medical procreation anymore. I happen to work a few blocks from the best clinic in the world for this procedure; it's where I had the tests done.

My mind wanders and I dream about what this could mean. Maybe it isn't too late after all. Not too late to cook together in a sun-drenched kitchen, Michael's arms wrapping around me from behind as he kisses my neck. Not too late to hear the pitter-patter of tiny feet running down steps. Maybe it will be a little girl, with brown curly hair like his, who will chase after our dog, laughing. Maybe it's not too late to wake up in Michael's arms every day for the rest of my life and, still sleepy, to feel my heart burst with joy. Maybe it's not too late for this new dream, which feels so familiar yet brand new at the same time.

I wriggle out of bed and go to his kitchen. I was in a splurging mood yesterday after I got the news, so I got two oranges and a tiny pack of real coffee as a surprise for him. He doesn't know about the test results yet, so I want us to celebrate properly when he wakes up. He'll be thrilled, I know how much he wants a family.

I peel the oranges, eat a segment with a smile, and make toast and coffee in the brand new French press. There's just enough for one cup. I make myself a tea and then I arrange everything on a tray and bring it, still naked, to the bedroom.

I put the tray on his bedside table and slip back into his arms as he blinks slowly awake and pulls me close, wrapping his arms around my waist as he spoons me.

'Mornin' gorgeous,' he rumbles, sleep making his voice hoarse. 'This is a nice surprise. I'm pretty sure I didn't have a beautiful redheaded time traveller in my bed when I went to sleep yesterday evening.' He bites my neck and kisses me.

'Your beard tickles, stop it.'

His hand moves to my breast and he plays with my nipple, softly rubbing it until it hardens. Squeaking and giggling, I fidget until I'm facing him. Without his glasses, he looks different, more vulnerable; his eyes are puffy and his curly hair is a mess. He makes gruff sounds and pulls me tightly against him.

I kiss him, scattering little pecks all over his face and then, on impulse, start drawing a path down his torso with my lips. Kissing all the way down to his cock. He takes a sharp breath as I close my lips around him and lick the drop nestled there, its taste mixing with the flavour of orange in my mouth.

31

DEANN

 *ew York, NY, USA, October 23, 2082*

I'M SURROUNDED by a sea of people, shoving me in all directions. Oh joy.

I let myself be carried by the flow and wash up in a huge cathedral-like mall. It's inconceivably large and filled to the brim with a Black Friday crowd on steroids. Standing in the main atrium, buffeted by the distracted shoppers, I stare up at a dozen floors, wondering how far they extend in all directions.

Olivia's plan could actually work and with one week to go, we're nearly ready. I've been cooped up in her room for three weeks and I had to threaten mutiny if she didn't agree to let me run this errand. She looked unsure, but in the end she relented and wired the funds to my account, so I could get some of the supplies myself.

Shaking off my cabin-fever, I walk down the alleys,

happy to be back in civilization. I don't think I could have taken another day in St. Louis, that backwater blighted by recession, invaded by Dust Bowl refugees, full of mediocre people; poor, unsafe, ugly. Good riddance. I feel a twinge, thinking about Jada's kids, and try to squash it. But for some reason, it lingers.

Soaking in the luxury shops, the smartly dressed women, the fast pace and sense of purpose, I try to enjoy my outing, but something seems to be missing. Maybe something like a soul.

I stop for a minute, trying to puzzle out what is wrong with me. Barely a year ago, I would have loved this. Buying a Tod's purse while tipsy on complimentary champagne was my thing. But today, I feel... I don't know...

I want to get rid of all these feelings yet I can't. I carry the sorrow for my lost friends like a chain coiled around my ankle. I can still move and function, but it rattles, it hurts, it's heavy.

The artificial lights make the sordid look glittery. Shiny, beautiful strangers who don't give a flying fuck if I live or die power-walk down the aisles, looping around me in meaningless circles. With a pang, I realize that I would give anything to spend one more hour in the company of my dispossessed, unfashionable, dead friends. This shopping trip is starting to feel like a mistake.

Giant TV screens blare announcements and show images of the news, advertisements and reality TV. It looks like Times Square but it's all around me. Entire walls are moving, filming shoppers as they amble by and superimposing their faces on sylph-like models sashaying down catwalks. The ads swallow up the passers-by, digesting them into their make-believe world of wealth and desire.

Garish, jarring images surround me everywhere I go. It's

as if I'd been sucked through a TV screen into a sugary
world of brightly colored, artificial absurdity. I walk at
random, having forgotten what I'm here for.

Already exhausted by the noise and crowds, I make my
way to the supermarket and find the alley where the guns
are displayed. There isn't any sales person around, so I just
pick up the various types; semi-automatics, automatic rifles,
miniature ladies' guns with hot pink plastic handles, shiny
Dirty Harry guns with absurdly long muzzles.

After a while, I choose a mid-sized gun that fits comfortably in my hand and isn't too heavy. It's a Glock 22 but much
lighter than the 2016 models, as it's made from a plastic and
metal alloy. More importantly, it's advertised as a 'vintage
piece' because it's not fingerprint- or DNA-locked.

I spend another fifteen minutes picking ammunition for
it and debate whether to get a holster but decide against it. I
keep expecting someone to come over. Maybe to ask me if I
need help or whether I have a permit. But I might as well be
picking a blender for all the notice I garner.

There are no cashiers at the exit. So I do a self-checkout
with my burner iMode. The screen asks: 'Paper or plastic?' I
stare at it for a minute and then swipe my iMode, shaking
my head in disbelief.

Now that I'm done, the prospect of going back to lock
myself up in the smelly little hideout is unbearable. For
weeks now, I've pored over the research, surrounded by my
ghosts, drowning myself in the work, coming out only at
night to buy food from small stores. Olivia comes by every
evening and we plot my return, discuss what messages I
should bring back, talk about what she'll do once I'm gone.

I've nowhere to be, so I spend some time window-shop-
ping and people watching. The mall feels surprisingly
familiar. Every surface is shiny and clean, everyone looks

wealthy. Teenage girls move in herds, teenage boys skulk, young mothers try to get their progeny to behave and older people look lonely and lost.

The contrast with St. Louis is doing my head in. After the clinic's near famine conditions, this feels wrong. There is food everywhere here and it is too bright, too shiny, too perfect. There is something completely fake about this place. Maybe I am on a TV set after all and all the food is plastic and all the people are actors.

I eventually drift into the food court and have Chinese. I try not to think too much about what I'm eating. God only knows how they can make General Tso chicken. Maybe it's chicken. Probably not. I eat my meal, sighing as I take in the plastic tray, the plastic plate, the plastic cutlery, the plastic water bottle. Maybe they've already put the toxin in sodas here as well; who knows? I seem to be the only black person here. I listen in on a group of teenagers at the next table.

'Genevieve just took her vow of abstinence yesterday,' one of the girls is saying. I scoff and lower my head. Teenagers and sex are pretty much destined to collide. Not much a chastity ring can do to counter raging hormones.

'Good. How many is that now?' a serious-looking boy asks.

'Ninety-nine percent of the senior class, Myles.'

'Good, good.'

They're exceptionally beautiful. All of them are thin, well dressed, groomed to perfection. The girls have well hydrated, glossy hair that cascades to their waists. Their complexions are diaphanous, clear and healthy. The boys are closely shaven, preppy types. Wiry muscles slide under their immaculately pressed shirts. They're all wearing white from head to toe. Frowning, I glance at their plates; they're eating leafy greens, actual lean meat. No soda. Just water.

They must be spending an arm and a leg on this meal alone. They're so young. I wonder where they get the money.

'They're striking, aren't they?'

An old woman, sat opposite me at the table, stares at me. She's plump and her hair is gray and tied up in a messy bun at the top of her head. There are several long necklaces dangling from her neck into the ample cleavage of her flowery blouse.

'Come again?'

'The Beautiful Ones,' she says with a slight Latino accent, pointing with her chin as she continues to eat her ice cream. 'First time you've come across them?'

I nod, reluctant to make contact. I wasn't supposed to stay out so long. I can already hear Olivia fussing. Curiosity wins, though.

'Who are they? Celebrity kids?'

'No, they're no one special, just youngsters who live in this area.'

'What did you call them?'

'That's just what the media call them: the Beautiful Ones. They had to give that generation a name, I suppose. You know, Baby Boomers, Generation X, Y, Millennials, Alphas. Similar groups are cropping up all over the country. It seems these kids are going to be the next generation.'

'I heard about the Alphas,' I say, thinking about Olivia's encounter with the ultra-violent youth group. 'Are they the same?'

'No, Alphas are just run-of-the-mill rich kids who get bored and act out their aggression on the poor. The Beautiful Ones are different. They're not violent. They're just... I don't know, turned off, I guess.'

'Really?' I ask, interested. 'What are they like?'

'See for yourself,' she shrugs. 'They just stick together,

looking gorgeous, mostly. They don't talk to anyone but each other and they have no interest in sex whatsoever.'

'Oh, that will come.' I smile. 'That chastity vow nonsense usually passes by the time they get to college.'

She finishes her ice-cream cone and throws the young group a distrustful glance. 'Maybe,' she says, dubious. 'They don't feel much of anything. I doubt they'll ever muster enough interest in anyone other than themselves. Sex requires a minimum of interest for the other as an object of desire. These kids just seem to care about food and looking perfect. No one can figure out why.'

The long-limbed, beautiful teenagers get up and move away as one. The crowd parts to let them through. There is a sort of aura around them. They're magnetically attractive but there's also something disturbing about them.

We both watch them walk away.

I turn back toward the old woman and start to ask her, 'Interesting. Do you know whether...'

She's staring at something beyond my shoulder, brows furrowed. I turn around and freeze. My face is plastered on the giant screen behind my seat, with the word 'Wanted' and a phone number to call.

'You should have said you were famous, hija.' Her eyes bore into me as she starts to rummage in her bag.

32

OLIVIA

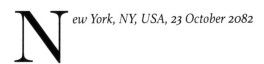

ew York, NY, USA, 23 October 2082

WE'VE TAKEN separate routes to work. He's still not telling anyone about us. I suppress a twinge of anxiety and tell myself it's ridiculous to feel like a mistress. My intestines squirm with apprehension. Am I making the right decision by staying here? Only one week to go before I find out, I suppose.

A hubbub of anxious conversations interrupts my self-absorbed thoughts. My colleagues seem more worked up than usual today. I shouldn't get sloppy in the home stretch. Especially with DeAnn in my flat and Groebler on to us. I need to focus.

'What's happening?' I ask the woman in the cubicle next to mine.

'Big wig from the DoD.'

Michael's voice tickles in my ear: 'Olivia, can you come to Conference Room 162-05, please?'

Michael and I have set up the iModes so that if either of us says the other's name or if we're within a small radius of each other, it translates immediately as a message in his ear bud or mine; it's simpler, as we work so closely on everything together.

'Coming.'

I hurry to the meeting room on the 162nd floor and get in as discreetly as I can. The usual partners are there in a meeting with the Secretary of Defense. Sitting down, I unfold my iMode screen unobtrusively and start to take notes.

'...the Coalition's tried conventional warfare. We've encouraged underdeveloped countries to fight each other and upgraded their arsenal to maximise casualties. We've financed civil wars based on ethnic rivalries, border skirmishes and land grabs. We've facilitated coups by mentally unstable dictators. Believe me, we've tried everything, but over time we've come to realise that these are counterproductive.' Secretary Matthews makes a steeple of his fingers above his bloated stomach.

'How so?' a law firm partner asks.

'Wars always trigger baby booms, so as soon as the conflicts we facilitate are over, the local populace start breeding again and we're back to square one or worse. There's no point in continuing to pour money down the drain, it's pointless. The budget will be better spent importing food. We're abandoning the war-financing strategy altogether.'

'Are you sure you want to proceed? The backlash—'

The Secretary's aide holds his hand up and interrupts the partner who is attempting to speak. 'Look, Tanner, this isn't up for debate. The Coalition is proceeding as per schedule; we have the backing of Australia, Russia and the KEW. As Jensen just pointed out, our tests have been successful. We're going live within the next twenty-four hours.'

'So soon. Should we not wait until—' Tanner starts.

'No,' the grey-suited man interrupts again. 'This is non-negotiable. We have a dozen rogue states and enemies lined up, which need to be kept in check, we just need to pick one to make an example of. The time has come to reveal our hand.'

'It would make our jobs a lot easier if you could manufacture outrage in the public. People will be more willing to accept this if it looks like retaliation for a perceived provocation,' Michael's manager says.

'We've got the perfect red herring in place. We've just suffered a terrorist attack on our embassy in Uganda. We'll use it there. We know that the chemical compound works on the Ugandan population. We've tested it there already, it's the ideal environment for the first tactical deployment.'

I do a quick online search; the newspapers haven't caught wind of the story yet.

'Really? Terrorism against the US, in Africa? That's not happened in years,' Tanner says.

The DoD aide laughs, and it's an unpleasant sound. 'A desperate mob raided the abandoned building for food and water. Our personnel had already been evacuated months ago. But there's enough material damage to the building to justify retaliation. We should do it as soon as the footage hits the press. We've already arranged for the breaking news to be positioned as a top story.'

'That'll work.'

I look up at Bartlett, unable to believe he could be quite

so callous. I've been working with this man for eight months, I thought... I don't know what I thought.

The DoD man nods. 'My team is working on it as we speak. We'll whip up a media frenzy about the "terrorist" act and leak enough information about this to convince the public to support an armed response. Your role is to make sure we've completed all our legal preparations before we use the weapon. We're ready to strike. What we need to know today is what we'll do in case of legal repercussions.'

Michael's manager stays silent for a moment, then says, 'Well, at the very least, the US could be declared in breach of UN resolution A/RES/29/3314, as we are striking a sovereign state without provocation—'

The Secretary of Defense interrupts him: 'That is precisely the reason we hired your firm. Under no circumstances – do you hear me, Bartlett? – under no circumstances must this ever be seen, referred to or interpreted as an act of aggression. This is self-defence pure and simple. We are facing a national security issue, gentlemen. Overpopulation is as serious a threat to our continued survival as a war. Make no mistake, we need to retaliate now before it's too late. If we don't strike them first, they'll kill us, in the long-run. It will be called famine, malnutrition, water shortage, but in fact it'll be their people taking over the world and stealing resources from our children's mouths. It might look cruel but it's a pre-emptive strike to preserve our way of life.' He pauses, his large belly quivering, 'It's us or them.'

I need to do something. Up to now they've only sterilised a few hundred people; could they really deploy this on a national scale? Neuter an entire country? How can they justify hurting these people just because they're a different skin colour? How could that possibly be relevant in any way? We're all one species, one humanity; we need to find a solution all together, not work against each other. Why can't these people see that?

The Defense Secretary's face is impassive and there's something toad-like about him, a slimy coldness that makes me shudder. The movement makes him turn his head slowly and look at me. For the first time, after weeks of meetings, he actually *sees* me. I'm no longer part of the furniture.

Wishing I were still invisible, I lower my eyes, hoping he won't pay me any more attention. It only lasts a few seconds but I'm shaken.

'OK, it's settled then, Mr Secretary. Thank you for letting us know,' Bartlett says, as he gathers his tablet. 'We'll prepare for the public opinion backlash and anticipate any legal defence, as required.'

The meeting finally ends and the DoD team leaves, perhaps to go see a PR team or a polling company. As I walk out, I hear Michael's involuntary 'pop-up' messages in my ear. He doesn't really mean for me to hear this conversation but I do anyway because we're within the pre-established radius.

'Good meeting, John.'

I only hear his side of the conversation, of course, as the device guesses the words he's saying based on the motions of his throat.

'Yes, I agree, the next few days should be interesting.'

'That should bring the price of corn and wheat right down.'

I think back on the conversation he and I have had about the tests being morally wrong. I know what he's doing. He's just maintaining a persona for work. His real opinions are much closer to mine.

Once I'm back on my floor, I retreat to the kitchen and

under cover of making myself a cup of tea, I text A. and DeAnn. 'Toxin deployment today. Uganda is target.'

We've been trying to get the press to publish the story and to alert people to the threat. But unfortunately without the support of UN Under-Secretary-General to give our case credibility, nobody's taking us seriously anymore. Still, we've got to try. DeAnn's burner iMode is the only one we can use without bringing the full weight of the Programme and the Department of Defense on us. So we keep trying to tip off the newspapers. So far, in vain.

'You alright?'

I jump out of my skin.

Work-Michael sounds neutral, pretending we don't know each other that well. I suppress my disappointment. What did I expect? He can't very well kiss me here, in the middle of the bloody office kitchen. I hide my iMode bracelet behind my back and lean against the kitchen counter while he closes the door behind him.

'I... wish there were something I could do. Warn people.' I shake my head, thinking of baby Jonathan. I'll warn the orphanage as soon as I can sneak to the loo undetected.

'I guessed as much.' He shakes his head.

'But you know that it's wrong, don't you? Tell me you know it's wrong.' I say, turning the engagement ring around my finger.

'There is no Right and Wrong, with a capital letter, anymore. That squeamishness is a luxury of another age. The truth is relative. There is nothing you or I could do; we're merely cogs in this machine and it's too late anyway. Let's just keep working for a better world. We can win the next elections. The next government will surely be Democrat. In the meantime, we need to accept the reality we live in and keep our heads down.'

'We shouldn't just do nothing at all. Maybe if I could get the press to—'

'You mustn't, under no circumstances, Olivia,' he whispers, taking my hand.

It's the first time he's touched me in the office. He presses my hand, then lets it go but he stays close.

'Look, things aren't as clear-cut as you think. We need to make compromises. Keep our jobs. They'd have you fired or worse if you breach client–attorney privilege and warn the press. This isn't some movie, we aren't heroes, we're just regular office employees and we need to earn a living, pay our bills, put food on the table.'

He reaches up and tucks a strand of hair behind my ear. I relish the feeling of his fingers wrapped around mine but he sees the doubt in my eyes.

'Try to think of these things like this: when we have children, we'll want to do everything in our power to make sure they have enough food, water, money. We can't afford to question things too much. These people have had every chance to control their fertility. We need to look after our own now, put our country first, our children first.'

He said '*our children*'. Butterflies frolic in my stomach as I take in his warm, affectionate eyes, his beard, his kind face. Maybe he's right.

Is this the kind of moral compromise I'm going to have to make, now that I've decided to stay?

33

DEANN

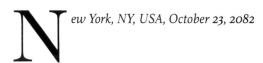

ew York, NY, USA, October 23, 2082

MY GIANT FACE starts to spread on every screen in the mall, like a contagion. It's my GeneX security badge photo. Thankfully, everyone is absorbed in their iBubbles and no one is actually looking at me.

Frozen in place, I stare at the old woman. If she yells, it's over for me. In this crowd, this far away from the exit, I'll never make it. As she rummages in her bag, I stare at her and hold my breath.

She extracts a baseball cap and a pair of sunglasses.

'I just bought these for my tropical vacation.' She snaps the tags and pushes the items on the table, looking me in the eyes. 'They'll suit you. You should try them on.'

I can't find any words. I nod in thanks and put them on, head still down. She smiles and gets up, saying, 'Silly me, I forgot to buy sunscreen. I should go before the mall goes into lockdown.'

I nod, feeling a lump in my throat.

'Don't you hate it when you get stuck in these endless ID check lines?' Then she pads away.

I hurry out of the mall as fast as I can without breaking into a run, my heart thumping. By now, every screen in this place is showing my face. Groebler must have found out that I'm in New York. The net is tightening.

This is probably the only time in my life, I'm happy to find myself at rush hour in public transports; the sweat, the greasy food wrappers, the elbows poking me in the ribs, the heels trampling my toes; I'm grateful for all of it, as I keep my face down and the cap screwed on tight.

The weight of the gun and bullets feels like an anvil, in the plastic bag looped around my wrist. This was too big a risk. We should have sent Chubby to get the weapon, Olivia's boyfriend.

By the time I make it back to Grand Central Station, it is packed with commuters. Their faces empty, they walk forward without stopping, without talking to anyone, isolated in their iBubbles. They shove slower travelers out of the way. Others are not people to them, they're just obstacles. 'Me, me, me' they seem to clamor with their disdainful, hollow faces; their fast, clipped steps urging, 'Faster. Move out of my way. I matter more than you.'

I hurry across the vast gloomy hall. Several centuries of soot permeate the air, coalescing with the cloying heat to form an unbreathable soup. I wend my way through the crowd, jostled and pushed, but when I stop in a corner to catch my breath, I see it. My face on the station's ad boards with text scrolling below it: 'Wanted for questioning', and a number to call.

Damn it. It wasn't a localized scan at the mall. I'm on fucking national TV now.

I stick out like a sore thumb here. The diversity that once made this city great seems to have leaked right out of it. Everyone around me is white. Somebody shoves me and I stumble. I need to extirpate myself from this crowd before someone recognizes me.

Shit. Cops. They're checking the exits.

I hunker down against the wall as fear grips me. I'm trapped.

On the floor at my feet, homeless men and women are lined against the marble walls, shoulder-to-shoulder, hip-to-hip. There must be at least a hundred of them in this hallway alone. The stench of piss, vomit and alcohol is unbearable. I'm starting to get up to make a break for it, when a thin young man tugs my sleeve, gently whispering, 'Get down!'

Two cops appear round the corner, machine guns slung on their shoulders as they walk past us, patrolling the area.

Still crouching, I turn toward the young man to thank him but he gestures for me to sit and I crumple on the flattened cardboard next to him. While I stare anxiously at the hall's to-ing and fro-ing, trying to find an escape, I sense his eyes on me, scanning my face and double-checking it against the billboard behind me.

'It's you, isn't it?'

The BOLO clearly mentions a reward, so I hold my breath and straighten up, getting ready to run. But he pats my arm and extracts a jacket from his pack, which he wraps around my shoulders. Despite the heat and the stench, I let him do it, as understanding slowly dawns on me. He gets up and gestures for me to grab his pack, then he takes the cardboard bed and leans heavily across my shoulder and we limp toward the exit.

When we get to the door, the cops make a disgusted sound and part to let us through.

One of the policemen spits at our feet. 'Get the hell out of here, you fucking scum.'

Keeping our heads down, we continue on to the square outside until we're safely out of range in a side street.

Speechless, I return the stinking jacket and the pack to the young man and with a little gesture, he says goodbye and starts to go down the alley, away from the station.

He really helped me. Just like that old woman. I don't understand why; he had nothing to gain by it. Puzzled, I detail his scrawny figure as he hobbles away, then I turn my head toward the direction I need to go, hesitating.

'Wait!'

I catch up with him and swipe my iMode against his. 'Thank you.'

His eyes widen when he sees the amount and he smiles, then resumes limping slowly to wherever he's going.

I never really paid attention to homeless people before. Why would I have? Now, though, I wonder: who are they? Who were they before? Why did he show me kindness when it would have been less trouble to denounce me? Was that psoriasis on his face? Why isn't the state taking care of these people?

Absurd questions. Who cares? And even if I cared, what could I possibly do about it? Nothing at all. I don't like this change in me. It was more comfortable when I didn't care.

I'm watching the young man's back recede down the small alley feeling bittersweet and jarred when a text message jolts me out of my thoughts, making me flinch.

'Toxin deployment today. Uganda is target.'

34

OLIVIA

ew York, NY, USA, 23 October 2082

I OPEN the door of my tiny flat and call out: 'DeAnn?'

She gestures to me from the sofa.

I remove my coat and my shoes and go sit next to her; she's in her bubble but when she sees me, she presses a button on her iMode collar and Dr Herault's face appears on the TV screen, as DeAnn's bubble retracts.

'Yes, Doctor Herault, it's what we discussed a few weeks ago. Were you able to convince the Ugandan media to publish the story? Did you manage to evacuate the hospital?'

'No, DeAnn,' the doctor replies. 'It was impossible. The press isn't interested in incurring libel lawsuits from multinational companies. Uganda's government has pretty much disintegrated and could never have stood up to the US's full might even if it hadn't. Headquarters said that they were not aware of any imminent threat and that, in any case, it's not in our NGO's remit to evacuate locals. Our mission is to help people where they are.'

'But Annaëlle—' DeAnn starts.

'Are you sure it's really happening?' Dr Herault inter-rupts. 'I've put my reputation on the line for you, DeAnn, and as you can see, everything is fine here.'

'Doctor Herault,' I chime in, 'what are you still doing there? Are you still in Kampala? I can't believe it.' I turn to DeAnn. 'Didn't you explain everything to her?'

'I did,' DeAnn says, frustrated.

The French doctor looks dubious. 'I can't believe anyone would be capable of unleashing a Mass Sterilisation Agent on an entire country and, anyhow, the technology doesn't actually exist,' she says. 'I have a lot of work to do and I need to terminate this call now. You can call again in a few hours if you like.'

DeAnn is more agitated than I've ever seen her before. 'Annaëlle, you've got to eva—'

The roar of low-flying planes erupts, drowning out our voices, and Dr Herault runs out to the clinic's front porch to look up at the sky. Through her iBubble, we see the clinic behind her and all the people's faces turned upwards. People are pointing and shouting at each other, over the noise.

'Holy Mary, mother of God,' I say quietly.

'Can you see?' Dr Herault asks, flipping the viewpoint, so we see the same thing as her.

Small ogival objects fall from the planes' bellies. There are hundreds of them. They look like a swarm of black insects but as they get closer to the ground they seem to grow in size until we can see that they're bombs. What on earth? The Sterilising Agent is normally laced in liquids, what's this?

Dr Herault points to the missiles, speaking in rapid Luganda to the people in front of the clinic, gesturing for them to come inside. They look at her confused. A handful start to run.

The high-pitched whistling sound increases in shrillness. Dr Herault screams orders and runs outside towards her patients just as two of the bombs strike the front yard's beaten dirt. There's a huge detonation and a wave of red dust and shrapnel explodes outward in all directions.

Dr Herault is knocked off her feet and for a moment, we only see the sky.

So blue.

We hear her struggle with her breath.

Then, hundreds of voices start to shriek in agony all around her.

I grab DeAnn's hand, pressing it hard in mine, eyes riveted to the bright blue screen.

Yells turning into moans.

A flock of bird flies across the blue sky above Dr Herault's iMode.

Then silence.

35

DEANN

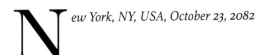

ew York, NY, USA, October 23, 2082

'DOCTOR HERAULT? Doctor Herault? Are you alright?' Olivia is on her feet, shouting, as if trying to reach the French doctor through the TV screen.

'Annaëlle, are you OK?'

My friend moves, and, as she sits up, the sky disappears. In front of her, the patients who were pointing toward the sky a minute ago are lying motionless. The old doctor hurries to the side of a young man who is writhing on the packed dirt floor, clawing at his face. It's as if the air he breathes is on fire and he's trying to scratch his nose and his mouth off. As Dr. Herault tries desperately to treat him, the man spasms and a pink foamy discharge spurts onto his chin.

A few yards away, a gaunt woman is on her knees, throwing up, but as the French doctor tries to assist her, she collapses and goes into convulsions as well. The child next to her is choking on blood-streaked foam, his wheezing agony unbearable to watch. They're nearly all lying on the floor, backs arched, faces contorted in agony.

Alerted by the screams, the hospital staff runs into the courtyard, but as soon as they reach the entrance, they collapse, scratching at their throats as well. We follow Dr. Herault as she hurries inside.

We hear her pant as she runs.

We see her hands closing door handles and window latches.

We run from room to room with her, as she tries to look for her patients, her colleagues.

But they're already dead.

All of them.

She walks into an operating room. A patient is lying on the table, her abdomen still splayed open for her operation. She's clearly dead. The nurse and surgeon are my friends, I recognize them. They've collapsed on the operating room floor. Their chins stained with vomit and blood.

Dr. Herault approaches them, tries to shake them awake. My hand tightens around Olivia's as I itch to shake them too. We've both turned to stone, standing in front of the monitor, unable to sit, unable to talk.

Dr. Herault takes the surgeon's pulse, then that of the nurse and the patient. Nothing. She frantically wipes the pink foam off her fingers stifling a sob and then she walks to the next room. We hear her muttering incoherently to herself in French.

She hurries from room to room, trying to shake my friends and colleagues awake, until finally she reaches the staff room. Someone moves. My heart leaps with hope. Someone's still alive!

'Andreas! *Tu es vivant!*'

It's the German doctor who mended Kitsa's arm. He's bent over someone, checking their vitals. He turns as Annaëlle enters the room and I recognize the woman he's trying to help, it's the nurse who yelled at me the day I met Omony. She's dead.

Andreas walks straight over to the old French woman and wraps her in his arms. For a long while, we only see the fabric of his stained white coat shaking, as he's wracked with sobs. Finally his lined face comes into view.

'Annaëlle, are you on the iMode? Can these people send help? Do they know what's going on?' he says.

Dr. Herault breathes in and she flips the iBubble's point of view again. The old woman's face is covered in the court-yard's red dust and streaked with tears, forming rivulets from her eyes to her chin.

'DeAnn, are you still there?' My friend's voice is shaking and she looks ten years older.

'We're here, Annaëlle.' I sound odd, husky.

'I didn't believe you. I didn't... I could have...' Annaëlle says, crying.

'There's nothing you could have done,' Olivia says gently.

'How...Why are Andreas and I still alive?'

My mouth works but no words come out. I can't bring myself to say what my mind is thinking. But finally the words come out, even though I don't want them to. It's as if saying it aloud will make this nightmare real.

'It must be a genetic weapon that only targets a specific DNA profile. You're both white.'

'Everybody else...' the old woman starts and falters, 'everybody else will...'

'Die. Yes.'

'I need to go, DeAnn. I need to check.'

She hangs up. Olivia and I look at each other.

The world feels like a colder, darker place.

Olivia slumps down on the sofa and turns on the news. The massacre is splattered there, on a loop, on all the news channels. Just as they planned. Just like Olivia said they would. The supposed terrorist attack on the American embassy, the self-defence gambit, the convincing lies about retaliation. White reporters drift through the streets of Kampala, trying to find survivors. We watch all night. They find none. Not a single one.

Olivia and I stay up, unable to stop watching, wiping angry tears away. The massive death toll keeps rising all night, as news trickle in of several air raids above Kampala and all the major cities in the country.

Shortly before dawn, debates break out about whether this was a field test for a new type of weapon. The exhausted journalists wonder if it's fake news. Conspiracy theorists start wondering why it killed only Ugandans and not relief aid workers. Videos begin to surface of people collapsing all around someone who isn't affected. Little by little, the journalists start piecing it together and in the early hours of the morning they're all reporting the same thing: a Genetic Targeting Weapon has been unleashed: 209,000,000 people are presumed dead.

Olivia's face is red and tearful as she keeps repeating the names of the dead like a broken record on the phone. She's frantically trying to call people who can locate her missing loved ones.

I know there's no point. Akello and the rest of Rosebell's friends are probably all dead and so are her parents and kind old Auntie Itungo; I didn't even need to hear it from Amy, the American expat, I already know no one escaped.

As the sun rises above Manhattan, I try to think of individual faces. Sellers at the market, my former colleagues, people I talked to on the street. But I can't actually comprehend that they're all dead. My brain can't visualize it. The footage on the news is vivid and nearly unwatchable. Yet my brain can't process it. The numbers are too large. All Ugandans wiped off the face of the planet at a single stroke.

How could anyone think this would be a solution? It's so incomprehensibly immoral. How could they not try to find another way to curb overpopulation? Any other way.

Reports start to trickle in of people dying at the borders with Congo, Tanzania, Sudan, where the wind pushed the substance farther.

Obviously they couldn't guarantee that the effects wouldn't spread more widely than intended. How could they be so reckless? How can they even know that it would kill only their target? It's wrong to use the weapon on anyone. But it also seems uncontrollable to me. This is an unknown technology, who knows what effects it might have once it's released? I guess the military didn't care either the first time the British released mustard gas in the trenches or when Truman bombed Hiroshima.

That's what it feels like. Like the world will never be the same again. There's a before and an after. Today, the 23rd of October, is a day that will change History.

In exactly eight days, I will leave for 2017. It's the only way now. The only way to prevent this from ever happening again.

DEANN

ew York, NY, USA, October 31, 2082

COULD we have done anything to prevent it? Should we have tried harder to sound the alarm?

The only solace we found was that Olivia's friend Edigold and her two children listened to her advice and left the country. We couldn't find any of the other people that Olivia had tried to warn.

I've barely slept for the last week, absorbed in the material I'm finding on the web. It looks like the perpetrators of this atrocity modified the smallpox virus. It's clever; smallpox is so virulent that even one airborne particle is enough to infect someone. Once they found a way to aerosolize it, they stripped it of its viral content but they kept the 'casing'. From the symptoms, the scientific community is extrapolating that they coupled the virus with a lethal respiratory irritant that attacked and destroyed the lungs of target subjects.

So it wasn't just MSA8742 that GeneX were working on. They also had an outright extermination weapon.

At first, I was relieved to confirm that the St. Louis facility I'd worked at had only worked on the sterilization sequence. I couldn't have forgiven myself if I'd missed something that huge. But a few days in, I started wishing I'd had the data, because then, maybe, I *could* have done something to stop it.

The news outlets are having a field day, spinning theories, looking into culprits and root causes. Discussing mechanisms and range, political ramifications for the world order and economic fallout. None of them discuss the elephant in the room: overpopulation combined with deep-seated racism. No one finds it palatable to discuss that. Instead, they talk about the usual: money, the economy, the power plays, the bloodshed, the price of grain, the stock markets' upheaval since the bombing. Anything rather than discuss the root cause. Overpopulation is a topic that's just not politically correct enough. Too mired in sex, race and religion for anyone to take on. Still. Even after all this.

There have been demonstrations practically non-stop every day since the truth broke out. Outrage finally started to seep through the ambient apathy. But no one is actually going to do anything at all about it. That's the sad truth.

Foreign governments have for the most part condemned the use of the weapon by the US and the Coalition. Sanctions were applied, fingers wagged sternly. But I suspect the other Security Council countries all immediately started funding their own genetic projects to try to replicate the chemical compound and wipe out their own ancestral enemies, rivals and neighbors, probably out of fear of being wiped out first.

I sigh and force myself away from the computer screen, knuckling my eyes. Olivia comes back from the communal bathroom just as I'm putting the kettle on. She slept here again last night. Today is the day I leave.

'All-nighter again?' she asks.

I nod and scald my palate on the burning hot tea.

'Found anything?'

I've spent the last week researching as much as I can. I need to bring back as much information as possible.

'I've been thinking about prevention,' I say, rubbing my face, feeling my eyes sting. 'Clearly, the iBubble couldn't keep the substance out of Doctor Herault's lungs.'

'The iBubble is probably porous, to let air in while you're on the phone. Maybe a gas mask might protect someone?'

Olivia looks exhausted as well, she's brushing her hair, getting ready to go to work, while I vent my frustration and powerlessness on her.

'Maybe, but who would we give the gas masks to? We have no idea who the Coalition will target next.'

The TV is on mute and a bar scrolls at the bottom of the screen, listing the latest developments. I let Olivia put on her makeup in peace and go seethe in front of the news. Obviously, the Coalition are milking this for all they're worth.

Olivia comes over, hair pulled back in a ponytail and tugs on a work jacket. 'Anything new?'

'The Coalition countries are getting sanctions lifted and blackmailing the UN Security Council into giving them a pass on the Beijing Treaty, just like Woody predicted.' I bite the inside of my cheek, regretting the mention as soon as it's out.

Olivia bites her lip, a distraught look on her face. 'In hindsight, I realize Woody was assassinated to prevent him from blowing the whistle before they were ready to strike. He died because of me. They thought he knew.'

'You couldn't have known the lengths they were prepared to go to keep this a secret—'

'But don't you understand? It's all my fault. We might have been able to blow the whistle if I'd put two and two together after the dead village near Camp Askaris, the experiments, the autopsied bodies... it was obvious. I should have guessed.'

'Stop it, Olivia, no one could have imagined the scale of this. You're hurting yourself for nothing. I didn't guess either and it's my job.'

'I should have known, I should have...' Her eyes well up.

My hand moves to touch her shoulder but I stop and close my eyes. I feel it too, the guilt, the responsibility.

'Woody was right, Olivia, when he told you that you can't put the cat back in the bag. Once the technology exists, it's too late. The only option is to go back now and prevent this abomination from ever being invented.'

Tonight, I'm leaving and she'll be stuck here forever.

'Are you sure...?'

I let the question hang, searching her face for doubt or fear and finding none.

I can't believe she's staying.

For a guy.

She nods, wiping a tear with the back of her hand.

'I don't know how you can still muster enough energy and enthusiasm for *any* man at our age.' The One. What a fairy tale. 'Life is much easier when you don't really care about anyone.'

'I know that you think that.' She shakes her head, smiling as her long red hair sways behind her like a fox tail. 'But you've changed, DeAnn,' she says, as she slips her coat on.

Maybe she's right. Over this last year, at the contact of so much death, I've felt a change in myself. I want a different kind of life now. All the emotions I'd batted away before – the empathy, the love, the heartbreak – they rise in me, and I tolerate them. Life does feel messier. But maybe more worth living as well.

I sigh. 'Well, if that's what you want, then you should go for it.'

After all, she's right: I've got this. I can bring back the information about this future to the Cassandra Programme. I could explain it and make sense of it with or without her.

So be it. If she wants to risk her life and her future for Chubby, good luck to her.

'We can't leave the chip here, though,' I say.

She stops, her hand on the doorknob. 'We've talked about it, DeAnn, I'll be safe once the deadline's passed and the chip loses its ability to travel back.'

'I've been thinking about this overnight. We don't know what the Programme might be able to do with it. We can't risk them getting their hands on it. I'll get a scalpel and suture material and remove it safely.'

She swallows and a shadow slides on her face. Suddenly, she looks afraid and lonely. But it's only for a moment.

Tonight, we leave for Boston and by midnight I'll be gone.

37

OLIVIA

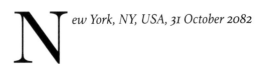 *ew York, NY, USA, 31 October 2082*

I'M LYING on a hospital table, my legs akimbo and a penis-shaped camera rummaging in my vagina.

When the clinic called this morning, the nurse said that there was no other slot for months, so I said yes. A simple procedure, they said. Mild anaesthesia. 'In and out in a few hours', then I'll be fertile. They'll give me a course of drugs that should increase my chances of conceiving to about 85 per cent, over the next year. That's the same odds as a woman in her early twenties.

I didn't have time to tell Michael about the operation today. After he asked me to marry him, we had long conversations about our life together and he asked me to go ahead and have the operation as soon as possible, but I didn't think it would be so soon; I just got the call, grabbed my bag and came to the clinic.

The clock on the wall ticks away the minutes one by one, excruciatingly slowly. I can make it back into the office and pass this off as a long lunch break. I should still be OK to meet DeAnn at the rendezvous point and drive up north with her tonight.

The nurse is talking to my business end about the demonstrations downtown. *Déjà vu* doesn't begin to cover what I'm feeling right now.

'It's hard to feel safe anymore with all *these people*,' she frowns distastefully, 'breaking storefronts, rioting and spewing UN propaganda.'

I squirm and wince, as she prods an organ.

'Of course, it's all lies and fake news perpetrated by the UN to justify hammering America with even more sanctions. When will it ever stop? We aren't doing anything wrong. Just protecting our way of life against terrorists.'

I bite my lip and force myself to shut up; they killed 209,000,000 people and somehow the US is the victim here.

'And the Negroes side with the Africans, no surprise there. I bet they're happy enough that the government is fighting for them when they go to the supermarket and they find full shelves. Traitors. Blacks should all go back to wherever the hell they came from.'

I shouldn't even bother answering her. What would I say? That the sight of African Americans protesting against the atrocities in Uganda is the first glimmer of hope and decency that I've seen since arriving in the US? That their supposed lack of patriotism is actually basic human empathy?

'I think the demonstrators are all American,' I mumble as she removes the device and hands me paper towels.

'Well then, they should be patriotic enough to understand that the president removed all those Rwandans to save us.'

'I'm pretty sure it's Ugandans.'

'Potato, potahto. They're all the same. Frankly, we should invent a similar technology to rid ourselves of all the scum rioting downtown.'

'Mmmh,' I say vaguely. I could argue with her until I'm blue in the face and probably not convince her of anything. Racism, nationalism, patriotism; they seem to be beyond reason. I wonder if every country inevitably retreats inwards when the going gets tough. I crane my neck towards the monitor in her hands.

'Can we operate?'

She taps on her transparent tablet and says with a saccharin smile, 'The doctor is going to be able to go ahead with the procedure today. You just wait here, honey. I'll come back with the anaesthetist.' She disappears. Not knowing quite what to do, I lie on the consultation table, feet in the stirrups, feeling vulnerable and exposed as hope soars in my chest.

38

DEANN

ew York, NY, USA, October 31, 2082

N

I PULL down on the baseball cap, trying to hide my face from cameras as I add forceps to my basket. Pincers, alcohol, thread and a surgical needle pack are already rattling at the bottom as I browse the shelves, trying to think of what else I'll need to remove the chip. Ah yes, adhesive bandages, maybe some local anesthetic. I shake my head. Such a bad idea to stay here, Olivia.

At her side, I realize now that I didn't love any of the men I dated. I chose Trevor based on his resume online. I chose Omony because he was my intellectual equal and he appreciated me for my mind. I liked it; it was less messy that way. No risk of feeling unwanted emotions. The last thing I need is to wonder if a man loves me or if I'm good enough for him or if he'll stay. Too much fucking effort.

Olivia seems to feel too much and I perhaps too little.

Maybe there is a way to be a forty-two-year-old who still believes in love and is able to keep her shit together when she finds it.

Anyway, I'm leaving tonight and it's none of my business. Once, long ago, I might have tried to talk her out of it, but I find that most people will do whatever they want to do, no matter what you say. So I save my breath and shut up.

I haven't been out of the apartment much over the last few weeks. Colonel Groebler was clever enough to find me in St. Louis and given the constant shocks I get whenever I see my face on the internet or on TV, I guess they know I'm in Manhattan and they're actively looking for me here.

After the shopping mall fiasco, I've stayed indoors as much as possible and have avoided being scanned by staying on the fringes and relying on Olivia for supplies but she wouldn't have known exactly what to purchase and I needed to be sure the surgical tools would do the job. So I decided to run this last errand myself.

I pay for my two items, relieved that it's not a human cashier but on the other hand, who knows what this machine is registering about me and where the data is being sent. I adjust my baseball cap and look around discreetly, trying to see if anything on the machine can scan my irises, my fingerprints or my DNA. I don't think so, but then again, since pretty much everywhere scans you these days, it's difficult to keep under the radar. I shouldn't stay out too long. It's risky.

I was so keen to learn about the future and to experience all the new technologies. I thought it would make me rich. But now I'm looking forward to going back tomorrow. I long for a simpler world where human interaction is still possible. Here, it seems there's either too little or too much of it all the time – and none of it fulfilling.

I take my purchases and step out of the pharmacy, one of the few physical ones left in New York. We couldn't risk sending this to Olivia's address. If I were discovered, it would give away her location and she needs to stay safe after I'm gone.

OK, so far, so good. It looks like I've escaped scot-free. I pause on the store's threshold and take a breath before diving into the flow of humanity on the sidewalk. A storm is brewing. The sky is really dark. It's only two o'clock but there is an end of the world feeling about the gloom. The sky is greenish and it looks much dimmer than when I went into the pharmacy.

Somewhere in the distance, angry people are chanting slogans. On the sidewalk, throngs of pedestrians are moving past. Just a normal day in Manhattan. I'm glad I won't have to deal with the crowds soon.

I tighten my coat around me and pull on my gloves, trying to figure out what the commotion is all about. One last check of my backpack: I won't get another chance to buy medical supplies. I need to remove the chip from Olivia's arm before we take to the road today. She's insisted on accompanying me but I'll drive, so her stitches won't matter. In a way, I'm glad she's accompanying me, it's better if she's there to help me leave and erase any traces of our passage after I'm gone.

Taking a breath, I step off the store's threshold and dive in. After weeks of voluntary imprisonment, the crowd feels too dense, the current too strong.

The yells are getting closer. It sounds like a demonstration, maybe another one about the Beijing Agreement or more likely another protest about the Uganda massacre.

As I walk briskly in the direction of the subway entrance, I can't help but go toward the demonstrators. They come into view now; black men and women, their faces calm and dignified, as they march holding placards, demanding justice. But what justice can there be for the Ugandan people? They're all dead. It's too late. Nothing can repair the damage. We can't bring them back. They're probably demonstrating less out of anger than out of fear. Fear that we're next. If only they knew. MSA8742 is probably already withering their future from the inside out.

I need to hurry. I can't risk staying out any longer.

I'm a few yards away from the subway when tires screech and three black SUVs skid to a halt, at the edge of the crowd.

The doors open and I freeze.

Colonel Groebler gets out and scans the crowd, looking for me.

Our eyes meet.

And he smiles.

39

OLIVIA

New York, NY, USA, 31 October 2082

I FRET and bite my lip, glancing at the consultation room's door. Where is that bloody doctor?

I need to get back to work. I need to be at the rendezvous with DeAnn at five.

I've been trying to reach her for the last couple of hours. Things are getting so real now. I can't help but feel that she's leaving me behind. Although technically, it's me who's choosing to stay. I've called her at least fifteen times but I can't find her. My iMode is lying on the steel table, just out of reach, its screen blank. Nothing. Where is she?

I feel dizzy just thinking about the procedure. I'm so close. One operation away from my new beginning. This is crazy. I'm excited. Yet my intestines feel like slippery eels, tangled up and burning. I usually have that sensation when

I'm about to be interviewed. Or when I'm about to make the wrong decision. I don't know which one it is today.

My iMode buzzes, startling me. Finally! I reach for it with the tip of my fingers, slipping against the metal table's edge as I stretch my arm and try not to fall off the examination table.

'DeAnn?'

I hear a crowd chanting loudly, angry cries and muffled police announcements.

'DeAnn? Is that you? What's wrong?'

I sit up and hold a finger to my ear bud, straining to hear over the noise.

'Olivia! The Programme... me...'

'What? Can you repeat?'

Someone says, 'Run!' and then the staccato of machine guns erupts in the distance, faint but clear.

'Oh my God, DeAnn, are you OK?'

There's a huge explosion and the line crackles, followed by panicked screaming and indistinct thuds, as if the iMode on the other side was being banged around.

I fight with the stirrups, trying to extirpate my feet out of them.

'DeAnn? DeAnn?'

The line goes dead.

I'm dialling her number frantically over and over when the nurse slips her head through the door and glares at me. 'Can you keep it down? There are other patients here.'

I stare at her, unable to understand what she's saying. Something really bad has just happened to DeAnn. I grab the remote control lying on the worktop. The nurse protests, but I don't care.

The news channels show images of people scattering in the street, covered in blood. The screen changes to a helicopter view of a huge crater in the middle of the road and demonstrators running away. There are bodies everywhere. Breaking news banners display a casualty headcount, which scrolls up as I watch, horrified. I stare at the screen trying to find a familiar silhouette. I can't find DeAnn. Oh God, what if she's dead?

I look down at my naked bottom half through the opened hospital gown and make my decision.

I rip up the bandage on the back of my hand, remove the drip, ignoring the blood, and wipe the lubricating gel away.

'What do you think you're doing?' the nurse says, trying to hold me down.

'Sorry, something really important has come up. I need to go.'

I push her off and get dressed as quickly as I can, grab my bag and run out of there, frantically dialling back DeAnn, to no avail.

'Hey!' the nurse calls behind me. 'You can't just leave.'

I skid to a halt in front of the lift and press the button three or four times. 'Come on, come on.'

'What could be more important than your future?' The bloody woman makes me jump. She's glowering at me, arms folded, judgemental and stern.

I stop staring at the lift button and turn to her. Everything is suddenly so clear.

'You're right. Nothing's more important than the future. That's why I have to go back.'

The lift doors open and I rush in, pressing the buttons until the doors close on the nurse's flabbergasted face.

There's no point going to the scene of the terrorist attack. It will be crawling with police officers by now. DeAnn is dead. She has to be. She sounded so close to the blast when it happened. And if she were alive, she's have picked up her phone. Jesus, Mary, Joseph, what if she's really dead?

I take a shaky breath, pushing down the tears. If she's dead, I need to go without delay; the mission rests on my shoulders now... and the weight of the responsibility is crushing me already.

She said the Programme found her. How is that possible? We were so careful.

I need to get to the car. I stupidly left the keys in my workbag, under my desk.

Slaloming through the throngs of people crowding the pavement, I run back to the office, receiving dirty looks from pedestrians as I jostle my way through. I don't care. None of these people exist yet. None of this has happened and there is still time to change it – the Mass Sterilisation Agent, the Genetic Cleansing Weapon, the fate of Uganda. All of it. I must go back to 2017 and change this future.

I can't believe I was about to sacrifice the mission just because I wanted to be happy.

Elbowing my way through the crowd, I finally arrive, panting, at the foot of my office building. I scan my badge and run to the lift, thinking fleetingly that my belly doesn't hurt anymore. My gut was literally telling me that I was making a mistake and I waved it away, pretending it was pre-operation nerves. I knew better.

The lifts take forever.

I've tried DeAnn again half a dozen times as I ran, but her phone doesn't even ring. Has she been blown up? Oh God, I can't think like that. I need to stay positive.

I arrive on my floor and make an effort to breathe. Smooth my hair down. Wipe my palms on my skirt. Smile. I walk calmly to my desk, sweat beading on my forehead. It feels like everyone is staring at me. But they just look up for a second and then, indifferent, stare at their screens again. Calm down, Olivia, calm down.

Dunking under my desk, I kneel to retrieve my bag, slipping my hand in the outer pocket to check that the car key is in it.

Time to go.

Head bent under my desk, I hear a familiar voice saying: 'Mr Quisling, can we please have a word in private? I'm with the Programme.'

My heart jumps in my throat and every part of me turns cold.

No, no, no.

It can't be.

The room starts to spin.

Trying to remain as inconspicuous as possible, I risk a look. I shouldn't, but I need to see with my own eyes. Still on my knees, I raise my head just above the desk and peer around my cubicle wall. A few meters down the carpeted corridor, Michael is holding the door open for a man in black fatigues. I can only see the back of him. A gun holster is strapped around his muscular chest and his hair is cut short. He turns as he enters the office and I have to clamp my hand over my mouth to keep myself from screaming.

It's Burke.

40

DEANN

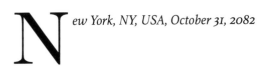 *ew York, NY, USA, October 31, 2082*

I RUN.

I run as fast as I can.

I leave the subway entrance behind me and make for the crowd of demonstrators. There must be hundreds of thousands of them.

I don't stop to look at Groebler.

I just run.

The protesters part to let me through, then the crowd closes in behind me, but the flow is going the wrong way; toward the Colonel and his men. Pressed on all sides by protesters, I fight against the current, elbowing my way through the mob.

His stare burning on the back of my neck, I try to burrow further into the crowd, expecting his hands to close around me any second. I keep pushing through, panicking.

An opening emerges in the crowd on my left, revealing a narrow alley. I rush in, wading through the mass of people and find myself in the tight space between two buildings. My iMode is ringing constantly, so I turn it off and shrink into the small street.

Crouched into a small ball, I try to think about what to do.

Legs and feet walk past, an endless stream of demonstrators. They're mostly African American. Here, a dad carries his daughter on his shoulders. There, a group of students, arm-in-arm, hold a homemade banner. I spot an old man, walking with a crutch, slowly but he's here. People chant, yell and shake their placards. I can't see whether the narrow alley behind me leads anywhere. The walls are grazing my shoulders but it's a way out.

I need to check if there's an exit that way. I have to make it out.

I hurry in the darkness of the alley toward the back; it's so narrow in parts that I can only go through like a crab.

The sky is too dim, something's wrong. Where is that storm?

Foul-smelling garbage containers block my way, as I pad on wet cardboard boxes flattened on the ground. Something scurries to my right.

End of the alley.

Shit, it's a dead-end.

The back wall is impossible to climb. There is no escaping that way. There's only one way out: into Grobler's waiting arms. I kick the fucking wall and contain a scream of frustration, I can't afford to make too much noise.

I need to escape. I must go back and make the rendezvous point. I can't fail. I check my iMode and see that I have a dozen missed calls from Olivia.

Rage and powerlessness are pooling inside me. I take a deep breath and dial my partner.

'Olivia, listen, I might not make it back to the meeting point on time, I'm stuck.'

She can't hear me. I double back and hurry down the alley, trying to get close to the street again. Maybe there's better reception there. Also more noise.

I run back to the mouth of the alley, holding the ear bud pressed to my ear as I try to hear what Olivia's saying. Skidding to a halt when I reach the street, I crane my neck, hugging the wall to assess the mass of demonstrators. Shit. There they are, Groebler and his men; they're elbowing their way past the alley and into the heart of the demonstration. They missed me.

Crouching, I hold a finger to my collar and one to my ear, straining to hear, hoping she's getting this.

'Olivia, the Programme has found me. You need to prepare the car and wait for me at your office. I'm on my way.' Then I add, even though it costs me to say it, 'If I don't make it in an hour, that means I'm dead. Hide, stay safe. I'll call you again if I make it.'

She keeps saying 'What?' I can't tell if she heard any of this. I need to find a spot with better reception. She *has* to know that the Programme has found me, and her life is in danger.

Someone's shouting a slogan and the crowd chants its response. Looking for an opportunity to rush back in, I steel myself to plunge back into the throng when someone yells 'Run!' and the unmistakable sound of a machine gun's rat-tat-tat erupts, soon followed by wails as people start shrieking and running haphazardly, their slogans against injustice replaced by shouts and screams of terror.

Stunned, I peer around the corner, feeling the rough

brick under my palms. There's a child bawling – not far away, but where? The mob is in complete panic now. Howls of pain erupt nearby. Hundreds of people are running to safety and they're not stopping for anything. A woman's keening voice pierces through the crowd's clamor.

A cloud of dust and smoke is billowing out, plunging the street in chaos, obscuring everything, covering the demonstrators with dust. I'm going to get trampled if I try to go against the current now.

Making my decision, I start to run with the crowd and that's when a sharp explosion bangs like a deafening firecracker. The huge detonation reverberates in the street as the shock wave shakes the ground under my feet. I'm thrown backward by the blast and fall hard on the grainy asphalt. My head hits the pavement and darkness engulfs me.

41

OLIVIA

ew York, NY, USA, *31 October 2082*

Burke.

Burke is alive.

How? I killed him myself.

This is a nightmare. A horrible, horrible nightmare. My hand twitches as I re-live stabbing him in the throat. He collapsed with the full weight of his dead body pressed on top of me. Bile rises as I struggle for air. I can't breathe.

I can't breathe.

Sitting back on my haunches under the desk, I gasp for air, panicking. My colleague looks at me strangely, but I ignore her and focus on my breathing. She rolls her eyes and continues typing.

Burke's not dead.

He's alive.

He's here.

He found me.

Oh my God, Burke's with Michael. He's going to hurt my love. Terror rises as I recall DeAnn's anguished description of her manager's tortured face.

No, no, no.

I need to stop him.

Just then, my iMode sputters and Michael's voice rumbles in my ear. He forgot to turn off his collar, as usual. Except these aren't instructions on the notes I should be taking.

'Thank you for coming so fast.'

Burke says something but I can only hear what Michael answers.

'Yes, the Secretary of Defense spotted something the other day when he looked at the paralegal in question. He asked to have everyone in the board meetings screened again and the search widened.'

I can't hear what Burke says.

'A terrorist? Are you sure? O... Miss Sinclair doesn't seem...'

Panic grips me. Please Michael, don't defend me. Don't say that you know me.

'Are you with the Department of Defense?'

Burke says something. No doubt a lie.

'I knew something was off after she had a heart-to-heart with the UN Under-Secretary-General minutes before he was assassinated. But I never suspected...'

This is obviously an act that Michael's putting on to buy me some time.

'Yes, I recognised the woman who's wanted for questioning.'

Of course, Michael saw DeAnn at my place the other night. Why would Burke ask Michael about her unless... did they already catch her? Is that what I heard over the phone? What do I do? I have to try to help her. But I can't leave Michael here, at Burke's mercy.

'Miss Sinclair must be on her lunch break. She'll be back soon. You can use my office to wait.'

So far Michael's doing a good job of confusing Burke by pretending to cooperate. But it's only a matter of time before he's unmasked.

Oh God, oh God, oh God. Burke is going to hurt Michael. I need to help him escape. I can't stay in 2082 but I'm not going to let Burke kill my fiancé. I'm hyperventilating. This is not good. Not good at all.

42

DEANN

ew York, NY, USA, October 31, 2082

WHEN I COME TO, my ears are buzzing with a high-pitch noise. My cheek is on the ground, the gravel encrusted in my skin, burning. Something warm is running down the side of my face. I try to get up but my head is spinning.

There was something I needed to remember. What time is it? Where am I? My head feels like it's full of cotton.

Unable to focus, I watch from my spot on the ground as a dozen white men wearing black and camouflage approach. Maybe the police have arrived.

'Over here,' I croak, but no sound comes out; it's as if my throat is coated in dust. Swallowing, I shake my head to dislodge the tinnitus but that only makes the floor spin.

Still sprawled on the ground, I struggle to get up but the men don't see me. Instead, they walk over to a young black woman with curly hair and a red hat who is trying to crawl away from them, a look of pure fear on her face. They close in on her from behind and when she glances over her shoulder and starts to plead, they shoot her in the back.

The sound explodes, piercing through the ringing in my ears, as the woman's body spasms and falls still. Shocked, I slam my cheek back down against the asphalt, trying to make myself as small as possible. My ribs are bruised and my heart is rattling the bars of its bony cage like a crazed prisoner.

Who was she? It could have been me. If they had heard me, I would be dead by now. My face stings and I realize the salt of my tears is mixing in my cuts. The road is covered with bodies and grey dust. It's hard to breathe. The last thing I need is snot blocking my nose. Get it the fuck together, DeAnn.

The men walk methodically through the blast's survivors and shoot them.

'Twenty-two,' a guy with a breaking voice says.

'Hey, don't let that one get away!'

A shot rings, making me flinch. Laughter.

'Twenty-three.'

'Got a live one over here!' another one shouts.

The slaughter elicits excited cries from the thugs; they call out to each other, cursing, laughing, as my people collapse to the ground, their falling abrupt and final, as their knees buckle and their bodies drop like sacks. Horrified, frozen, I can't move. I can't think. I can't feel anything other than abject terror.

'Twenty-four!' the half-bass, half-falsetto voice cackles.

The gravel digs into my knees and my palms, as I try to crawl away.

The shooters move in formation. Professionals? Groebler's men? No, no. They're young, disorganized. They wear the familiar red armbands with a black twisted cross against a white circle.

'Twenty-six.'

I can hear one of them getting closer to me but I don't dare move or look back. So I hold very still hoping he's not coming for me. Yet.

He stops a few yards away. I can only see his boot planted on the side of a child's head. The little boy is seven at most, his blue eyes striking against his brown-colored skin. The soft curls of his afro are squashed under the grimy sole of the young man's combat boot. The mother's wounded, her arm hangs loose at her side, bleeding, but she wrenches herself up and grabs the man's leg, fighting to get the attacker away from her son. He nearly falls backward and his friends laugh.

'Fucking jig!'

Blushing, the teenager pulls the trigger and her head whiplashes, a spray of blood splattering her executioner's jeans.

'Twenty-seven.'

From my spot on the ground, I can see the child's eyes widening. He's heard the sound of his mother's death but the man's foot is pinning his head down against the road and he can't move. He looks straight at me, eyebrows raised, mouth open, dread consuming him.

The black boot comes down and I close my eyes at the sickening crunch and wet noises that follow.

'Hey, Matt, try crushing their skulls with your boot, it's fun.'

My brain starts to work again.

Alphas.

They're Alphas.

I need to get away.

Just as I get on all fours, I hear boots pounding the street, accelerating. Someone's spotted me. The gravel rips through the skin of my palms as I scramble to get up but something slams against me, knocking me to the ground.

I struggle and then he flips me with a kick. I'm on my back now, staring into his jeering face, holding my painful side as he stands over me.

'Hey, we got a live one here,' he says and his voice breaks mid sentence, ending in a croak.

He takes aim; I'm so close that I can see the pimples on his chin. He's not even old enough to shave.

I wonder what it will feel like.

I can't see anything but the darkness down the barrel of his machine gun.

That's it, then.

That's how I die.

The young man says, 'Twenty-nine.'

43

OLIVIA

ew York, NY, USA, 31 October 2082

I PUT MY BACKPACK ON. I'm glancing over at the exit, biting my lip, when Michael leaves his office.

'This is a very, very bad idea, Olivia. Very bad,' I mutter, as I straighten up and walk calmly towards the loo, trying to stay out of view from Michael's office. Oh God, I hope Michael's going to be OK, he must survive this. I'd never forgive myself if he gets hurt because of me.

I get into the men's room and lock the door behind me. He's washing his hands. As I sneak in, he looks up and freezes.

'Olivia! You're back. Where have you been?'

His eyes dart towards the locked door behind me.

I rush to him, hugging him, breathing in his scent. When I let him go, he turns to the dryer, which starts its wailing.

I stare at his back, taking in the familiar bulk of his shoulders, the unruly brown curls, the faintly ridiculous twentieth-century suit.

'Michael, you have no idea how dangerous Burke is. You're not safe. If he learns that we're together, he'll torture and kill you.' I glance at the time. 'We need to go now.'

I turn around to open the door. Silence envelops us when the dryer stops. I look over my shoulder. He hasn't moved an inch. His eyes are little more than slits behind the tortoiseshell glasses. His moist hands hang at his side.

'What are you talking about, Olivia? You're the dangerous one.'

I turn to face him, stunned, my back to the locked door, looking up at his beloved face.

'I called in Captain Burke as soon as the security clearance report came back.'

Michael reported me? No, no, no. This can't be.

'I should have known when your friend arrived in the middle of the night, looking like she wanted to murder me. But I told myself it couldn't be the same person that Homeland Security had been looking for on national TV. Imagine my surprise when I found out that the authorities are looking for you too. Sweet Olivia Sinclair.' He snorts. 'Oh yeah, that's right, it's not even your real name.'

'You have it all wrong. I'm just trying to do something right, something for the greater good. You said yourself that it was wrong to experiment on Ugandans and wipe them off the face of the planet. I thought you understood. I thought...' I trail off.

I sound absurd.

He glares at me.

We can iron this misunderstanding later. I need to get

him out of here, he's in danger. I must make sure he's safe before I go back to 2017.

'Michael, you said you loved me, was that true?' I ask him.

'Yes.' But he says it like a question.

'You said you wanted children – that you wanted to marry me.'

He shrugs.

'I don't understand it, then. Why would you rat on me?'

'This all went out the window when you made it to the top of the most wanted list. I can't believe I fell for your bull-shit story about time travel, I'm such a fool!' He looks morti-fied and angry.

'But it's true, I—'

'Save it for the agent who's come to collect you.' He tries to push past me but I'm rooted to the spot. 'Move out of my way, Olivia. I can't be seen to be your accomplice. It's bad enough that some people in the office suspect we've had an affair, even though I was careful to keep it a secret. Imagine if they knew we were engaged, I'd be fired. Thrown in prison.' He shakes his head. 'I've got to look out for myself. If I'm the one to turn you in, that'll count for something.'

'But you said you wanted me to stay,' I say, pathetically.

He rolls his eyes. 'Olivia, grow up. It's over.'

I feel as if he's just punched me in the stomach.

'What did you expect me to do? Leave it all behind just to be with you? My career, my family, my whole life and everything I've worked so hard to build?'

'I was going to do that for you.'

The words struggle to squeeze out from me, past the ball of grief in my throat. I clench my jaw shut and hold back the tears. Once again, I've grabbed handfuls of my skin and torn my chest wide open, cracked my ribs aside to expose my beating, bleeding heart. And once again, a man has reached in and squelched it. Every time. Every bloody time. The sound of his fist dripping my heart's blood is marking the seconds as we stare at each other.

The shape of his eyes changes from wariness to pity.

'There's no time for this.' He sighs. 'Get out of the way; I need to let Captain Burke know you're here.' He pushes me roughly aside, shaking his head. 'I can't believe I proposed to a terrorist.' He chuckles. 'Talk about a bullet dodged.'

And that's when my anger awakens. I let him fumble with the lock, as I take the gun out of my rucksack. I stare at the back of his head. My fingers remember the feel of his soft brown curls, as they tighten on the Glock's barrel.

I hit him as hard as I can and he collapses with a loud thud, crumbling into a fat mound on the filthy floor.

Oh no! What have I done? I check his pulse and gasp with relief when I find one. Torn between concern, sorrow and anger, I heave his unconscious body away from the door; then I pull the engagement ring off my finger and throw it on the floor next to his unconscious form. I won't need it where I'm going.

By now, my internal alarm bells are screeching. Time to go. Palms slick with sweat, I squeeze through the gap as inconspicuously as possible, then turn around and shut the door calmly. The weight of his slumping body keeps it closed, so that it feels locked. No one will find him for a while.

I walk steadily to the lift, not looking left or right, just in front of me. My bleeding, dripping heart is bungee-jumping up and down my chest, as I reach the lobby. I smile to the receptionist, call the lift and wait, feeling the hair on the back of my neck lift up.

I force myself not to look back. Burke is in Michael's

office, just a few meters away. The lift pings and I nearly jump out of my skin.

I get in and clasp the handrail behind me. As the doors close, I breathe shakily and hands on my knees, take in lungfuls of air. OK, I can do this, I can do this. The doors finally open again with a ping. The underground parking lot. Where did I park that bloody car?

DeAnn is dead. Michael betrayed me. Burke's on my trail. There is nothing for me here anymore. I made the right decision at the clinic. I need to go back to 2017 and fulfil my mission.

Also I need to keep my shit together. Can't drive and cry at the same time. It's not safe.

44

DEANN

New York, NY, USA, October 31, 2082

I'M LOOKING down the barrel of the rifle. It's oddly peaceful. I wouldn't want it to hurt. But I'm not that scared about death itself.

What bothers me the most, actually, is that I'm not done. I realize all of a sudden that I wanted to learn how it felt to love someone. Really love someone before I died. To leave a legacy. To make a difference in someone's life.

It's weird. As I stare death in the eye, I don't think about my career or achievements or the mission. I just think about Kitsa, my spunky, lovely girl jutting her chin forward; I feel my dad's frail, papery embrace; and unexpectedly, my friend Jordan comes into focus, his kind eyes, his soft smile. The warm feelings surge out of nowhere.

Yet here I am, lying on my back in the street, bleeding

from cuts on my cheek, my forehead and my arms, ears buzzing, a terrorist pinning me down with a boot on my chest. Thinking of love.

Life is funny sometimes.

I laugh.

The Alpha lowers his gun and glares at me, puzzled. 'Why are you laughing, you cun—'

His eyes go wide as his chest jolts. He falls to his knees, a surprised expression on his face. Behind him Groebler appears, walking calmly toward me, holstering his gun.

'Well, Miss Carpenter. What a pleasant surprise. We all thought you were dead.'

He pulls me roughly to my feet and, rolling up my sleeve, inspects my forearm.

'Still there. Excellent.'

One of his goons wrenches my arms back and I feel a tie pulling tightly around my wrists. Then Groebler drags me toward the car, his fingers digging in the back of my neck as I stumble, still in shock. Blood trickles down my face and my legs feel like Jell-O, but all things considered, I just have a few scrapes and bruises. I'll live.

Or maybe not.

The Alpha's friends, realizing they're under attack, start bellowing and firing their machine guns in our direction. Groebler pushes me down behind the fuming carcass of a car as bullets smash against it, riddling the metal with holes. As we crouch there, hunkering down, Groebler shouts to his men.

'Stay behind, cover our exit! Meet me at the airport at 1600 hours.'

For a short instant the bullets stop clanging against the carcass as his men start to return fire. Groebler springs to his feet and pulls me with him, as we make a run for his car. The street looks like a battlefield. It's littered with corpses and shrapnel. Everything and everyone's covered with dust. Gunshots erupt nearby again. I stop in my tracks, involuntarily hunching down. But he drags me forward, unfazed, as his team tackles the rest of the Alphas.

I follow Groebler reluctantly, aware that I have nowhere to run and more importantly, that I have no weapon. Damn it, the gun. I should never have left it with Olivia.

He shoves me in the back of the car, buckles my seat belt for good measure, to make sure I can't move, and sits in the driver seat then he drives off, leaving his men behind.

'Cat got your tongue?' he says pleasantly, glancing at me in the rearview mirror. 'We'll fix that, don't worry.'

Torture then. I guess they want to know who helped us escape Uganda, and who managed to place me in the lion's den at GeneX. They'll probably purge the Programme, make sure there are no Resistance members among them anymore.

'We're on our way to pick up your little friend and then we're off to London tonight. We should make it with plenty of time to spare before our agents' departure tonight.'

Shit. They figured out that Olivia's still alive. I glare at him with all the loathing I can muster.

'Oh, don't look at me like that. You didn't seriously think that we'd let you go back with those microchips? They're invaluable. You don't have any qualifications; you're just fucking amateurs. We're doing the world a favor by taking over your mission.'

'Why can't you just let us go back?' I ask him. 'We're all supposed to be on the same side. We're Programme agents too.'

'Oh, get off it. I'll never be on the same side as a kaffir bitch like you. If you went back, you'd try to save everyone. And your friend the liberal snowflake would do the same. You think it hasn't been tried? Raising awareness, appealing to the public's sense of responsibility? That's how we got in this situation in the first place. Free will.' He sneers. 'The world's a fucking shambles because of you. You people must be kept under control.'

'Groebler, listen...'

He interrupts, me, uninterested, his eyes fixed on the road: 'With your chips, our Helenus agents will be able to change the world's fate. We'll position the right people in government, provide the Mass Sterilization Agent formula to them early on. Can you imagine what we'd achieve if we could produce and test it before 2020? The Genetic Cleansing Weapon will be deployed worldwide *before* resources go scarce. We'll live in a new Eden created for the few chosen ones.'

He's going toward Olivia's office. Fuck. How did they find out where she works? Have they already caught her? Maybe she's already dead.

He pulls up in front of Olivia's office building. My hands are hurting, the hard plastic strings dig painfully into my wrists. The cuts on my face are stinging and anxiety is starting to gnaw at my insides. Outside the SUV, nothing is happening; we stay parked here, waiting. What for? The afternoon sky seems awfully dark.

After fifteen minutes or so, the passenger door opens and *Burke* climbs in. It can't be.

'Hey, DeAnn,' he says jovially.

'I thought you were dead,' I answer, keeping my face expressionless.

'Nah. I lost a lot of blood but the artery wasn't cut. I lived.'

'Too bad. I should have slit your throat when I had the chance.'

'Nice to see you too.'

'Where's Red?' Groebler asks.

'Don't know. Her boyfriend said she went out for lunch.'

Groebler glances at the time.

'Bit late for lunch. You think he's lying?'

Burke shakes his head. 'Shifty bastard, but I think he was telling the truth. He was shitting his pants the whole time we spoke. No wonder the little weasel went to the toilets. He was still at it when I came down.' They laugh.

'We're better off intercepting her outside the building anyway,' Groebler says. 'Less conspicuous.'

'Agreed. She has to come back at some point. We can't miss her.'

'How did you find us?' I ask him.

'Facial recognition at the pharmacy,' Groebler says casually.

Burke adds, pretty pleased with himself: 'Yeah, today's like an early Christmas. After we found you in St. Louis, we figured that Olivia was probably also working on getting info on GeneX, so we monitored all security tipoffs related to the company.'

Groebler says, 'You were last seen in New York during your little shopping trip. So when Red's boyfriend called to denounce a colleague, we figured it might be her.'

'He probably needed the promotion or something,' Burke sniggers.

Groebler turns toward me with a smile, his fake teeth in a neat white row in his too-tanned face. 'And *voilà*. Here we are. In the nick of time too. A few hours more and we'd have missed our window of opportunity for our little trip to 2017. Looks like it's going to be our lucky d—'

He never finishes his sentence, the car rocks violently sideways with a deafening sound of buckling metal. Glass shards explode and I'm projected against the backseat as my neck whiplashes and the SUV rocks violently backward.

45

OLIVIA

N *ew York, NY, USA, 31 October 2082*

DISENGAGING THE DL OPTION, I manoeuvre carefully out of the parking lot. Driving is not my forte, so I make sure not to scrape the car on the walls. It was already hard enough to find a vehicle that can be put in manual and to convince a garage mechanic to disengage the iMode connection and the GPS tracker; the last thing I need is to attract attention and potentially compromise the vehicle. I drive past the barrier, wince as the gear sticks in the wrong position, belatedly downshift and pause to look in both directions, forgetting which side of the road I'm supposed to drive on.

I don't know what to do.

Should I try to go look for DeAnn at the explosion site? There's only a few hours left until our window closes and we're stuck here forever. The dashboard watch glows green, proclaiming how late it is. I need to get on the road now if

I'm going to make it. She would want me to put the mission first. Otherwise, all the work we've done this year will be for nothing. I need to go. I just wish there were something more I could do for DeAnn.

I pull out onto the street slowly. There's hardly anyone; it's not rush hour yet. A strange storm is gathering above the city. The light is all wrong, green and ominous. I drive attentively – and that's why I notice a black SUV parked in front of my law firm's building. That's odd. I know for a fact that it's not allowed to be there. I had to ask for a special permit at reception this morning to park in the building's basement.

I'm staring curiously at the SUV as I drive past when I realise who is in the car: Groebler in the front and DeAnn, looking banged up but alive in the back seat. Just as I drive away, Burke climbs in.

Burke who enjoyed hurting me. Burke who murdered all the Kampala test subjects as if they were rats. Burke who's going to hurt and kill DeAnn. But what can I possibly do about it?

I tuck my backpack behind the driver's seat as I do a lap around the block, picking up speed, my heart beating wildly in my chest. Pressing down on the accelerator, I clasp the steering wheel, my knuckles white. Burke and Groebler were talking and their eyes go wide when I swerve, but it's too late. The motor revs as I push the pedal to the floor and plough into them.

The crash is deafening. The lightweight, modern bodywork of their car crumples under my vehicle's old-fashioned steel. Groebler was closest to the point of impact, the bonnet of my car rams into him. I close my eyes and clench my jaws as he disappears in the folds of mangled metal.

The shock of the impact radiates through the wheel as

the seat belt engraves itself across my chest, compressing my ribs and half choking me. The airbag explodes in a shower of white dust and a horn starts to blare.

Dazed, it takes me a minute to gather my wits, my foot is stuck in the crumpled metal. I pull but I can't get out. The car starts to smoke.

Fighting with the airbag, I manage to undo my belt and dive my head under the dashboard to work out what's wrong. My shin is imprisoned in the crushed metal. Getting increasingly frantic, I pull and push but to no avail. The smoke makes my eyes water, a pungent smell of gas is pervading the smoky air of the cabin.

Finally, with the strength of panic and despair, I manage to yank my foot out of my shoe and extract my leg. The metal clings to me, ripping through my trousers and gouging a long rip through my shin as I scream with agony.

Bloodied but free, I get out of the car as fire starts to lick the back seat, choking on the toxic fumes. I open the back door, get my backpack gingerly out of the melting, smoking floor and stagger forwards, pulling to get the gun out.

Holding the weapon in my shaking hand, I limp towards the totalled car, feeling oddly clear and woozy at the same time; it must be the adrenaline. I can't help but glance at Groebler's disarticulated form, projected through the windshield. His corpse has merged with the crumpled bonnet of my car in an odd tango between man and red-splattered metal. A heave swells in my throat and I throw up on the road.

Wiping my chin, I hoist the backpack on my shoulders, wipe my palm on my trousers and adjust my grip on the Glock. The passenger window is smashed and Burke's head is bleeding, his head lolling on the headrest.

The light seems really dim for this time in the afternoon

and I can't see very well. I yank DeAnn's door open and stare at her anxiously. She's limp in the seat belt's embrace, not moving at all. My stomach drops as I lunge forwards to check her breath. She's alive. I breathe a sigh of relief and climb in hurriedly.

Glancing out the broken windshield, I see gawkers approaching and the building's security guards calling for back up.

Shit, shit, shit.

I fumble with her seat belt, struggling to reach around my friend's unconscious form and at last, manage to unbuckle it. Feeling like a target is painted on my back, expecting to be yanked backwards any minute, I heave and pull DeAnn into my arms, as police sirens wail, getting louder and louder. Somewhere close, car doors are slammed and men shout. I pull her out of the car; she's still insensible but I manage to lay her arm around my shoulder and hoist her out of the wreck.

The bitter smell of burning plastic pricks my noise and a cloud of dark smoke surrounds us, choking me. DeAnn moans, her head lolling on my shoulder. I limp away from the car, just as it starts burning.

Blue lights bathe everything but something's wrong, it's too dark; it's not just the car crash's smoke that's shielding us from view. It's like night has fallen all of a sudden.

'Police! Freeze!'

I throw a quick glance over my shoulder and my jaw drops. Behind the police car, advancing at unimaginable speed, an enormous black cloudbank is hurling towards us. The cops, seeing my face, turn around and I watch agape as the cloud swallows them. I only have time to breathe in deeply before it swallows DeAnn and me.

The black sand burns and stings as it gets in my eyes. Coarse specks burn like embers as they burrow under my half-closed lids and inside the wound on my shin. The wind blasts inside my ears, howling. Sand fills my nose with grains that feel like mad bees ricocheting inside my nostrils, invading my lungs.

DeAnn isn't able to walk much. She's woken up but she's wobbly. I raise the neck of my shirt over my nose with my free hand and do the same for DeAnn. I adjust her weight on my shoulder and hobble as far away as possible from the policemen and the place they last saw us.

But if I can still run inside the black cloud of dust, so can they. My only advantage is that I know my way around these streets; I have worked here every day for the last few months.

I need a plan.

On impulse, I touch my iMode collar and mouth a desperate command as we stagger away. The cloud of black dust is getting thicker and it's nearly impossible to see anything now, we're suffocating. Millions of little dust particles are swirling around us.

My hair stands on end as little bolts of static electricity light up the air about us with blue flashes. I can't see DeAnn anymore. I know she's there because I can feel her weight on my shoulder, but she's disappeared in the pitch black. The darkness is oppressing. Panic starts to gnaw at my stomach. We're not going to make it.

The iMode bracelet's feeble light is the only thing I can see now, as my free hand tentatively searches for a way forwards. My hip hits something hard and I stop. It worked. The driverless cab is in front of me. Thank you, God. I open the door and push DeAnn inside.

'St Peter's Church,' I croak into the interface and swipe my iMode on the reader.

The driverless cab rides placidly through the city plunged in darkness. Fine black dust swirls like a swarm of demons taunting people, pulling their hair, as they hold their sleeves to their faces, running panicked, trying to get indoors.

'What on earth?' I whisper in awe, crossing myself.

'The black blizzards are from Kansas,' DeAnn says woozily.

'DeAnn, you're awake!'

'No thanks to you. You're crazy, Snow White.' She closes her eyes.

I release a breath I didn't know I'd held.

'Just be grateful I didn't kill you. You've had it coming, you know. You really should try being nicer to me.'

Her lip curls up in a crooked smile, but she doesn't lift her head; she looks pretty banged up, there's blood dripping from a gash in her forehead and her ear looks battered, her face is covered in thick dust. I fish out a tissue and some water from the backpack and hand her the bottle, while I clean up her face as best I can.

Fifteen minutes later, the taxi stops in front of the church. Well, hopefully it does because I can't see anything at all.

I make one last call with the iMode.

'We'll be there in five hours.'

'Understood.'

The communication cuts off.

I take a deep breath, then fight with the car door, the wind pushing it back against my arm. As soon as the door cracks open, the wind howls in, throwing sand around the cab, lifting our hair, swirling into our clothes, invading our eyes and noses. I push with a groan and extirpate myself from the cab then hold the door open with my hip, as I bend to help DeAnn out.

We don't have much time. They'll be able to figure out where we went within the hour, as I used my iMode to get here.

When we're finally both out, I speak another command and, holding my finger to my collar, swipe my bracelet against the pad. Then, pinching my ear bud out, I yank the iMode off my wrist and my neck, grab DeAnn's as well, and throw everything inside the cab, slamming the door shut.

Squinting against the sand, the wind buffeting my hair, pushing me, slapping my face, I watch the cab drive off. I hope that will do the trick. I don't think it will, though, not for long anyway.

Right. Time to go.

We climb the stairs and I drop DeAnn on a pew while I run towards the sacristy. Hoping, praying, that my gamble will pay off.

'Miss? Is everything alright?'

I skid to halt by the altar and exhale when I see him.

Father Raymond; the little boy I taught how to sing.

The old man looks at me and his eyebrows shoot up, his eyes wide.

'Miss Olivia?'

46

DEANN

R *oute I 84 USA, October 31, 2082*

'FIFTEEN MILLIONS TONS of dust have unfurled over New York City today in the largest dust storm ever to reach the East Coast since the 1930s,' the radio drones on. 'Dozens of casualties have already been confirmed and reports of severe material damage are coming in as New York City officials are—'

I turn off the button and focus on the road.

I slept for a while and now it's my turn to drive. I've been at the wheel since we crossed over into Massachusetts. If we make it back to our own time, I'll treat Olivia to a few hours of driving lessons. But in all fairness, she did OK.

What I perceived as her weaknesses – her caring for others, her sociability, her chatty chirpiness – is what got us out of New York alive. She's resting, her face pressed against

the passenger window. Asleep, she looks even more innocent and sweet, although I know better now. I smile again,
thinking about our escape and her stroke of genius at the
church.

She nearly gave the old man a heart attack. He fell back
into the pew when he saw her.

She knelt down next to him and spoke soothingly. The
seventy-year-old simply looked at her, his mouth working
silently, no words coming out.

When she grinned and said, 'We don't want any fishes in
the choir', he clamped his mouth shut and looked at her
with wonder.

'How can this be? By what miracle?'

'Raymond, I'm so sorry, there's no time to explain.' She
said, as she helped him to his feet.

'Is it really you, Miss Olivia?' he asked, taking her proffered hand.

'Yes, Raymond, it's me,' she said, smiling, as she dusted
herself off.

The priest looked stunned. 'But they said you disappeared. We all thought you were dead...'

She took a step back and sat on the bench next to him,
explaining things in rushed whispered sentences. I didn't
hear it all but guessed the gist of it.

'Do you trust me?' she said finally.

He nodded.

'Then please help us, Raymond.'

'Anything. Just tell me what you need.'

'A car.'

'I have a pick-up truck. But it's really old. Not very good.
It's not even a self-driving one.'

'Actually that's perfect. Can we borrow it?'

'Of course.'

He hurried into the sacristy and came back a few minutes later with a bottle of water, a bag of food and old-fashioned car keys.

'It's out back.'

'Thank you, Raymond. Thank you.' She held his hands in both of hers while he stared at her face, as if committing it to memory. Then she gave him a big old hug.

WE'VE BEEN DRIVING the old electric pick-up truck ever since.

11.07 p.m. Less than an hour to go before midnight. I have no idea at what hour we were supposed to be at the rendezvous point. I'm mean, we've worked out that it has to be within a twenty-four-hour window, as it's been a year since our departure. But God knows when the chips will actually stop working. Maybe we've already missed the time. Does it have to be a certain hour for it to activate or does it just activate on the right day at midnight?

Nearly there.

If it stops working at midnight, we're cutting it awfully close.

It's not exactly like Professor McArthur had the time to tell us before we jumped forward. Not for the first time, I hope the Professor made it. I hope the Cassandra Programme still exists. Otherwise, assuming we can even go back, we'll make it out of here and find ourselves in the hands of Helenus as soon as we arrive. Out of the frying pan and into the fire.

We'll cross that bridge when we get to it. If we ever get to it. Whatever.

Olivia wakes up, blinks, rakes her fingers through her red curls sleepily and looks out the window. 'Where are we?'

'Massachusetts.'

We drive a long time in silence.

'Olivia, something's been bothering me.'

'Mmmh?'

'Why did you risk your life to save me? You had the car, the gun, the location. You could have just left. That was the rational thing to do.'

'When I thought you were dead... I... I nearly did leave.' She glances at me, biting her lip. 'But the minute I saw that you were alive, I could never have left you, you're my friend.'

'That's really stupid.'

'You're smiling.'

'No, I'm not.'

I try to put myself in her shoes.

'What about what's-his-face, chubby lawyer boy? Didn't you want to escape with him instead and live happily ever after?'

'Nah.'

'Turned out to be an asshole, I hear.'

Her smile falters, then she recovers. 'I had to choose between saving the world or getting my knight in shining armor.' She stares at the dark road ahead. 'So I chose the world.'

'Well, I'll be damned. Girl, you finally got it.' I laugh. 'Can I have an amen?'

'Oh shut up, Oprah.' A smile twitches at the edge of her lips as she wipes the corner of her eye.

I drive through the darkened streets, hunched over the wheel, searching the surrounding neighborhood for our destination until the MIT cupola appears, surrounded by stately columns lining its courtyard.

I park, feeling trepidation; we're so close now.

Olivia is saying, 'Oh, it's just as I remembered', when a knock on my window makes us both flinch.

A slender woman, wrapped in a hooded coat, is standing beside our pick-up truck, her gloved hand poised to knock again. I roll down the window and she drops her hand to her side.

'You're late.'

'We were busy,' I answer.

'You might be *too* late.'

'Then let's not stand around chatting.'

The college grounds are plunged in darkness and the woman's hood is up, so I can't see her face. We follow her warily as she winds her way silently through the colonnade and across the campus.

Finally we make it to a small side door and she keys in a code, holding it open as she gestures for us to go in. Given the day we've just had, I half expect sirens to start blaring and armed men to tackle us to the ground as we enter. But nothing happens. We slink like shadows into the darkness and continue to follow her in silence as she darts through the corridors.

She clearly knows where she's going. I've slipped our gun in the back of my belt, just in case. Olivia carries the backpack.

Eventually, she stops in front of a door marked 'restricted access'. She rummages in her bag, pulls out a key and unlocks the padlock. The metal chain slides to the ground with a clinking noise that sounds excruciatingly loud. Wincing, I glance at both sides of the hallway but nothing moves.

As we step into a small dusty lab, the smell of decay and mold grips my throat. The abandoned space clearly has been out of use for years; white tarps cover the desks and machinery, shadows move and dust swirls like ghosts disturbed by our visit, as the mysterious woman hurries toward the far end of the lab.

When she reaches the door at the back of the room, she places her hand on the doorknob, but before she can go inside, I touch her arm and stop her.

'Before we go any further, I want to know who you are.'

She turns toward me, eyebrows raised, and I realize that she must be at least ninety years old. Maybe more. She seems beyond old: her skin is crisscrossed with wrinkles and it looks parchment thin. She's so thin and slight that it looks like she might break with the slightest shove.

She says she's part of the Resistance, that she's Cassandra. But what if she betrays us like everyone else?

One thing is sure: I don't recognize her.

'I'm glad we finally get to meet, DeAnn.' She extends her hand.

I shake it, thinking 'how quaint', but it feels important to establish contact. Her hand is very small, dry and cold.

Olivia is frowning. She looks like she's trying to remember the lyrics of a long forgotten song, a faraway look in her eyes.

'I know you...'

'Yes, we met in London... behind the scenes, with Madison.' The old woman says, lowering her hood. Her hair is short and bristly on one side and shoulder length on the other. The white strands gleam like cobwebs in the moonlight. Three studs shine in her ear and a tattoo pokes out from under the neck of her shirt.

'No. No, I met you before that,' Olivia says pensively.

'I didn't think you'd remember. It was a very long time

ago for me,' the old woman says with a smile. 'Come, it's nearly midnight. We need to move on before the portal closes.' She opens the door and I suck my breath in.

Olivia gasps as well, as she grabs her forearm.

47

OLIVIA

M *IT, Cambridge, MA, USA, 31 October 2082*

I KNOW THIS WOMAN. I'm sure of it. I remember feeling concern or puzzlement about her. When was it? Who is she? She's so old that it's really hard to tell who she might have been once. She opens the door and then, I remember.

My father brought me here once. A lifetime ago. In my mind's eye, the room just beyond the door lights up with sunshine. A sunshine more than eighty-nine years old.

I step through the threshold and I'm eighteen again.

DAD HAD INVITED me to come visit him on one of his projects. He never invited me to anything. This was very exciting, MIT! It was full of boys. American boys! I wore a mini skirt and maybe a smidge too much makeup. But it was

1993 and I could get away with it. My curly red hair reached down to my waist and I was positively giddy. My dad actually wanted to share something with me about his interests. This was going to be a good day.

He let me into the lab and gave me a little spiel. I didn't listen very closely. There was so much to look at. The computer stations were full of geeky-looking students. I was distracted by the clicking noises of the programmers' typing and the trip's excitement. Dad realised I wasn't listening and with an indulgent look, he cleared his throat.

'Young lady?' He put his hand on the doorknob and turned to look at me, a big grin on his face.

I smiled, I was so proud of him; my father had brought all these people together. He was the leader here. I had no idea what it entailed but it sounded really scientific.

Yet even though he was so important, sometimes Dad was like a big kid. His salt-and-pepper hair was mussed. His chin jutted and he wiggled his bushy eyebrows playfully.

'Ready to see something you've never seen before?'

His tie was a bit askew and he'd pulled back the sleeves of the Savile Row blazer he used to wear all the time.

I hurried to his side as he opened the door and when I glanced inside, all thoughts of boys and makeup flew right out of my head. The pyramid was so tall that it touched the huge hangar's ceiling. It was enormous and glowing from the inside with a bright white light. My father grinned from ear to ear.

'What do you think, sunshine?'

LIKE AN ECHO, the door opens again but, in the dark, the carcass looks different. It's old now, and dusty. My dad's voice whispers something as a draft lifts the corner of a white sheet draped over one of the working stations. Awed by the size of the device, I crane my neck up, staring at the seemingly never-ending structure. The room is so dark that I can't even see the ceiling.

Glancing at DeAnn, I step cautiously forwards. But as soon as I've stepped over the threshold, my microchip jolts me. An itching sensation flashes through my arm and as if in answer, the pyramid wakes up. A low hum sends a tremor across the silent room, when the structure's glass floor starts to glow feebly.

I press my hand on my forearm and wince as the chip begins to pulse. My father's playful grin fades, swallowed by the dust of time and the memory of impending pain.

The pyramid stirs, white light radiating from the bottom, reaching higher and higher, dimly lighting the whole room as it inches upwards.

A. turns with a smile, but her face falls, as she looks past me, to the lab's entrance.

When I turn back to the door, to check what she's seen, a lone silhouette steps forwards and I take an involuntary step back. A familiar mocking voice emerges from the shadows.

'Good evening, ladies,' Burke says with a smile, coming out of the dark towards us, raising his gun. 'Good, good, your microchips are still working, then.' He nods to A. 'Thank you for bringing them to me.'

48

DEANN

M IT, *Cambridge, MA, USA, October 31, 2082*

'You betrayed us!' I shout, glaring at the old woman.

Olivia's face is stricken. She looks like a pillar of salt, completely unable to move.

'I... Listen...' A. starts.

'Everybody shut the fuck up!' Burke cocks his gun and points it at my head.

The gun's nozzle is cold against my temple. Its touch spreads tentacles of fear to my spine.

We fall silent.

'Olivia, darling, I have to say, your driving hasn't gotten any better.' He chuckles.

Burke doesn't look right. There's dried blood on the side of his face and he's covered in black dust, which accentuates the bitter wrinkles around his mouth. He's holding his left arm bent at the elbow and the angle is wrong. There's dust and debris in his buzz cut.

Olivia looks like she's going to pass out. A sheen of sweat coats her face and throat. She's pale and her eyes are wide. That won't do. Come on, Olivia, snap out of it. You were doing so well lately, so fierce and determined. Don't let Snow White take over.

I need to find a way out of this. The gun is just there, tucked in the back of my belt. If I could only reach it.

A. looks at me and shakes her head.

'OK, love, come here.' Burke gesture to Olivia.

Olivia walks toward him, as if entranced.

'Take these.' He hands her nylon strips to bind us.

'Tie up DeAnn. Hands in front. You,' he taps the barrel of the gun against my head, 'go sit next to the old hag, back to the pyramid.'

I move slowly toward A. and we both sit on the floor, hands raised.

Olivia takes the strips and then pads over to us. She ties my hands at the wrists. I try to catch her eye but she's looking down at our hands, subdued. Noticing that he doesn't instruct her to tie up the old woman's hands, I glance at A. suspiciously. She seems so defenseless and regretful. Could she really have been manipulating us from the beginning?

When she's done, Olivia stands up, leaving A. and me sitting on the floor. Burke gestures with his gun for her to come back. It's loaded and cocked for God's sake. He could blow our heads off inadvertently. I guess he doesn't care, as long as he gets the microchips.

'So, this is what we're going to do,' Burke says, jubilant. 'Olivia, you and I are going to go back to 2017 as per my original fucking plan. And D. over there is going to graciously provide me with a one-way ticket, aren't you, D.?'

Nobody answers him.

'I've radioed in our location, so my colleagues will be here in a few minutes, but I'm afraid we'll be long gone by the time they get here.'

'Burke, you can't—' I start.

'Don't interrupt me, you fucking cunt.'

He pulls Olivia close, caressing her cheek with the gun's muzzle. 'I had to run ahead of everyone else to make sure I'd be the one to escort Olivia home.'

'So all you're interested in is saving yourself? Living in a time before the famines began?' A. spits, her lips twisted in a bitter half moon.

'Of course. Why should I let someone else go back in my place? I've earned this. I'm going back so I can make sure this shit show never happens. We need to cull the fucking vermin before they start proliferating.'

His words echo through the gloomy hangar as A. forges on: 'Don't you understand the uncontrollable ramifications if you live for decades in the past. The *past*, Anthony. No one should live outside their timeline...'

'Ha. That's a bit rich coming from you.'

A.'s face sags and she seems even older all of a sudden.

'That's right, I know who you are, old woman. How do you think I traced them here? I tracked *you*,' he hisses.

A. continues, undeterred, 'If you know who I am then you must understand the risks. Remember your training, Captain Burke. You could kill us all. The temporal paradox alone...'

In a fluid motion, he throws a long serrated knife toward me. It lands point down, swaying a few inches in front of my feet. A. and I flinch, startled.

'Shut the fuck up! Who are you to give me lessons? What has your generation ever done for us? You're responsible for the way the world turned out. You made me who I am.' He scowls, taking a ragged breath. 'Olivia, bring back the strips.'

It's as if my partner's just turned off. She sleepwalks back to Burke obediently and hands him the remaining nylon strips. He reaches for them but then in a darting motion, grabs her face, squeezing her cheeks so hard that it parts her lips. Her eyes widen but she doesn't move, frozen, the white of her eyes showing.

He moves her face from side to side. 'I see you've healed.'

He rubs a rough finger against the light pink scar on her lip.

Then pulling her toward him, he kisses her hard. She struggles as his fingers dig into the flesh of her cheeks, leaving angry red marks.

Burke releases Olivia, but before she can take a step away from him, he grabs her arm, twists it behind her back and marches her over to us, holding her close to his body and pointing the gun to her head.

'You, take my knife,' he orders, and A. takes the knife planted in front of me. 'Open her up.'

That's it. He's going to remove my chip.

As A. leans toward the knife, I bend my elbows and bring my hands toward my mouth, desperate to prevent her from cutting me.

I'm struggling against my bonds, trying to break them apart when I realize that the nylon zip isn't actually that tightly fastened.

Clever girl.

49

OLIVIA

M IT, *Cambridge, MA, USA, 31 October 2082*

MY SHOULDER SCREAMS, and my arm feels like it will pop outside of its socket. But I can't move. I can't breathe. My brain is completely frozen. I just want to wake up from this nightmare.

I lick my lip where he's just bitten me. The pain feels far away, the blood tastes salty. It's as if I am wrapped in cotton. I know that this is happening but maybe it's happening to someone else. It doesn't seem real or terribly important.

His breath is warm and humid against my ear.

'Soon, love,' he whispers, when he feels me squirming.

The gun is rammed against my head and every time he moves, the metal knocks against my temple, digging painfully into the soft spot there.

A. is kneeling next to DeAnn, the knife already in her hand but DeAnn is having none of it, she's twisting about, struggling to get up and trying to break apart the restraints on her wrists.

As Burke looms behind the three of us, in front of me the pyramid is pulsating with white light. A vibration rises from the floor, through the soles of my feet, climbing through my body like a nervous tremor, rattling my teeth.

'Go help. Hold her still.' He releases me and pushes me forwards.

I stumble and fall next to the two women, feeling Burke's gun aimed somewhere between my shoulder blades. The scar where McArthur injected my microchip starts to throb. My veins are lit from within, the red glow eerie and mesmerising under my transparent skin highlights the chip nestled in the black-green branches of my veins.

My heart speeds up pounding uncontrollably against my ribs as the scorching pain builds up, searing through my forearm.

Jolted by the twin of my fiery pain, DeAnn stops fighting.

Our eyes meet.

Time stops.

The foggy silence is deafening as I stare into her dark brown eyes. We're connected. Months of friendship, support and trust are tugging at my mind, insisting that I do something, but I can't remember what. It's like looking through a mirror. Her lips are moving silently. I watch them move, captivated.

There's something I need to remember about midnight.

The red-hot microchip seems to wriggle under my skin. She grimaces with pain, just as I scream. We both know what this means. We know what's next. I have to wake up. NOW!

The fog around my brain rips apart, burnt by the heat and the pain. DeAnn is actually screaming.

'Olivia! Wake up! OLIVIA!'

I look at my hands and realise I'm holding her wrists, preventing her from fighting back. I release her and she twists to show me the gun in the back of her belt. Before I can think, I grab it and swinging around as I get up, I aim the weapon at Burke.

'Release DeAnn!' I yell at A. over my shoulder, keeping my gun trained on him.

A. slashes through DeAnn's restraints and lets the knife clatter to the ground. My friend scrambles to catch it and starts cutting through the restraints on her ankles with jerky movements.

'Go!' I shout, gesturing for A. leave. 'For fuck's sake, run! They're coming!'

Throwing an uncertain glance at Burke, the old woman darts for the door and disappears into the pitch-black shadows. I hope she'll make it.

'She won't go far.' Burke says, his eyes boring into mine.

I hold the gun, the heavy weight and unfamiliar grip strange in my hand. Burke looks at me with a smirk and deliberately trains his gun on DeAnn.

'You've tried to kill me before, love.' He twists his face, to show me the ugly raised scar on his neck. 'I don't think you really wanted to, or you'd have succeeded.'

His smile broadens as the muffled sound of boots beyond the door reaches us.

'It's over, Olivia. Just give up. You're surrounded and about to be outnumbered.'

He steps forwards and I take a step back, feeling the gun's weight in my sweaty palms.

'When they arrive you'll die, Olivia. I won't be able to stop them this time. I'm your only chance of survival.'

DeAnn snorts, somewhere behind me.

He snarls, 'Who do you think kept you both alive this past year? It was me.' Then he turns to me, and his face changes. I recognise the old charming Anthony and keep retreating, aiming with both hands.

'They wanted to kill you right away, Olivia, you've got to believe me. I was the one who told them you could be turned.' The sound of boots gets louder and we hear shouted instructions through the lab's far door.

'There are still three minutes left, it's not too late, Olivia. I can still save your life.' His eyes slide over to DeAnn, as he adjusts his aim. 'If you just let me.'

I take another step back and feel DeAnn backing towards the pyramid too. 'Stay behind me,' I whisper to her.

'Look at you, Olivia,' he sneers. 'You're ridiculous with that gun in your hands. You're not meant for this life, love. You're an amateur and you know it. Let me take over. I'm a professional; I'll make sure you're safe from what's coming through this door.' He jerks his chin back as his gun keeps trying to lock on DeAnn.

Making sure I'm between them, I wave DeAnn backwards towards the small glass door in the pyramid's side.

'Come on, Olivia, you know that the world can't be allowed to reach the state we're in today. I need to go back to 2017 and change the outcome. I just need one chip and I don't want to kill you. You know that if she goes back, she'll let her people proliferate and we'll all fucking go extinct. What did that nigger ever do for you anyway? You don't even like her.'

His iMode is counting down rapidly with a ticking

sound, so I risk a glance. 11.58 pm. Oh God. Only two minutes left and then we'll be stuck here and at his mercy.

DeAnn and I reach the door and she opens it just as the hangar door crashes open and a dozen men burst in, all wearing black fatigues, body armour and automatic weapons. The pyramid is radiating light everywhere now. We're never going to make it. There's at least twenty of them.

Burke shakes his head as his eyes harden. 'Too late,' he whispers. 'Now you die.'

His gun still aimed at us, he turns towards the armed men and yells, 'Take them!'

They start swarming towards us and he smiles at me. Bloody cocky bastard. He doesn't care if I die and he doesn't believe I'll fire. I can't let him change the world. Even if I die in the next few minutes I have to try to stop him.

I take the shot. The sound tears through the brightly lit space like a thunderclap, as the recoil pounds into my shoulder. DeAnn pulls me by my waist and we fall backward slamming the door open as we fall in. Above our heads, several of the pyramid's panels burst into shards where we were standing a few seconds ago.

A shower of broken glass shatters in my face.

'Olivia, duck!'

Dazed, I close my eyes and raise my arms to protect myself, screaming. It feels as if we're underwater – everything seems to have slowed down. All I can focus on is the tinkling sound of the glass falling on the ground around us. Some are sparkling in DeAnn's hair. Like little diamonds against her shiny black curls.

My arms are bleeding from dozens of cuts, but I can't really feel them because of the chip burning like an ember wedged inside my flesh.

Eyes on the shattered glass door, I back away, holding

the gun steady in my shaking hand, as I aim at the small opening.

Just as I reach DeAnn, her mouth forms a surprised 'O' and that's when the pain hits me. Blinding, searing pain scorches through my whole body. It feels like my whole body is on fire, the heat radiates outwards and then my whole body ignites and bursts.

Through DeAnn's screams and the tears of pain, I see Burke step into the pyramid, limping from a gunshot wound in his thigh. His left arm dangles by his side and his face is unrecognisable, distorted with rage and loathing. He aims at my face and fires.

A white light explodes and everything disappears.

50

OLIVIA

B *oston, MA, USA, 1 November, 0:03 am*

'WAKE UP. COME ON, WAKE UP!'

Blood, blood everywhere. On my hands, on DeAnn, on the glass floor. I kneel next to her, as she lies unconscious on the pyramid floor, pressing both of my hands on her wound. She jumped in front of me when Burke fired. Why on earth would she do that?

I look all around us, panicked; where is Burke? Letting go reluctantly of DeAnn, I straighten up, looking for the gun. Wasn't it just in my hand? I thought I was holding it.

The room beyond the pyramid is silent and dark. Wait... the glass panels were broken, now they're whole. The shards of glass are gone. The pyramid's door is closed, the glass intact.

Wiping my sweaty face with the back of my hand, I look down. I'm naked. Are we...?

DeAnn moans and her eyelids flutter. 'Olivia?'

Thank you, God, thank you, God, thank you, God, thank you.

'Don't move. You're wounded. I'm off to get help.'

'I'm OK.' She struggles to sit up.

Typical. The woman is a bloody tank. But it's too painful; she collapses back on the floor and presses her hands on her abdomen.

'We need to... Burke...' she pants, visibly in pain.

'We made it. We made it. We're back.'

'Really?'

'Don't sound so surprised. We're bloody awesome. We're Programme agents, of course we made it.'

Her face relaxes and she slumps back on the floor. 'Oh good, good.'

She seems really faint. Blood is oozing through her fingers.

Should I stay and stench the flow or should I go get help? I hesitate for a split second, then make my decision.

'I'll be right back.'

I walk over and open the pyramid's door tentatively. Nothing. The room is dark and quiet. It must be late. There's no one here.

Tiptoeing out into the darkened corridor, I make my way, stark naked, to a deserted campus memorabilia shop just a few doors down. There. Tracksuits with the university logo. That will do.

Wiping the blood off my hands and my face, I hurry back to DeAnn and help her dress. Before she faints again, I hoist her arm on my shoulder and pull her towards the exit.

'Get me to Jordan.'

'Well, that might be a bit far away. Also probably not as

warm as you'd think, this time of year,' I joke, trying to get her to stay awake.

'Oh, shut up,' she chuckles weakly. 'Jordan, my friend. He lives nearby. He's a professor at MIT medical. Valentine Street. I can walk there, I think.'

'Are you sure? We should try to flag down campus police, instead.'

'Just walk.'

Adjusting her arm on my shoulder to make sure I bear most of her weight, I drag her out of the building in the pitch-black night. It must be past midnight here too, of course. I orient myself, thinking stupidly that we should take Raymond's pick-up truck. But of course it won't be parked here for another sixty-five years.

DeAnn gives me woozy directions, as we hobble through the dark streets. A few passers-by in Halloween costumes look at us curiously.

'Drunk,' I smile, limping forwards.

They don't give us a second glance but moments later, we pass a group of women dressed in red gowns with stiff white bonnets. There're at least twenty of them.

'Are we sure we came back to the right year?' DeAnn whispers, her voice rasping.

Agape, I watch them go by. Is this an alternate reality? What the hell is this? The young women are eerily quiet as they walk, two by two in an orderly procession, their heads bowed down.

The campus feels strangely subdued for a Halloween night. The temperature is mild but it's starting to rain. I can feel my friend fading so I walk on, as fast as I can, worried about the colour draining from her face.

Ten minutes later we stumble in front of a modern timber-framed house. I bang on the door but no one answers. My right arm is completely numb and I can feel DeAnn's knees giving way, as her weight on me increases. Her head starts to loll.

'No, no, no, DeAnn wake up!'

I make a fist and bang on the door as hard as I can, screaming.

51

OLIVIA

B oston, MA, USA, *1 November 2017*

A LIGHT COMES on somewhere on the first floor and I hear heavy footsteps going down a staircase.

A man's voice shouts, 'Who is it?'

'Your friend DeAnn needs help!' I yell, desperation rising.

I let go of the door and wrap both my arms around DeAnn instead, as her knees give out completely. The door flies open and a man appears on the threshold, wearing nothing but boxer shorts. He's wielding a baseball bat, ready to bash me in the head with it.

But when his eyes fall on DeAnn, the baseball bat clatters to the floor, as he lunges to catch her.

'DeAnn? DeAnn!' He scoops her in his arms as she collapses.

I follow them inside, hurrying behind him as he rushes

to the kitchen. The man swipes everything off a large wooden table, then deposits her carefully on it.

She seems to be dropping in and out of consciousness. I press on her wound, feeling the MIT jumper soaked with blood between my fingers. He hurries away and comes back with a medical bag, towels and disinfectant.

'Who the hell are you? Did you do this to her?' he yells, as he opens the bag and tears open a pack with this teeth.

'No! I'm her friend. She told me to come here. She said you'd help.'

'What the fuck happened?' He fills a syringe with something.

'She was shot.'

'What?' He pushes me out of his way and pulls up the sweater, uncovering the round wound on the side of her stomach. Dark red blood gushes out of the jagged tear as he lifts her on her side and inspects the exit wound. 'OK, hold her like this,' he says and starts to work, focusing intently on her with practised, precise gestures.

Two inked snakes are coiled around a winged pole on his shoulder. My panicked mind freezes for a moment as I think *Helenus*. But it's only a combat medic tattoo.

Under my bare feet, the small kitchen floor is slick with blood while I continue holding my friend tightly in my arms, watching as her face slackens and she turns grey.

Jordan and I say very little, both focused on her. I help as best I can, wiping away the blood from the gaping hole, passing him what he asks for.

But when she fades and he starts to give her CPR, I take a few steps back, encounter a wall and slide against it, sitting hard on the floor. I stare at my bloody hands and look up when Jordan climbs on the table to try to coax her heart into starting to beat once more.

DeAnn's body sways limply as he pushes with both hands on her sternum. Her arm drops off the table. Her face is expressionless.

She's gone.

She can't be.

Dead.

52

OLIVIA

S urrey, England, 24 December 2017

HOLDING THE TRUNK OPEN, I push a musty jumper out of the way and try to disentangle the Christmas lights. I pull too hard and a shoebox tumbles open, spilling its glossy paper innards all over the attic floor. My father's smile spreads everywhere, gripping my heart, reaching up from the faded seventies photos to capture me in a delicate web of sorrow and regret.

Somewhere in the house, Bing Crosby's honeyed voice croons about coming home for Christmas, slowly revealing that he won't be making it back. That he'll be there in spirit only. Like most of the people I love. For a moment, I lose myself in the past, as I detail my brother's hollow, dark eyes, Mum's twirling chiffon dress, my young, happy dad catching her dancing waist.

'Olivia, have you found the Christmas lights?' Mum yells

from somewhere down below, in the distant present, out of sight.

'Not yet!' I lie.

With sorrowful thunks, I group the photos in small packs and return them to their shoebox grave. But as I push the mothball-scented memories aside to cram the photos back in the trunk, a dozen notebooks come into view. They're leather-bound, dog-eared, ink stained. Frowning, I lift one up and my breath catches.

21 DECEMBER 1970, Poolesville, Maryland.

Calhoun has probably lost it. Turned religious, four horsemen and all that hogwash. Had to cut him loose today. He wasn't best pleased about it, but after twenty-five mice experiments all yielding same result, clearly no money to be made out of this. Mice colony slipped into overpopulation and behavioural sinks started appearing again (violence, deviance, etc.) as usual.

[illegible note]

Mice utopia now collapsing despite no predators or disease. Calhoun can't figure out why they always all die. Several thousand mice already gone.

One thing's sure: overpopulation always brings on full species extinction as soon as obsessive grooming mice appear. Wonder why TBO have no interest in sex or social interaction and only care about their own appearance.

[Something scratched out.]

Note: Potential to salvage project?

—Search for possible ways to delay/stop/reverse TBO mice advent.

—Try placing TBO mice out of source environment, to check whether they ever return to normal social/reproductive behaviour.

—Confirm whether extinction really irreversible once the Beautiful Ones appear.

MY CAT RUBS herself against my knee, making me flinch. She's been glued to me ever since I came back. She's snuggles up in my lap and starts to pump and purr for all she's worth.

Lost in my thoughts, I scratch absentmindedly below her chin. 'What do you think, Bubblesqueak? I wonder if Martin might have been...'

A quick leaf through the rest of this notebook reveals no other mention of overpopulation. There are countless other experiments, though.

'Sunshine?' My mother's voice comes faintly from downstairs. 'Your friends are here.'

Springing to my feet, I pile up the dusty notebooks, stack the rolled-up Christmas lights on top and climb down the ladder, holding the pile stable under my chin, as Bubblesqueak clings on to my shoulder.

As soon as I'm downstairs, I put on my wellies, a warm coat and run out.

The garden is covered in a fine layer of snow, apples have frozen on our tree and the desiccated wisteria is clinging to the red-brick walls. The cottage sparkles with frost in the afternoon light as I hurry over to the gate and open it.

The car drives in, tyres crunching on the snow, and parks. I smile in anticipation as the passenger door opens.

DeAnn comes out slowly, looking pale but alive.

Alive.

Jordan comes round and pauses to hug me warmly. 'I've taken care of it,' he whispers in my ear.

'You're sure your contact will protect us?'

'If my contact doesn't manage to convince the Programme, I'll take you both to a safe place.'

He moves around the car and opens the boot, retrieving their suitcases while DeAnn is being greeted enthusiastically by Mum.

Jordan and I stand back and a bemused smile etches itself on the corner of his lips as he watches DeAnn try to fend off the hugs.

'I don't know how I got this lucky,' he says, 'but let me tell you, if it ever comes to it, I'll lay my life down for this woman.'

I can see he really means it.

He turns and beams at me. 'And I'm in your debt, Olivia. I know just how much I owe you, so if you ever need my help, you just say the word.'

As he hurries over to the passenger door to help DeAnn navigate the icy ground, I feel a twinge of sadness about what I've lost. But when my friend pulls herself up with a wince, I also realise how much more I could have lost and a surge of gratefulness soars in my chest. Wrapping my arms around DeAnn, I squeeze her tight and hold her for a while.

Thank you, God.

Thank you.

When I let her go, she avoids my eyes but I can see that she's touched. What can I say; I give very good hugs.

DeAnn walks slowly, clutching my arm, while Jordan gets their luggage inside the house, smiling as Mum chats with him. Once DeAnn is safely plopped on the sofa next to Bubblesqueak, I go make them tea.

Yes, tea will help.

∾

CHRISTMAS EVE PASSES by really quickly. This year I don't feel the sadness and emptiness of other years. Hope, love, and friendship are sitting at our table once again. The cottage sings with light and warmth. The house smells of mulled wine and cloves.

Over dinner, Jordan tells us stories of his time in the navy and in an elegant, subdued way, he makes it sound like he had no merit, when in fact, I know he was awarded a medal of honour. We eat more than we need, drink exactly as much as we should and sing less than I want.

Eventually the others go to bed while DeAnn and I take a tour of the garden. Our feet, in sparkly ballerinas and elegant stilettos, crunch on the frozen grass. I wrap my shawl around her shoulders and tip my face up towards the deep blue sky and the myriad of stars shining above us. I've missed stars.

The wine still warming us, we giggle at the thought of waking Jordan and my mother as I show her the turkey spending the night in a vast tub of marinade in the garden shed.

Finally, when she starts to flag, I pretend to be cold and we come back inside to sit by the fire, as logs crackle, spraying showers of sparks up the dark chimney. We chat late into the night, eating chocolates and drinking port as I detail her paleness, the dark under her eyes, the new wrinkle that's appeared on her forehead.

How lucky I am that she survived. My friend.

She taught me strength.

'Are you alright?' I whisper, eyes on the flames.

'Yes, yes. Much better.'

'Jordan?'

'Yes, we're together.' She smiles. 'I've known him for years. This feels right. I can be myself around him. Hard, if I need to. But mostly, I find that he brings out happiness in me and a willingness to love and give.' She falls silent for a minute. 'It's a process.'

'I'm so happy for you.' I should get up and put another log on the fire but I don't want to disturb this fragile moment.

'I told him everything.' She throws me a sideways glance.

'I know. Is that... wise?'

'I trust him with my life. He should know. Dating me can be dangerous.'

'You don't think that the Programme bought our story?'

'Maybe... I don't know.'

'I wonder where Professor McArthur and Andrew Catterwall are.'

Fear mixes with anguish in my stomach as I remember Dad's friend. Theodora McArthur cared about me. Now that I understand more, I realise that she saved our lives at the cost of hers.

'Probably dead,' DeAnn says. 'Critchlow's done well. He was probably a Helenus agent inside the Programme all along.'

'I did wonder about that. He managed the Programme's armed operatives and was in charge of security. It seems really too convenient that he survived the attack and managed to remain in the Programme.'

DeAnn makes a small, disenchanted sound. 'At least Aileen saw the sense in submitting to them. We need an ally on the inside.'

Biting my lip, I wonder how much of a support Aileen Foley will be for us really. The slender, soft spoken admin girl didn't exactly strike me as strong or self-assured when we met her during the selection process.

'Do you think we did the right thing?' I say. 'Falsifying the dates and names, and keeping so much to ourselves?' I add a log to the fire. 'We need the Programme's influence to get governments to take action before overpopulation reaches a critical stage. So how can we fulfil the mission if we lie to them? How can they effect any real change if we don't tell them everything?'

'Maybe that was true when the Programme was Cassandra. Now that they're probably Helenus, who knows what they would do with the real information? We only disguised the dates and locations to protect ourselves and the people who helped us. We can't divulge anything that could help Burke or Groebler find us.' She sighs as emotions war across her face. 'No, we already discussed this fifty times. We did the right thing, Olivia, and I'm not just saying that.'

'Well, at least we gave them the most salient elements about that future. That's the main thing, right? They can still take action based on that.'

'Yes, I agree. The way I see it, there are only three options for governments and international organisations, going forward.' She holds her fingers up as she enumerates: 'One: impose a one-child policy on a global level as soon as possible.'

'Only one? Maybe two children would be more likely to work. And how will governments impose this in democratic environments? Maybe they could prohibitively tax families who go over two children?' I stop and try to imagine my own pro-natalist government doing this. They would never do it, not in a million years. I sigh. 'It's unlikely, to be honest. Governments will never do this.'

'Agreed.' She pauses. 'Alright, then let's move on to two: accelerate economic and social growth in all underdeveloped countries to trigger the demographic transition.'

I nod. 'Yes, that's certainly the more viable option. What's your third?' I ask.

'Three: deploy the Mass Sterilisation Agent within the next twenty-five years,' she says sombrely.

'What? How can you think that sterilising people is still an option? After everything we went through? How can you say that?'

'There will come a time when we'll be robbed of all choices. Nature will decide for us and put an end to our species if we don't control our numbers before it gets to that stage. You told me about this yourself,' she says, pointing to Dad's notebooks, which I showed her earlier this evening. 'As soon as the Beautiful Ones emerge, we'll know that over-population has reached an irreversible stage and that we'll be heading for extinction.'

I sigh. I know she's right, unfortunately. 'Did you read the article I sent you about the young Japanese who are starting to forego sex?'

'I did, and you see – nature might take its course sooner than we think,' DeAnn swallows her port and pours herself another.

'Well, thankfully, we don't have the formula for that terrible chemical, so releasing MSA8742 is a non-option.'

DeAnn looks down at the flames and moves a log with a poker.

53

DEANN

S urrey, England, December 24, 2017

I CAN'T TELL HER. I really can't.

I know the Mass Sterilization Agent's formula. I memorized it.

I went one step further, actually.

The fire crackles, releasing sparks as I nudge it with the poker. The enormity of what I did overwhelms me again, making me shiver.

I drank the soda.

After they executed Jada. I just took a bottle from the pallets at the clinic and drank the whole thing.

Now, I carry MSA8742 in my blood.

I'm patient zero in 2017.

Nobody can know. Not even Olivia. It's too dangerous.

Olivia is still talking. I tune in to what she's saying, looking at her kind, naïve face. There's no way I can tell her what I'm doing. Her cheeks are pink from the fire's heat and she's gesturing with her hands, enthusiastically.

'...but what if governments don't do anything? What if they lack the foresight or the authority over their own populations to impose any fertility control?'

'We can't wait for governments to do the right thing here. We need to do something ourselves. Something to prevent overpopulation before it happens.' I hesitate, thinking of the toxin pumping through my veins.

'Yes, you're right.' She worries her lower lip. 'The single most important difference we can make is through education and access to family planning. If we empower young women to take charge of their fertility, we can prevent this future. Not through war and genetic holocaust. Simply by spreading awareness.'

She misunderstood me. But I hope she's right. I really do.

Olivia looks like she wants to say something else. She hesitates then takes a breath and dives in.

'DeAnn, you know, we can't be sure that the Helenus will do anything with the information we brought back. Maybe if we raised awareness about overpopulation being a danger to our survival as a species, if we could just get the public to understand this, then surely people would reduce their fertility of their own accord, don't you think? Governments wouldn't have to impose a one-child policy then.'

'You really are impossibly optimistic, Olivia. I don't think people will do the right thing neither in the bedroom nor in the public sphere. At some point, it will come down to coercion.'

'I can see your point but I think... I think there may be another way.' She hesitates again. I look up from the fire. 'Change only ever happens because a large number of people start thinking that something is an important issue,' she continues, trying to find the right way to put it. 'So we need to reach a tipping point where most of the public is aware of the overpopulation issue and wants to do something about it. If we reach that point, then governments will have to listen.'

'There are only two of us, that's not enough to start a movement. What difference can we possibly make?'

'Maybe two is enough. Especially if it's the two of us.' She smiles. 'I think it's possible to bring about change, through a cultural shift, through ideas. That's how. We start sharing our experience.'

'Are you crazy? They'll have your skin if you reveal anything about the Programme. The new guys don't kid around. They probably only let us live because we convinced them that we became Helenus during our year away.'

'No, no, I don't mean revealing real secrets from the Programme, that'd be too dangerous.'

'Then how? Most people don't read obscure scientific papers and UN forecasts about demographics. Most of them just watch mainstream media, which, by the way, keeps peddling sentimental inanities about motherhood and apple pie.' I shake my head. 'I kid you not. They even rejoice when we pass the threshold of another billion.'

'But think about it. It's just like you said – most people read novels, watch TV, go to the movies, keeping up with mainstream culture. Maybe if we gave them the message in the form of a story, we could reach more people?'

I think about it for a while. 'Yeah. That could just about work.'

'I've started writing a novel...'

'You're kidding.'

Olivia smiles. 'Will you help me with it? I want to get it right.'

'Yes, of course.'

I can't believe I used to hate this woman. I smile back, hoping she'll succeed, hoping I won't have to resort to my solution.

Pushing away the thought, I say, 'Well, if we're sharing confidences, then I should tell you. I'm quitting my job and moving to Boston.'

'Why?' she asks.

'Well, in part, for Jordan. But mostly because I'm taking a new position in a local hospital.'

What I don't tell her is that the less demanding job means I'll have time to work on my side project: researching the toxin. I'll work on it discreetly, after hours, and make sure I leave no trace of my activities.

On the one hand, I want to work on finding an antidote for it. But on the other hand... Maybe I'll start by figuring out how to remove the targeting of African genes. It's essential for the chemical in my blood to become ethnicities-agnostic. Used as a universal deterrent, perhaps it could nudge humanity in the right direction.

'What about your high-powered career in genetics?' Olivia asks.

'I need a less stressful job, so I can concentrate on my side activity.'

I've already invested all my savings in the medical devices and computer companies that were widely used in 2082. As soon as the iMode is invented, my stock market shares will skyrocket. I'll invest the dividends to fund my research.

I understand now why there was no trace of me anywhere in the future. I was looking in all the wrong places. I'm going to live in Boston, not Baltimore. It's still early days, but I can sense that I'm probably going to marry Jordan. I'll change my family name and that's likely why I didn't appear anywhere. And the kind of research I'll do will never garner any awards, it will always be secret.

'Really?' Olivia asks. What side activities?'

'I'm going to head a not-for-profit organization that mentors young people of color. It's a charity that pays their college tuition fees and ensures that they go to college in groups. So that when they start to feel alienated by the mostly white culture, they can support each other and make sure they all graduate together. You know, education is directly correlated to fertility rates. We need more educated, empowered women in the world.'

'Amen to that,' Olivia says with a smile.

The fire crackles and she gets up to add a log.

Outside, snow starts to fall.

54

OLIVIA

L *ondon, England, December 2017*

I GO HOME a few days after DeAnn's visit. She and Jordan looked happy. It's incredible how much my friend has changed in one year. She seems to have opened up to her feelings. She's so much kinder and happier. I wonder what I've found at her side, in 2082? Maybe my strength.

I wave to my mother as she drives off, then I push my front door open and place Bubblesqueak's box on the floor. The cat meows and escapes as soon as I release her. Probably to go hide in a closetful of jumpers or something.

I close my front door. Home at last. Back in the Shire.

Like Frodo, I'm not sure how to integrate back into my normal life anymore.

I gather the scattered mail from the doormat, remove my shoes and go make a cup of tea. With milk and sugar. Diets are for wimps. I'm very happy the way I am, after all. And come to think of it, I don't particularly want a boyfriend anymore. Maybe one day but not now.

For the moment, I'm enjoying being on my own.

I bring the tea, the post and my bag upstairs to my brand new office. The small white desk looks inviting, with its comfortable chair, its pots of pens and an orchid, over-looking my snowy garden. How could I not see before how lucky I am?

I had all this before: my house, my job, my friends, Bubblesqueak, my loving mother. But I didn't appreciate any of it, all I could think about was what I didn't have.

Now I see clearly. We have enough food and water, we have breathable air. We still can make a difference in this world. These are precious gifts.

I sip my tea and look at the frosted trees in my backyard, then I pick up the top letter and think of how to call my novel. '*There and Back Again*?' I smile to myself. No, I'll have to think of something else, that one's already taken.

The first envelope is large; I open it distractedly and read:

Dear Ms Sagewright,

As discussed with you last month, we are delighted to start the process to get you approved as a single adopting mother.

ALSO BY O. M. FAURE

THE CASSANDRA PROGRAMME SERIES:

The Disappearance (prequel)

THE BEAUTIFUL ONES (TRILOGY):

Book 1: *Chosen*

Book 2: *Torn*

Book 3: *United*

If you enjoyed *The Beautiful Ones* trilogy, then you will love *The Disappearance*, the action-packed prequel that explains how the Time Travel Programme got started.

Grab your FREE copy of *The Disappearance* today simply by visiting www.omfaure.com!

BIBLIOGRAPHY

This book is based on scientific studies, UN forecasts and real data. If you would like to know more, please consult the sources listed below. A list of book club topics to discuss is also available when you join the Readers' Club at www.omfaure.com

Overpopulation Analysis:

- Cafaro, P. and Crist, E., *Life on the Brink: Environmentalists Confront Overpopulation,* Athens, Georgia: The University of Georgia Press, 2012.
- Ehrlich, P., *The Population Bomb*, New York: Ballantine Books, 1971.
- Emmott S. 'Humans: the real threat to life on earth', *Guardian*, 29 June 2013.
- Furness, H., 'Sir David Attenborough: If we do not control population, the natural world will', *Telegraph*, 18 September 2013.

- Jowit, Juliette, 'Three's a crowd', *Guardian*, 11 November 2007.
- Meikle, J., 'Sir David Attenborough warns about large families and predicts things will only get worse', *Guardian*, 10 September 2013.
- Remarque Koutonin, M., 'Isn't it Europe that is overpopulated rather than Africa?', *Guardian*, 11 January 2016.
- Roberts, D., 'I'm an environmental journalist, but I never write about overpopulation. Here's why.' *Vox*, 29 November 2018
- Bloom, D., 'Demographic Upheaval.', *Finance and Development, a quarterly publication of the International Monetary Fund*, March 2016.

UN Forecasts on Population:

- United Nations, Department of Economic and Social Affairs, Population Division, 'World Population Prospects: The 2015 Revision'.

Japanese Celibacy Syndrome:

- Haworth, A, 'Why have young people in Japan stopped having sex?', *Guardian*, 20 October 2013.

Food and Water Scarcity:

- Banigan, M., 'At bug-eating festival, kids crunch down on the food of the future', *NPR*, 14 September 2017.
- Johnson, G., 'The great nutrient collapse', *Politico*, 13 September 2017.

- Lederer, E. M., '20 million people in four countries facing starvation, famine: UN', *The Associated Press*, 10 March 2017.
- Menker, S., 'A global food crisis may be less than a decade away', TED Talk, August 2017.
- Runyon, L., 'Will the Government help farmers adapt to a changing climate?' *NPR*, 18 March 2017.
- Wiebeı, K., Lotze-Campen, H., Sands, R., Tabeau, A., van der Mensbrugghe, D., Biewald, A., Bodirsky, B., Islam, S., Kavallari, A., Mason-D'Croz, D., 'Climate change impacts on agriculture in 2050 under a range of plausible socioeconomic and emissions scenarios', *IOP Science* 25 August 2015.

Bio-chemical weapons:

- Adam, D. 'Could you make a genetically targeted weapon?', *Guardian*, 28 October 2004.
- Charlet, K., 'The new killer pathogens: countering the coming bioweapons threat', *Carnegie Endowment for International Peace*, 17 April 2018.
- Hessel, A., Goodman, M., Kotler, S., 'Hacking the President's DNA', *The Atlantic*, November 2012.
- Howe, C., 'DNA targeted warfare', *Front Line Genomics*, 7 November 2017.
- Wade, N., 'What science says about race and genetics', *Time*, 9 May 2014.
- Video 'Intense Sarin Gas Weapons Test', Military.com, 10 December 2012.

Dust Bowl:

- *Black Blizzard*, Amy Bucher, 2008, retrieved from: Historychannel.com.
- Documentary: *Surviving the Dust Bowl*, by Chana Gazit, retrieved from PBS.com

Immigrant Population Fertility Rates:

- Browne, A., 'UK whites will be minority by 2100', *Guardian*, 3 September 2000.
- Cygan-Rehm, Kamila, 'Do immigrants follow their home country's fertility norms?', FAU Discussion Papers in Economics 04/2013, Friedrich-Alexander University Erlangen-Nuremberg, Institute for Economics, 2013.
- 'Immigrants boost America's birth rate', *The Economist*, 30 August 2017.
- Livingston, G., '5 facts about immigrant mothers and U.S. fertility trends', *Pew Research Center*, 26 October, 2016.
- OECD/European Union, 'Socio-demographic characteristics of immigrant populations', *Indicators of Immigrant Integration 2015: Settling In*, Paris/European Union, Brussels: OECD Publishing, 2015.
- Watts, J., 'Immigration: UK births to women born abroad reach record number', *Independent*, 25 August 2016.

Making Diamonds from CO2

- Reissman, H. 'This tower sucks up smog and turns it into diamonds', Ideas.TED.com, 31 October 2017.

Pro-natalist societies:

- Autumn Brown, J., and Marx Ferree, M., 'Close your eyes and think of England: pronatalism in the British print media', *Gender and Society*, Sage Publications, February 2005.
- De Paulo, B., 'The cost of choosing not to have kids: moral outrage', *Psychology Today*, 12 March 2017.

ACKNOWLEDGMENTS

This book benefited immensely from the careful edits of my wonderful editor, Sue Lascelles, whose suggestions were invaluable in injecting more life and action into the novels.

I want to thank my fantastic sensitivity reader, Isabelle Felix, for greatly improving this book by bringing her bubbly energy, her in-depth cultural knowledge and her methodical diligence to her edits.

I'm eternally grateful to Tara Biasi, Graeme Maughan, Jeremy Gray, Luke Tarrant, Clare Kane, James Young and Ahize Mbaeliachi for their unflinching feedback and the countless hours we spent reviewing and critiquing each other's work. Thank you for your insights and for the fun conversations.

A special thank you as well to Brandon Lowry and Jason Burnham for providing me with their expertise on matters of genetics and medical procedures out of the kindness of their hearts.

I'm also very grateful to Matt Jones, for helping me enhance the fight scenes thanks to his military experience and his considerable writing skills.

The books would not look the same without Stuart Bache's brilliant covers. His patience and hard work were as remarkable as his talent.

Finally, a big thank you to all my beta-readers who took the time to read early drafts of this trilogy and painstakingly point out all the ways it could be improved (and there were many): Tony King, Nina Vox, Amanda Gabrielle Jones, Anne Loiseau, Nicole Turner, Lashelle Roundtree, Evelyn Laurencin, Alastair Pugh, Tenko, Martin Lye, James Collector, Charles Thomas, Dorothée Tonnerre and Nina Pugh, you guys rock.

ABOUT THE AUTHOR

 O. M. Faure studied political science at Sciences Po in Paris, before obtaining a Master's degree in International Affairs at The Fletcher School of Law and Diplomacy in Boston.

She has worked at the United Nations in Geneva and has extensive experience as a change and transformation manager in several banks over the last twenty years.

Today, she is a Principal at a Scenario Planning consulting firm, and she lectures and coaches at the Hult International Business School.

Based in London, O. M. Faure is a feminist, a Third Culture Kid, an enthusiastic singer, and a budding activist.

facebook.com/omfaure

twitter.com/OM_Faure